HELL QUEST by Gar Wilson

A U.S. spy satellite has landed in the middle of an Ethiopian war zone. Storming the ravaged wasteland to search for the hardware, Phoenix Force joins a deadly scavenger hunt that includes Libyan commandos, Communist-backed terrorists and a CIA maverick. Each side wants the Intel contained in the satellite. The men of Phoenix must get to it first—at any cost.

DEATH LASH by Dick Stivers

Former members of the Iron Curtain's most brutal secret police have fled Eastern Europe for the U.S., offering a wide selection of services—from assassination to supplying arms. Gaining access to vital government Intel, this covert group unleashes a plot that threatens U.S. security. If ComBloc thugs haven't heard that the Cold War is over, Able Team will drive the message home—with steel and flame.

DIRTY MISSION by Gar Wilson

DEA agents have uncovered a cocaine supply ring aimed at U.S. military personnel in Europe. Washington is alarmed that officers in sensitive positions may be affected. Phoenix Force, dispatched to Britain to stop the deadly trade, unearths an arms-for-drugs conspiracy. In a lightning strike, the Stony Man warriors prove that America, when compromised, does business the hard way.

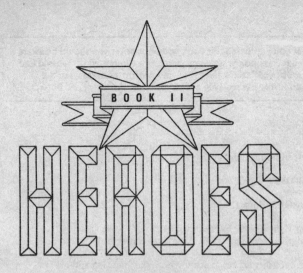

BOOK II

HEROES

HELL QUEST
DEATH LASH
DIRTY MISSION

A GOLD EAGLE BOOK FROM
WORLDWIDE ®

TORONTO • NEW YORK • LONDON
AMSTERDAM • PARIS • SYDNEY • HAMBURG
STOCKHOLM • ATHENS • TOKYO • MILAN
MADRID • WARSAW • BUDAPEST • AUCKLAND

First edition August 1992

ISBN 0-373-62405-0

HEROES: Book II

The publisher wishes to acknowledge the following authors for their contribution to the individual works:

William Fieldhouse—HELL QUEST
David North—DEATH LASH
Mike Linaker—DIRTY MISSION

Contents

HELL QUEST

by
Gar Wilson

A Phoenix Force novel

1

The Ethiopian sun seemed to bake through the canvas roof of the cab to the truck as Calvin James drove the battered old deuce-and-a-half. The Chicago-bred commando reached for a canteen on the seat beside him. The water was warm but welcome as he took a long swallow and peered through the windshield at the plain adobe buildings in the distance.

"That's Goba," Yakov Katzenelenbogen announced. He was in the front seat next to James. The Israeli warhorse had a map of the area stretched across his lap. "The capital city of Bale Province."

"That's a city?" James remarked. The black American thought Goba resembled an obscure Mexican village from a distance.

"It's probably bigger than it looks from here," Rafael Encizo said. "None of the buildings appear to be more than two or three stories high. They're not tall enough to be particularly visible from this distance."

James grunted. He guessed Goba would be another depressing collection of hovels and undernourished people living in poverty that made the worst American slums seem like Beverly Hills by comparison. They had passed a dozen small towns and villages that fitted this description since they'd crossed the border at Kenya. Ethiopia seemed to be a land of sheer misery unlike anything he had seen before. What most disturbed James was that he knew the villages he had witnessed thus far were considered affluent communities by Ethiopian standards. They could expect to see far worse as the journey continued.

Dressed in a khaki short-sleeved shirt, matching trousers and boots, James was more comfortable than his companions. Encizo wore a Cuban army fatigue uniform with the rank of captain on his collar and cap. Encizo's family had been wiped out by Castro's forces and Encizo himself had participated in the abortive Bay of Pigs invasion, been captured by the Communists and imprisoned at El Principe, one of the more than two hundred political prisons in Cuba. Understandably he despised wearing the uniform of Castro's military.

Katz's clothing was the most unusual and seemed the most uncomfortable, yet the Israeli didn't appear to mind. Katz wore a white linen cassock and a simple white miter. A copper Coptic cross with ornate arms hung from his neck. Katz's jawline was covered by a beard that matched his iron-gray hair, and dark glasses concealed his blue eyes. Although Katz's features were Semitic, he was a European Jew and had to maintain his disguise with care to carry out his role as a Coptic priest from Egypt.

The Israeli's right "hand" was covered by a black glove. It appeared realistic, unless one noticed that the fingers remained extended and rigid. Katz's right arm had been amputated at the elbow, the result of a battlefield injury during the Six Day War. The prosthesis he wore was less functional than the device with trident hooks he favored, but the gloved "hand" would attract less attention.

"I hope David and Gary arrived all right," Encizo remarked. The Cuban's dark features seemed grim as he tugged at the brim of his cap to guard his eyes from the merciless glare of the sun.

"We've made it so far," Katz replied. "And our route has been a lot riskier than theirs. Still, I'll be glad when we make contact with them. In a country like Ethiopia no one's really safe and the authorities can be unpredictable."

"And ruthless," James added.

David McCarter and Gary Manning were the other members of the elite five-man unit known as Phoenix Force. They had flown directly to Addis Ababa from Australia. McCarter and Manning were disguised as Australian journalists and claimed to be in Ethiopia to interview the current leaders. Among the sites the "reporters" wanted to cover was a new sugar refinery near Goba. If all went according to plan, McCarter and Manning would slip away from the watchful eye of the authorities and meet the other Phoenix Force members at the preplanned site outside Goba.

The mission had been put together in a hurry. Infiltrating a country like Ethiopia was difficult and dangerous under any circumstances. The limits of time and poor relations between the United States and Ethiopia made the task harder and riskier.

James, Katz and Encizo had crossed the border the night before. Ethiopian security along the border wasn't very strict these days. Kenya had more to fear from Ethiopia than the other way around. Getting in was easier than they'd expected, but they did encounter occasional roadblocks. With Encizo impersonating a Cuban officer, most of the blockades simply waved them through without asking questions. Cuban military advisers in Ethiopia were still regarded with some respect by most of the various guerrilla factions operating in the country.

Goba was larger than it appeared at first. It was also densely populated. Some people wore colorful dashikis, but most wore casual Western-style attire. A few were dressed in robes and keffiyehs. The Arab influence in Ethiopia was also apparent in the city itself. A mosque as well as an Ethiopian Orthodox church were located in Goba.

Few vehicles prowled the streets of the town. Most were army trucks and jeeps. The Phoenix vehicle appeared to be another military rig and attracted little attention. Aside from the novelty of a priest in the same vehicle with a Cuban officer, there was nothing unusual about the truck. Since the Ethiopian Orthodox Church was closely related to the Egyptian Coptic Order, the fact that the priest wasn't a black African didn't seem particularly strange. The people of Goba didn't choose to be curious when they saw a military vehicle with a Cuban officer. It was difficult enough to survive in the country without poking one's nose into matters that could prove lethal.

Most of the people of Goba were busy in the marketplace. They appeared to barter for goods rather than pay for merchandise with cash. The majority of Ethiopians didn't have money. The national currency was the birr, worth less than fifty cents American currency, but many Ethiopians were unaware of this. They could spend their entire lives without ever seeing a birr, or meeting anyone who ever had one.

A group of people sat in a circle at the edge of the city and listened to an Islamic holy man. Soldiers were scattered throughout Goba, and a few troops stood near the Muslim congregation. They seemed to listen to the sermon with suspicion rather than piety. Now that the government of former President Mengistu had been overthrown, Ethiopia was a hotbed of factionalism with a variety of armies jockeying for power. All assemblies, religious or otherwise, were viewed with wariness.

"Well, I don't think I'll stop and ask for directions," James commented as he steered the truck around the Islamic congregation. "Since we managed to get this far, I guess we can find the clinic now that we're here."

"We know it's outside the city to the northwest," Katz declared. "It shouldn't be too difficult to find."

They continued to circle Goba until they spotted the peak of a tent in the distance. James headed for it like a homing pigeon for its roost. The clinic was nearly six miles outside the city. A large canvas tent, it was marked by the familiar Red Cross symbol. Aside from a truck parked beside the tent, the area seemed deserted.

James drove to the tent and parked next to the vehicle. The three Phoenix commandos emerged from the rig. Encizo, an AK-47 assault rifle across his shoulder, also carried a 9 mm Czech-made CZ Model 75 autoloader in a hip holster, a pistol similar to a Browning Hi-Power. The Phoenix trio walked to the front of the tent.

Two Ethiopian soldiers suddenly appeared and pointed their Kalashnikovs at the commandoes. An arm extended from the canvas flap of the tent, a Russian Tokarev pistol in its fist. The muzzle was aimed at Encizo's head. A dark face peered from the interior of the tent and smiled at Encizo. The pistolman said something in Amharic, the office language of Ethiopia.

"*Maf-hem-tish,*" Katz declared, aware many Ethiopians in the southern provinces spoke Arabic. "I didn't understand. None of us speak your language."

"Any of you speak English?" the man with the Tokarev asked.

"Yes," James replied as he raised his hands to shoulder level. He did his best to imitate the not-quite British accent found among English-speaking Kenyans. "We all speak it, to some degree at least."

"Good," the pistolman stated. "Then that stinking priest will understand if I tell him to shut up. I hate Christians, especially Arab Christians. They have no respect for Muhammad or the Koran, even though they come from the cradle of Islam."

"Put that gun away," Encizo snapped, trying to use the rank on his collar to gain authority over the Ethiopian troops. "What do you think you're doing? I'm an officer in the Cuban army."

Encizo started to lower his arms, but one of the soldiers snarled and thrust the barrel of his AK-47 under the Cuban's chin to warn him to keep his hands up. Encizo knew better than to argue with armed opponents under such circumstances.

"I can see your rank," the Ethiopian with the pistol snarled contemptuously. "You Cubans are no longer welcome in my country."

"You have everything wrong," Encizo replied. "If you'll put away those guns and take us to Dr. Abraha, I'll forget this little outburst."

"How generous," the man with the pistol said with a laugh. "Come in. Let me introduce you to the doctor."

The soldiers outside the tent confiscated Encizo's AK-47 and Czech pistol. They didn't take the Cuban's Gerber Mark I boot knife or James's Blackmoor Dirk in a belt sheath. Obviously they figured no one would be crazy enough to pull a knife against opponents armed with assault rifles. Satisfied, the soldiers herded the Phoenix trio into the tent. Two more Ethiopian troopers were inside the canvas structure with the pistol-packing fellow who spoke English.

The man with the Tokarev appeared to be in charge, but he wore only a dark green undershirt, trousers and boots. Although his rank wasn't displayed, it seemed likely he was an officer because he spoke at least two languages. He barked orders in rapid Amharic. One of the stooges at the mouth of the tent nodded and hurried away, while the other stood guard outside. The other two soldiers watched the three visitors with amusement. They were tough-looking enlisted men, each fairly well built by Ethiopian standards. One held a Kalashnikov, the other a panga machete with a twenty-eight-inch blade. The crimson stains on the sharp edge didn't look like catsup.

The soldiers' cockiness and lack of concern about Encizo's bogus officer status worried Phoenix Force. So did the blood on the machete. The leader of the band strolled between two rows of cots that served as improvised hospital beds. At the opposite end of the tent was a wall of canvas that served as a room divider.

"Let me get Dr. Abraha," the man announced. He walked backward as he spoke, studying the three strangers. "What are you doing with a priest, Captain? I thought Christians didn't like Communists."

"The priest is with a relief program," Encizo answered. "I can show you the paperwork. Our truck is loaded with food and medical supplies."

"One of my men is checking it now," the leader declared. "Why would Cubans help a Coptic priest?"

"The Russians are playing this *glasnost* game," Encizo answered with a shrug. "They want to give the world an image of more openness and cooperation with the West. Cubans can be humanitarians, too. My superiors figured it would look better if an officer was sent. Unfortunately I got the job.''

The African laughed. ''Doing your duty. Must make you feel pretty good. A good obedient Cuban soldier.''

He backed up to the canvas and disappeared from view. The three Phoenix commandos glanced at the remaining soldiers. The man at the entrance peered inside and grinned at the captives. The fellow with the machete started to make short practice strokes with the long, thick blade. His companion kept a rifle trained on the trio. The three Phoenix veterans had been in tougher situations before, but this was the sort that could get them all killed in the blink of an eye.

The leader of the troops reappeared from the canvas. His arm was extended and hidden from view behind the sheet. The man smiled at the prisoners.

''You want to see the doctor?'' he inquired in a mocking tone. ''Here he is.''

The guy's arm swung away from the canvas. He held the handle of a bayonet in his fist. A severed human head was stuck on the end of the long blade. The tip of the bayonet was jammed into what remained of a neck. Flies buzzed around the lifeless features of the decapitated head. The eyes were rolled up in the head and only the whites were visible. The mouth hung open and insects crawled along the tongue. The head had formerly belonged to a black man, about forty years old. The skin had a gray appearance, and blood formed a crusty, reddish-brown stain along the abbreviated neck.

The Ethiopians laughed in unison as if this were a clever practical joke. Their leader tossed the severed head to the Phoenix Force. It fell near Katz's feet. The Israeli didn't want to look at it. He had seen worse, but he wanted to keep his attention on the soldiers. Aware that a Coptic priest would be awestruck and terrified, Katz cried out in alarm and backed away from the severed head.

"Jesus," James hissed with disgust as he turned from the decapitated present to the leader of the troops. "What did you do this for? I just want to deliver this Egyptian and the supplies so I can go back home."

"You delivered everything," the smug ringleader declared. He had stuck the Tokarev into his waistband and reached for the pistol as he spoke. "But none of you are going home."

"One moment!" Katz urged, and raised his arms. The sleeves of his cassock slid down to reveal the hard plastic shell to the forearm of his prosthesis. The gloved fingers were stiff as he gestured toward the leader. "If you're going to kill us, may we at least know why?"

"Haven't got time, priest," the man replied. He looked at the henchman with the machete. "Denke!"

Denke smiled and nodded as he stepped forward with the big jungle knife in both fists. His partner kept the AK-47 ready. The guy at the entrance of the tent used the barrel of his rifle to push back the flap to get a better view. The ringleader strolled closer, hand poised on the butt of his Tokarev. He wasn't in a hurry to draw the pistol. Since they were close enough to Goba for gunshots to carry to the city, the gang seemed keen to eliminate their victims as silently as possible.

"May our Lord in heaven preserve our souls," Katz said as he gazed up at the canvas ceiling of the tent. He lowered his eyes and fixed a stare on the face of the trooper with the Kalashnikov. "And may He forgive you!"

Katz pointed his prosthetic "hand" at the gunman. Flame suddenly appeared from the tip of the gloved index finger. The report of the .22 Magnum round sounded like a bazooka in the confines of the tent. The soldier's head recoiled, and his eyes rose as if to stare at the small scarlet dot in the center of his forehead. The Kalashnikov fell from the man's fingers, and he wilted to the dirt floor in a lifeless heap.

The shot stunned the other soldiers. James and Encizo were aware of the single-shot "finger gun" built into Katz's prosthesis. They were ready for the Israeli to make his move and immediately took advantage of the distraction. James charged the man with the machete and leaped forward to throw all his weight into a flying roundhouse kick. His boot smashed into the forearms above the panga. The kick jarred one fist from the handle of the machete and deflected the big blade. The Ethiopian still held on to the jungle knife with his other hand, but James grabbed the guy's wrist before he could swing the machete.

The black commando pulled his opponent toward the entrance, twisting the captive wrist. He used his free arm to deliver a short, hard karate stroke. His elbow clipped the Ethiopian under the jaw.

A burst of automatic fire snarled, and James felt his opponent jerk in a wild spasm as bullets punched through the man's back. Exiting from the man's chest, the projectile tore a hole in James's shirt at his rib cage, but at an acute angle. The Chicago tough guy was too busy, too pumped up with adrenaline, to realize how close he'd come to death.

James wrenched the machete from the dying man's fingers and shoved the quivering figure at the gunman at the opening of the tent, who had inadvertently shot one of his comrades. He swung his rifle barrel around the hurtling form to avoid blasting him again. The body landed in front of him, its frozen, glassy eyes seeming to accuse him of gross ineptitude. The soldier glanced at his dead comrade too long. Calvin James closed in and swung the panga.

The long blade swung across the frame of the gunman's AK-47, slicing off two of the trooper's fingers. Still, he tried to raise the rifle with his other fist. James stamped a boot on the barrel to pin it down as he swung the machete once more. The sharp edge struck the Ethiopian in the side of the neck. It hacked through muscle and bone with a single stroke. A fountain of blood seemed to burst from the stump of the soldier's neck.

When Katz fired the first shot, the ringleader of the troops had grabbed for his pistol. Encizo launched himself at the African, whose attention had been fixed on Katz. The man cursed in his native tongue as he tried to reaim the pistol at the Cuban. Encizo clamped a hand around the guy's wrist and shoved it upward. The Tokarev barked a harmless round through the canvas roof.

Encizo slammed the heel of his free hand into his opponent's breastbone to keep the man off balance. He grabbed the African's undershirt and rammed a knee into the soldier's groin. His opponent wheezed in breathless agony. The Cuban swept a boot toward the Ethiopian's ankle.

The ringleader landed on his back, Encizo on top of him, still holding the wrist above the Tokarev. With his other hand Encizo drew the Gerber knife from the belt sheath. He drove the double-edged steel blade between the soldier's ribs. The man shrieked as Encizo plunged the sharp steel into his opponent's heart.

Hearing shots, the trooper who had been sent to investigate the truck headed for the mouth of the tent, AK-47 in his fists. James had claimed the rifle from the man he had decapitated. Katz had also taken a Kalashnikov from his slain opponent. Both men were ready when the last soldier approached. They opened fire before the trooper could train his weapon on the pair. Half a dozen projectiles shredded the soldier's torso. He collapsed to the ground in a thrashing fit of death. His body soon lay still.

"Everyone okay?" Encizo asked as he wiped the blood from his blade on the dead ringleader's shirt.

"Yeah," James replied. He examined the tear in his shirt and realized how it had happened. "But things sure could have turned out different."

"They could have turned out better," Katz said grimly. He glanced down at the severed head of Dr. Abraha on the floor. "We've lost our contact. The only man who could have been our guide and translator, and the only person with enough connections to help us reach Argus. This mission may be over right now and we'll have to return empty-handed."

"If we manage to return at all," Encizo added.

2

The Phoenix Force mission to Ethiopia had begun when the President of the United States met secretly with Hal Brognola, the operations chief of Stony Man. The President explained to the cigar-chomping Fed that a satellite had been struck by a meteor and knocked out of orbit. It had gone down in Ethiopia. Officially it was a Nimbus model meteorological satellite, but the President wouldn't be involved if that was true, and he certainly wouldn't be meeting with the head of the most top-secret enforcement agency in the United States.

Stony Man had the tightest security of any clandestine outfit in America because it consisted of a small, highly professional number of personnel. Brognola himself was the only man who knew everyone involved and the details about all Stony Man assignments. Even the President wasn't privy to most of this information, although he assigned the majority of the missions to Brognola, who in turn passed on the responsibility of actually carrying out the missions.

Experts in unconventional warfare, espionage and antiterrorism were required for these assignments. Mack Bolan, the fabled Executioner, had helped Brognola create Stony Man and select the supercommandos for Able Team and Phoenix Force. The latter, assembled from top specialists throughout the world, was possibly the most efficient five-man army ever created.

Brognola met with Phoenix Force in the Stony Man war room less than an hour after he left the White House. The Fed had a detailed report of the incident in Ethiopia at his place at the conference table as he addressed the commandos.

"All of you are familiar with the term TECHINT and its importance to our national security," Brognola began. "Well, one of the National Security Agency's most advanced TECHINT satellites has fallen from the sky and landed in Ethiopia."

TECHINT was an acronym for "Technical Intelligence." It referred to information gathered by technical or mechanical methods, including a variety of different forms of electrical eavesdropping and surveillance. Spy satellites were among the most advanced TECHINT sources. Brognola opened a file folder to consult his notes as he continued.

"This one was a new LASINT version of the Argus," he continued. "That was one of the most successful of the DSP-647 black launches in the seventies and eighties."

"Are we supposed to know what the hell you're talking about?" David McCarter asked gruffly. The tall Briton was infamous for his impatience.

"I didn't know some of this stuff myself until I got this NSA data," the big Fed admitted. "Okay. A 'black launch' is a secret rocket launch to put a TECHINT satellite in orbit. The DSP stands for Defense Support Program, and the 647 series was a covert launching platform system."

"And LASINT refers to Laser Intelligence?" Encizo inquired.

"That's right," Brognola confirmed. "How'd you guess?"

"When HUMINT is an abbreviation for 'Human Intelligence' and SIGINT stands for 'Signals Intelligence,'" the Cuban replied dryly, "it wasn't hard to figure out what LASINT means."

"Actually, the term applies to two different types of TECHINT," the Fed explained. "There's LASINT that concerns gathering information about laser research by foreign governments and LASINT connected with laser technology used for our own intelligence-gathering methods."

"That's all we need," James muttered. "More acronyms for something that's already covered by about nine different clipped-down intel terms."

"Yeah," Brognola allowed. "But in this case it does serve a purpose because the Argus is equipped with new laser technology. Laser beams are used to increase the range and accuracy of radio waves, and they can bounce images onto TV cameras from twenty miles away. According to NSA, this new LASINT Argus makes the DSP-647 models look like old plate cameras by comparison."

"Argus," Katz repeated thoughtfully, tapping his chin with the curved steel hooks of his prosthesis. "In Greek mythology Argus was a monster with a hundred eyes until Hermes killed it and Hera put the eyes in the tail of the peacock. It sounds like the Argus satellite certainly has the equivalent of a hundred eyes, each of which makes the most observant eagle seem nearsighted."

"But the satellite didn't fly so well," Gary Manning commented. The big Canadian poured a cup of black coffee as he added, "Maybe the NSA should have named it the Icarus instead."

"Satellites don't really fly," McCarter stated. Among his talents, the Briton was an ace pilot.

"Yeah," Manning replied dryly. "I'm aware of that."

"Actually, the satellite was in orbit for a long time," Brognola explained. "Several months. It made hundreds of passes at a thirty-degree longitude around the world. It received radio broadcasts, made videotapes and transmitted data to NSA listening posts in ten locations. Argus was hit by a meteor and ceased to transmit, but there's every reason to believe it continued to record and store information before it finally went down."

"What countries did it record and what kind of data?" Manning asked.

"Thirty degrees longitude would put it over Mexico, the southern part of the United States, possibly Cuba and the West Indies, as well," Encizo commended. The Cuban had spent time at sea and was familiar with nautical maps.

"Probably passed over China and India, as well," McCarter, the pilot, added. "And the Middle East."

"You guys are good," Brognola remarked. "As for what Argus recorded, we don't know for sure. From previous surveillance transmissions the NSA is pretty sure there are recordings taken of military installations in more than a dozen countries. These include the People's Republic of China, Libya, Syria, Egypt and Israel."

"A hell of a lot of governments would like to get their hands on information like that," James said with an impressed whistle. "Especially any of the nations that might have their security jeopardized by the Argus recordings."

"Uncle Sam and the NSA want those recordings, too," the Fed declared. "We damn sure don't want them to fall into the hands of the Libyans, Syrians, Russians or even the Israelis. No offense, Yakov. You know how the espionage game is played. You've been doing it longer than anyone in this room. I don't have to tell you that national security requires keeping secrets from our allies as well as our enemies."

"Absolutely," Katz agreed. "Each country has its own ideas about national security, and they're all concerned with self-preservation first. I can tell you one thing—if Israel suspects what that satellite is, it will send someone into Ethiopia to get it. Israel happens to be much closer to Ethiopia than the United States."

"That's true," Brognola admitted the obvious. "But the Israelis wouldn't be able to pinpoint the spot where Argus went down. The NSA locked onto the Argus with specially designed tracking systems, so we know its exact location. It's all here in the files, along with maps and topography charts, even information on regional weather patterns. There's also a diagram of Argus that explains how to remove the recordings from the satellite. It's all on microdots, so it isn't bulky and can easily be carried in the storage wafer, which is only slightly bigger than a credit card."

"The wonders of modern technology," James commented without enthusiasm. "Why the hell didn't the NSA destroy Argus when it went out of control?"

"They didn't mention that in the report," the Fed answered. "My guess is they waited too long and Argus went down before they could nail it."

"Unless I'm really misinformed," McCarter began, "Ethiopia is a predominantly black African country. Except for Cal, the rest of us would stand out like four albino crows in a murder."

"A murder?" Brognola looked at the Briton with raised eyebrows.

"A flock of crows is called a murder of crows," Manning explained. "David's right for a change. He also has a point about us trying to operate in a clandestine manner in Ethiopia. Unless we can change pigment like a chameleon, we're going to have trouble fitting in."

"What do you mean *we,* paleface?" James commented.

"It seems to me it would make more sense to use black agents," Katz added. "Doesn't the NSA or CIA have personnel in Ethiopia, or at least cutout operatives hired to work for them?"

"Yakov, you know what happened to American intelligence organizations in the 1970s," Brognola began with a sigh. "It just about went down the drain after the Watergate scandal and the Church Commission. The operations in the Middle East took a beating, and we're still paying for it because American intelligence in that part of the world is so weak. The espionage apparatus there got strongly reduced, and it still hasn't been built up. That's one of the reasons Americans are still held hostage in Lebanon. Our intelligence operations in Africa got hit even harder, and now they're almost nonexistent in some countries in that part of the world. Ethiopia is one of those countries."

"From what I understand it's a rough country any way you look at it," Encizo remarked. "The U.S. isn't on good terms with the country, and no one knows who's really in control at any given moment. They've had a civil war for decades, and starvation is endemic. Not exactly a vacation spot."

"That's about the size of it," Brognola confirmed. "That's also why we haven't been able to establish a solid intelligence network in Ethiopia. There are a few cutouts from free-lance intel outfits and loners on the Company payroll still working in Ethiopia, but they're not trained in combat skills. You see, Argus went down in a particularly chaotic part of the country. The satellite is virtually surrounded by potential battlefields.''

"That's great,'' Manning said with a groan. "So we have to go into a war zone to get this thing? It'll be open season on us.''

"We're putting together cover identities to get you guys in,'' Brognola assured Phoenix Force. "But I won't lie to you about the risk. It'll be damn high. Even greater than what you guys are used to. It won't be easy.''

"It never is,'' Katz replied. "Will we have a contact?''

"There's a doctor working in a southern province who's been feeding information to the CIA,'' the big Fed answered. "The guy has really been giving intelligence to both the CIA and the Kenyan National Security Service. Kenya is worried about its neighbor and doesn't trust Ethiopia. We can get some cooperation from Kenya to help get you guys across the border.''

"That's nice,'' James muttered. "What if the Ethiopians have already found the Argus? After all, it landed in their country, and I think they've got a rather large population.''

"About fifty million,'' Brognola stated as he consulted his notes. "No reliable census has been taken in Ethiopia, so that's an estimate. It's believed the population will probably triple by the year 2000 if it continues to grow at its present rate.''

"I always wondered about that,'' McCarter said sarcastically. "The Ethiopians may have found Argus. We could go into their country for nothing. That would be mighty disappointing.''

"That's possible,'' the Fed allowed. "It'll also be bad news if they realize what it is and get their hands on the microdots. Argus is disguised as a weather satellite. If they do find it, hopefully they won't find the recordings.''

"I doubt the Ethiopians have high-tech space-tracking gear," Katz remarked. "But a number of the Middle Eastern countries do. Certainly Israel, Saudi Arabia and Egypt are capable of tracking the satellite and probably know it's American and suspect it isn't just a weather satellite. Jordan, Syria and Libya probably have the necessary technology, as well. Any of these countries might send some people in to try to claim Argus. Maybe they won't know the precise area, but they'll certainly have some idea based on their own radar intelligence. RADINT, if we're to use the jargon of the computerized age of espionage."

"That's possible," Brognola had to admit. "But you'll have another advantage. Argus has a special UHF frequency ground-tracking system built into its hull. You can activate it by using a receiver unit radio designed for this purpose. If you can get within four miles of Argus and switch on the radio, the signal will be activated in Argus and should lead you straight to it."

"Unless that was damaged when the meteor hit it," McCarter said as he took out a pack of Player's and fired up a cigarette. "A shame the damn thing didn't burn up when it plunged to earth. It would sure have saved everyone a lot of trouble."

"If you didn't have trouble, you wouldn't know what to do with yourself," Manning told the Briton.

McCarter thought for a moment. "Yeah, I guess that's true."

"Well, don't worry," James remarked. "It sounds like we can expect enough trouble to keep us all busy on this mission."

No one at the table was about to argue with this prediction.

3

Rafael Encizo stepped out of the tent to make certain no more Ethiopian soldiers were around. Katz discovered a backpack on the dirt floor between two bunks. He opened it and found that the pack was stuffed with small bottles and vials. The Israeli handed the pack to James.

"Looks like medical supplies," he remarked.

"Yeah," the black commando confirmed as he examined the contents. A former hospital corpsman with the U.S. Navy SEALs, James had continued to study medicine since leaving the service. "Penicillin, chloroform, that sort of stuff. Looks like the soldiers helped themselves to Dr. Abraha's medical supplies."

"Think they were looking for drugs?" Katz inquired. "Morphine, heroin, that sort of thing?"

"Could be," James said with a sigh as he tossed the pack onto the bunk. "If so, they killed Abraha for nothing."

"Waste," Katz said sadly, shaking his head. "We'd better get out of here. The shots will probably attract attention, and we're going to have a hard time convincing any Ethiopian soldiers that we killed five of their comrades in self-defense."

A scraping sound drew their attention to the canvas partition. Katz and James immediately swung Kalashnikovs toward the noise. A bulge in the canvas moved toward the opening. James advanced, AK-47 held ready, while Katz covered the black commando.

A shape appeared at the rim of the partition and fell to the ground. James stared down at a woman strapped to a chair. She lay on her side, a gag tied around her mouth. Her white cotton dress was torn.

"Jesus," the tough guy from Chicago rasped as he knelt beside the woman and dropped his AK-47.

He drew his Blackmoor Dirk and cut the leather straps that held the woman fast. She used a freed hand to grip the front of her dress and bunch it together to cover her breasts. James removed the gag as the young woman looked up at his sympathetic expression. He winced when he saw the bruise on the side of her face and the blotch of blood at the corner of her mouth. Moist streaks marked the trails of tears on her cheeks.

"Don't be afraid," he said softly, hoping she would understand his tone if not his words in English. "No one will hurt you now."

"Thank God," she replied in the same language. "If you hadn't arrived—God, I was terrified."

James helped her to rise. She was an attractive black woman, tall and sleek with graceful curves and coffee complexion. Her large dark eyes, above high cheekbones, were expressive and bright. A mane of curly black hair framed her oval face. James tried to avoid revealing his admiration for her beauty. He supposed the soldiers had intended to use her body against her will, and didn't want to make her feel uncomfortable in the presence of another male.

"Here," James said, offering his canteen. "Did you work for Dr. Abraha?"

"I work for the Kenyan National Security Service," she replied as she accepted the canteen and took a long drink.

"My name is Victoria Yatta. Dr. Abraha was working for us as well as your CIA. In a sense he was actually working for me, although I am a registered nurse and assisted him here at the clinic."

"Where are the patients?" Katz inquired, glancing at the rows of empty bunks.

"They stopped coming about a week ago," Victoria answered. "Pressure from the local military. They didn't trust Abraha and were suspicious of his politics. He tended to help too many people the ruling faction considered questionable."

"Is that why the soldiers . . . did this?" James asked.

Victoria dabbed blood from her lip. "Those dirty little buggers were working on their own. Renegades, I reckon. There are a number of bands of soldiers who have simply decided to desert and go into business on their own. Nothing more than bandits. They probably figured the clinic was an easy mark, but I don't think they were carrying out any sort of action approved by any recognizable faction. Of course, here in Ethiopia, it's hard to say."

Encizo entered the tent and announced that he hadn't found anyone outside. He was surprised to see the lady. "Who's this?" he asked.

"We'll handle introductions later," Katz replied. "Right now we have to decide whether to go on with our original plans or head back in the direction we came from."

"You're here to find the fallen satellite, aren't you?" Victoria inquired.

"You know about that?" James asked as he stared at her in astonishment. "I guess that's a dumb question because you just mentioned it."

"Of course I know about it," Victoria confirmed. "I was working with Abraha. I knew everything he was involved with. The satellite went down in Tigre Province, right near the border where Wollo meets Tigre from the south and Gondar meets at the west. Correct?''

"So much for security," Encizo muttered.

"That's going to be a difficult journey, and you'll have to travel close to six hundred miles to reach the site," Victoria declared. "Are any of you familiar with Ethiopia or speak Amharic or Tigre?''

"No," Katz admitted. "Now that Abraha is dead our mission seems pretty close to hopeless. If we go back to Kenya, we might be able to smuggle you across the border."

"Absolutely not," Victoria insisted. "I can help guide you. I've been all over this bloody country."

"Maybe you don't understand how dangerous this could be," James began. He immediately resented his choice of words when Victoria's eyes flashed in response.

"I happen to be a professional, sir," she declared. "And I've been operating in this country for more than a year. Perhaps you think I can't take care of myself because I'm a woman and you found me strapped to that chair, but I was caught off guard and unarmed. Abraha didn't do any better against those bastards than I did."

"We don't know what we might be up against out there," Encizo said grimly. "Aside from the chaos and confusion everywhere, there might be others trying to locate that satellite. We could find ourselves under attack from any one of a dozen sources. That's no place to have someone who isn't experienced in combat."

"I've been in the war zone before," Victoria answered. "I've worked with Red Cross personnel for relief programs for the starving masses who are victims of drought as well as the war."

"That's not the same," James told her. "The Red Cross provides a certain degree of protection. Nobody wants to fire on the Red Cross because it's an internationally recognized humanitarian organization. There's almost always some sort of media or press coverage when the Red Cross handles something like this, and that provides a measure of added protection."

"You're doing this for your country," Victoria began. "I want to do it for mine, too. Kenya is much closer to Ethiopia than the United States."

"Everybody's giving us geography lessons," Encizo muttered.

"Kenya has good reason to be concerned about Ethiopia," Victoria insisted. "If the Ethiopians find that satellite first, they may sell it to Libya or Syria or even the Russians in order to get more weapons and technology. Right now Ethiopia is busy with its own problems, but eventually it may decide to claim more territory. We don't know who's going to come out on top in this country, or what the intentions will be."

"The lady is volunteering," Katz stated. "She's not a civilian and she has made some valid points. If we're to continue with our mission, we need help. Ms. Yatta is aware of the risks. The decision is up to her."

"I don't like it," James commented. He looked at Victoria as if he questioned her sanity. "You're sticking your neck out farther than you realize, Victoria."

"It's my neck," she replied. "I also speak Amharic and Tigre fluently, and I have a working vocabulary in Tigrinya and several local dialects. I'm really more qualified than Abraha to assist you."

"All right," Encizo said in frustration. "Let her come along if she's that determined. We don't have the time to continue this debate. Troops from Goba are probably already on their way.''

The sound of an engine growling interrupted the Cuban. Encizo turned and pointed his AK-47 at the tent opening. James scooped up another Kalashnikov and tossed it to Victoria. He and Katz still carried their confiscated assault rifles.

"I hope you know how to use that," James told Victoria.

She canted the AK-47 across a shoulder and glared at the American. James didn't notice. He had already joined Encizo at the front of the tent. Katz moved to the opposite end of the tent and checked for other openings. The Israeli glanced at the headless corpse of Dr. Abraha behind the canvas partition. The grisly remains were framed by a pool of blood. Katz resumed searching for another entrance in case opponents hit them from more than one direction.

Peering outside, Encizo saw a cloud of dust rise from the direction of the engine noise. James covered the Cuban as he moved to the corner of the tent, thrust the barrel of his AK-47 at the dusty fog and swung around the canvas to confront the potential threat.

The Cuban discovered the source of the roaring engine: it was a Land Rover about a hundred yards from the clinic to the northeast. It drove around in circles, stirring up a lot of dust while going nowhere. Encizo didn't see anyone in the vehicle. He immediately realized that someone had braced a stone or heavy object on the gas pedal and tied down the steering wheel to fix the Rover in its orbit.

It was equally clear why this had been done. The vehicle was intended to distract them while whoever did it approached silently on foot.

"Don't shoot, mate!" a voice called. "It's just us."

Encizo and James recognized the familiar cockney accent. They turned to see David McCarter appear near the trucks parked alongside the clinic. The Briton held an Uzi machine pistol in his fists, the stubby barrel pointed toward the sky. Gary Manning emerged from the back of the truck James had driven to the clinic. The big Canadian also held an Uzi.

"Sorry if the stunt with the car gave you a start," Manning said as he swung down from the tailgate of the rig. "We heard shooting as we were headed here and when we were close enough we looked the place over with binoculars. When we noticed a corpse in front of the tent, we figured it might not be a bad idea to approach with caution. Just in case."

"Glad you made it," James greeted. "We kind of wondered if you two managed to slip away from the military watchdogs in Goba."

"They wouldn't let us come to Goba, after all," McCarter explained. "So we just sneaked away in the Rover at Addis Ababa instead. Not that hard." He glanced down at the dead Ethiopian soldier. "What happened here?"

"I'll explain later," Katz declared as he and Victoria emerged from the tent. "We need to get on the road again as soon as possible."

"Is this Dr. Abraha?" the Briton inquired. "If so, he's wearing one hell of a disguise."

"This is Abraha's replacement," James said dryly. "It's sort of a long story."

"I need to get my things," Victoria declared, and headed back inside the tent.

"Her things?" Manning asked with a frown. "Don't tell me she's going with us?"

"If you don't want us to tell you, we won't," Encizo replied as he headed for the truck. "But you'd better get used to her company. She's going to be with us for a while."

"What happened to Abraha?" the Canadian asked.

"Well, I guess I could sew his head back onto his body and we could bring him along," James commented. "But he still ain't gonna be very good company."

"I hope Ms. Yatta didn't hear that remark," Katz said, a tone of disapproval in his voice. "She obviously knew Abraha for some time, and I doubt she'd appreciate that sort of levity."

"Yeah," James admitted, slightly embarrassed by his lack of sensitivity. "You're right, man. I guess I'm a little uptight right now. Maybe it's male chauvinism, but the idea of taking a woman on a mission as dangerous as this one really doesn't sit well with me."

"I suggest you try to get along with her as best you can, because she's riding with you in the cab of the truck," Katz told him.

"What?" James replied with a blink of surprise. "What happened to our original cover identities?"

"Too risky," Katz answered. "Too many people in Goba noticed a Cuban officer and a Coptic priest in the truck. If they saw us headed in this direction, they'll soon connect us with the shootings and the slain soldiers. Ethiopia might not be the most technologically advanced nation, but I'm certain they have radios. Let's not make it easy for them to spot us when we keep moving north."

"So they won't be looking for a black guy and a black woman in the cab of the truck," Encizo remarked, approving of Katz's logic. "Good idea. Cal and Victoria won't attract as much attention that way. If I need to play a Cuban officer again, or if you want to be a priest again, we can hop out of the back of the truck and perform for the audience.''

''The back of that truck is gonna get pretty uncomfortable,'' Manning commented. He patted the Uzi machine pistol. ''But I'm glad the authorities didn't search the rig and come across our gear hidden among the sacks of food and crates of supplies.''

''All things considered,'' Katz began, ''we've been fairly lucky so far. Of course, you know how luck tends to be in a mission. It can go from good to bad to worse. We can't count on it and must rely on strategy and skills.''

''Business as usual,'' McCarter said with a shrug.

Victoria reemerged from the tent. She had changed her tattered dress and hastily donned a brightly colored dashiki. She carried a cloth suitcase and the backpack that contained the medical supplies the renegade soldiers had intended to steal.

''I was already packed,'' she announced. ''We may come across people who need these antibiotics and medicine. Dr. Abraha would want them to go to those who truly need them.''

''Hell, lady,'' Manning said dryly, ''we might need them ourselves before this is over.''

''That's better than needing funeral shrouds,'' Encizo commented as he climbed into the rear of the truck.

4

Major Dawa wanted to leave Eritrea. The province was firmly controlled by the Eritrean People's Liberation Front. Dawa commanded a battalion of infantry troops loyal to the deposed President Mengistu. In reality, though, he was a soldier without a government.

More accurately, Dawa had started out with a battalion. His forces had been whittled down to less than two companies. The officer was bitter and angry about his current circumstances. Now he was the rebel, and his former quarry the hunters.

Dawa was fighting for his life these days. Initially he had also held the vain hope that when the dust settled in Addis Ababa, someone would appreciate his determination to hold out against the Eritreans. Without Eritrea Ethiopia would be cut off from the Red Sea and effectively landlocked.

The EPLF had picked off several of his soldiers in hit-and-run attacks, using their superior knowledge of the rugged terrain to disappear into the environment. Dawa was all by himself and could no longer count on aerial support as he had in the past before the various guerrilla factions had put an end to his president's regime. Even after all this time he found it hard to accept that he was the one more likely to have bombs dropped on him. Necessity, however, had taught Dawa to think like the Eritrean rebels. After all, he had survived this long against seemingly impossible odds.

Right now, though, Dawa didn't give a damn whether or not Eritrea seceded from Ethiopia. He just wanted to get out of the dissident province without losing any more men and return to his family in the south. Dawa had a wife and five children. He hoped they were alive and well but realized the unlikeliness of such a prospect in war-torn, famine-ravaged Ethiopia.

The major tried to push such thoughts from his mind as he led the troops across the harsh, sun-baked plain. Desert shrubs and elephant grass dotted the landscape. Some scrawny antelope sensed the approach of the soldiers and bolted along the ravine of a dried-out stream. The antelope were a good sign. It meant the EPLF probably weren't in the area or the animals would have run from them, as well. Besides, the rebels seldom missed a chance to bag an antelope for dinner.

Dawa was relieved. He didn't want to encounter any more EPLF troops. The major had no desire for more war and wanted only to fight his way out of Eritrea.

A sudden burst of machine gun fire destroyed Dawa's hopes. The muzzle-flashes erupted from two different areas of the ravine, cutting down Ethiopian soldiers near Dawa. The major managed to throw himself to the ground in time to avoid a stream of full-auto fire. One of his men collapsed across him. He felt the soldier's body convulse against him and the hot blood pump from the dying man's wounds.

Dawa stayed down, the corpse draped across his back as he aimed his Soviet-made PPSh-41 submachine gun at the glare of the ambushers' weapons. The other side had the best cover available and took full advantage of it.

Dawa heard more of his men scream as the attackers sprayed the soldiers with machine gun and autorifle slugs.

The major returned fire with his subgun. Dirt flew up in chunks along the edge of the ravine. A mud-smeared face popped into view for a fragment of a second. Dawa saw a bullet hole in the Eritrean's forehead and realized he had managed to take out one opponent.

The other ambushers continued the assault. Bullets raked the soldiers' position and pinned them down while mud-stained tubes with burning fuses were hurled from the ravine. Dawa and his troops covered their heads as best they could before the dynamite sticks exploded. Dirt and debris showered the survivors. Some of the objects that fell on the soldiers were bloodied pieces of their slain comrades.

We're finished, Dawa realized grimly. There was no way they could retreat, and the other side had all the advantages. The major closed his eyes and tried to recall a prayer from his childhood.

Then a series of explosions erupted, one after the other, to create a continuous bellow of violent fury. Dawa hugged the ground as the explosions rocked the earth. Yet he wasn't pelted by more shrapnel or debris. The blasts didn't occur among his troops. Screams accompanied the explosions, but they didn't come from his people.

Dawa looked up and saw the glare of bursting projectiles within the ravine. Mud, uprooted plants and human body parts flew from the trench. Automatic fire snarled, and several figures appeared from across the ravine, dressed in spotted camouflage uniforms and caps, similar to regulation Ethiopian army fatigues.

Assault rifles blazed ruthless salvos into the remaining shapes within the ravine. Two mud-covered rebels crawled from the bank, both clad in the dark shirt and shorts that was the unofficial uniform of the EPLF. One was a young woman whose face had been half ripped off by shrapnel.

The mysterious gunmen blasted the two EPLF survivors without mercy. Their bodies quivered and jerked from the impact of the slugs. A tall figure with a white scarf drawn across his lower face marched to the ravine and pointed a large blue-black pistol at the wounded and dying in the ditch. Calmly, he finished off the few injured rebels who had survived the attack.

"Are you all right?" Sergeant Kiflom, Dawa's senior NCO, inquired as he pulled the dead soldier from the major's back.

"I think so, Sergeant," Dawa replied, unsteadily rising to his feet. He stared at the strangers who had rescued them from the ambushers.

"Do you know who they are, Major?" Kiflom asked as he watched them approach.

Dawa had no idea. As they drew closer, he saw that they weren't Ethiopian despite the uniforms. They weren't even black Africans. Their features were dark but Semitic. The tall man with the big pistol seemed to be in charge. He wore dark glasses with gold frames and had a trim black mustache. Although none of these men wore emblems of military rank, the tall man walked with an arrogant swagger that suggested he was accustomed to command. His uniform seemed tailored for his athletic physique, and a bulky wooden holster hung from his belt. It resembled the buttstock of a rifle.

"Greetings, Major," the man announced as he slid the pistol into the wooden scabbard. "It appeared you could use some help against the Eritreans."

Dawa stared at the wood holster and tried to place the man's accent. He spoke Amharic fluently but pronounced words with an accent that suggested Arabic was his native tongue.

"You never saw one of these Stechkin machine pistols before?" the Arab leader inquired, patting the wooden case at his hip. "It's Russian, of course."

"Very interesting," Dawa said dryly. "You probably saved our lives, and we do appreciate that, but I'd like to know—"

"Who we are?" the man guessed, displaying a smile. "I'm Captain Rashid al-Jabal of the Libyan army, a special unit known as the Asad Asifa."

"The Storm Lions?" Dawa said with a frown.

"You speak Arabic?" Jabal inquired. "The Storm Lions are commandos. We're used for special operations such as this."

"That brings me to the question I most wanted answered," Dawa began. "What are you doing here, Captain? To the best of my knowledge there has been no authorization granted for Libyan forces to enter Ethiopia."

"Fortunate for you we were here," Jabal replied. He glanced at the slain Ethiopian soldiers strewn across the ground. "If we had been a minute or two later..."

"The fact I haven't already placed you and your men under arrest is due to the gratitude I feel for the rescue, Captain," Dawa assured him. "However, you haven't answered my question."

"We're here to carry out a mission to protect Libyan national security and very likely the security of your nation, as well," Jabal answered. "I'm afraid you aren't authorized to know any details about this mission, Major. Besides, you don't have a government to report to anymore, do you?"

Dawa glared at the Libyan. "Sergeant Kiflom! Place these men under arrest."

"That's not a wise decision," the Libyan officer warned as he gestured toward two of his men.

Dawa looked at the weapon of one of the men and frowned. It resembled a mounted machine gun with a short barrel and a huge muzzle. A big drum magazine was installed along its side. The other man carried a large ammo box with a rope handle. Both soldiers smiled without mirth as they met Dawa's gaze.

"Did you wonder how we were able to fire so many grenades into that trench?" Jabal asked with a smile. "What you're looking at is a Soviet-made AG-17 automatic grenade launcher. It fires 30 mm cartridge-style grenades with explosive warheads at a rate up to three hundred rounds per minute. You already saw what it can do. Care for another demonstration?"

"Are you threatening us?" Dawa demanded, stunned by the Arab's behavior.

"Not at all," Jabal assured him. "But you're not going to ruin my mission. I have only a dozen men in my unit, but they're highly trained and very well armed. We came prepared to fight the EPLF but if necessary we'll fight you, as well. If you'll simply give me some information about the terrain and what sort of opposition we can expect from the Eritreans, we can part company here and thank Allah for allowing us to help each other."

Dawa smiled. Perhaps the Libyan could help him escape from the north. "Maybe we *can* work something out."

5

The truck rolled along the grasslands. Some hyenas scrambled away from the carcass of an antelope as the vehicle approached. The beasts brayed with the haunting, maniacal laugh associated with the species. Crouching in the high grass, they watched the truck, uncertain if it presented a threat or not. As the mechanical invader passed without further bothering the hyenas, they cautiously returned to their meal.

Calvin James peered out the windshield and scanned the surrounding area. Victoria Yatta noticed he had slowed the truck and seemed to be looking for something. She didn't see anything of special interest about the area aside from the pleasant abundance of lush vegetation. They were approaching Lake Zwai near the heart of the Ethiopian Plateau. Plant life benefited from the underground streams that branched out from the lake.

"This is one of the most tranquil areas in Ethiopia," Victoria told the American commando. "No need to worry about being attacked here Mr.—what should I call you?"

"The name on my passport is Daniel Manyoni," James answered, scanning the surroundings as he spoke. "Best if you use my cover name. As for this place being safe, there's no such thing as a safe area when we're on a mission, and we always have to consider the possibility of being attacked. The clinic back in Goba was suppose to be safe, too."

"I must admit I was wrong about that," Victoria said quietly as she looked down at her hands.

"Sorry," James said with a slight shrug. "I shouldn't have mentioned it. Actually, I'm really not looking for soldiers, bandits, rebels or other human opponents. I figured there might be a lion or a leopard hanging around."

"There aren't many big cats in Ethiopia anymore," Victoria informed him. "They don't have proper wildlife preserves here like the ones we have in Kenya. I'm afraid you'll be disappointed if you think you'll see lions and elephants running about all over Africa."

"Yeah," he assured her. "I've been to other African countries before. Haven't seen a lion in the wild yet. Sort of hoped I might after we passed those hyenas."

"You think hyenas are scavengers that eat only kills left by predators?" Victoria asked with amusement. "That's a popular misconception. Hyenas are hunters as well as scavengers. As often as not hyenas will bring down game and a lion will chase them off and steal their kill. Animals aren't terribly concerned with the labels men give them. Hunters can be scavengers and vice versa."

"I've known some people who were the same way," James commented. He applied more pressure to the gas pedal and gradually increased speed. "Guess we oughta try to put a few more miles between ourselves and Goba."

"Yes," Victoria agreed. "But we might be going toward an even greater problem. We're headed for Addis Ababa. Those two white men who joined us were formerly at the capital city and slipped away from security personnel. Correct?"

"That's right," he confirmed with a nod. "They also borrowed that Land Rover in order to meet us at the clinic."

"You mean they stole government property," she said grimly.

"The government will get it back when they find out where it is," James replied with a shrug. "Of course, that Rover will need a new transmission after going around in circles for so long. They're lucky it didn't get shot up, as well."

"We'll be lucky if we don't get shot with those two in this vehicle," Victoria declared. "Going back to the Addis Ababa area seems extremely foolhardy to me. If they're looking for the whites and discover them in our truck, we'll be fortunate if they just expel us from the country."

"If they're looking for my pals, they'll be searching vehicles going from Addis Ababa, not toward it," James explained. "The authorities don't have any reason to think they'd head back to the capital."

"Perhaps," Victoria admitted reluctantly. "But they might stop this vehicle and search it if they suspect it's connected with the killings of the men at the clinic. Not to mention the murder of Dr. Abraha."

"Well, that's a risk we gotta take if we want to find that satellite," James told her. "You knew this was dangerous when you decided to come along."

"It really bothers you that I'm a woman," she replied, her tone dripping venom. "Do you have this sense of superiority toward all females? Perhaps it's just that you regard Africans as backward savages, or maybe you just have this attitude toward black women. Your friends are whites. Don't you feel comfortable with your own color?"

"Jesus, lady," James muttered. "You're dumping a lot of crap on me that I don't deserve."

"I know a lot of blacks who consider themselves inferior to whites," Victoria continued. "Black Africans mostly. What do you fellows call yourselves now? Afro-Americans? As if being black in America gives you any idea of what it means to be an African."

"Man, we can't win either way with you," James said with a slight chuckle. "I'm not sure where to start denying your accusations. Maybe I shouldn't even bother, because I'm not so sure you'll listen if I do."

"Tell me what I'm wrong about," she invited.

"First, it doesn't really bother me that you're a woman," James assured her. He glanced away from the windshield to look at her lovely face. "Under different circumstances I'd be delighted to be with you because you're a woman."

"Sexual attraction?" she inquired. The question surprised James because it sounded less hostile than most of her remarks.

"So shoot me for being heterosexual," he replied. "I just don't like the idea of getting you into a dangerous situation. The fact that you're a woman will make me worry about you more than I would if you were a man. Sorry, but that's the way I was raised. I'm more protective toward women than men. You may think that's terrible, but that's the way I feel."

"I can take care of myself," she insisted. "Probably better than Abraha could have if he accompanied you."

"Yeah, but you're a lot prettier than he was," James answered. "I don't know if he would have accused me of being a bigot and an Uncle Tom. I don't like hearing that even from a woman as good-looking as you."

"Perhaps I was a bit too defensive," Victoria admitted.

"Defensive?" He shook his head. "You were downright insulting, Victoria. So I've got white friends. What's so awful about that? Those four guys in the back of this truck are the best men I know. I don't care what color they are. They've put their lives on the line more times than even I know about because they believe things like freedom, world peace and civilization are worth fighting for. Each of them has saved my life more than once. You expect me to apologize for feeling close to them?"

"I didn't know—"

"I'm not finished," James declared. "I'm not ashamed of being black or Afro-American or whatever term would be okay with you. As it so happens, I worked my ass off ever since I was a kid in a shitty ghetto on Chicago's South Side in order to make something of myself. Sometimes things were harder for me because I was black. Damn right I had problems due to discrimination and prejudice, but I never used that for an excuse to give up. I have medical training and a degree in chemistry. I speak three languages fluently and I've got working vocabularies in a couple of others. I've got a second *dan* black belt in tae kwon do, and I've been decorated for valor in the United States Navy when I was with a SEAL unit in Vietnam and by the San Francisco PD when I was on one of their SWAT—"

He stopped in midsentence, aware he was telling Victoria too much. James was furious that he had rambled on about himself and given too many details about who he was and what he had done. That was no way to maintain security, and he felt like biting off his own tongue for letting it flap so freely.

"You sound proud of what you've accomplished," Victoria commented gently.

"The point is, I earned it," James explained. "I earned the GI Bill that let me go to college so I could get a good education. I'm proud of what I've done on a personal level as well as proud of it as a black man who proved he was as good as any white dude. Most of them didn't have to go through half the shit I did to get somewhere in life."

"And where did it get you?" she inquired.

"Oh, driving a truck in Africa," he said with a grin.

They stopped outside a village near Lake Zwai. The city of Asselle, the capital of Arusi Province, was only a few miles away and visible in the distance. Asselle resembled Goba from their position. The city would probably be similar to the provincial capital of Bale in many ways, including the likelihood that the streets would be patrolled by the Ethiopian People's Revolutionary Democratic Front, the largest, most stable guerrilla group in the country. Phoenix Force figured the village would be a safer area to eat and to refill the fuel tank.

McCarter lifted the hood and checked the oil, radiator and battery. In the heat the radiator needed more water than usual and, although the water level in the battery was not low, he filled it just to be on the safe side. Satisfied the vehicle was in good working order, the Briton joined the others at the rear of the truck.

Katz, still dressed as the Coptic priest, ate a C-ration can of chicken and dumplings with a mess kit spoon in his left hand. On his right arm he still wore the stiff prosthesis with five metal fingers. Aside from the built-in .22 Magnum, the gloved limb had no advantage except for cosmetic appearance. However, the Israeli hadn't exchanged the device for a more functional prosthesis.

Encizo, clad in the Cuban officer uniform, sat on the tailgate with a C-ration tin and a canteen cup of coffee for dinner. Gary Manning, who had brewed the pot of coffee, consumed a second cup as McCarter leaned against the tailgate and took a pack of Player's from his shirt pocket. The Briton shook out a cigarette and fired it up.

"Isn't somebody missing here?" he inquired.

"Calvin and Victoria are in the village," Katz answered as he finished his rations. "They took some medical supplies and went to see if any of the locals need antibiotics, vitamin supplements, that sort of thing."

"They both have medical training," McCarter mused as he puffed his cigarette. "I wonder what else they found out they had in common during the past five or six hours."

"It's not a good idea to get emotionally involved during a mission," Encizo remarked.

"It's not a good idea to get emotionally involved period," McCarter said sardonically.

James and Victoria approached the truck. Both carried canvas bags. The American commando handed his container to Katz. The Israeli was surprised to discover it was filled with loaves of bread and eggs.

"The villagers insisted on paying us," James explained. "They gave us about two dozen eggs, some pancake bread and something that looks sort of like pumpkin seeds."

"Lentils," Katz announced when he saw the seeds. "My mother used to make lentil soup. I probably won't manage as well as she could, but I might try to reproduce her recipe if there's time when we make another stop. How did it go in the village?"

"A lot of vitamin deficiencies," James answered. "Kids with night blindness due to lack of vitamin A. Scurvy, rickets, other ailments associated with malnutrition. They aren't exactly starving, but they sure as hell aren't healthy.''

"Typical for Ethiopia," Victoria stated. "Those people probably live better than most. There's little we can do for them and even less that we can hope to do for the millions of others who suffer under far worse conditions."

"We're not here to save Ethiopia," Katz reminded them. "I'm afraid that's beyond our ability."

"The United States is more concerned about their military surveillance satellite than the lives of Africans," Victoria said bitterly. "How many billions does the American government spend on defense? Far more than it spends on foreign aid to Third World nations."

"The United States has sent hundreds of millions in aid to Ethiopia," Katz replied calmly. "Not to mention millions more to other African countries, including your homeland of Kenya. Since you've brought up the subject, Kenya happens to be far more prosperous than Ethiopia. How much has your government been doing to assist its less fortunate neighbor? Both of your countries, as well as the vast majority of other African nations, belong to the Organization of African Unity. How much has the OAU done to help Ethiopia? How about nations like Japan and the oil-rich Arab countries? Do you feel as hostile toward them as you do toward the United States?"

Victoria was too angry to reply. James came to her rescue and asked how much farther they had to go before they reached the Argus.

"About two hundred and fifty miles," Encizo replied. He glanced up at the dark twilight sky. Parrots cawed loudly from trees near the lake, and several herons soared above the waters. "It'll be dark soon. We should keep traveling all night."

"Agreed," Katz said. "You and I will take the front seat for a while and give Manyoni and Ms. Yatta a chance to get some rest."

"Good idea," Encizo agreed as he continued to admire the blue-and-gold sky. "African sunsets are always so beautiful. Have you noticed that?"

"Yeah," Manning answered. The Canadian loved nature and enjoyed being far from civilization whenever possible. "It's been said that Africa has a special allure. The beauty and savagery of nature are juxtaposed here unlike anywhere in the world. Thousands of cultures and an extraordinary variety of art and languages, customs and traditions, are all found in Africa. The claim is once you've been here, it's in your blood and eventually Africa will draw you back."

"My God," McCarter snorted. "We've been called back to this part of the world four or five times now. Nothing romantic about that attraction for us. Each time we've returned because Africa is also a continent filled with civil war, Third World despots that run their countries like junior Adolf Hitlers, and extremists of every sort who resort to murder and fanatical conspiracies. We're not here to do an article for *National Geographic,* you know."

"Sometimes you really are a pain in the ass," Manning told him.

"I hate to interrupt this charming conversation," Katz said dryly, "but we have to concentrate on our mission. May I also remind both of you that discussing past operations, even to the extent of simply mentioning how many times we've been in Africa before, isn't wise in the presence of outsiders like Ms. Yatta."

"You don't trust me?" the woman demanded.

"It's not a matter of trust," the Phoenix commander replied. He cast a sharp glance at James. "It's just basic security precautions. Right, Manyoni?"

"Yeah," James confirmed with a nod. He realized Katz had somehow guessed he might have been a bit careless with Victoria while they were together in the front seat. Sometimes James wondered if the Israeli could read minds.

"We're bound to come across more roadblocks and military units as we go farther north," Katz continued. "We'll need a better ruse than what we've got."

"You should have thought about that before you started this mission," Victoria remarked, eager to poke a hole in Katz's apparently impregnable armor of professionalism.

"We did," he replied. "Dr. Abraha is connected with the Red Cross, and we could have adopted new identities as volunteers to assist the victims of famine if he was with us. His death has caused an obvious problem now. Mr. Sanchez can continue to impersonate a Cuban officer, but we might encounter genuine Cuban military advisers when we get farther north. That cover won't hold up very well then."

"Besides," Manning said, "the Cubans aren't too welcome here these days, either."

"The best bet is to steer clear of Addis Ababa," Encizo stated as he consulted a map.

"The roads in this country are in pretty bad condition, and traveling where there aren't roads is even tougher," Manning remarked. "Still, the latter will be the more practical choice under the circumstances. It won't save us any time, but we might face more serious delays if we get stopped by the Democratic Front or some other faction."

"Hopefully they won't be checking vehicles coming from the south at night with much enthusiasm," McCarter commented. "Unless, of course, they're looking for the blokes who killed those renegades."

"If they managed to identify those slime buckets, they'll know they were deserters," James commented. "I don't know how high a priority they'll place on finding their killers. And it's unlikely they'd suspect a Cuban officer and a Coptic priest, even if somebody did see our truck headed toward the clinic back at Goba."

"Well, I guess we'll find out," Manning replied. "One thing that worries me is that after we find Argus—assuming we do find it—we still have to get out of Ethiopia. Our original plan for leaving the country died with Abraha."

"We'll have to figure that out later," Katz replied. "When we get past Addis Ababa, we'll try the radio and see if we can establish contact with the NSA listening post in Sudan."

"You think they'll have any valuable advice?" Encizo asked. His tone expressed doubt.

"Right now I just want to make sure they're aware we're still here and that they haven't gone to sleep at their station," the Israeli answered.

"Well," McCarter said with a shrug, "I reckon there's some small comfort in knowing that if we don't make it out alive, at least somebody will know we were here."

"Very small comfort indeed," Manning stated gruffly.

6

Chaim Levi shuffled past a row of beggars. More than one held out a single open palm and displayed the stump of his other wrist. They had probably lost the other hand as punishment for being thieves, or at least for having been convicted of that crime. Sudan had adopted this practice since September 1983 as part of their Islamic penal codes.

Levi reached inside his robe for a few coins to toss to the beggars. Voices replied with thanks and blessings as the beggars scooped up the alms. Levi looked away from the ragged group, eager to get beyond them. He had been uncomfortable and paranoid since he'd arrived in Qallabat. Being near the maimed beggars increased his consternation.

Dressed in Arab garb and keffiyeh headgear, Levi resembled dozens of locals in the streets of the town. No one paid him much attention, but he couldn't shake off the creeping sensation that somehow they knew he was an Israeli agent.

Levi was more anxious than usual due to the meeting with the American. Being assigned to the Sudan was more depressing than threatening for a Mossad agent. Although Sudan's population was seventy percent Arab, it wasn't particularly hostile toward Israel and had generally stayed out of the major conflicts in the Middle East.

However, the American presented a new problem for Levi.

The Israeli pushed through the beaded curtain at the entrance to the coffee shop. The small establishment was crowded with more than a dozen customers clustered at the flimsy wooden tables. Alcoholic drinks were illegal in Sudan, another result of the strict observation of Islamic law. The coffee houses were therefore more popular than ever. Not that everyone in Sudan could afford the price of a cup of coffee. The largest African country was also one of the poorest.

Levi found the American easily enough. A small slender man with a hawklike nose and a black mustache, the NSA agent was also clad in traditional Arab garb, but Levi recognized him. He had met Jerome Halpern in Tel Aviv more than a year earlier.

"Asalamu a'laykum," Levi said in the traditional Arab greeting. "Peace be with you."

"And may peace be with you," Halpern replied with the equally traditional response. "Please sit down."

"Thank you," Levi said.

He sat at the table. A waiter took an order for two cups of coffee, Kenyan blend, and a plate of dates. The agents waited for the man to leave before they spoke in soft whispers. Levi and Halpern understood Hebrew and English, but they used Arabic to avoid attention.

"I was surprised to find you here," Halpern stated. "A man with your background isn't generally sent to a little town like this. Does it have anything to do with the fact that Qallabat is along the border to Ethiopia?"

"One might ask you the same question," Levi replied.

Halpern grunted. Levi knew he was with the NSA SIGINT department when he was in Israel. The American's expertise was satellite surveillance systems. Since

Levi was in Qallabat due to the Argus that went down in Ethiopia, he suspected that was the reason Halpern was there, as well.

"You know we're both on the same side," the American told him.

"We have different interests," Levi reminded him.

Halpern frowned. The American NSA and the Israeli Mossad did have different goals. The National Security Agency was concerned with gathering intelligence on virtually every level. It spied on the military and espionage networks of other countries, including allies as well as those hostile toward the United States. Since America was a world power, it had interests everywhere, and the NSA operated as an enormous "snoop" organization that relied largely on high-tech equipment. It was the largest U.S. intelligence network and the least familiar to the American public. The NSA was less inclined to indulge in traditional cloak-and-dagger activities than the CIA and other intelligence outfits.

The Mossad had only one concern—the preservation of Israel. Unlike the United States, Israel wasn't terribly concerned with the welfare of its allies, because it wasn't a superpower. The Mossad used "human intelligence" or agents in the field more than technical intelligence. Mossad was also far more apt to use "direct action." It had only limited interest in matters in parts of the world that were of no immediate importance to Israel.

The waiter brought the coffee and dates.

"Have you been doing any astronomy lately?" Halpern asked. "The night sky is so clear here. There's so little industrialization to pollute the skies."

"Astronomy is more your hobby than mine," Levi replied as he sipped his coffee. "Is there something special I should know about in the night sky here?"

"This is absurd," Halpern said with a sigh. "We both know what I'm talking about."

"Then why don't you just say it?" Levi asked guardedly.

"Do you have people in Ethiopia looking for it?" the NSA man asked suddenly. "We could join forces in an emergency. That might be best for both of our establishments."

"That's a very generous offer," Levi responded. "But I think it's unnecessary."

Halpern glanced around to be sure none of the customers were eavesdropping. He bit off half a date and chewed it as he thought how to handle the Israeli. The Mossad had obviously sent a team into Ethiopia to try to locate the Argus satellite. Levi wouldn't be there otherwise. There was also little doubt that Levi assumed there was an American team looking for the fallen spy satellite, as well.

Cigarette smoke drifted across the dimly lit café and formed a gray haze between the two men. It seemed ironic, as if the smoke were a symbol of the obscurity they were trying to maintain. Neither would admit to the facts that each knew to be true. The natural enmity between Levi and Halpern didn't help the situation. Both tried not to allow personal attitudes to get in the way of the job.

"Frankly," Halpern began slowly, "the merchandise your people are looking for belongs to my...employer."

"Not if we find it first," Levi answered. "Rightful possession of salvage. Besides, it's more important to us."

The NSA agent understood what the Israeli meant. The Mossad was aware the Argus had passed over Israel and recorded data about the country's military bases, missile silos, production factories and other potential targets that Israel's enemies would find valuable in an attack on the

Jewish state. Likewise, Argus had accumulated similar details about several Arab nations that Israel could use for a strategic advantage if a conflict occurred with one or more of these countries.

"I appreciate your position," Halpern told him. "But isn't it also in your interest to ensure the merchandise we're searching for doesn't fall into Arab hands?"

The Mossad agent nodded. "Yes, and that's why we're determined to get our hands on it first."

"If you won't cooperate with us," the American said, "I suggest you warn your people not to interfere if our people get to the merchandise first. That could be a big mistake."

Halpern and Levi studied each other silently. Finally Halpern rose from the table. "If you change your mind, contact me. You know how."

Levi nodded. There was an American embassy in Khartoum.

"Leave a message for Mr. Roberts," Halpern continued. "They'll get in touch with me."

Levi watched Halpern pay the waiter and leave the coffee shop. The Mossad agent ordered another cup of coffee and spent the next half hour thinking about the circumstances of his mission. The Israeli team in Ethiopia was top-notch. It was led by Captain Uri Moshin, a former commando in the Israeli Independent Paratroop Battalion. He commanded two other Israeli agents and eight African mercenaries, including four veterans of the Eritrean People's Liberation Front. Levi considered the EPLF members of the team to be its weak links, but that was mostly because he didn't trust the Marxist politics of some of its members.

The team was really on its own. Moshin could radio the Mossad listening post in Qallabat, but Levi could be of little direct assistance to the men in the field. The presence of the NSA made his job even more difficult. Halpern and his SIGINT expertise meant the Americans would certainly be monitoring radio waves to gather information about the Israelis stationed in Sudan.

Levi hoped Moshin and his team could reach the fallen spy satellite before the Americans and get across the border to Sudan without a confrontation. He didn't want Moshin and his men to be forced to use violence against the U.S. unit. Nonetheless, Captain Moshin's first obligation was to Israel and her national defense. He would do what was necessary to retrieve the American spy satellite for the Mossad.

Levi finished his coffee and left the shop. The Israeli had to get a message to Tel Aviv and warn them that the mission was now complicated by the interference from friendly forces.

7

Victoria Yatta watched Calvin James take something from the supplies in the back of the truck. The black American removed a shoulder holster rig from a sack, then drew a blue-black pistol from the holster. He removed a loaded magazine from the butt of the autoloader, pointed it at the canvas ceiling and pulled back the slide to examine the chamber and barrel.

"Do you think those guns will be necessary?" Victoria inquired.

Seated in the rear of the truck, Gary Manning and David McCarter had weapons close at hand, as well. The husky Canadian was curled up on some bags of grain with an AK-47 resting beside him and a shoulder holster rig on the sack above his head. McCarter was sprawled across the floorboards with a rolled-up blanket for a pillow. The Briton actually wore a shoulder holster with a Browning Hi-Power under his left arm and cradled an Uzi machine pistol in his arms as he slept. He seemed as comfortable with the weapons as a child in pajamas with a teddy bear.

"Well, we'll have a hell of a problem if we need these guns and we don't have them," James commented as he inspected his pistol. "After all, they've still got a lot of fighting going on here. The civil war really isn't over yet."

He worked the slide to chamber the first round and placed the handgun on a sack of powdered milk within easy reach. The pistol was a Walther P-88, the most advanced in the fifty-year tradition of double-action autoloading pistols. The P-88 had been adopted as the standard side arm for all members of Phoenix Force except McCarter, who stubbornly refused to part with his Browning Hi-Power.

James removed the Uzi machine pistol from his weapons bag and inspected it. A smaller version of the world-famous Israeli submachine gun, the Uzi had the same excellence in design that had earned it recognition as one of the best—if not the best—close-quarters autoweapon in the world. The Uzi machine pistol was another standard weapon for Phoenix Force, although James and Manning favored assault rifles over subguns.

Satisfied that the Uzi was in good condition, James put it away and began to disassemble one of the AK-47s they had confiscated from the renegade soldiers at the clinic. He would have preferred the more familiar M-16 assault rifle, but the Kalashnikov was a better choice for Ethiopia because it was the standard military weapon, so parts and ammunition were more readily available. James had used AK-47 assault rifles many times in the past. It was a good weapon, and James had confidence in his skill with the Soviet-made firearm.

Victoria quietly watched him clean and oil the Kalashnikov parts. This American was a strange man, she decided. A paradox, in her opinion. He was both healer and warrior. An intelligent and compassionate man, yet tough and obviously deadly when necessary. She found him attractive and compelling as well as good-looking. Perhaps he was just short of handsome, but his personality and magnetism were more appealing than perfect features or the style of a male model.

"Have you done this sort of thing often?" Victoria inquired.

"Enough times to know they're all different and each mission has its own special problems," James answered. "You never really have a clear idea of what to expect until you're right in the middle of an assignment. Even then you only have a fifty-fifty chance of guessing what will happen next. You pretty much have to play it by ear when you do this sort of work."

"Play it by ear?" Victoria said with a frown. "Oh, yes. I understand. Don't you ever want a normal life?"

"I'm not even sure what that is," he answered with a slight laugh. "Seems like something I saw in a dull movie once. I don't figure I'm cut out for that sort of life."

"You don't want a wife, family, children?"

"A little late for that now," James stated with a trace of regret in his voice.

"You can't be older than forty," Victoria told him. "You're still young enough to start a family."

"That's not it," James explained. "When I joined the…group I belong to, there was a price. I set myself up to put my life on the line over and over again. Eventually I won't come back from one of these missions. Sooner or later I suppose that all of us will be killed in action. It's remarkable we've survived as long as we have."

"They won't let you quit?" she inquired.

"I can't quit," he stated. "How can I walk out on four guys who are like my brothers and know they're still risking their lives in the field? Besides, we've made a lot of enemies over the years. Terrorist outfits, intelligence organizations with the KGB at the head of the list, criminal syndicates, assorted fanatics and God knows what else. If I decided to give up this business, get married and settle down, it means my wife and kids and whoever else happened to be close to me would be potential targets for any band of assassins that might come after me looking for revenge. That's part of the price, too."

"That's sad," Victoria said sincerely. "I already planned to get out of the covert operations part of Kenyan national security. Now I'm sure of it. I'd like to be a wife and mother before I'm thirty. I don't want to be a widow or have my children become orphans, or worse, get them killed in a car bomb intended for me."

"Well, I sure don't blame you," James assured her. "That's too big a sacrifice to ask anyone to make."

"You made it," she declared. "You've denied yourself the warmth and comfort of a family and sons to carry on your family name, whatever that might be."

"Yeah," the American agreed. "But I made that choice. They didn't ask me to make it. I volunteered. I wasn't some naive kid who got conned into enlistment by a shrewd recruiter. I knew exactly what I was doing. Well, pretty much."

"No regrets?"

"Hell, there are always regrets regardless of what you do with your life," James answered with a shrug. "For now we'd better get some sleep while we've got the chance. You and I will be in the front seat in about six hours. That'll come soon enough."

"I think I'm finally relaxed enough to go to sleep," she said with a smile. "After everything that happened today, I wouldn't have thought that possible. Thank you, Daniel. You've helped more than you realize."

RAFAEL ENCIZO DROVE the truck as the headlights cast twin beams through the darkness. Katz sat beside him, a powerful transceiver radio on the floorboards by his feet. The Israeli wore a headset around his ears and spoke into a microphone in Arabic. Encizo didn't understand the language and simply concentrated on the road, if one could call it that.

Katz ended the transmission and switched off the radio. He slipped off the headset and donned the miter to complete his disguise as a Coptic priest. The robe concealed the bulge of a Walther P-88 jammed into his waistband.

"Sounds like you got through to the NSA base," Encizo remarked. The terrain was flat and almost featureless, so he glanced away from the windshield to look at Katz's face. "Anything of interest from the Sneaky Petes in Sudan?"

"Well," Katz began, "I naturally communicated indirectly with the case officer at the post. I continued to play my role as Father Raouf, contacting a Coptic Church bishop in Sudan to tell him I had arrived in Ethiopia with the relief program. If anyone was listening, it shouldn't have sounded very suspicious. Of course, that might depend on who's listening and why."

"The KGB is probably monitoring radio waves here," Encizo said. "Probably the Ethiopians, too, but the Russians have better equipment, and they're more skilled at the TECHINT side of espionage."

"The Russians haven't been devoting much time and energy to Ethiopia lately," Katz reminded his Cuban teammate. "I don't think they'll be a major concern here."

"Maybe not," Encizo answered, "but the same might not be true about the Cuban advisers. Gorbachev's doctrine of *glasnost* hasn't caught on in Cuba. Fidel Castro still considers his government to be a 'revolutionary Communist regime.' Supposedly a Russian journalist spent some time in Cuba recently and complained, 'I don't know what we're going to do with these people. They're still reading Lenin.' "

"The Cuban military is an additional concern," Katz agreed, "but I think we might have serious competition from another source. Jerome Halpern, the NSA agent in Sudan, told me my mission in Ethiopia was important because the Muslims and 'the small yet stubborn Jewish' influences in Ethiopia are trying to steal away our Christian followers.' "

"He's playing the part of a Coptic bishop," Encizo remarked. "Maybe he figures that means he has to sound radical and intolerant. A lot of people think other religions are comprised of extremists and zealots."

"I don't think so," Katz replied. "Halpern was stationed in the Middle East for years. He certainly knows the Coptic Church isn't some sort of fanatical cult. He's also Jewish, but went to extra trouble to warn me about 'stubborn Jewish influences.' I'd say he's referring to the Israelis. Halpern must have discovered the Mossad is also trying to find the Argus."

"We figured that might happen," Encizo replied. "At least the United States and Israel are allies."

"I wouldn't count on that meaning too much to the Mossad team in the field," Katz warned. "Israel knows the satellite has detailed video recordings of their military systems, defense network, vulnerable targets and whatever else Argus recorded when it passed over their country. I can't blame them for not wanting that sort of information to fall into *anyone's* hands."

"Actually, I can't blame the Libyans, Syrians, Ethiopians or anyone else for feeling that way," Encizo admitted. "You think the Mossad would attack us to get the data in the Argus? Never mind. Dumb question. Obviously they would."

"If I was still with the Mossad," Katz began, "I wouldn't let an American team leave with the information from the Argus. The same applies to us. We can't let the Israelis claim it, either."

"You were with the Mossad for a long time, Yakov," Encizo said.

Katz knew what Encizo was getting at. "Yes, but I live in the United States and I work for the U.S. government," he assured him. "I certainly don't like the idea of fighting fellow Israelis, but if there's no other way, we won't have a choice."

"Let's hope we get to the Argus first and manage to avoid all the competition, including the Israelis," Encizo commented. "We do have the advantage of the UHF ground-tracking device to help us locate the satellite when we get closer to where she went down."

"Provided the transmitter in the Argus wasn't wrecked when it fell to earth," the Phoenix commander replied. "I wish Brognola had set up a route from Sudan instead of Kenya. We would already be in the area where the satellite went down if we had crossed the border in the northwest instead of from the south."

"Hal said the operation could be put together faster in Kenya," Encizo remarked. "I think we were victims of politics and red tape again. Stony Man can always manage to cut through some red tape, but not everywhere right away. Apparently the scissors worked faster in Kenya than Sudan."

"True," Katz agreed, "but I suspect the Mossad managed to get a team into Ethiopia from that direction. I hope they have only a vague idea where the spy-in-the-sky went down. Otherwise this trip could be for nothing."

"Even if the Israelis have reached the area first," Encizo said, "they don't have the tracking device, and they'll have to deal with the various warring factions. The Argus went down right in the middle of a lot of potential battlefields. That's bound to slow them down.''

"The only problem is we'll have to deal with the same conditions,'' Katz reminded him. ''Not to mention whatever else we might encounter between here and there.''

"Yeah," Encizo said grimly as he peered through the windshield at the drab terrain surrounded by the shadows of night.

The landscape appeared bland and nonthreatening, but the Cuban realized Ethiopia was dangerous and unpredictable. It was unlikely their mission would be either peaceful or simple. Phoenix Force was never called upon to handle a milk run.

8

The roar of the churning water was a comforting sound. Captain Moshin and his men spent the night inside a cave near the frothing white waters of Tisisat Falls. The noise was a reminder that their position was about as safe as they could expect while in Ethiopia. The waterfalls offered good camouflage for the Israeli officer and his ten-man team. Trying to find any safe haven in Ethiopia was no small feat, and they took advantage of the discovery to get some badly needed rest.

Kanwonkpa woke Moshin at 4:00 am. The Israeli had elected to take the last watch and stand guard at the mouth of the cave. He told the Liberian mercenary he could go back to sleep, but Kanwonkpa displayed a broad smile and shrugged.

"There's just another hour or two until sunup," the merc declared. "I think I'll just stay up."

"Your decision," Moshin replied as he got to his feet and stretched.

The cave was damp and musky and the stench of rotted animal remains lingered, although they had removed the debris when they moved into the enclosure for the night. Moshin suspected Kanwonkpa was willing to stay up instead of remaining inside the cave with the smell that seemed locked into the rock walls. The captain reached for his web belt and buckled it around his waist. He welcomed the familiar weight of the .357 Desert Eagle in a holster at his hip. Ammo pouches, grenades and a bayonet also hung from the belt.

Moshin gathered up his AK-47. He would rather have the more familiar Galil rifle, but all the men in his team carried the Kalashnikovs and wore spotted green-and-brown fatigues to better suit their mission in Ethiopia. The captain had used his backpack for a pillow, and a poncho lay on the floor of the cave to keep his body from the damp. He rolled up the poncho and returned it to the pack before he headed for the mouth of the cave.

The others continued to sleep. Moshin glanced at the lumps in the shadows that barely seemed human in the dark. They appeared to be sleeping as soundly as stones despite the less than ideal conditions. Of course, they were all familiar with hardships of many sorts and they were exhausted from traveling all day and much of the night on foot. Moshin saw Kanwonkpa at the opening to the cave as he approached the entrance. The Liberian's face was briefly illuminated as he raised a match to the cigarette at the corner of his mouth.

Kanwonkpa's features were strong and dark as coral. He was a tough soldier for hire who had served in mercenary units throughout Africa. The Liberian also spoke several languages, including two major tongues used in Ethiopia. Moshin communicated with Kanwonkpa and the other Liberian mercs in English, the official language of their country.

"Here's some tea," Kanwonkpa offered as he handed the captain a metal canteen cup. "It's cold."

"Naturally," Moshin replied. "Thank you."

The Israeli peered out at the lush green vegetation that surrounded the waterfalls. Some monkeys chattered among the branches of nearby trees. It was a beautiful, tranquil setting. Moshin was aware that this was a rare exception in Ethiopia. There was little beauty to be found in this troubled country.

Moshin sipped the tea and contemplated the mission. He could throttle the Mossad operations officer who had given him this assignment. They had a mission that seemed close to impossible. Tel Aviv knew the general area where the American satellite had landed and they were convinced it was more than a weather satellite. Moshin certainly hoped so. He hated to think he and his men were risking their lives just to obtain recordings of climate changes in the Mediterranean.

"The EPLF men in our group say Gojam Province is probably the most agreeable area of Ethiopia," Kanwonkpa remarked as he blew smoke at the trees beyond. "I believe them. The Abbai River is also called the Blue Nile. It brings life to this area. Agriculture flourishes here, but not enough to feed all the people, of course."

"That's what I've heard," Moshin replied.

"The terrain will be more difficult the farther in-country we go," Kanwonkpa said as he finished his cigarette. "This country is a lot bigger than Liberia or Israel. We still have a lot of territory to cover."

Moshin nodded. They were trying to find a mechanical needle in a figurative haystack. He had established radio contact with Levi at the Mossad post in Sudan only to learn that the Americans had also sent a team to recover the satellite. There was also a fifty-fifty chance Libya or Syria had a unit in Ethiopia. Moshin was tempted to turn around and head back to Sudan, but the mission was of vital concern to Israel. It would be bad enough if the Americans had detailed data on Israel's national security. If Arab governments that refused to acknowledge Israel's right to exist got to the satellite first . . .

That was the greatest incentive to carry out the mission and claim the fallen satellite. Moshin wished he had more hope for success. His communications NCO had monitored radio frequencies in the hope of detecting the competition, but they hadn't been very successful. They found some military messages by the Democratic Front to the south and a couple of Eritrean broadcasts. And the radio scan picked up a faint broadcast of a conversation in Arabic that sounded promising for a moment, but it proved to be a discussion by two members of the Coptic clergy.

Moshin was satisfied with the men in his unit, and if the mission failed, it wouldn't be due to the caliber of his team. The two Israeli sergeants were veteran paratroopers and commandos. Moshin had been an NCO until 1984 when he enrolled in an officers' candidate training program and earned his commission. He had great respect for the enlisted men and noncoms, since he had spent some time as one of them.

The veteran EPLF members in the team were motivated by the promise of arms. Two of them were actually Ethiopian Jews who weren't concerned with Eritrea one way or the other. They were part of the mission because Israel would grant them citizenship and property in the southern district of Israel.

Kanwonkpa and the other three mercenaries had more than financial gain in mind when they accepted the mission. Their country, Liberia, was extremely dependent on aid from the United States and Israel.

The Liberian mercs might have accepted a mission with the Americans if the CIA had contacted Kanwonkpa's people before the Mossad had hired them. Their sense of loyalty would be just as great toward their U.S. allies as those of Israel. Luckily the Mossad got the mercs first.

Moshin had no doubts about Kanwonkpa and his Liberian teammates.

"Captain," Kanwonkpa whispered tensely, a hand cupped over the glowing tip of his cigarette.

Moshin immediately realized the merc was hiding the lit end of the cigarette from something he had seen in the shadows outside the cave. The Israeli crouched low and gripped his AK-47 with both fists as he scanned the area. Bushes and giant ferns stirred along the hill three hundred feet away. He glimpsed the barrel of an assault rifle and the top of a cap among the foliage.

Kanwonkpa ground out the cigarette. He looked at Moshin and rapped knuckles against his own skull in a gesture of self-criticism. Moshin shook his head to assure the Liberian it wasn't his fault. They hadn't thought anyone would be stalking them in the Tisisat Falls area. Kanwonkpa's cigarette may have attracted whoever was approaching the cave, but there was no time to waste on thoughts of what they should have done.

Moshin pointed at the sleeping members of their commando team. Kanwonkpa nodded and headed toward the napping figures to wake them silently. The Israeli officer stepped from the cave and crept behind some moss hanging from the rock ridge above. Using the moss as camouflage, he peered between the strands to watch the approaching figures.

The shapes crept closer, effectively using natural surroundings to conceal themselves as well as possible. Moshin couldn't see them clearly, but there seemed to be at least three shapes among the shadow-draped foliage. He couldn't determine if they were Democratic Front soldiers, EPLF guerrillas or any one of a number of other factions. Moshin had to assume the worst. The Israeli heard the shuffling of his men within the cave. They needed to get out of the confined area. If the men outside were planning an attack, they could simply lob grenades into the mouth of the cave to blast Moshin's team to bits.

The captain felt his stomach and throat constrict with fear. His heart seemed to beat so fast and hard that Moshin thought the sound might betray his presence to the mysterious figures that drew steadily closer to the cave. The Israeli slid his finger into the trigger guard of the AK-47 and held his breath as the first intruder stepped into the moonlight.

He was dressed in a tattered camouflage uniform. The man was obviously one of the many ragtag soldiers infesting Ethiopia these days. Still, he was well-armed with a Kalashnikov and several F-1 grenades attached to his webgear. The trooper stared up at the cave. His mouth fell open and he started to raise his weapon. Moshin realized the man had spotted him along the edge of the cave.

The Israeli thrust the barrel of his AK-47 toward the soldier and opened fire. A trio of 7.62 mm slugs slammed into the Ethiopian's chest. Moshin glimpsed the ragged bullet holes in the trooper's tunic as the muzzle-flash cast harsh light on the twitching figure. The soldier dropped his weapon and tumbled sideways down the hillside.

As more assault rifles responded to Moshin's Kalashnikov, the captain retreated around the edge of the cave. Bullets chipped bits of stone from the shelter. Moshin pressed his back against the rock wall, teeth clenched as he felt a stray round hiss inches near his face. Kanwonkpa moved to the mouth of the cave and yanked the pin from a grenade. The Liberian thrust his arm around Moshin and exposed it briefly to hurl the grenade.

Kanwonkpa shouted in pain and withdrew from the opening. Moshin glimpsed the mercenary's left hand and saw blood spurt from the second knuckle of his ring finger. That was all that remained of the digit. A bullet had chopped off most of the finger. The sound of the grenade explosion signaled Moshin to return to the offensive. He whirled around to fire at the enemy.

Moshin saw two figures on the hillside. One was maimed and bloodied by the explosion. The other held a hand to his shrapnel-torn face but still tried to point his rifle at the Israeli. Moshin sprayed the pair with his Kalashnikov and watched them topple downhill.

The captain bolted from the cave, followed by Sergeant Gehmer. The Israeli NCO backed up his commander as Moshin headed toward the enemy position. He found no more opponents on the hillside. Gory remains of human beings suggested at least one opponent had been torn apart by the grenade explosion and others by Moshin's rifle fire.

Automatic fire erupted from trees and bushes at the base of the hill. Moshin and Gehmer ducked as bullets whined against rocks above them. The others emerged from the cave and aimed their weapons at the muzzle-flash of the enemy's weapons. Streams of full-auto slugs blazed from their rifles. One of the EPLF recruits fell backward and tumbled back into the cave. Blood stained his uniform shirt.

Sergeant Rabin, the other Israeli NCO, fired a grenade launcher. A 40 mm shell hurtled into the Ethiopians below. The explosion sent tattered figures sailing into the trees. Screams announced that other opponents had been injured by the blast.

Moshin and Gehmer charged down the hill. Three of their African teammates followed the pair while the others remained with Rabin to supply cover fire. Dead and wounded Ethiopians littered the ground. One corpse was on fire. The grenade blast had ignited some flares in his webgear. Flames consumed the dead man's uniform, and the stench of charred flesh drifted from the remains. The burning body served as a grisly campfire, illuminating everything around it and exposing other Ethiopians among the bushes and trees.

The captain and his companions closed in while the rest of the unit pinned down the enemy with cover fire. The renegade soldiers were kept busy while Moshin and the men who joined the charge advanced. Their Kalashnikovs blasted the Ethiopian gunmen. Bodies fell among the bush as the commando team effectively turned the tide of the battle to their favor.

Moshin exhausted the ammunition of his AK-47. There was no time to reload, so the captain dropped his rifle and drew the Desert Eagle. He rushed to a tree trunk for cover as the enemy exchanged fire with his teammates. The Israeli gripped the big .357 autoloader in both hands and leaned around the trunk to aim at two Ethiopians. Moshin squeezed the trigger.

The Desert Eagle recoiled in his fists as the pistol roared. A soldier's head burst open and the man fell lifeless. The other Ethiopian swung his Kalashnikov at Moshin. The captain ducked as bullets hammered the tree trunk. Leaves, loosened from the branches, showered down on Moshin's bowed head. Suddenly a shape lunged from a nearby cluster of ferns, a panga in the figure's fist.

Moshin glimpsed a furious ebony face and saw the long blade of the machete slash diagonally at his skull. The Israeli dropped to the ground. His back slid down the tree and his rump touched earth as the panga chopped into the trunk above his head.

The Ethiopian's face registered surprise at missing his target with the machete. The soldier pried the blade loose from the tree and prepared to swing the big jungle knife once more. Moshin raised his Desert Eagle and squeezed off two shots from his seated stance. The trooper seemed to hop backward with each slug as the .357 rounds tore into his lower abdomen and stomach. He slashed the panga in a wild gesture, but the Ethiopian had staggered out of Moshin's reach. The captain exhaled as the blade sliced air near the tip of his nose.

Moshin fired a third shot into the soldier's chest, throwing him back into the bush. Moshin was ready to fire again, but the man's body slumped lifeless across the ferns. His ears ringing, the Israeli gradually realized the shooting had ceased.

Gehmer stood by the tree. "Captain, are you all right?"

"Yes, I think so," the captain replied, his breathing ragged.

Moshin got to his feet. His legs felt unsteady. He inhaled deeply to calm his nerves. The stink of the burning corpse assaulted his nostrils. Moshin nearly gagged on the smell. He glanced around and saw that the enemy had been wiped out. Gehmer placed a hand on his shoulder.

"We won, Captain," the sergeant said softly. "You can put your pistol away now."

The officer nodded and returned the Desert Eagle to its holster. He noticed that one of the Liberian mercs had been killed in the firefight. Moshin recalled that Kanwonkpa and another man in his unit had also been hit. He hoped they hadn't been seriously injured.

"These renegade pigs are all over the countryside," Galadi, one of the EPLF vets in Moshin's group, announced. "They must have thought we were another band holed up in the cave. I wonder how they found us."

"It was my fault," Kanwonkpa confessed as he stumbled downhill. The merc clutched his maimed left hand in his right fist. "I was careless with that cigarette."

"Don't dwell on it," Moshin told him. "Sergeant Gehmer, see to that wound unless somebody else was hurt worse."

The NCO bandaged Kanwonkpa's injury. One of the Africans started to urinate on the burning corpse. Moshin was repulsed by this, although he realized the man might not have intended an indignity. He told the fellow to put out the fire with some dirt instead.

Rabin and three others descended. Another man who had been in their unit was dead. Moshin shook his head. They had been whittled down to nine men. Kanwonkpa was wounded but seemed fit to travel. Galadi suggested they salvage ammunition and supplies from the slain Ethiopians.

"Do it quickly," the captain replied. "We have to get out of here. Don't take any more than we can carry without weighing us down. From now on we'll have to travel as light as possible."

"All things considered we were lucky, Captain," Rabin remarked as he broke open his grenade launcher to feed a fresh 40 mm cartridge-style shell into the breech. "They could have wiped us out if they had been better organized and employed a bit of sound strategy."

"We lost two men, Sergeant," Moshin reminded him. "With that kind of luck we'll all be dead before this is over."

9

At daybreak Calvin James resumed driving. Victoria Yatta joined him in the front seat while Katz and Encizo climbed into the rear of the vehicle for a well-deserved rest. The truck continued north across an ugly, dry region. The earth was cracked in a spiderweb pattern. Tough grass and leathery weeds sprouted from the fissures, but otherwise the area seemed as lifeless as the surface of the moon.

"We've passed through Shoa Province and reached Wollo," Victoria announced, her voice grim as if warning James they had ventured to the entrance of hell itself. "From here on we'll be in one of the worst areas of Ethiopia."

"This hasn't exactly been Acapulco so far," the American commented dryly. "You mean there are gonna be even fewer laughs up ahead?"

"You might not be capable of laughter after Wollo Province," Victoria said seriously. "This place could break the stone heart of a gargoyle."

James peered out at the bleak surroundings. It was as dismal as any stretch of earth he had ever encountered, and the oppressive hot winds from the Danakil desert region swept in from the east as if to ensure the climate remained as uncomfortable as the setting. The area and the heat reminded James of the Gobi Desert, which Phoenix

Force had passed through during a previous mission in Mongolia. Yet this seemed even more grim and forbidding than the Gobi had been.

"You've been here before?" James inquired as the truck bounced along the uneven surface.

"Yes," she answered. "I was in this area with Dr. Abraha as part of a relief program. All Four Horsemen of the Apocalypse are found here. I sometimes wonder when the other seals will be opened."

"The seals?" James wondered aloud. A former SEAL in the Navy, he was surprised by her remark.

"In the Book of Revelation," Victoria answered. "In the Bible."

"Yeah, I've read it," he assured her, "but it's been a while. What seals do you mean?"

"In the sixth chapter of Revelation it speaks of seven seals," Victoria began. "The horsemen of war, famine, pestilence and death emerged from the first four. The fifth reveals the souls of those slain for the Word of God. Of course, thousands have already died for their faith throughout the world."

"I'd say that's been happening for a long time," James agreed. "What about the sixth seal?"

"Natural disasters and omens," she replied. "Earthquakes and blood on the moon. The sun turns black and stars fall to earth."

"A satellite falling from the sky would look like a shooting star," James mused. He immediately wished he hadn't thought of this comparison. "I'm not so sure I want to know about the last seal."

"The seventh seal reveals seven angels with trumpets," Victoria stated. "They herald more omens followed by the rise of the Antichrist, Armageddon, the end of the world."

The truck rolled on without incident in the early hours of the morning, then James noticed a group of tents up ahead. There seemed to be dark stones surrounding the tents. As the vehicle drew closer, he realized these "stones" were actually crowds of people. They sat motionless in clusters around the tents. James also noticed large dark birds sailing gracefully in the sky above. They were vultures that clearly sensed the presence of death.

"Oh, my God!" James rasped when he got a better look at the crowd.

Thousands of people had gathered in the area. They were emaciated, with blank eyes and parchment-dry skin that seemed drawn taut across bone without fat or muscle. Clad in rags or draped in tattered sheets, the figures seemed more dead than alive as the truck advanced. Many of the people were too weak from hunger even to turn to look at the truck.

The horror of starvation was as terrible as any battlefield. Worse because the victims of famine and neglect confronted opponents that couldn't be slain with a bullet or a blade. People who resembled living skeletons held out open palms in a desperate if feeble gesture. Pleading for help, their eyes seemed sunken deep into the sockets and their lips trembled, too weak to utter words.

Some were strong enough to stumble toward the truck, palms pressed together as if in prayer. Small children wandered about naked, crying as parents tried hopelessly to comfort them. Flies hovered around their faces. Most were too weak even to brush the insects away. The children cried without tears. They didn't have enough moisture left in their bodies to produce any kind of liquid. Mothers held infants to their leathery breasts, and the babies suckled on dry nipples. The mothers had no milk left.

Sorrow and anger formed a clenched fist in James's stomach. He wanted to avert his eyes, but he couldn't. Not looking at this anguish wouldn't make it go away. This wasn't a television commercial for funds to help stop world hunger. James couldn't conveniently switch the channel or turn off these images.

He had seen poverty before. Raised in a ghetto, he had known hardships that had seemed unbearable. Now he was ashamed that he had ever complained about having little. Compared to the people gathered in this remote camp of ghastly deprivation, James had been born in a palace with luxuries and opportunities all around him.

"We've got supplies in the truck," James suddenly announced as he stepped on the brake.

"We don't have enough to do any good," Victoria told him. She gestured at the windshield. "Look at them. There must be thousands. We don't have enough food for one-tenth of these people."

"I know," James said bitterly. "But we gotta do something. We can't just drive by and not even try."

A hundred scrawny scarecrows, their faces and limbs scarred by skin diseases, staggered to the vehicle. Mouths hung open to reveal rotten teeth and raw gums. They seemed more dead than alive, walking corpses that were slowly rotting as they waited for death.

James emerged from the cab of the truck. Begging figures held out their hands for alms and followed him to the rear of the vehicle. Gary Manning had pushed back the tarp and stared out at the sea of suffering. The Canadian's face was pale and his eyes wide as he looked at the horrific sight.

"Hand me those medical supplies," James urged. "I'm gonna see what I can do for the people with infections and disease. Then we can pass out as much food as possible."

"Sweet Jesus," Manning whispered. His expression told James that the big Canadian's thoughts were identical to his own. "We don't have enough, Cal."

"I know," James said with frustration. "But at least we can give them something, man."

Manning located some crates of medical supplies and started to hand them to James. McCarter climbed from the tailgate and stared at the crowd with astonishment. Encizo handed him a sack of powdered milk. The Briton took it and nodded woodenly as if physically stunned by what he saw.

"This looks like something out of Dante's Inferno," McCarter remarked. "The damned souls on the floor of hell."

"This is worse than hell," Encizo said. "Hell is for unrepentent sinners. These people have been damned although they're innocent."

Katz emerged from the truck, still dressed as a Coptic priest. Many of the emaciated Ethiopians cried out and flocked to him. They dropped to the ground and kissed the hem of his robe. Katz solemnly blessed them and recited Bible scripture in Arabic. The Israeli felt awkward leading the masses in Christian rituals, but they found comfort in his presence and the words of their faith. The fact that he wasn't an ordained priest or even a Christian didn't seem to matter. The masquerade offered them some spiritual hope. Most were beyond a chance for physical redemption.

"We can't stay here long," Katz warned the others. "I don't know if we should have even stopped. There's almost nothing we can do for these people."

"We can feed some of them," Manning insisted as he gave a bag of grain to a group of desperate Ethiopians.

"There isn't enough to give them all a single mouthful of food," Katz replied. "We'll only build up their hopes rather than give them any real help."

"Maybe we should concentrate on the people who need help the most," the Canadian suggested.

"Might do better to try to strengthen the ones who aren't already too weak from hunger," McCarter said. "Maybe they'll have a better chance, and perhaps they'll even be able to help the others."

"I certainly can't make a decision about who should live and who shouldn't," Katz said as the images of Nazis making selections for the camps nagged at his brain. "It may be best just to leave the food and let them deal with the moral crisis."

A number of parents approached Katz with infants. One spoke Arabic and explained that they wanted him to baptize their children. Katz was reluctant to carry out this Christian sacrament in the guise of a priest, yet he was familiar with the rites and knew most Christians considered it acceptable for a person who wasn't a member of the clergy to perform baptism in an emergency. Considering the grave condition of the starving children, Katz was satisfied it was an emergency.

"Pass me my canteen," Katz told Encizo. The Cuban remained inside the truck to avoid alarming the Ethiopians, since he was dressed in a Cuban military uniform.

Encizo handed him the canteen and watched Katz baptize the first child. The Cuban was impressed by how the Israeli carried out the sacrament. He knew he wouldn't have been able to perform a Jewish rite as convincingly.

James and Victoria tried to search out people they could treat with antibiotics and disinfectants. Many of the crowd suffered from infections and skin problems due to days without bathing and exposure to harsh weather.

Several had fallen into comas and others were strangely fatigued in a manner that seemed unrelated to starvation. These individuals actually refused food when offered. James was puzzled by these ailments.

"Trypanosomiasis," Victoria explained as she searched through a medical kit. "African sleeping sickness carried by the tsetse fly. I can treat some of them with organic compounds that contain low-level arsenic."

James nodded, aware that arsenic, a poison, was used in some medicines. Victoria gave the compounds only to those with early stages of the sleeping sickness disease. The more advanced cases were beyond treatment. They would never wake from their comas.

An old man spoke with Victoria in Tigre. James noticed that whatever the man said sparked anger in the lovely Kenyan lady. She wasn't upset with the old fellow, however, and gave him some painkillers with verbal instructions about using the pills. Victoria moved next to James and explained what the man had told her.

"Most of these people were driven out of their homes by nearby fighting," she said, bandaging a woman's arm after applying a disinfectant cream to a lesion. "There are still some old Mengistu troops operating in the region, and now they're preying on the general populace."

"So this was done on purpose," James said, shaking his head.

James and Victoria made the most of their medical supplies and tried to ration them out to as many people as possible, but there were just too many. Although they helped more than two hundred sick and injured, hundreds more pleaded for assistance. Victoria sadly told them there was no medicine left, and James opened his leather kit to show them it was empty. Two children reached out for the bag. James let them have it and managed a weak smile.

People squatted around bags of grain and powdered food. They had torn open the canvas and scooped out fistfuls of food to devour it in a desperate feeding frenzy. For every person who had something to eat, ten still went hungry. James saw the frustration and sorrow on the faces of Manning and McCarter as they had to turn away from the crowd when they ran out of food.

Katz had completed as many baptisms and blessings as time allowed. He assembled a large group of Christians among the crowd and recited the Lord's Prayer in Arabic. Some Muslims in the congregation joined them. They knelt and faced Mecca while Katz spoke. Perhaps the Islamic members uttered their own prayers to Allah and simply participated for the comfort of being part of an assembly of worshipers, finding at least the illusion of strength in numbers.

Rafael Encizo suddenly appeared from the rear of the truck. He held the CZ-75 in his fist as he held his arm high and squeezed the trigger. The report of the pistol startled the crowd. Encizo snapped orders in curt Spanish, telling the others they had wasted enough time and had to move on.

They realized Encizo had decided to play the villain to make it easier for them to leave. James and Victoria returned to the front of the truck while Manning and McCarter climbed into the back. Katz finally joined them. James started the engine. He saw that several Ethiopians sat on the ground with the medic kit the children had taken from him. They were tearing the bag into strips and pounding the portions with rocks. Then they started to chew the leather.

The truck rolled forward. Some of the Ethiopians were reluctant to get out of the path of the vehicle, apparently hoping they could get more aid if they could delay the departure. James steered the rig around the group and managed to avoid running anyone over. Pleading faces stared at him from the windows. The commando forced himself to concentrate on the area ahead.

"I never went through anything like that before," he muttered. "I've seen some terrible things before, but nothing worse than that."

"Yes," Victoria said softly. "I tried to warn you, but I know nothing can really prepare a person for something like this. It doesn't get any easier when you do it again. Or the next time or the time after that."

"It's selfish, but I don't want to go back there," James admitted. He slammed a fist against the steering wheel. "Damn it! The U.S. government gave Ethiopia millions in foreign aid to help the victims of famine. There were rock concerts in America and Great Britain to raise funds for the same cause. They came up with millions more."

"There were other charities, too," Victoria told him. "Close to seven hundred million dollars in aid flooded into Ethiopia, most of it from the United States and Western Europe."

"So why is this still going on?" James asked. But he already knew the answer. "Because of the chaos, all the fighting, the civil strife."

"That's right," Victoria said bitterly. "You Americans were generous but naive. Some of the organizations sent people to supervise the distribution of money and food, but most of it never actually got to the people. Some of it went into the pockets of Mengistu and his henchmen. Some of it helped buy arms for the various guerrilla factions." She stared grimly at James. "Corruption breeds like flies in this unhappy country."

10

After visiting the starving people, it was hard for Phoenix Force to believe there were actually towns and cities in Wollo Province. Nonetheless, they had to steer clear of places like Waldia and Lalibeta as they moved farther north. The truck had already passed Dessye, the provincial capital of Wollo. It was important to avoid the cities because one or more of the various guerrilla factions would have troops posted there.

They stopped briefly to stretch their muscles. McCarter checked the truck to make sure it was still in good condition and do some preventive maintenance. None of the men of Phoenix force or Victoria Yatta wanted anything to eat. After the encounter with the starving masses, they didn't have much of an appetite.

"This area seems pretty sparsely inhabited for such an overpopulated country," McCarter commented as he fired up a Player's.

"Ethiopia is almost three times the size of California and has a population of roughly fifty million," James answered. "That's less than twice the population of California. There are still some parts of the Golden State that aren't heavily populated."

"Much of Ethiopia is virtually uninhabitable," Victoria added. "You've seen that for yourselves. Yet the majority of Ethiopians are still farmers. They can't produce enough food for all the people here. The droughts and war certainly haven't helped."

"I've never seen a country more depressing than this," Manning confessed as he scanned the harsh, dry land.

Miles of barren earth stretched out before them. A few hardy bushes that appeared to be mostly thorns and some ugly trees without leaves appeared to be the only vegetation. The knotted, dark limbs of the trees resembled gnarled fingers of blistered giant hands that jutted up from the ground.

"I could drive for a while if you want to take a break from behind the wheel," Encizo volunteered. "It's not likely we'll come across many people if we keep going the same route we've used so far."

"Naw," James answered. "I'd just as soon keep driving until sundown. If anybody other than a black man is at the wheel, it'll attract attention. You can drive after dark. Safer then."

"That might work as long as we don't come across a blockade of soldiers who decide to search the truck," Manning said grimly. "Sanchez isn't going to be able to bluff his way through military troops that include real Cuban officers, and Miller and I are going to be damn hard to explain. Besides, Cubans don't seem a whole lot more popular than Americans."

"Powell's right," McCarter said, using the Canadian's cover name. "Father Raouf is going to have some trouble trying to convince anyone he's a Coptic priest with a relief program, since we handed out almost all the supplies and food."

"I know," Katz agreed. "If we come across any more victims of starvation or the war, we can't stop to offer help again. We have only enough rations and medical supplies left for our own use. I know it's hard. We'd all like to do whatever we can for the unfortunate people of this country, but right now that means we can't do a damn thing for them.''

"You're right," James reluctantly admitted. "I wish you weren't, but that's the reality of our situation."

"Our mission is to find the Argus and get the microchips from the recording unit," Katz reminded them. "That's going to be hard enough, since there's a lot of fighting concentrated in the area we're headed for. Then we have to get out of Ethiopia after we get the data. That might not be so easy, either."

"We'd better come up with some sort of convincing cover to explain our presence," McCarter said as he tossed his cigarette onto the ground and crushed it under a boot. "Right now we look as suspicious as a bloke dressed in a Nazi uniform at a bar mitzvah."

"I wish you'd come up with a different comparison," Katz said dryly, "but the point is still valid. The only idea that I can offer is that Powell, Miller and I wrap ourselves with bandages to cover the color of our skin and the rest of you can try to convince the military we're locals who were badly burned in a fire."

"I'm not looking forward to being wrapped up like a mummy in this heat," Manning admitted. "That sounds like a real long shot."

"Frankly I think it might work better if you continue to play the role of Father Raouf and I get bandaged up as one of the wounded," Encizo reluctantly declared. "My disguise as a Cuban soldier is wearing awfully thin and might be more of a liability now."

"I hate to dump more kitty litter on the parade," James began, "but I don't speak Amharic or any of the other local languages unless you count English. The only ID I have is a Kenyan passport. No matter how we handle this, it's gonna be awfully suspicious.''

''Perhaps I can convince the soldiers you're a deaf mute,'' Victoria offered.

''I don't think that'll really make anyone less curious about our vehicle,'' McCarter told her. ''With a deaf mute driver, a woman apparently in charge, a Coptic priest from Egypt and three chaps bandaged up so much one can't tell if they're black or white, well, a fellow would have to be terribly dense not to think this was a rather odd combination.''

''Any military blockade with a commander smarter than a garden snail,'' Katz said, ''would insist on searching the truck. They'd find our weapons for sure, and we can't abandon our firepower if we're going into a war zone. They'd probably unwrap the bandages, as well. I would in their position, even if I believed the burn victims might be genuine. I wouldn't take the chance the enemy might be using a disguise. I'd unwrap the bandages enough to determine if the alleged burns were there. You can bet your last parabellum round they will, too.''

''You're right,'' Encizo said with a sigh. ''I hate the idea of pulling out of a mission without seeing it through to the end, but maybe we should seriously consider heading west for Sudan and forget about the satellite. It won't do anyone any good if we get killed or captured by one of the guerrilla factions because we stubbornly tried to carry out an assignment that had gone so wrong that it was virtually impossible to complete.''

''I never thought I'd hear you make a suggestion like that,'' McCarter commented.

''I don't remember ever being in the middle of a mission and all the problems seemed this insurmountable,'' the Cuban answered. ''Victoria's the only one of us familiar with this country, and she doesn't know this area well enough to help us travel secretly past the military forces here.''

''We can't do that with the truck,'' Katz declared. ''If we go on with the mission, we'll have to travel on foot. That will make our odds a bit better. If the rest of you want to pull out, we change direction right now and head for Sudan. What do you say?''

''We've never backed out of a mission, and I don't want to bloody start now,'' McCarter announced. No one was surprised by the Briton's reply.

''As reluctant as I am to agree with Miller,'' Gary Manning began, using McCarter's cover name, ''I think we should see this through. The microchips from the Argus could wind up with the Russians, Libyans, Syrians or somebody else who isn't exactly friends with the U.S. or Western Europe, let alone Israel. That's too great a risk to just walk away from.''

''We've got this far,'' James declared. ''I'd hate to turn back when we're so close.''

''Well,'' Encizo said with a sigh, ''I already expressed my reservations about this, but we've taken on big odds in hostile territory before. If everybody else agrees, so do I.''

''Victoria?'' Katz inquired. ''The final vote is yours.''

''What if I say we should pull out?'' she replied as she studied Katz's face to determine what the Israeli genuinely thought.

His expression remained calm and impassive as he said, ''This has to be a unanimous decision. The rest of us have done this sort of thing for quite a few years. You're professional, but you've never been faced with the dangers and risks we're headed for. There may be violence on a level you can barely imagine. Some of us may die before this is over. There's a possibility none of us will survive."

"You sound as if you're trying to frighten me," Victoria replied with a nervous smile.

"You should be frightened," Katz told her bluntly. "I'm not going to lie to you about how dangerous this mission is. I won't understate how important it is, either. Kenya has as much interest in keeping the Argus from falling into the hands of Ethiopia or Libya as we do."

"Those are strong reasons to continue with the mission," James said urgently. "But we may not be able even to get close to the satellite. Maybe one or two of us ought to escort Victoria to the border and the rest of us go on with the mission. The guys who reach Sudan can contact the NSA post and try to help as much as possible from there. Could be they can put together an effective plan to get the other team out of Ethiopia as quickly and safely as possible."

"No," Victoria declared. "I'm staying with you. Perhaps I don't know this province well, but I know it better than any of you. I can also act as a translator, and the simple fact that I'm a black woman makes me the least conspicuous of this unit. African men are among the most chauvinist in the world. That's especially true of Ethiopians. They won't be nearly as suspicious of me as they'd be of any of you."

"Victoria," James began, but he knew she was strong-willed and he wouldn't be able to talk her out of this decision.

"It's settled," she insisted.

"All right," Katz said with a nod. "According to my last radio contact with the NSA, the heart of the war zone is still nearly a sixty away. Let's make the most of the truck while we can use it. We should be able to cover another fifteen or twenty miles before we have to abandon it. It'll be close to sundown by then, and it'll be safer to travel on foot after dark.''

"Sounds like the best plan we can put together under the circumstances," Encizo agreed.

"Then let's get on the road again, mates," McCarter urged with customary eagerness. The Briton sensed they would soon be involved in action, and he was anxious to be on a battlefield once more.

"Maybe we should bring along some valium for him in the future," Manning muttered, tilting his head toward McCarter.

"If we have a future," James said under his breath.

After another six miles, the truck encountered different terrain. The earth rolled slightly in a series of tiny hills. Boulders and rock formations lined the area. James glanced suspiciously at the stony structures as he drove the vehicle across the bumpy surface. Victoria, once again seated beside James, noticed his apprehension.

"Is something wrong?" she inquired.

"I'm probably just paranoid," he replied, "but this place is an ideal setting for an ambush."

An object suddenly flew from the peak of one of the rock formations. James glimpsed the projectile and stomped on the brake pedal. It resembled an oversize Ping-Pong paddle and didn't appear threatening from a distance. Nonetheless, James reacted as if it was a serious attack. He stopped the truck and pulled Victoria to the floor.

"What . . . ?" she began, startled.

He covered her with his own body and bowed his head beneath the dashboard. An explosion roared outside the vehicle. The truck trembled from the shock wave, and a loud crack erupted above James's head. He felt something fall across his back and realized that part of the windshield had broken off and dropped on him.

"Stay down!" James ordered as he reached for the Walther P-88 holstered under a seat cushion.

The others had immediately reached for weapons when the truck had abruptly halted. The explosion triggered them into action. Encizo and McCarter hurried to the tailgate while Manning hauled a canvas sack of grenades from the supplies. Katz crouched by one side of the truck and braced an Uzi machine pistol across his prosthesis. The Israeli peered through a gap in the canvas tarp along one of the wooden ribs.

Several figures moved in the surrounding rock formations. Katz saw vague shapes of heads and shoulders as well as a glimpse of a rifle barrel. Automatic fire snarled from the rocks. Bullets tore at the ground outside. Apparently the ambushers didn't want to hit the truck. They probably hoped to seize the merchandise from the vehicle.

Encizo spotted two armed figures by some boulders. The Cuban, AK-47 in his fists, looked at McCarter. The British ace, an Uzi close to his chest, tilted his head toward the opening. Encizo grunted and shrugged. McCarter had volunteered to be the first from the vehicle. Encizo expected this from his bold teammate and didn't envy the Briton's position.

The Cuban warrior pushed back the tarp with his rifle and fired at the figures by the boulders. The bullets startled the ambushers. As they ducked behind the rocks, McCarter leaped from the tailgate. His boots hit the ground, and he swung his machine pistol toward the stony clusters across the clearing. The Briton sprayed a volley at the rocks to discourage any possible opponents from trying to open fire from that position.

Other ambushers rose from stony cover to point Kalashnikovs at McCarter. They were unaware of Katz hidden inside the truck. The Israeli thrust the stubby barrel of his Uzi through the gap in the tarp and triggered the machine pistol. Katz saw a dark head snap back from the impact of one or more slugs. The skull split open to spray blood and brain matter against the rocks. Almost decapitated, the corpse slumped from view and the others ducked for cover.

Manning rushed to the end of the truck and covered Encizo as the Cuban jumped from the tailgate. The Canadian commando used his AK-47 to keep the enemy busy while Encizo and McCarter bolted for cover by some boulders.

Another paddlelike object sailed from the rocks, falling near the rear of the truck. Manning saw two tube-shaped sticks held to the paddle by wire. Fuses sizzled at the crimped ends of the sticks. The Canadian demolitions expert immediately recognized dynamite. He nearly leaped from the truck to grab the paddle and throw it back at the enemy or extinguish the fuses. However, he realized if he jumped outside he would be exposed to the ambushers' fire.

Yet if the dynamite exploded it would almost certainly destroy the truck and kill everyone in the vehicle. Manning had to act quickly. Indecision would be fatal. The scant seconds of burning fuse was all that stood between life and death. The Canadian pulled the canteen from his belt and hurled it at the paddle with one hand, raising the buttstock of the AK-47 to his shoulder with the other.

Clasping the front stock, he snap-aimed as the canteen fell to earth near the dynamite. The Canadian warrior relied on years of training and experience with firearms as he squeezed the trigger. If a bullet struck the dynamite, it could detonate the explosives. He had to trust his skill and accuracy as he fired at the canteen.

Three 7.62 mm slugs slammed into the canteen. The impact tossed the container into the air as water spilled from bullet holes. The spray descended from six leaks caused by entrance and exit holes in the canteen. Water doused the crimped ends of the dynamite. The fuses sputtered and the burning tips were soaked and extinguished.

Encizo and McCarter saw Manning's plight and fired at the rock formations to draw the attention of the ambushers. Manning took advantage of the distraction to jump from the tailgate. Bullets tore into the ground near his feet. Dirt splattered the Canadian's legs as he dashed to the paddle and scooped it up before he ran for the boulders. A stray round hissed inches from his ear, and more clods of dirt hopped up from the ground to shower the paddle in his fist. The ambushers had tried to set off the dynamite with bullets and missed by more than half a foot.

The Phoenix pro from Canada bolted for the boulders. Manning fired his Kalashnikov at the rocks, holding the rifle by the pistol grip with one fist. He dived around the nearest boulder as bullets struck stone. Chips pelted Manning's hunched back even as he scrambled to cover. The commando was breathing hard and was damp with sweat as he glanced up at McCarter and Encizo.

"You still in one piece, mate?" the Briton asked.

Manning nodded, unable to speak. He leaned against the boulder and caught his breath as he removed the pack of grenades from his shoulder. Manning placed the sack next to his partners and reached for a small pack at the small of his back.

The Canadian demolitions expert unfastened the Velcro straps to the pack and removed it from his belt. Opening the pack, he reached inside for the packets of C-4 plastic explosives in the case, took out a small glob of the white taffylike substance and jammed it between the sticks of dynamite wired to the paddle. Then he reached into a jacket pocket for a detonator and a miniature timing mechanism.

Encizo and McCarter, busy fighting the ambushers, barely noticed what their Canadian partner was doing. Encizo extracted a spent magazine from his Kalashnikov and reloaded. McCarter took two grenades from the sack, tossed one to Encizo and hooked the other to his belt. The Briton started to draw the magazine from his Uzi machine pistol when movement among the rocks above their position drew his attention.

Looking up, McCarter spotted two figures creeping down from the top layers of stone. He raised the Uzi and only glimpsed the opponents as he pointed the weapon at the pair. They were young, black and slender. Both wore dark bush shirts, shorts and caps. They carried AK-47s and ammo belts crisscrossed on their chests. McCarter fired at the closest gun-totting ambusher before realizing it was a young woman.

The last two parabellums snarled from the Uzi and slammed into her torso. McCarter's stomach twisted into a knot when he saw he had shot a woman and heard her scream. A bullet punched through the hollow of her jaw, burned through the roof of her mouth and plowed into her brain.

She fell lifelessly from the rock ridge and plunged to the ground as her male companion pointed his rifle at McCarter. Encizo drilled the man with a trio of copperjacketed rounds. His body jerked from the force of the high-velocity slugs. The man triggered his AK-47, but the stream of bullets sliced well above the three Phoenix warriors.

The gunman dropped his weapon and tumbled down the rocky monuments. McCarter hastily swapped magazines to reload his Uzi, ducking as a salvo of enemy slugs ricocheted against the boulders. The fire came from the rock formations across the clearing from their position. The fury of the attack suggested that two or more opponents were firing at the three Phoenix pros.

"Let's give them a real jolt," Manning suggested as he finished preparing the detonator and timer for the C-4.

Encizo and McCarter yanked the pins from their grenades and lobbed the explosive eggs over the boulders. The grenades landed among the rock formations covering the enemy. Manning set the timer to his own demolitions device. When he heard the grenades explode, the Canadian rose and hurled the paddle at the ambushers' position.

The reason the mysterious attackers had strapped the dynamite to the paddle was to allow the sticks to be thrown greater distances and deliver twice as much destruction as a single stick of dynamite. The same principles allowed Manning to hurl the paddle with greater accuracy and range than his partners' grenades. The paddle spun high above the cloud of dust and stony debris of the grenade explosions. It began to descend on a cluster of rock formations. The detonator set off the C-4 packet and ignited the twin sticks of dynamite, as well.

The blast was devastating. It tore huge chunks of stone from the structures and sent several opponents hurtling from cover. Bloodied and dismembered by the explosion, the corpses fell to earth like monstrous hail. Ghastly remains of human beings littered the ground, accompanied by more rock fragments and a large fog of dense dust and powdered stone.

The explosions drove a few ambushers from shelter. Male and female figures, all clad in the same makeshift uniform, darted across the rocks in a desperate effort to escape the horrendous fate that had struck down their comrades. Encizo and McCarter trained their weapons on the fleeing opponents but held their fire. The women among the group caused them to hesitate. It was also clear that these were irregular guerrillas of some sort.

Three ambushers approached the truck. One sprayed the cab with a volley of Kalashnikov rounds while the others jogged forward. James and Victoria, still huddled beneath the dashboard, heard glass shatter and metal groan. James glanced up at the windshield and saw that the view had been eclipsed by a broad metal shape. He realized the latch to the hood had been broken by a bullet and it had popped open.

The Phoenix pro figured if the open hood blocked his view, it also prevented the attackers from looking through the windshield. Broken glass fell from his back and shoulders as James sat up. He opened the driver's door and swung from the cab, ducking low, using the open door for cover. Pointing the Walther P-88 under the door, he stared across the sights to aim at the closest opponent.

The startled ambusher swung his Kalashnikov toward James, but the American crusader already had him lined up and squeezed off two shots. Both 9 mm rounds hit the gunman in the solar plexus. One bullet powered upward to burst the man's heart. The fellow uttered a loud groan and fell as if hit in the chest by an invisible baseball bat.

Another opponent fired into the truck door, which vibrated violently. One bullet pierced the door and hissed just two inches from James's elbow. The tough guy from

Chicago didn't realize how close the projectile came. He was too busy leaning around the edge of the door, aiming the Walther at the second gunman.

Unable to see the man's entire body, James blasted the opponent's right leg. The man screamed as the high-velocity blow knocked him off his feet. James saw the gunman hit the ground and nearly fired again. However, the guy had dropped his AK-47 and was clutching the wounded leg with both hands. The Phoenix pro didn't want to kill a man who was no longer armed and didn't present a direct threat.

The third opponent was sprinting for some boulders. The shapely legs and curved hips and bosom revealed that the figure belonged to a young woman. James let her run to cover. More gunfire erupted from the surrounding rocks. Bullets plowed into the ground near the commando's position, and James slid under the truck as slugs hammered the door and punched holes through the metal skin.

Victoria began shouting from inside the cab. James wasn't certain what language she spoke, but he thought the words and voice inflection resembled Tigrinya rather than Amharic. She repeated her name several times. Eventually the ambushers ceased fire. Victoria opened the passenger door and emerged from the vehicle.

"Get back inside!" James told her as he crawled under the truck toward her position.

"Tell your friends to hold their fire," Victoria replied, her tone confident, almost commanding. "I think I can get the rebels to agree to a truce."

"Rebels?" James inquired, not really surprised. "You mean they're EPLF? Why the hell did they attack us?"

"If you'll give me a chance," Victoria said sharply, "I'll try to find out. Now tell the others to hold their fire."

The others had already ceased fire after the other side appeared to terminate their attack. The silence allowed a voice from the rocks to call out clearly from his hiding place. The words were in Tigrinya, followed by an English equivalent.

"I'm coming down!" the voice announced. "I'm coming alone and unarmed! If you don't kill me, we can talk! Agreed?"

"Agreed!" Victoria answered firmly.

11

Katz climbed from the rear of the truck and walked around the vehicle as James emerged from beneath the rig to stand next to Victoria. The Phoenix commander still wore the cassock and Coptic cross, but the Uzi machine pistol in his fist made the disguise of a priest less than convincing. James thrust his Walther pistol into his belt and looked at the Israeli.

"Maybe you should go back to the rocks with the others," James told him. "This could be a trick."

Katz replied by kneeling and placing the Uzi on the ground. He started to remove the robe as a lone figure appeared and approached from the summit of some rock formations. Tall and slender, the young man descended the stony surface. He was unarmed and seemed grimly determined. The rebel's expression revealed he also had doubts about confronting the Phoenix warriors.

James moved his hand away from the P-88 in his belt, but he was unwilling to put the pistol on the ground. Katz folded the cassock across his prosthesis. The Israeli also carried a Walther autoloader in his belt. He held his artificial limb close to his body and concealed the pistol with the robe draped across the prosthesis. The middle-aged Israeli was deceptively harmless in appearance, and he had learned to use this to his advantage. Many opponents had underestimated Katz. Most paid for this mistake with their lives. Katz seemed to have discarded his weapon and even removed his disguise to avoid offending the rebels who might regard his priestly garments as blasphemy. Yet Katz was still dangerous and capable of defending himself if necessary.

The other three members of Phoenix Force remained behind the boulders. They were alert to the possibility that the representative from the EPLF might be a decoy sent to draw their attention while the other rebels moved into position for another ambush. Although Phoenix had clearly gained the upper hand in the battle, they realized the rebels still outnumbered them and had them surrounded. If the EPLF had enough ammunition, explosives and water, they could pin down the commandos and eventually wait them out to destroy them.

The spokesman from the rebels approached James, Katz and Victoria. His angular face was strong with a determined jawline and fierce eyes. He didn't carry a weapon, but he moved with catlike grace and silence acquired by a lifetime of guerrilla warfare. There was no trace of fear in his face as he stared at the trio near the crippled truck. Wounded EPLF members groaned, and the man James had shot in the leg cried out for help as he lay in the dust, hands still clasped to his damaged limb.

"My name is Ebrahim," the rebel spokesman announced. "Group commander of this cell of the Eritrean People's Liberation Front. We've heard of Victoria Yatta before. She is said to be Dr. Abraha's nurse and credited with helping many of my countrymen who suffer from starvation and illness."

"I have tried to help," Victoria replied. "These men are my friends. This is Daniel Manyoni and Father...Raouf."

"They are well-armed and skilled fighters for members of the relief program," Ebrahim commented. "Several of my people are dead."

"We acted in self-defense," James told him. "What the hell did you ambush us for in the first place?"

"You weren't EPLF and you were driving an old army truck," the rebel leader answered. "In Ethiopia that is enough to assume hostile intentions."

"You thought we were renegade government soldiers?" James demanded. "Sounds to me as if you guys have gotten a little trigger-happy over the years. After all, you're in control of this area now, aren't you?"

"We've learned not to take chances when we see potential enemies. Old habits die hard."

"That's wonderful," James snorted. "Are we gonna kill each other now? I'm sure you dudes want to get even with us for wastin' some of your comrades and, of course, we'll object to being slaughtered. Does that mean we don't have any choice except to die together?"

"You're not the enemy," Ebrahim remarked. "In fact, you don't talk like an African of any nationality. You use expressions I don't understand. The whites among your group might not be Cubans—" he pointed a finger at Katz "—but this one is no priest. Foreigners don't come to Ethiopia without a reason. Who are you people and why are you here?"

"We came to retrieve something of interest to the U.S. government," Katz explained. "America isn't your enemy, you know."

"They were when our war first began," Ebrahim stated, his voice loaded with venom. "Your country supported Haile Selassie. You didn't care what he did to Eritrea and you condemned us because of our Marxism."

"Mengistu and his Communist government weren't exactly your salvation, guy," James reminded him.

"That's true, but that bastard is gone now." The rebel spit on the ground. "As for you, how do I know you're not spies for the American CIA come to gather information about us?"

"Oh, shit," James muttered with disgust.

Katz cut him off quickly. "The CIA would have sent in black agents to avoid attracting attention. The reason we're here instead is because this had to be handled faster than the Company could manage with their ponderous bureaucracy. We can't waste time because there's little to spare before the Democratic Front, Cubans, agents from certain Arab countries or someone else claims our prize before we can get to it."

"And what is this thing of such value that you're willing to march into a war zone to find it?" the rebel inquired.

"It's best if we don't tell you," Katz answered. "What I can tell you is this item would be very valuable to a lot of people, all of whom are unlikely to be friends of Eritrea."

"You still haven't told me what value this mysterious merchandise has for everyone."

"I know you still have problems with the Democratic Front and some of the other guerrilla factions. Eritrea is far from independent yet. The object we seek could be bartered for millions in weapons and supplies—booty that might find its way into the hands of your enemies."

"I see," Ebrahim said solemnly. "What if my people helped you locate this thing? Would your government be willing to send us weapons and supplies as a reward?"

"Yes," Katz said without hesitation. "I can't promise you unlimited aid, but you'll certainly get food and medical supplies in abundance, at least a million dollars' worth in aid. Perhaps two or three times that much. The exact amount isn't up to me to decide, but I can promise you increased aid delivered in a covert manner."

"And how long will this take?" the rebel demanded. "We need it now, not four years from now when your country has another President who might not oblige this clandestine agreement."

"The assistance will began two days after we leave Africa with the merchandise," Katz assured him.

"You made a fine offer," Ebrahim admitted. "What if we don't help you?"

"We continue on our own just as we planned to before this unfortunate incident occurred," the Israeli said. "It may be more difficult to do this without you, but we won't stop now. The EPLF aren't the only people with determination, Ebrahim."

"I must discuss this with my comrades," the rebel leader said. "You killed many of our brothers and sisters. My comrades will want revenge, of course, but I might be able to convince them that this was a tragic mistake. It's one that I must accept full blame for since I ordered the ambush on your truck. If you hear a single shot, it will probably mean my comrades decided to execute me." Ebrahim glanced down at the ground. "I can't blame them if that's what they wish to do."

Ebrahim's actions had forced Phoenix Force to kill several people in self-defense, including at least one woman. If the rebel felt guilty about this, James figured that was as it should be. "I'm gonna see to that guy I shot in the leg. You can send down other wounded for treatment if you survive."

The rebel boss glared at James. The American met his gaze without flinching. Ebrahim suddenly smiled without humor and nodded. "Agreed," he declared. "I see we understand each other."

"To a degree maybe," James replied. "But I wouldn't have ambushed this truck without knowing who was in it. That's something I don't understand. I don't like killing people, Ebrahim, especially when it's over a misunderstanding."

"I think I'm lucky you're not among my EPLF comrades," Ebrahim remarked. "My fate might already be sealed if you were my judge."

"If you guys join us, I *will* be among your group," James told him. "You screw up like this again and you're damn right I'll take you out."

"Daniel," Katz rasped. His tone warned James to control his temper.

"It's all right," Ebrahim assured him as he turned to head back to the rocks.

Victoria and James attended the rebel with the wounded leg. The man had passed out, so he didn't resist their help. Katz moved to the boulders and told the other Phoenix warriors about the conversation with Ebrahim. McCarter, Encizo and Manning remained behind cover, ready for battle in case the deal went sour. Minutes crawled by and the sun seemed determined to sweat them into dust. The groaning of the wounded ceased, and the only sounds consisted of the trickle of water from the truck's punctured radiator and each person's own heartbeat.

Vultures congregated in the sky. The great dark birds seemed to be waiting patiently for the opportunity to descend upon the dead littered across the area. Phoenix Force found the waiting more frustrating. It seemed as if hours had passed since Ebrahim had climbed the rocks to meet with the other EPLF cell members.

At last the rebel leader and more than a dozen of his comrades appeared from the peaks. Five more EPLF followers appeared from other rock formations. Their faces revealed that most of them were unhappy about calling off the attack. Yet they carried Kalashnikovs canted to shoulders and didn't threaten the Phoenix warriors or Victoria. Nearly half the rebels were women. None appeared to be older than thirty, and they all had the weary, hardened appearance of seasoned soldiers.

"We've discussed the situation," Ebrahim announced as he handed his AK-47 to a woman next to him. "Nearly all of us have agreed to join forces with you to locate whatever it is you seek."

"Nearly all?" James asked with a frown. "What does that mean?"

A large male member of the EPLF tossed his rifle to one of his comrades and stomped forward. His broad ebony features were filled with rage, and he glared at the Phoenix pair as if he hoped he could burn sheer hatred through their flesh to destroy them by willpower. The man held a panga in his fist and suddenly thrust the machete at the ground. The point pierced the earth. The long blade and handle wobbled slightly as the man stepped back from the panga.

"Meneke isn't willing to agree to our terms," Ebrahim said grimly, tilting his head toward the angry young man. "I don't blame him. His wife was killed in the battle."

"So he wants to kills us, huh?" James commented. He glanced at Meneke and saw that the answer was obvious. The man was seething with anguish and rage.

"Not you," Ebrahim replied. "Just me."

The other rebels began to back away to make room for Ebrahim and Meneke. Both men stood roughly twelve feet apart with the machete between them. Victoria started to step forward to try to stop the duel that seemed imminent. James placed a hand on her shoulder.

"These folks are already pissed off," he told her. "They seem to be putting most of the blame on Ebrahim instead of us. Let's not do anything to change their minds."

"That's terrible," Victoria replied, shocked by James's attitude. "One of these men could get killed."

"Several people already got killed because of Ebrahim," James reminded her. "This is obviously some sort of test for Ebrahim, or the other EPLF members wouldn't let this duel take place. It's up to them. Let them deal with it."

"He's right," Katz agreed. "It's not our place to get involved with this. I can sympathize with Meneke's point of view, but I rather hope Ebrahim wins. Otherwise it's hard to say what the rebels will decide to do. That includes what they might decide to do about us."

Ebrahim and Meneke squared off. They bent their knees and arched their backs, arms extended and fingers open. They carried no weapons. Each man tried to watch his opponent and also judge the distance to the machete planted in the ground between them. Meneke was bigger than Ebrahim and appeared to be physically stronger and and perhaps a couple of years younger. His anger and grief could make him even more dangerous, yet it would also be apt to make the man rash and careless.

He lunged for the panga, reaching for the wooden handle. Ebrahim charged forward and lashed a boot into Meneke's shoulder. The kick knocked the larger man to the ground. Ebrahim grabbed the machete and yanked the blade from the ground as Meneke quickly rose.

The angry young widower had scooped up a fistful of dirt and hurled it into Ebrahim's face. The rebel commander pawed at his eyes with one hand and slashed blindly at his opponent. Meneke dodged the panga stroke and stepped forward to chop his fists across Ebrahim's forearm and wrist. The blows struck the machete from the ringleader's grasp.

Meneke slammed a backfist at Ebrahim's face and rammed a knee into his opponent's abdomen. Ebrahim doubled over with a gasp, and Meneke wrapped an arm around his neck to apply a front headlock. Squeezing hard to form a viselike choke hold, Meneke began to throttle the smaller man.

Ebrahim dug the fingers of one hand into the crook of Meneke's elbow to ease the pressure around his neck. His other hand jabbed a short uppercut between Meneke's legs. The big man wheezed painfully and trembled from the pain in his manhood. However, he held the headlock with one arm and grabbed the seat of Ebrahim's shorts with his other hand. Meneke suddenly pulled hard to lift Ebrahim's feet off the ground and threw himself backward.

The rebel leader sailed head over heels. Both men hit the ground, but Ebrahim landed from a greater height with greater force. He groaned from the stunning impact to his spine. Meneke rolled over and clutched his bruised crotch with one hand as he reached for the machete with the other.

He grabbed the handle and started to raise the big jungle knife. Ebrahim, on all fours, suddenly lunged into his opponent. The rebel leader grabbed Meneke's wrist behind the machete and twisted hard as both men sprawled across the ground. Meneke's free hand seized Ebrahim's hair at the back of his head and pulled hard, but Ebrahim held on to the wrist and continued to twist with all his might. Meneke's fingers opened, and the panga fell once more.

Ebrahim raked his fingernails across Meneke's face.
The big man moaned as blood oozed from scratches on
his cheek. Still powered by rage, Meneke shoved hard and
forced Ebrahim onto his back. He straddled his opponent's chest and grabbed Ebrahim's throat with both
hands. Squeezing forcibly, he began to strangle the cell
leader.

Ebrahim extended his arms over his head and clasped
his hands. He swung them forward and smashed the
doubled fists into the bridge of Meneke's nose. The big
man's head bounced from the blow and blood oozed from
his nostrils. Ebrahim hammered his fists against Meneke's wrists to break the grip at his throat and hooked a
punch at Meneke's jaw. The widower toppled sideways as
Ebrahim started to rise.

Meneke reached out with both hands and grabbed
Ebrahim's arm with one hand and his shirtfront with the
other. He pulled hard and rolled onto his back. Raising
his knees, he clipped Ebrahim across the shins. The EPLF
cell leader tripped and tumbled forward, falling to the
ground. Meneke scrambled after him and reached for his
opponent's neck with both hands.

Ebrahim turned to face him. Too late Meneke saw he
had actually thrown Ebrahim to where the machete lay.
The rebel leader held the big panga in both fists. Ebrahim swung the machete. The heavy blade struck Meneke's closest wrist and chopped off the hand with a single
stroke. Blood fountained from the stump as Meneke
screamed in agony. His severed hand convulsed on the
ground and fingers clawed wildly in a muscle spasm.
Ebrahim swung the machete in a cross-body stroke. The
edge caught Meneke in the side of the neck. Crimson
squirted from the severed carotid as Meneke fell, the blade
still lodged in his neck.

"Oh, my God!" Victoria gasped, and looked away, one hand clamped across her mouth.

Ebrahim slowly got to his feet and stood on shaky legs. He breathed hard to catch his breath and looked at his comrades. Heads nodded, satisfied that the duel had been fought fairly and that Ebrahim was the rightful victor. He turned to face James and Katz.

"It's settled," he declared. "We're going with you."

12

The truck was ruined. The radiator, battery and fan belt had been punctured by bullets. Parts of the engine block had been damaged and all four tires were pierced by slugs. Phoenix Force had intended to abandon the vehicle, anyway, but were forced to do so sooner than anticipated. The commandos hauled out the remaining supplies, including the rest of their weapons and sets of tiger stripe fatigues.

Phoenix Force donned the combat attire and discarded their previous disguises. They were relieved to be dressed for combat, with weapons readily available instead of hidden and out of immediate reach. Ebrahim and the other EPLF rebels were startled by this transformation. These five foreigners had already impressed them with their skill and cunning in combat, but the rebels hadn't expected the strangers to be so well armed.

All five members of Phoenix Force wore shoulder holsters with pistols under their arms. They also carried Uzi machine pistols with shoulder straps, and grenades, knives and ammo pouches were attached to their belts. James, Encizo and Manning also carried AK-47 assault rifles. Katz strapped the transceiver to his back and the others carried packs with supplies and rations.

Ebrahim wondered what sort of men he had made a pact with. They were clearly not the soft weaklings he considered typical of Americans. One thing was certain: he would rather have them for allies than enemies. Ebrahim hoped he wouldn't regret the alliance, as the five mysterious commandos apparently could handle themselves in almost situation.

Victoria was also surprised when she saw the Phoenix warriors in full battle array. She had also changed clothes and now wore khaki shirt and shorts to better suit the uniform of the EPLF. Victoria carried James's medic kit as well as her own and extra canteens of water. The Czech-made CZ-75 pistol was holstered on her hip. Encizo had given her the handgun after he retrieved his Walther P-88 and shoulder rig from their gear.

Katz took advantage of the opportunity to exchange his "five-finger" prosthesis for the more practical and versatile trident device. The steel talons could do almost anything flesh and blood fingers could do, and a few things human digits couldn't accomplish. The Israeli was glad to have the familiar prosthesis again strapped to the stump of his right arm.

The EPLF collected weapons and supplies from the bodies of their slain comrades. They didn't bury the dead. Nearly three decades of civil war had taught them to be pragmatic if somewhat callous about such things. Combat veterans learn that the dead are dead. Burial ceremonies and other niceties had to be ignored because the living took first priority.

Ebrahim's group consisted of twenty-nine members. Five had been injured during the battle. Three others were assigned to stay with the wounded and help them travel to an EPLF camp in Tigre Province to the east. The remaining twenty-one rebels joined Phoenix Force as they headed north.

Katz finally shared some details about the NSA satellite. He told Ebrahim why the Argus was so important and the general vicinity where it had gone down. The rebel leader grunted and shook his head. Ebrahim informed them that the area was rife with brigands and renegade government troops.

"That's why we ambushed your truck," he added. "Major battles have been fought there in recent days."

"The second horseman," James commented, thinking out loud.

"What's that?" McCarter inquired, overhearing the black commando.

"Oh," James said with a shrug, "Victoria was comparing the Four Horsemen of the Apocalypse with the situation in Ethiopia. Wasn't the second horseman war?"

"Yes," Manning confirmed. The Canadian was more familiar with the Bible than either of his teammates.

"Seems to me that horseman has been galloping over the earth for a bloody long time," McCarter commented.

"He's sure been making the rounds in Africa," James added. "Ethiopia, Mozambique, Angola and God knows where else. More than half the nations of Africa are on the verge of revolution. Every year there's at least one coup. The whole continent's a political powder keg."

"Yeah," Encizo replied as he joined the conversation, "but that's not why we're here. Let's concentrate on one major crisis at a time."

"Ebrahim tells me there's an old rock quarry four miles from here," Katz declared. "His group has been using it as a temporary base in Wollo Province. We can go there and wait until nightfall before we move on to the satellite landing site."

"Sounds good to me," McCarter replied. The Briton tugged at the brim of his sand-colored beret to shade his eyes from the sun. "I'll be glad to get out of this heat for a while."

"Before we go much farther I want to make another radio spot check with the NSA post in Sudan," Katz stated. "I don't want Halpern and the others to go to sleep over there. We might need them to get out of this country."

"We sure want to be able to do that," Manning commented. "Ethiopia makes Vietnam look like Disneyland. This has to be the worst mission we've ever had. Thousands of starving people, and we can't do anything for them. We're attacked by people who aren't even the enemy. In fact, I'm not even sure who the enemy is this time."

"Anyone who tries to prevent us from getting the Argus satellite," Katz answered grimly. He recalled the previous radio contact with Halpern and realized the enemy might include Israelis. "Regardless of their nationality."

The Phoenix commander unslung the transceiver from his shoulder to radio the NSA listening post. Once again he communicated with Halpern in Arabic and conversed in a cryptic manner, continuing the Father Raouf identity, although he had discarded the priestly garments. Wondering who might be listening, Katz spoke with the NSA agent as obliquely as possible while still relaying enough information to let Halpern know they were gradually getting closer to the fallen spy satellite.

SERGEANT RABIN, sitting on the ground with a canteen cup of tea, listened to the voices from the radio. Captain Moshin's unit had spent the day traveling northeast toward the Gondar/Wollo border. After its encounter with the renegade soldiers, the Israeli's team had stayed on the move since dawn. Finally the captain had told the men to break out some rations, and they were now resting beneath some shade trees.

"Have you found anything on the radio?" Moshin inquired as he finished consuming a small can of chicken and dumplings.

"Nothing important, Captain," Sergeant Rabin answered as he slipped off the headset. "Just that Coptic priest talking to his bishop again."

"They conversed in Arabic?" Moshin asked with a frown.

"That's why I understood it," Rabin confirmed. "If they'd spoken one of the African languages, I would have told one of the mercenaries to translate for me."

"Did they use the same frequency?" Moshin asked.

"Yes," the NCO answered. "It's a rather strong wavelength and the priest seems to be closer to our position, so he came through quite clearly. In fact, they're probably overriding any of the military broadcasts from standard field radios."

"Interesting that a Coptic priest would have such efficient equipment," Moshin commented suspiciously. "What are these Arabs talking about?"

"The priest was babbling about how some locals are helping him find his way around and guiding him to a church where an Ethiopian Orthodox priest is expecting him," Rabin answered.

"Are they still on the radio?" Moshin demanded.

"No," the sergeant replied. "The conversation was brief but boring."

"And you're certain their accent was Egyptian?" the officer inquired. "Not Syrian or Libyan?"

"Nile dialect," Rabin assured him. "I can't quite place the accent as Cairo or Giza or whatever. They both sounded almost as if Arabic wasn't their native language."

"Curious," Moshin said thoughtfully.

Rabin's head suddenly snapped back and his eyes expanded as loud beeping from the headset painfully filled his ears. Moshin heard the beeping as well and recognized it as a variation of Morse code used by the Mossad base in Sudan. The commo NCO took a pencil and notepad from his pocket to jot down the message. Then he took out a small black codebook to decipher it.

"It's from Levi," Rabin announced, although he realized Moshin was already aware of this. "He says, 'Priest—American—same as you.' Maybe I got that message wrong."

"I don't think so," the captain told him. "Levi's warning us that these so-called priests are actually American agents. 'Same as you' means the one here in Ethiopia is looking for the same thing we are."

"How could he know this?" Sergeant Gehmer asked as he overheard the conversation. "Levi's in Sudan. How can he make a judgment of this sort?"

"I don't know," Moshin admitted. "The Americans' contact must be CIA or NSA with a post in Sudan. The same as our Mossad station. Levi either traced the radio waves to the American base at his end, or he might have simply recognized one of the voices on the radio. A surprisingly large number of CIA and Mossad agents know one another. Actually, one of the voices sounded slightly familiar to me."

Moshin shook his head. The voice couldn't have belonged to the man with one arm he had encountered several years earlier in Israel. He tried to dismiss the notion because it seemed too incredible, and he didn't want to think that his team might be pitted against the five mysterious supercommandos led by the one-armed colonel.

"Captain?" Gehmer inquired. "Is there something we should know about these men?"

"We already know it," Moshin replied. "The Americans are our competition. They're not our enemies, but we can't let them get the satellite. We'll never get the information from the device if they claim it first."

"Judging from the frequency of the broadcast and how strong it was," Rabin said, "I can figure out fairly precisely where it originated. Let me get out the map and try to chart a course for us."

Kanwonkpa approached the Israelis. Sergeant Gehmer noticed that the bandages on the Liberian's injured hand needed to be changed. He unwrapped the bloodied dressings and examined the stump of Kanwonkpa's maimed finger.

"You need stitches," Gehmer said in thickly accented English.

"Go ahead," Kanwonkpa replied. He extended his arm toward Gehmer, but his attention was fixed on Moshin as he said, "I don't understand much Hebrew, but it's obvious you've been talking about something important."

"We have a possible lead to the location of a team of American agents also seeking the satellite," Moshin answered. "It's likely they have a good idea where the device went down. If we can catch up with them, they may lead us to the satellite."

"Americans?" Kanwonkpa said with a frown. He glanced at Gehmer as the unit medic threaded a needle. "When I signed up for this job, I realized there would probably be fighting. I won't hesitate to do battle with the Ethiopians or the Arabs. However, the United States is an ally to Liberia as much as Israel is. I don't like the idea of killing men from a friendly nation, especially a country so closely associated with Liberia's past."

"The Americans kept your people as slaves and returned you to Africa because they didn't want you to live among them," Rabin remarked. "I wouldn't think that would make them such favorable allies."

"Our economy would fall apart without American support," the mercenary admitted. "The same is true for Israel. If we kill those men, we could bring considerable misfortune to our countries."

"I doubt the U.S. would cut off support and funding," Rabin replied. "The Americans worry about their public image, you know."

"They also worry about national security the same as we do," Moshin reminded the NCO. "Relations between Israel and the United States have been strained from time to time. The Americans won't sever relations if we get the satellite, even if we have to kill some of their agents to do it. Still, our relations will certainly suffer. Besides, I also have no desire to harm any Americans."

"But we may not have a choice," Kanwonkpa said grimly.

"Unfortunately that's true," Moshin admitted. "I just pray it doesn't come to that."

13

The limestone quarry had been abandoned years ago when the war extended to Wollo Province and digging became too hazardous and new construction virtually stopped in the area.

Ebrahim's cell had discovered the quarry shortly after they moved into Wollo Province. It had been forgotten by the locals and ignored by Mengistu's military. Phoenix Force hoped the site would remain secure as they followed the EPLF rebels to the quarry.

Drab gray stone walls surrounded them as Ebrahim led the way along an incline into the pit. The soil was dry and striped by gouges from machinery once used in the quarry. Ebrahim gestured toward rock piles by the stony walls.

"That's what's left of the digging that was formerly done here," the rebel leader explained. "The rock piles and gouges in the stone walls offer us shade and concealment if any enemy forces approach this quarry."

"Not bad," Manning remarked as he scanned the area. "But attacking forces could pin you down and saturate the quarry with grenades to take out your forces."

"We always have sentries posted at the peaks to alert us to danger," Ebrahim explained. "They'll determine if approaching forces are about to launch an attack or are simply passing. If it's the former, they'll warn us to prepare to fight. That means we get out of the quarry as fast as possible to avoid being boxed in. This place could become a communal grave for us."

"So if any enemies pass by, you'll lie low and wait until they're gone?" James inquired.

"That depends on the size of the unit," Ebrahim answered. "If it's small enough for us to take it, we'll attack. If it's a large, well-armed unit, the prudent action would be to radio our comrades in the field and report the progress of the enemy force. We would inform them of the size of the unit, weapons, direction it is headed and other important information."

"Practical enough," Katz said as he took a watch from his pocket. "It's almost 1700 hours. That means there should be approximately two hours until nightfall. Let's get as much rest as possible. We won't get much after we're on the move again."

"I don't know how much rest we can get in two hours," McCarter complained.

"Three hours," Katz corrected. "We'll wait an extra hour after twilight to be certain it's dark enough to cover our movement. That's still not much, but it'll give us time to relax, eat and check our weapons before we have to leave."

"We should take advantage of whatever time we've got," Encizo agreed. "We still have a fair piece of ground to cover before we reach the Argus."

"It may take days to find the satellite after we get to the area where it crashed," Halima, an attractive female member of the EPLF, declared. "We can't spend that much time on this venture."

"We have a device for tracking the satellite," Katz assured her. "Unless the mechanism of the Argus was damaged when it hit the ground, we should be able to locate it once we get within range."

"I hope that's true," Ebrahim commented. "Battlefields aren't the best places to spend long hours searching for something that might not even exist."

"We'll find out," the Phoenix commander replied.

The rebel leader assigned two men to stand guard. Ebrahim and Halima headed for a rock pile that formed a semicircle with the rock wall blocking off the open end. Ebrahim slipped off his pack as he approached the barrier. Halima pulled a blanket from under her pack and began to unroll it as they climbed behind the wall of stones.

"Looks like they've got their own style of relaxing," McCarter remarked as he watched the couple vanish from view.

"When men and women are together in circumstances that could mean this day is their last," a wiry rebel with a keffiyeh wrapped around his head said, "it isn't surprising they should seek the pleasures of the flesh when possible."

"What if the woman gets pregnant?" James inquired as he noticed other EPLF couples had chosen sites for coupling and moved toward their selected compartments.

"When evidence of a child within a woman occurs," the rebel answered, "we transfer her back to Eritrea where she gives birth at one of our camps. Sometimes the women have their babies in Keren or another city."

"That must present some serious problems," Manning remarked. "By the way, we haven't been introduced.

"My name is Muhammad," the rebel answered with a short bow. "A large number of us are Muslims. Many of us don't share the politics of the Marxist leaders of our movement, but we have a common desire to accomplish an independent Eritrea."

"And what kind of government do you hope to set up?" Katz inquired.

"From our point of view," Muhammad replied, "almost anything will be an improvement. I doubt that we'd adopt a system of democracy such as you have in America, but we would tend to be more agreeable toward your country and the other nations of the West. After all, that's where the food and medical supplies have come from to try to help the victims of war and famine. Keren is probably the best example of this. The Catholic relief center is there."

"Is that why you'd take pregnant women to that city?" James inquired.

"Exactly," Muhammad confirmed. "It's still difficult to get enough food to survive, but Keren is the best place to get a fair share of the supplies. Keren is a modern city with fine hotels and architecture by Italian craftsmen. It's an example of what all of Eritrea could be one day, but that will be far in the future."

"What becomes of the children?" Victoria asked, concern in her voice.

"If they survive, they'll be raised by village elders until they're old enough to go to training camps," Muhammad said.

"To be taught to fight in future wars," Manning said with a frown.

"We've overthrown Mengistu, but Eritrea still isn't free. I think there will be much more fighting."

"Have you ever thought about leaving Eritrea?" Encizo inquired. "I was born in a country that became a Communist dictatorship when I was a child. I was a member of a guerrilla army of counterrevolutionaries for a while, but eventually I had to accept the fact that we would never be able to overthrow the government from within. I moved to another country and started a new life."

"Eritrea is my home, and we are winning," Muhammad replied. "I don't know where I'd go, anyway. Besides, I now believe I will live to see a free Eritrea. It would be a shame to leave after so long a fight."

"We can sure understand that," McCarter assured him.

"Please make yourselves as comfortable as possible," the rebel urged. "If any of you need anything, I'll be happy to do what I can. Right now isn't a good time to disturb Ebrahim. I'm sure you understand."

"Not too hard to figure that out," James said. "We'll let him enjoy himself. Nice that somebody can in this country."

"I think we should do an inventory of our medical supplies, Daniel," Victoria suggested. "We might as well find some shade and get comfortable."

"Okay," James agreed. "Pick a spot."

Victoria led him to a ring of stones not occupied by an EPLF couple. McCarter grinned as he watched them walk away. The Briton looked at Encizo and saw a sly smile on the Cuban's face, as well.

"You reckon somebody else is going to enjoy himself?" McCarter said in a low voice.

"Not us, amigo," Encizo replied with a shrug. "Let them have some privacy. We can check our weapons and gear while they inspect...uh, medical supplies."

"Never heard it called that before," the Briton commented with a chuckle.

Victoria placed the blanket on the ground. James was startled by her actions. Although his teammates had already guessed the couple would be doing more than inventory, James hadn't expected Victoria to want to make love. Under different circumstances he would have eagerly initiated such a union. However, in the middle of a mission with danger and death surrounding them it seemed the wrong time and place.

Not that he didn't find Victoria desirable. James had found her physically attractive since the moment he'd first set eyes on the lady from Kenya. During their journey across Ethiopia, James had gotten to know Victoria. She could be abrasive, a bit short-tempered and opinionated, but she was also intelligent, compassionate and courageous.

"I don't think we need to check the medical supplies again, Daniel," Victoria announced as she sat on the blanket. "Is there something else you'd rather do?"

"Oh, yeah," James admitted. "There's definitely something I'd like to do."

He watched Victoria unbutton her bush shirt. The swell of her breasts appeared at the gap. James's gaze traveled across her dark, shapely legs and thighs. Victoria bent a knee and interlaced her fingers around it as she looked up at James with a questioning expression.

"I don't intend to embarrass myself," she announced. "I need a little encouragement. That is, if we understand each other."

James glanced at the rock wall that surrounded them. It was more than a yard high and would conceal them if they stayed on the blanket. Assured that they would have as much privacy as possible under the circumstances, James lowered himself to the ground beside Victoria.

He placed his hands on her shoulders and kissed Victoria gently on the lips. She responded willingly and they kissed again. Their mouths pressed together hard and lingered in warmth and pleasure. His tongue ran across her teeth as Victoria cupped a hand around the back of his head to pull him closer.

They lay across the blanket and embraced. Their lips parted, and James looked into Victoria's large, beautiful eyes. He saw desire in her eyes and knew she would see the same longing in his, as well.

"I do want you," he whispered. "I just want you to be sure about this, Victoria."

"I'm sure," she replied softly. "I've been sure for a while now, and I want us to do this because there might not be another chance."

"To be honest I was planning to romance you when we got out of this mess," James confessed with a grin. "So I'd want to make love to you even if things were different."

"Let's not wait," Victoria urged as she unbuttoned his shirt and caressed his chest.

James felt the biological yearning build as Victoria's touch became bolder. His hand stroked her thighs as he started to shrug out of his shirt. Victoria leaned forward and kissed his neck. Her tongue slid along the hollow of his throat as her fingers fondled him to feel the firmness of his desire.

"Will you tell me your real name, Daniel?" she asked.

He looked at her thoughtfully. "My name's Calvin," the Phoenix warrior said. He found the words almost caught in his throat due to the sudden emotion he felt.

"Calvin," Victoria said thoughtfully. "If you don't mind, I think I'll stick with Daniel instead."

"Yeah," he replied ruefully, "that'll be fine."

14

Captain al-Jabal ran a cleaning rod through the barrel of his Stechkin. The Libyan officer had disassembled the Soviet machine pistol to clean and oil the weapon while the unit rested by a creek near the Tigre/Wollo border. A soldier named Hamel lovingly cleaned the big AG-17 automatic grenade launcher, the most formidable weapon in the Storm Lion arsenal. Then he loaded the drum magazine with 30 mm cartridge grenades.

"I hope these blacks know where we're going, Captain," Hamel commented to his commander. "Ethiopians are such a backward people."

"That's enough of that sort of talk," Jabal warned as he began to reassemble his Stechkin. "Major Dawa and his men have been doing a good job. Some of them understand Arabic, so be careful what you say. If you can't control your tongue, don't speak."

Hamel grudgingly admitted that the captain was right and turned back to the AG-17 blast machine. Jabal finished assembling his pistol and slid a magazine into the butt well. The officer pulled back the slide to chamber a round as he glanced around the temporary camp. In spite of Hamel's remarks most of the Libyan commandos seemed to be getting along fairly well with the Ethiopian troops. Jabal's Storm Lions shared canned rations with

Dawa's men, and the Ethiopians collected edible plants and berries in exchange for the kindness.

Dawa was once again with Sergeant Kiflom as the NCO fiddled with their radio. He was listening to a conversation between two Coptic Christian clerics. Then he tuned in to a Democratic Front exchange, detailing the presence of an Egyptian Coptic priest, a black driver and a Cuban officer on Ethiopian soil.

"Captain," Kiflom said, "apparently this Egyptian priest and his band were first sighted in the south and were last reported in Wollo Province. Supposedly they were passing out goods to some poverty-stricken nomads in the area."

"That doesn't seem very sinister," Dawa remarked.

"Perhaps not," Kiflom replied, "but they were also accompanied by a black woman and two white men. Witnesses said they spoke English. Apparently the Cuban officer is a fake."

Dawa sat up, intrigued.

"The Democratic Front suspects they might all be working for the Americans," Kiflom continued. "The woman with them could be a Kenyan nurse who vanished at Dr. Abraha's clinic near Goba. The clinic was attacked by a gang of renegade soldiers. They apparently murdered Abraha and then were wiped out themselves."

"You think this odd collection of characters is working for the CIA?" Dawa asked.

"The important fact is that these foreigners seem headed toward the same area as our unit, and possibly for the same reason."

The Ethiopian officer considered this information. Dawa felt an ambivalence about the possibility that this mysterious team might be from the CIA. He would be glad to catch up with the American team if it could lead him to the satellite so that he could complete the mission and go home. Yet he was repulsed by the idea of going into the worst war zone in Ethiopia to hunt down a group of clever and obviously dangerous agents from the United States. Whoever they were, they had to be very tough and professional.

Dawa noticed Jabal approaching him. "We seem to have company. Apparently the Americans sent a team, as well."

"Hopefully they have a better idea of the location of the satellite than we do," the Libyan officer remarked.

"Better tell the men that the break is over," Dawa announced. "We'll be on the move again shortly."

CALVIN JAMES GOT DRESSED after making love to Victoria Yatta for almost an hour. She looked up and smiled as the Phoenix warrior slipped on his boots. She seemed to take her time dressing to allow him to admire her body for a few more minutes. James hoped this was because she wanted more of him after they finished the mission.

He reached for his shoulder holster and started to slip it on. Then, suddenly, the sky became darker. A massive shadow descended across the quarry. Startled, James glanced up. A great black disc covered approximately one-quarter of the sun.

"An eclipse," James said with surprise, looking away, aware that staring at the sun could damage his eyes even during during a partial eclipse. "I didn't know this was supposed to happen today."

"Neither did I," Victoria replied as she put on her clothes with greater haste.

Suddenly the earth trembled. Loose dirt and small stones slid down the rock walls. James finished donning his shoulder holster and grabbed the AK-47. A chill wormed up his spine as he recalled Victoria's comparison of events in Ethiopia to the prophecies from the Book of Revelation.

The darkness from the eclipse increased, and the ground shook harder. James tried to dismiss notions of omens and biblical warnings of the beginning of Armageddon, but he was unnerved by the events unfolding around him.

A shape appeared along the rock pile. Startled, James began to swing the rifle around. A hand caught the barrel before it could complete the arc. David McCarter stared at James and released the AK-47, motioning James to be quiet.

"If the earth moved for you two," he whispered, "you weren't alone. Three Russian T-62 tanks are rolling right by this quarry along with a brigade of Democratic Front infantry. So stay down."

"It's not an earthquake?" James rasped as he ducked low behind the rocks.

"I just told you it's some bloody tanks," McCarter snapped. "Let's hope those blokes are distracted by the eclipse."

Victoria moved closer to James and held his arm for comfort. The Chicago badass was glad he wasn't the only one upset by the coincidence of the eclipse and the shaking ground. More tremors shook the rock walls. James glanced up and saw the top of a tank turret above the summit of the quarry. A man's helmeted head and shoulders jutted from the open hatch, but the soldier didn't look down as the tank rolled by.

Minutes sluggishly passed while they waited tensely. The engines of the big armored vehicles sounded like the bellowing of mechanical beasts. James ducked low and held Victoria close until the rumble of the tanks finally became distant.

"Well, that was a bit close," McCarter remarked as he leaned against the stones that surrounded James and Victoria. "Lucky the sentries spotted them coming."

"They must not have seen the tanks any too soon," James muttered, buckling the web belt around his waist. "Those damn armor-plated monsters are headed north, same as us. I hope we don't run into them again."

"It's pretty obvious the Democratic Front is up to something," the Briton commented. "We might be headed for one hell of a donnybrook."

"I don't know anybody else who would call combat with tanks and heavy artillery a donnybrook," James remarked. "What would you call a nuclear conflict? A nasty altercation?"

"Oh, that would be a brawl," McCarter answered. "A very large and destructive brawl."

"He's not serious, is he?" Victoria asked James.

"The rest of us haven't been able to figure that out yet," the Phoenix pro from Chicago replied dryly.

Ebrahim and Katz approached them as James climbed over the rock pile. Victoria collected the medical gear and other supply packs before she swung over the low wall to join them.

"It got dark sooner than we expected," Ebrahim commented. "I forgot the eclipse was today. Other things were on my mind. I'm sure the rest of you understand."

"You knew about it?" James inquired.

"Of course," Ebrahim confirmed. "It's been mentioned on the radio for more than a week."

"We haven't listened to much radio except for military wavelengths and our own communications," Katz explained. "When we were briefed back in the U.S., they didn't include information related to astronomy. Maybe we should consult an almanac for such items before we leave for a mission.''

"Speaking of leaving," McCarter began, "does this mean we'll be moving sooner because it's already dark?''

"Don't be so anxious," Katz replied. "We'll be leaving soon enough, and I don't think there's much doubt that we'll see more action before this is over. In fact, there's a good chance we might find more than we can handle.''

15

Twilight followed the eclipse so closely that it seemed almost an extension of the solar phenomenon. However, the moon and stars cast a startling degree of light from the night sky.

Phoenix Force and Victoria Yatta followed the EPLF rebels. Ebrahim's group was familiar with the area, and the veteran guerrillas knew how to use the natural surroundings for camouflage to conceal their progress. There didn't seem to be much to hide from as they continued to travel north. The haunting howl of a hyena echoed from the arid plain, and bats sliced through the night sky on leathery wings. Aside from these nocturnal beasts, no other signs of life appeared.

There was no breeze, and the weather was hot and muggy even though the sun had set. The sand under their feet seemed to have absorbed the heat from the day and radiated it up at them. They felt as if they were walking over an enormous charcoal grill that hadn't completely cooled.

The region was bleak and eerie, with barely a sound except those made by themselves and the night creatures. They walked for hours until they saw a cluster of bushes with two figures seated beside it. The shapes were draped in blankets, heads bowed as if asleep. Neither moved as Phoenix Force and their companions carefully approached. James and Manning stationed themselves by a rocky ridge and adopted kneeling stances, AK-47s held ready. They covered the advance of Encizo, McCarter and Muhammad as the trio moved toward the motionless figures. The others also stayed back and let the three men check the quiet forms. It didn't seem to be a trap, but experience had taught them not to assume too much from innocent appearances.

The figures didn't stir when McCarter stepped closer, Uzi machine pistol held against his chest. Encizo glanced at the bushes and noticed that the stems were bare. He scanned the naked plants for signs of a grenade or other booby trap. The Cuban gestured for McCarter to go forward. Muhammad stepped next to the Briton as McCarter knelt beside the closest figure.

"Oh, God," the Briton rasped as he peered under the portion of the blanket that formed a hood around the figure's head.

A lifeless, emaciated face peered back at him with unblinking eyes. Ants crawled across the open orbs. A black beetle stirred by the open mouth of the corpse. The skin was drawn taut across the cheekbones and forehead, ash-colored with yellow blotches. McCarter couldn't tell if the face belonged to a man or a woman.

"They must have tried to walk to one of the relief stations and didn't make it," Muhammad remarked as he examined a bare stem. "There are scrappings on these. They must have eaten the leaves, stripped them off with their teeth. Perhaps they simply became too weak to keep moving, sat here and consumed the bushes, hoping it might give them enough energy to continue."

"I don't smell any stink," Encizo remarked. "They must have died fairly recently. The bushes weren't enough to save them from starvation."

"Probably dehydration and thirst," Muhammad stated. He pointed at claw marks at the base of the bushes. "They dug at the roots in search of water. Perhaps they drank whatever they found, then consumed the leaves in an effort to find more moisture. At last they just gave up and waited to die."

"You find this sort of thing very often?" McCarter inquired.

"Especially in Tigre Province," Muhammad said with a nod. "Ethiopia is littered with the corpses of desperate people who finally surrendered to death."

"I guess we just leave them," McCarter said grimly, aware they couldn't spare time to bury the dead. "There's something printed on the blankets," McCarter noticed as he lowered one corpse to the ground, pulling the edge of the blanket over the face.

"It's an old Ethiopian army blanket," Muhammad explained. "Many renegade soldiers have entered the black market and sell or trade supplies and food to civilians."

"The more time we spend here the more eager I am to leave," Encizo admitted.

"You shouldn't touch the bodies," Muhammad warned as McCarter prepared to place the other corpse beside the first one. "There may be tsetse flies inside those blankets. It's even possible scorpions or snakes are hidden among the folds."

"Nice of you to tell me," McCarter growled as he backed away. "This bloody country is so treacherous you can't even trust the dead."

"You don't like my homeland?" Muhammad inquired with a mirthless smile. "Neither do I. Not the way it is now."

They continued the long trek north. Although the terrain was difficult, they didn't have to hide from troops, and they covered at least three miles of the steaming ground an hour. After several hours, a sound similar to thunder rolled across the night air, and light flashed repeatedly in the distance. Popping sounds like strings of firecrackers grew steadily louder as they drew closer.

"There's a battle up ahead," Manning announced, aware the others had already figured that out. He raised a pair of binoculars and scanned the horizon. "About two miles away and right in the direction we're headed."

He saw the muzzle-flash of automatic weapons flare from trenches and knolls. Other volleys streamed from groups of soldiers that were partially hidden by the rolling terrain. He spotted a huge mechanical shape at one side of the conflict. The great barrel of the tank gun swung around, flame ejected from the muzzle and an explosion erupted along the knolls. Figures were blown from the site. The tank advanced, impervious to the rifle fire.

"Well," the Canadian began as he handed his binoculars to Ebrahim. "We know where those tanks wound up. I saw only one, but you can bet all three are involved in the battle."

"Those could be my people being slaughtered," Ebrahim declared, fists clenched tightly around the binoculars as he stared at the battle in the distance. "We don't always get along with the Democratic Front."

"What do we do?" Victoria asked, turning to James. "There doesn't seem to be much we can do against tanks, either, but still the EPLF has befriended us."

"You do what you want," Ebrahim announced grimly. "This isn't your war and there's no reason for you to fight this battle, but we can't allow our own people to be faced by such overwhelming forces and do nothing."

"The smart thing to do would be to circle around the battle zone and avoid the conflict," Katz said with a sigh.

"However, since we've joined forces with your group, Ebrahim, we can't let your people do this on their own provided it is your people being attacked."

"I'm pretty sure it is, and we appreciate your support," the rebel leader assured him, "but you might want to think twice about this. There's a high probability we'll all get killed."

"He's right," Muhammad added. "Even if Allah smiles on our efforts, there's little we can do against those tanks."

"A tank is like any other large opponent," Manning told him. "You don't fight a big powerful opponent on its own terms. You have to rely on cunning instead of strength and strike at the opponent's weaknesses."

"On a tank?" Halima asked, shaking her head. "What weaknesses does a tank have? Perhaps if we had some RPG rocket launchers we might have a chance."

"We have one thing on our side," James told the rebels. "The element of surprise. The Democratic Front soldiers won't expect to get hit from behind."

"You think that will be enough?" Ebrahim asked.

"I reckon we'll find out," McCarter answered with a fatalistic shrug.

THE DEMOCRATIC FRONT unit consisted of close to two hundred ground troops as well as the trio of tanks. A lieutenant colonel and a major were stationed behind the forces by a British Land Rover. The senior officer spoke into the microphone of a field radio while his executive officer observed the battle through binoculars. The NCO behind the wheel seemed relieved that the Rover wasn't moving. He wasn't eager to drive into battle. The two field-grade officers were clearly commanding their forces from a stationary position in the rear with no intentions of advancing until the EPLF soldiers were defeated. This suited the driver just fine.

The tanks steadily advanced across the battlefield. Huge monsters, they didn't fire their big 115 mm guns unless ordered to do so by the commander on the radio. Soldiers were positioned at the turret hatches to man mounted machine guns. They sprayed the trenches and knolls with steady streams of steel-jacketed slugs. Foot soldiers accompanied the tanks and fired AK-47s at the EPLF defenders.

Pinned down by the Democratic Front, the rebels were forced to duck low behind their cover. A few hurled grenades and paddles with dynamite bombs from the trenches and ridges. The projectiles exploded among the Ethiopian troops. Screams, like howling wind in a thunderstorm, were barely audible amid the roar of the explosions. Grisly corpses and dismembered limbs littered the dry, cracked earth. The machine gunners at the tanks ducked into their hatches for shelter.

The lieutenant colonel cursed into his microphone. He was about to order the tanks to shell the EPLF side again when a blurred line suddenly descended in front of his eyes. The officer barely glimpsed the wire loop as it swung over his head. The Democratic Front commander didn't have time to comprehend what was happening before the garrote tightened around his neck and throat.

David McCarter pulled the garrote and yanked the colonel away from the Land Rover. The Briton shoved an elbow between the officer's shoulder blades and turned to place himself back to back with his opponent. McCarter bent forward, the handles of the garrote still in his fists, and hauled the colonel onto his back. The man's legs thrashed the air as he hopelessly struggled. He died within seconds.

The Ethiopian major heard the scuffle and started to turn toward the colonel. He saw McCarter garrote the senior officer but had no chance to act. Calvin James jumped the major and reached around the man's left shoulder to grab his lower face. James muzzled the officer's mouth with his palm as he pulled the soldier backward and rammed a knee into a kidney.

James raised the Blackmoor Dirk and drove the tip of the dagger between the neck and shoulder of his opponent. The blade sunk through soft tissue behind the collarbone to sever the major's subclavian artery. The man convulsed in James's grasp as the driver of the Land Rover turned and gasped in terror.

The driver reached for an AK-47 on the seat beside him. James charged forward and shoved the major into the front of the Rover. The body crashed into the driver. The weight of the slain major struck the NCO hard and knocked him against the door.

Having dumped the corpse of the colonel, wire garrote still wrapped around its neck, David McCarter jumped to the front of the Rover and grabbed the stunned driver. He applied a viselike grip to the soldier's head and yanked hard. The driver's head and neck were forcibly snapped downward with McCarter's weight behind it. A loud snap announced that the vertebrae and spinal cord in the NCO's neck were broken.

McCarter pulled the dead man from the vehicle as Ebrahim rushed to the Rover and gathered up the headset and microphone. Although almost all of the Ethiopian troops were preoccupied with the battle, a few saw James and McCarter take out the commanders and their comrades-in-arms swarm forward from the rocks and shadows.

Several soldiers swung weapons toward the attack force. Katz and Encizo watched the Ethiopian troops, expecting this reaction. The Israeli and Cuban commandos had attached nine-inch silencers to the barrels of their Uzi machine pistols. The sputtering reports from the sound suppressors erupted before the soldiers could fire their Kalashnikovs. As the slugs ripped into their upper bodies, the Ethiopian soldiers twisted, trembled, staggered and fell. Only a couple managed to return fire before they collapsed.

An EPLF rebel among Ebrahim's people screamed, hit by the wild spray of AK-47 slugs. Ebrahim didn't turn to see how badly his comrade was hurt. The rebel leader concentrated on using the field radio. He keyed the mike and barked orders in rapid Amharic to the tank drivers not to fire their big guns but simply supply cover for the foot soldiers. Ebrahim hoped the men in the tanks were too stressed out to notice a different voice was giving them orders. It was also possible the lieutenant colonel had used some sort of code when issuing commands and that Ebrahim's orders would immediately be recognized as false. If that was the case, they would find out soon enough.

James pulled the corpse of the Ethiopian major from the Land Rover. The Blackmoor Dirk was still lodged in the dead man's flesh. As the Phoenix commando worked the blade free, there was a sickly sucking sound as skin and muscle protested the removal of the sharp, double-edged steel.

Manning and McCarter climbed aboard the Land Rover while James slid behind the steering wheel. He glanced back at Ebrahim's rebels, worried that Victoria might have been hit by the enemy salvo.

To his relief James saw Victoria beside a wounded rebel, her medical kit open. She seemed barely to notice as a stray bullet tore up a geyser of dirt near her, but James sucked in a tense breath and almost called out to her.

"What the hell are you waiting for?" McCarter demanded as he unslung his Uzi and gripped it with both hands.

James turned back to the battlefield, realizing he couldn't afford to delay any further. The tough guy from the Windy City turned on the ignition and stepped on the gas pedal. The Rover rolled forward with the three Phoenix commandos ready to plunge into the center of the battle.

Katz and Ebrahim led part of the rebel cell in a foot attack on the right flank of the Democratic Front forces while Encizo and Muhammad commanded the remaining team members in an assault on the left flank. Most of the enemy forces still didn't realize the Phoenix commandos and their EPLF companions had arrived until the strike force closed in.

The silenced Uzis of Katz and Encizo claimed more opponents, and the element of surprise was diminished as more and more Ethiopian troops saw their fellow soldiers fall. Even if they didn't hear the muted snarl of the silencer-equipped weapons, the troopers clearly saw the ragged bullet holes in the tunics of their slain comrades.

Foot soldiers whirled to confront their attackers. Rebels hurled paddle bombs at the troops. Others lobbed grenades or opened fire with Kalashnikovs. Explosions bellowed across the battlefield. Ethiopian troops were torn apart or thrown by the high-velocity punch of automatic weapons.

Encizo exhausted the ammo from his Uzi and switched to his AK-47. The Cuban ran toward the nearest tank, blasting soldiers as he went. Troopers tumbled from his path. Encizo didn't know how many were felled by his bullets or those of Muhammad and two other EPLF rebels who covered this advance.

Encizo soon reached the T-62 juggernaut as it moved ponderously across the field. He ran alongside the great tractor rollers of the metal beast, which seemed to make the earth quiver as it moved. It was unnerving to be so close to a war machine that weighed more than forty tons, but Encizo knew its crew likely hadn't noticed him. He was in greater danger of being shot by Democratic Front or EPLF forces among the trenches and knolls.

The tank was only a few yards from a trench. The rebels in the ditch ducked as the mighty mechanical beasts closed in. Encizo took a deep breath and bolted for the trench. He dashed past the tank and hit the ground in a wild slide like a baseball player desperately trying to reach home.

Encizo dropped into the ditch and fell against a startled rebel crouched behind a dirt wall. The Cuban's boots landed on something solid and uneven. He glanced down and saw that it was a corpse.

Encizo arched his back and moved to the tank as it began to pass over the trench. He ducked low and peered up at the undercarriage of the T-62. The big tractor rollers plowed loose dirt as the tank rolled over the ditch. Encizo pointed the barrel of the AK-47 at the track of the tractor and thrust it into the gears between the wheels.

The rollers came to an abrupt halt. The tank stopped, unable to move. The engine roared as the driver tried to force the huge vehicle forward, but the T-62 wasn't going anywhere as long as its tractor roller was jammed. Encizo climbed from the trench, followed by the EPLF rebel.

Encizo scaled the armor plating by the runner and mounted the tank. A hull machine gun barrel jutted from beneath the cannon of the T-62. Encizo plucked an object that resembled a black metal pen from a shirt pocket as he approached the hull gun. The Cuban pressed the clip of the implement, and a steel blade snapped from the end of the tube and locked in place.

The gadget was called a Guardfather and was designed for close-quarters self-defense. Encizo inserted the point of the Guardfather into the muzzle of the hull machine gun and jammed the blade into the barrel. Then the Cuban scrambled across the front of the tank to the driver's observation window. Hearing metal clang inside the tank, he drew his Walther P-88.

An explosion rocked the vehicle as flame sparked from the vents in the barrel of the hull machine gun. The crew had attempted to fire the weapon with the barrel clogged by the Guardfather and it backfired inside the tank. Encizo pointed the P-88 at the observation window and squeezed the trigger. The porthole was less than one foot long and half as wide, but the Cuban was only a few inches from the target and easily pumped two rounds through the reinforced glass.

The thick glass shattered. Encizo fired another round through the gap, pulled a fragmentation grenade from his belt and yanked the pin. After holding the grenade for the count of two, he thrust it through the broken window and promptly jumped from the tank.

As the grenade exploded, the hatches of the T-62 giant were blown open, and the mighty machine trembled as smoke rose from the gaps. Encizo looked up at the steaming hulk and sighed with relief.

James steered the British Land Rover alongside another big Soviet-made tank, while Manning and Mc-

Carter crouched in the back. The Canadian removed a yard-long piece of primer cord and tied a knot in the center. Manning curled the thick black cord into a ball and stuffed it into a pocket of his field jacket.

A bullet pierced the windshield, sliced past James's left shoulder and burrowed into the upper front seat. Fortunately the bullet came to rest in the upholstery. Another rifle round struck the windshield and ricocheted but cracked the glass in a road map pattern.

"Son of a bitch," James rasped as he ducked low and held on to the steering wheel to keep the Rover steady.

The shots came from the EPLF forces at the knolls. James didn't know if the rebels were firing at the Land Rover deliberately or accidentally. Either way the risk to the three Phoenix Force commandos in the British rig was increased. They didn't have much choice about how to handle the situation, since they were already committed to their strategy.

James pulled as close to the tank as possible, grateful the combat colossus moved so slowly. Manning jumped from the Land Rover, landed on the armor plating above the rollers and clasped the storage bin at the turret.

McCarter leaped next. James had slowed down the Rover a bit too much, and the T-62 was actually pulling ahead of the smaller vehicle. McCarter discovered that the tank wasn't as close as expected and that he was hurtling toward the rear of the metal titan.

His hands slashed the air wildly for a grip on the tank. Fingers closed on the long, thick stem of the antenna. McCarter braced a boot against the armored guard above the rear of the tractor roller. He swung forward and landed belly first across the transmission louvers at the rear of the tank. The Briton gripped the vents and hauled himself across the tank until he could get to a kneeling position by the turret.

Manning climbed the turret and wrapped the primer cord around the commander's hatch, linking both ends with an elastic cord. Then he placed a small C-4 charge against the knotted portion of primer cord and inserted a special blasting cap and detonator. The Canadian finished the task and started to climb from the turret.

He glimpsed the Makarov pistol just in time to roll away before the handgun snarled. Flame from the muzzle-flash streaked up the side of the turret. The Canadian commando realized someone inside the tank must have used a pistol port at the turret in an effort to take him out. That meant the enemy knew the T-62 was under attack.

McCarter heard the report of the Makarov, saw the frame of the blue-black autoloader shift around at the pistol port as the unseen gunman tried to train the weapon on Manning. Both Phoenix warriors had left their assault rifles and Uzi machine pistols in the Land Rover, figuring they would need full use of both hands and that small arms would be useless against the armored mammoth.

However, McCarter had his Browning Hi-Power and swiftly drew the pistol, clasping it in a Weaver's combat grip. McCarter aimed quickly and squeezed the trigger. A 9 mm parabellum round smashed into the frame of the Makarov. The bullet severely dented the slide of the weapon at the pistol port and sent the Makarov hurtling across the plates of the tank.

"It's clear now!" McCarter shouted to Manning.

The Canadian climbed down from the turret and joined McCarter at the rear of the tank. They ducked low and held on to the louver vents, waiting the few seconds for the charge attached to the hatch to go off. The C-4 exploded and detonated the primer cord. The blast tore the hatch off and shook the tank with a violent concussion wave.

Manning bolted back to the hatch and pulled the pin from a concussion grenade. As he tossed the explosive egg into the hole, he noticed that one of the lower hatches at the front of the turret had opened. A soldier emerged, pistol in his fist.

There was no time to reach for his own Walther autoloader or climb around the turret for cover. Manning reacted to the threat with instinct rather than thought. He dived from the turret before the soldier could spot him and aim his pistol. The Canadian crashed into the Ethiopian trooper.

The force of his hurtling body sent both men tumbling across the armor shields across the top of a tractor roller. They skidded along the plates to the front of the tank. Manning, who had the advantage because he had hit the soldier with all his weight behind the blow, remained on top of his opponent. He grabbed the Ethiopian's forearm and wrist above the Makarov and slammed the man's gun hand against the edge of the armor plating.

The soldier's fingers popped open, releasing the pistol, but he hooked his other fist at Manning's jaw. The Phoenix pro's head jerked from the punch, but Manning was a powerful man and as tough as steel. He returned a hard backfist that rocked his opponent's head and knocked loose two teeth. Manning hammered his fist into the other man's sternum and prepared to shove the dazed trooper off the moving tank.

The concussion grenade bellowed, and the forty-ton tank convulsed from the explosion. Manning and the soldier, shaken off the roller guard, landed on the slanted front of the tank and slid downward. Manning descended between the headlights while the trooper tumbled sideways over a mud shield at the front of the rollers.

The Canadian clawed at the nearest headlight for a handhold. He missed and his nails scrapped metal as his legs dangled and his belly slid along the edge of the tank's front. A shriek of agony seemed to erupt from the ground. Manning heard the crunch of broken bones and a sickly liquid sound. His stomach turned as he realized the soldier had fallen into the path of the tractor rollers and had been crushed under the monstrous treads.

He knew he could share the man's fate if he was careless. Manning struggled to keep his feet and legs away from the gears of the rollers as he tried to prevent himself from sliding to the ground. A hard cylinder jammed into his stomach. He grabbed the object with one fist and discovered a tow bar beneath the headlights and between the roller wheels.

Manning pulled hard and hauled a foot up to the bar, as well. He glanced up at the barrel of the tank gun overhead. The Canadian braced his boot firmly on the bar and held on with his fist until he placed the other foot on the tow bar. His pulse raced as he released the bar and stood erect on it, arms extended overhead.

He grasped the thick cannon barrel, climbed it hand over hand and walked toward the turret. Finally he mounted the turret once more and reached the commander's hatch.

Suddenly the tank stopped. Manning froze and reached for the Walther P-88. It seemed impossible that any of the crew inside the tank could still be conscious and able to operate the machine. The concussion grenade blast should have rendered everyone within the T-62 senseless if not dead. Yet Manning had learned not to rule out anything as impossible, so he drew his pistol in case the Ethiopian tank crew still had some fight left in them.

"Gary!" a familiar cockney voice called up from within the tank. "I managed to stop this thing, but I'm going to need some help getting these bodies out of here so there'll be enough room to use the bloody controls! If you're through playing around out there, you might give me a hand."

"Give you a hand, hell," Manning muttered, relieved to hear McCarter's voice. "I ought to give you a fist instead."

The foot soldiers and rebel forces continued to fight. Explosions and gunfire had cut down the number of Democratic Front troops to less than fifty. With two of the tanks taken out, the EPLF defenders who had previously been pinned down rejoined the battle actively and blasted Ethiopian soldiers with hails of AK-47 rounds.

Ebrahim's followers hit the troops from the opposite angle to trap the enemy in a deadly cross fire. Rafael Encizo, Muhammad and other EPLF guerrillas used the smoking ruins of the first downed tank for cover as they fired at the soldiers. Katz watched the Ethiopian military topple like blood-splattered tenpins. The Phoenix commander was reluctant to participate in the carnage. It no longer seemed to be a battle. The Democratic Front soldiers were already beaten, but the rebels didn't appear to have any interest in taking prisoners.

Suddenly the Israeli spotted a Democratic Front soldier in a kneeling stance with a long, tube-shaped weapon braced across a shoulder, a torpedolike object at its muzzle. It was a Soviet-made RPG rocket launcher, and the man was pointing it at the tank commandeered by Manning and McCarter.

The threat to his fellow Phoenix commandos immediately dispelled any hesitation, and Katz swiftly aimed his Uzi and triggered a 3-round burst. The man with the RPG stumbled backward, his chest torn open as he joined the dead.

The third tank, still commanded by the Ethiopians, stopped rolling forward and the turret turned slowly toward the heart of the battle. This had changed to the rear of the Democratic Front forces where the rebels were busy wiping out what remained of their attackers. The metal Goliath pointed its big gun at the Ebrahim cell members.

The tremendous bellow of a 115 mm gun sounded as if the devil had kicked open the doors to hell itself. Harsh orange light flared across the battlefield. The shell crashed into the turret of the enemy tank. Metal burst apart, and the cannon fell broken across the hull of the big T-62.

Manning sat at the command chair of the tank he and McCarter had captured. Unlike the behemoth taken out by Encizo, the equipment inside their tank was still in good working order because Manning has used a concussion grenade instead of a fragger. The Canadian peered through a periscope and studied the damage to his target. The last enemy tank was crippled and surely unable to use its big gun. Manning's shell had taken out the other tank's turret as well as its main weapons.

Grimly Manning turned the rotor wheel to extract the spent shell casing and feed another 115 mm projectile into the cannon. The Phoenix pro aimed at the rear of the crippled T-62, where the external fuel tank was located. He fired another round at the enemy machine. The explosion ignited the fuel container and blasted away most of the tail end of the tank. Flames rose from the metal wreckage. There was little doubt anyone could have survived.

Cheers sang out from the EPLF rebels as they claimed their victory. Men and women swarmed from the knolls and trenches. They took weapons and supplies from the slain Democratic Front troops. James drove the Land Rover in a semicircle to the site where Encizo and Muhammad waited by the remains of the first tank. The Cuban and Islamic rebel climbed aboard the Rover. James drove around the EPLF guerrillas as they rummaged through the pockets of dead soldiers.

Victoria had commented that the hyena was both a hunter and a scavenger, James recalled. This was true about most animals, including man. He realized the rebels had to take arms, ammunition and supplies from the lifeless troops. James himself carried an AK-47 he had removed from a dead man. It was a cycle of life in a violent world. The living preyed on the dead one way or the other.

"At least we won," Muhammad commented quietly.

"Yeah," Encizo said grimly. He glanced around at the corpses strewn across the battlefield. Dozens of bodies lay everywhere. His nostrils were clogged by the smell of smoke, cordite and the scent of blood.

They saw Ebrahim kneel beside a lifeless form among the legion of dead. The rebel leader gathered up the limp figure in his arms. James swallowed hard when he recognized Halima. Ebrahim pressed his face against his lover's crimson-stained head and sobbed.

Desperately James glanced around, looking for Victoria Yatta. He was relieved to see her, once again attending to the wounded among the EPLF rebels. He sighed and steered the Land Rover to where Katz stood. The tires rolled over a corpse as he approached. There were too many bodies to avoid them all. James brought the rig to a halt near the Israeli.

"You okay?" James asked. Katz's expression seemed pale and sickly.

"Such a waste," the Israeli replied, shaking his head. "We usually find ourselves pitted against terrorists and gangsters and others who make a conscious decision to commit evil. This was more conventional war, the type fought by strangers who are on opposites sides largely due to simple geography. It's even odder when you think that the Democratic Front and the EPLF have been allies."

"We are fighting for our independence," Muhammad assured him. "That never changes, and the Democratic Front now rules in Addis Ababa."

"I hope some good comes from all this," Encizo said.

"Perhaps sometime in the future," Katz said as he looked at Ebrahim carrying Halima's body away from the battlefield. "But at the moment I don't think we'll find much good here. The only thing more bitter would have been if we had lost the conflict. As it is, I don't know that we won anything."

16

Captain Moshin lowered his binoculars. The Israeli agent and his team had heard the distant sounds of battle and saw the flashing lights of weapons and explosions set against the shadows of the night. They were more than twelve miles from the battlefield, too far for Moshin to see any details of the combatants even with the binoculars.

"It seems to be over," he announced. "It must have been a pretty good-size conflict with hundreds of soldiers. I think we've all heard enough cannon fire to recognize it."

"Sounded like tank guns," Kanwonkpa remarked thoughtfully. The Liberian mercenary rubbed his bandaged hand. It itched, but he couldn't scratch it.

"The Democratic Front and the EPLF must have clashed in large numbers," Galadi, the rebel veteran, declared. "I wish I knew if my comrades won."

"One thing we can be certain of," Sergeant Rabin said as he switched on his radio transceiver. "The American team surely avoided this battle zone. Their group must be too small to get involved in such a conflict."

"But the satellite went down somewhere in this area," Moshin said. "They'll be out here searching for the prize just as we are."

"If they're still alive," Sergeant Gehmer added. "We haven't detected any radio messages from the bogus priest for some time. No word from Levi in Sudan, either. I know the Mossad thinks it's infallible, but Levi might have been mistaken."

"My radio scan isn't getting much," Rabin told the others as he listened to the headset of his transceiver. "There's a faint frequency some distance away. Democratic Front airwave. It's an observation post reporting the battle to command headquarters in this region."

"The Ethiopian troops involved in the fight aren't reporting it?" Galadi asked with pleasure. "That must mean the EPLF won. I don't know how they took out those tanks. Perhaps they got some RPGs from the bodies of dead Ethiopians."

"We really don't want to encounter the Democratic Front or the EPLF," Gehmer remarked. "But the latter would certainly present a lesser threat. It's probably in our favor that the Democratic Front lost the battle."

"Don't be so sure of that," Kanwonkpa warned. "How do you think the Ethiopians will react when they discover that the EPLF won this round? They'll probably send as many troops to this area as possible, and that may include air support."

"Our Liberian friend is right," Galadi declared.

"We need to keep moving forward," Moshin announced. "We'll have to remain alert to any threat from the Ethiopians, including air attacks."

"Still no broadcast by the Americans," Rabin said as he knelt by the radio. "They must be maintaining radio silence. They must be smart enough to realize that everybody else is probably monitoring the wavelengths now."

"Even the disguise as an innocent Coptic priest chatting with his bishop would attract attention now," Moshin replied. "They won't use the radio again as long as they're in Wollo Province. These people are obviously professional or they wouldn't have gotten this far. Don't expect them to make too many mistakes."

"We'd better not, either," Kanwonkpa added. "This country seems very unforgiving of mistakes."

MAJOR DAWA WAS overjoyed by the news. The guerrillas, according to the radio, were killing one another. Apparently the battle had occurred fifteen miles from Dawa's position. Despite the advantage of three T-62 tanks, the Democratic Front had been wiped out by the EPLF.

"The EPLF must be very strong in this area," Dawa said grimly.

"We knew this region was dangerous before we came to this province," Jabal commented. "Of course, Tigre Province was far from a safe harbor. If we're going to complete our mission, we have no choice except to keep going."

"With Democratic Front troops and EPLF guerrillas swarming all over the place," Dawa said, "every step we take is a dangerous one."

"A clandestine mission remains covert," the Libyan agent said with a sigh. "That's to be expected."

They had seen the fighting in the distance and heard the automatic fire and cannons. Dawa and Jabal had hoped the Democratic Front and the EPLF would wipe each other out, but the Eritreans had won and made their job even more dangerous. There was the possibility the EPLF would retreat and regroup after their victory. If their losses were great enough, they wouldn't wait for more Democratic Front troops to arrive.

"Do you have a family back in Libya, Captain?" Dawa inquired as he opened his canteen.

"Yes," Jabal answered. "A wife, a son and two daughters. My mother also lives with us. If I don't make it back, I know my brother will look after them. That's some comfort, I suppose."

"I have a family," Dawa said, taking a drink of water. "I haven't seen them in a long time. I don't even know if they're still alive."

"You must have hope, Major."

"Hope is a rare commodity in Ethiopia," Dawa replied. "Very rare."

VICTORIA YATTA and Calvin James finished tending the wounded EPLF members as well as time and their limited medical supplies allowed. A few of the rebels were also skilled in emergency first aid and combat surgery. Most had learned their abilities the hard way—on-the-job training in the trenches. However, they lacked the formal training and expertise of Victoria and James. The Kenyan nurse and Phoenix Force medic had years of experience as well as good medical training. The others quickly recognized their superior ability and agreed they should be in charge of the task.

They bandaged the victims of gunshot and shrapnel wounds as best as possible. There wasn't enough disinfectant, antibiotics or painkillers. James and Encizo had to clean the lesser wounds with water and give medication only to those in serious need. Katz approached them and announced that they would have to leave soon.

"How's Ebrahim?" James asked. "He must be pretty torn up about Halima's death."

"I'm sure he is," Katz replied. "But Ebrahim doesn't have the luxury of grieving for her, and he knows it. The living have to take precedence. Ebrahim is aware of this harsh reality, and he isn't about to let the rest of his people down, even if he's suffered a personal tragedy."

James looked at Ebrahim. The EPLF cell leader was conversing with four of the EPLF defenders rescued by Phoenix Force and Ebrahim's group. James guessed the survivors of the larger cell were trying to convince Ebrahim to remain with them. Despite the fact that they had been saved they had lost many comrades in battle.

Ebrahim embraced the others warmly, turned and headed toward the remaining members of his cell. Rafael Encizo was among them. The Cuban commando inspected an AK-47 he had confiscated from a slain soldier to replace the rifle used to jam the tank's tractor gears.

Gary Manning and Muhammad monitored military radio broadcasts while David McCarter pried open a storage bin on one of the T-62 tanks. The Briton found some food, a medical kit, a small tent and some tools. He took the food and medical supplies, intending to give the latter to James only after they left. The British ace wasn't callous toward the injured members of the EPLF, but he was concerned about the diminishing supplies of Phoenix Force.

James and Victoria had been behaving as healers instead of soldiers or agents. McCarter understood this and sympathized, although the self-preservation of Phoenix Force and the success of their mission remained his primary concern. They had been too generous with their supplies and couldn't afford to run out if any of their people were injured or became ill before they reached the border.

The five Phoenix commandos and Victoria Yatta joined Ebrahim's remaining followers. Halima hadn't been the only casualty among the group. Four were dead and five injured badly enough to remain with the larger EPLF force, which was better equipped to handle the wounded. Ebrahim's cell had been whittled down to twelve.

"The other EPLF cell would like us to stay with them," Ebrahim told the others. "They were very impressed by your skill and cunning. I might add that I was, too."

"One of those blokes who spoke English wanted us to stay and teach them how to use a tank," McCarter remarked. "He was pretty disappointed when I told him the tanks wouldn't do them much good, anyway, not as long as the Democratic Front have MiGs."

"Speaking of which," Katz added, "we should be on our way before they send planes and more troops in retaliation for what happened here."

"They're already mobilizing forces, according to the most recent military broadcasts," Manning stated.

"Hopefully their aircraft won't be equipped with infrared scanners or heat detectors so we can still make the most of the darkness," Encizo commented.

"We're not accomplishing anything here now," Ebrahim announced. "The battle is over. Now we have to find that satellite. I just hope this thing will still be there when we reach the site where it supposedly went down."

"If the Argus isn't there, a lot of people will be disappointed," Katz answered. "If the information from the satellite winds up in the wrong hands, some people may be more than disappointed. They may very well be dead."

17

The receiver unit was no larger than a pack of cigarettes and resembled a common transistor radio. Katz extended the nine-inch antenna as they moved toward the reported site of the fallen satellite.

The Phoenix Force commander was concerned that the UHF frequency ground-tracking system built into the Argus had been damaged when the satellite crashed. Katz recalled that Brognola had said the receiver would transmit a signal to the Argus that would trigger the tracking unit, which would then transmit a steady UHF wavelength to guide them to the satellite. The Israeli was a veteran of the "old school" of intelligence and was never terribly comfortable relying on machines and high-tech gadgets instead of individual human intelligence and abilities.

"Maybe someone else should operate this thing for a while," the Israeli said with a sigh. "It might know I resent it."

"I don't think that sort of sensitivity is programmed into the receiver," Manning assured him as he took the device from Katz.

Since leaving the battlefield, Phoenix Force and Ebrahim's rebel group had traveled for hours. The terrain was greener than that encountered earlier in Wollo Province. Elephant grass and trees covered the landscape. Hills extended before the Phoenix group. Night birds and monkeys called out and chattered from the branches. The chirping of tree frogs revealed there was water in the area.

Ebrahim regarded the small receiver unit with suspicion. Such contraptions were beyond his experience, and he had even less faith in them than Katz possessed. The EPLF leader wondered if any of the mysterious commandos knew how to use the radio properly. He was beginning to have serious doubts that they would ever locate the spy satellite.

A dull roar rolled through the night sky. They looked up and saw three dots in the dark firmament approach from the south. The Team and its allies ducked into the elephant grass and stayed low as the jet planes drew closer. They peered between long blades of tough grass and watched the MiGs slice through the night sky in a tight formation. The planes swung into a wide arc and passed over the hidden commando unit.

Hugging the ground, the Phoenix pros and their guerrilla companions tensely waited for the fighters to leave. Although this took only scant seconds, their nerves were taut and pulses raced until the sound of the turbo engines faded into the distance. The exhaust flames of the MiGs blinked on the horizon as the jets headed east.

"They're combing the province from the air," McCarter said as he got to his feet. "Obviously they don't have heat-sensor tracking equipment or they probably would have spotted us."

"We would have known if they had," Encizo added. "It took a while for the planes to cover this area, so they must not have much of an air force."

"If they have only one plane, they'd have more than we've got," James remarked. "I hope they don't keep searching by air after sunup. They won't need sensors or infrared to find us then.''

"It'll be dawn in a couple of hours," Ebrahim said grimly, "and we don't seem to be any closer to finding the satellite than we were twelve hours ago."

A soft beeping surprised Ebrahim. He glanced at Manning and saw a small orange light flash on the radio receiver's dial. Manning cupped a hand over the radio and examined the dial as he slowly moved the antenna from side to side. "The signal isn't very strong," he announced, "but there's no doubt which direction it's coming from."

"How far away is the satellite?" Victoria inquired.

"About three miles," the Canadian answered. "Give or take a yard."

"Then let's go find that damn Argus," James declared. "I want to see the thing that's responsible for this mission."

Less than an hour later they set eyes on Argus. It lay at the bottom of a deep gorge in the side of a rocky hill. It was shaped like a giant metal cork with a wide circular base and a boxlike top connected by skeletal steel framework at the center. A big, rectangular solar panel extended from one side of the satellite like an artificial wing. Another panel had been broken off and lost before the Argus had plunged to earth.

"There it is," Manning said unnecessarily as he switched off the receiver. The beeping ceased abruptly. "The NSA's monster with a hundred eyes."

Katz stared down at the Argus. The ravine was more than a hundred feet deep and littered with clusters of boulders and tangled clumps of weeds. The satellite was battered and dented. Even from a distance in the dim light there was no doubt that the Argus had been badly damaged. Considering it had been struck by a meteor and had plummeted from orbit to crash-land in the gorge, Katz thought they were lucky the satellite hadn't burned up or shattered like a wineglass.

The darkness began to surrender to the gradual light of predawn. With the Democratic Front hunting EPLF rebels, daybreak posed a greater threat to Phoenix Force and their allies. Katz suggested someone should stand watch at the top of the ravine while the others climbed down to the Argus.

"I have no desire to get a better look at that machine," Ebrahim assured him. "You go do whatever you need to do with the satellite. I'll stay here with some of my comrades and watch for the MiGs."

"Fine," Encizo said as he examined the rock walls to the ravine. "We didn't bring any climbing gear, but I don't think we'll need it. It's not that steep. We can almost walk down to the bottom, and there are plenty of available handholds for us among the rocks."

"Getting down there won't be a problem," James agreed, and handed his AK-47 to one of the rebels. "I just hope the recordings weren't destroyed."

"Better they're destroyed than fall into enemy hands," Katz answered. He turned to Manning. "You've studied the diagram of the Argus more than the rest of us. Figure you can get the recordings out of the satellite?"

"I've got a copy of the diagram," Manning replied, patting his shirt pocket. "I may have to check it to make sure I'm working on the right part, but I can handle it."

"That's a comfort," McCarter said dryly as he started to climb into the ravine.

James followed, and Victoria moved to the edge of the gorge, as well. He frowned and shook his head. James was about to suggest that she stay with the watch above.

"I want a closer look at this thing," Victoria said before he could voice his opinion. "After all, we've traveled across most of Ethiopia to find it. I'd like to see what all the fuss is about."

"Okay," James agreed, aware that it was pointless to argue with Victoria when she had her mind set on something. "Just be careful and stay close."

Manning and Encizo also handed their Kalashnikov rifles to the rebels at the top of the ravine. The Phoenix commandos needed to have full use of their hands as they descended the gorge. All five warriors were still armed with Uzi machine pistols and 9 mm autoloaders in shoulder leather. Muhammad and two other EPLF members also descended into the ravine.

Encizo's evaluation of the climb proved accurate. It wasn't difficult to descent the rock walls. The decline wasn't steep and only required a minimum of effort. Phoenix Force, Victoria and the three rebels soon reached the bottom of the gorge and approached the smashed shell of the Argus.

The damage to the satellite was more extensive than it had appeared from a distance. The metal skin was scorched and battered. The frames were smashed and twisted. Part of the base was bashed in. Vents at one side of the big disc had been pressed flat and other parts were missing entirely.

Manning opened his pocket and removed the diagram. The Argus was designed to resemble a meteorological satellite, and much of its styling was the same as a weather satellite's. The pitch nozzle and command antenna at the top had been broken off, and the altitude control no longer resembled an air-conditioner vent. It was mangled and beaten into a shapeless lump.

Chunks had been torn from the remaining solar panel. It looked like the giant wing of a mighty metal bird ripped apart by buckshot. Manning moved to the base of the Argus. The thermal control shutters and beacon antenna were wrecked. These were located along the rim of the satellite. The vital intelligence-gathering portion of the Argus was stored at the bottom of the base. An object that resembled a crushed helmet jutted from the center of the underside of the disc.

Manning consulted his diagram and grunted. The smashed contraption had been an infrared spectrometer and radio telescope. Next to it was a device that looked like a broken video camera. That was what it was, but far more sophisticated that the familiar civilian Camcorder. It had been equipped with a laser-directed image dissector system. Manning opened his pack and found a small battery-operated drill.

"How does it look?" Katz asked as he stood back to give Manning ample room to work.

"I'm not sure yet," the Canadian admitted. "I have to get some of this smashed-up junk out of the way in order to reach the panel to the recording section."

He pointed to a thick metal stem that looked like a broken sprinkler nozzle. "See that?" Manning inquired. "It was the location guidance antenna. The recorder should be inside the panel behind it."

"If you say so," Katz replied. He glanced up at the bright blue morning sky.

They had hardly noticed the dawn, but the sun cast rays of light into the gorge. This made Manning's task easier but increased the risk of being spotted by hostile forces. James looked at Victoria. She offered a weak smile and took one of his hands in both of hers. He squeezed her hands gently as they tensely waited for Manning to finish working on the Argus.

The Canadian knelt by the base of the satellite and inserted the drill into the side of the spectrometer. He triggered it and dug the drill bit into the battered metal. The bolts eased loose and the infrared scanner slid from the base to dangle by frayed wires. Manning turned the drill on the panel above the location antenna.

"Bloody lovely," McCarter complained. "We just stand around and watch. Might as well have stayed above with Ebrahim."

"So climb back up there," Manning growled in response as he shifted the drill bit to another corner of the panel. "I don't need a cheering section to do this."

McCarter muttered something under his breath and took a pack of Player's from his pocket. The Briton fired up a cigarette and impatiently waited while Manning worked. A loud snap of metal finally rewarded the Canadian's efforts, and the hatch to the panel fell open.

"Okay," Manning said as he checked the diagram once more. "This should only take another minute now."

He peered inside the compartment. A network of circuits and microchips lined the interior. Cords were attached to a metal plate, linked to the wrecked camera and spectrometer from within. Manning detached the cords and removed the plate. The Canadian used the drill to pry open the plate. At last he found a blue wafer, only slightly larger and thicker than a credit card.

"This is it, gentlemen," Manning announced. He glanced at Victoria and added, "And lady. This miniature disc has months of surveillance information stored on microchip recordings."

"It's so small," Muhammad said, amazed by the innocent-looking little water that was so important to several nations.

"No bigger than it has to be," Manning said as he slipped the wafer into his shirt pocket.

"Good," Encizo said with a nod. "Now let's get the hell out of here."

Suddenly automatic fire burst from the summit of the ravine. They looked up and saw three EPLF rebels at the precipice convulse from the impact of high-velocity slugs. They tumbled over the edge and fell against the rocky incline to roll lifelessly into the ravine.

"Son of a bitch!" James exclaimed. "We're under attack!"

18

Phoenix Force bolted for cover as the rattling reports of full-auto weapons continued. They heard screams and glimpsed more falling figures at the rim of the ravine. Manning and Encizo ducked behind the wreck of the Argus satellite for shelter. James dashed behind some boulders, pulling Victoria with him. Katz and McCarter darted for another set of boulders near the edge of the ravine. Muhammad and the EPLF pair who had accompanied him into the gorge also ran for cover.

The shooting above ceased. Phoenix Force and their four companions peered up at the bullet-ravaged bodies of the EPLF rebels who had been standing watch at the precipice. Some were sprawled along the edge and others lay, bloodied and broken, at the base of the gorge. Only two appeared to have survived the attack. A male and a female rebel managed to scramble over the edge and tried to reach cover among the rocks along the incline.

A figure appeared at the summit and pointed a Soviet-made PPSh-41 submachine gun at the rebel pair. Flame snarled from the weapon. The EPLF female warrior shrieked as 7.62 mm rounds punched through her back. She cartwheeled off the incline to hurl gracelessly to the unyielding ground below. The other rebel dodged behind a stone ridge in time to avoid another burst of enemy gunfire.

McCarter drew his browning Hi-Power and held it in a firm two-handed combat grip. The British pistol marksman aimed over a boulder, fixing the sights on the gunman at the top of the ravine. He saw the opponent's spotted army fatigues but noticed the man's face wasn't black. The features were Semitic. McCarter didn't know if the man was an Israeli or an Arab. Under the circumstances he still had only one choice of action.

The Briton squeezed the trigger. The range was a fair distance for a pistol shot, even for an expert Olympic-level shooter. McCarter didn't try anything fancy. He aimed at the upper torso and fired three rounds. The gunman's arms rose and the PPSh-41 fell from open fingers. McCarter saw his target topple backward and glimpsed a bloodstain left of center on the man's shirt. He knew the guy wouldn't get up again.

The other attackers kept away from the rim of the ravine. A large projectile shot across the gorge and slammed into the opposite wall. It exploded on impact and dislodged a minor avalanche of dirt and rock. The debris showered down on the boulders used by Phoenix Force and their allies for cover. Stones pelted the group and loose dirt slid inside shirt collars and splattered clothing.

Two more shells hit the same ravine wall. Nearly a ton of dirt and rocks crashed down on the boulders below. Commandos and rebels shielded themselves as best they could. One EPLF guerrilla, struck in the skull by a large stone, fell unconscious as dirt formed a pile on his senseless form. Another large rock smashed into Katz's Uzi, denting the breech. Encizo groaned as a chunk of stone hit him in the left shoulder blade.

"What the hell are they using on us?" the Cuban rasped as he rotated his left arm gently to try to judge whether or not the blow to his back had broken a bone.

"Either firing two or more grenade launchers or they've got an automatic launcher," Manning replied. "They must be afraid of hitting the Argus, because they're firing high. It's a hazing action. They either want to flush us out or pin us down."

"They're doing a pretty good job at the latter," Encizo commented.

The explosions stopped and the enemy held their fire. A voice shouted something in Amharic. Muhammad prepared to translate, but another voice from above the ravine called out in English.

"You CIA Americans!" it declared in a guttural accent. "You are trapped! Throw out your guns and stand in the open with your hands up. We'll let you live if we get the satellite!"

"That might be more convincing if you hadn't just gunned down several of our friends!" James shouted back. He gestured for Victoria to move with him to another position, explaining that the enemy might fire in the direction his voice came from.

"The people we shot were Eritrean Separatists!" the voice announced. "Dogs who seek to tear Ethiopia apart. I'm accompanied by Major Dawa, a high-ranking officer in the army of the new regime in Addis Ababa. We have authorization from the lawful government of this country. You are here illegally! You could be shot as spies! Surrender now and we'll see to it that you safely leave this country!"

Gary Manning opened his pack as he slithered under the Argus. Encizo wondered what he was doing, but most of his attention was fixed on the enemy position above. The Cuban peered around the base of the satellite and examined the summit. Their opponents were still keeping out of sight. They clearly had the advantage, and both sides knew it.

Manning emerged from under the Argus. He held a small electrical squib with a long wire that extended under the satellite. Encizo wasn't particularly pleased with the notion that the demolitions expert had placed an explosive charge so close to them.

"What are you doing?" Encizo inquired, not certain he'd like the answer.

"I'm going to try to buy us some time," Manning answered. He raised his voice to call out to the unseen opponents above. "You people want this satellite? You'd better back off, or I'll blow it to hell!"

There was a brief pause before the voice of Captain al-Jabal replied, "If you destroy it, you won't have the satellite, either, and we'll kill you, as well!"

"You'd probably kill us, anyway!" Manning shouted back. "Why should we reward you for that? If we don't get the Argus, neither will you!"

"You're bluffing, American!" Jabal declared. "CIA infidels aren't willing to sacrifice their lives for a cause! Don't waste my time with these false threats!"

Manning pressed the plunger to the squib. An explosion, similar to a giant firecracker, barked from beneath the solar panel of the Argus. The winglike extension burst apart and pieces of the panel spewed in all directions. Encizo gasped and ducked.

"That's just the first charge!" Manning called up to the enemy. "If you don't think I'll set off the other two, come ahead and you'll see me blow up the whole damn satellite!"

"You might have told me you were going to set off an explosion," Encizo whispered, still watching for any sign of the enemy.

"I didn't mean to startle you," Manning said calmly. "It was just a small charge of CV-38 low-velocity plastic explosives. Not much of a blast."

"Maybe not to you," the Cuban growled. "But to someone who isn't a demolitions expert and not expecting an explosion, it wasn't a pleasant surprise. Did you really plant more charges under the Argus?"

"No," Manning replied. "I don't want to blow up the satellite while we're using it for cover."

"I'm glad to hear that," Encizo said dryly. "Any idea what we should do next?"

"Not really," the Canadian admitted. "The only thing in our favor is that the enemy doesn't realize the Argus is just a pile of junk now. We've already got the data wafer, so it doesn't matter if the satellite is destroyed or not. As long as they still think the Argus is important, they won't be apt to launch a full-scale attack or bombard us with explosives."

A figure moved toward their position. Manning and Encizo started to move their weapons toward the shape, but they saw the familiar prosthesis and recognized Katz in time to hold their fire. The Israeli held a Walther P-88 in his single hand as he approached, back arched and head down.

"You two all right?" Katz asked as he moved next to the Argus.

"Dented," Encizo answered, "but not broken." His shoulder blade still ached.

"You're doing better than my Uzi," the Phoenix commander said. "It was dented and broken."

"Any idea about strategy?" Manning asked.

"Right now the enemy's reluctant to attack and they're staying clear of the cliff," Katz replied. "That means we can't see them, but they can't see us, either. If we move to the boulder by the wall directly under their position, it'll make it more difficult for them to attack us."

"They're not stupid," Encizo warned. "They'll know enough to divide their forces to hit us from more than one direction."

"We'll divide our force, too," Katz said.

He turned to see Muhammad drag the stunned rebel from the mound of dirt and discover that his unlucky comrade had already suffocated. Katz had seen James and Victoria move to some boulders by the ravine wall. Neither appeared to have been harmed by the flying rocks or shrapnel from the grenade blasts.

"We don't have much of a force left to divide," Manning observed. "On top of that none of us brought rifles and we're running low on 9 mm ammo for our Uzis and pistols."

"I'm glad you can look on the bright side of this situation, Gary," Katz said dryly.

JABAL SHOOK a cigarette from a pack and stuck it in his mouth. He was tempted to move to the edge, but the dead Storm Lion commando was a reminder that that could be a fatal mistake. Major Dawa and his men stood several yards from the cliff and stared at the bodies of the EPLF rebels they had shot down when they closed in on the ravine.

It had been easier than they'd expected until now. Sergeant Kiflom had monitored the radio waves with his transceiver and discovered the steady beeping sound on a UHF frequency. The communications NCO had suspected that it was a signal of some sort, and it was close enough to be connected with the "CIA agents" they were stalking. They simply followed the signal and discovered the group of rebels stationed at the top of the gorge. The sentries were paying too much attention to the sky, more concerned about the MiGs than an attack from ground level.

Dawa's troops and Jabal's commandos easily picked off the EPLF guerrillas. However, they appeared to be stalemated for the moment. Their unit couldn't fire down at the opponents in the ravine without jeopardizing the spy satellite, but the American team couldn't come up from the gorge without risking death.

Hamel paced nervously, his AG-17 grenade launcher cradled in his arms. The Libyan trooper was eager to use his prized weapon and resented the Yankees for preventing him from simply blasting them to bits with his Soviet launcher. Jabal gestured for Hamel to back away from the cliff. The other Storm Lions didn't seem to be in a hurry to confront the opponents in the ravine.

"I don't think they have much food or water down there," Dawa told Jabal. "Perhaps we can wait them out."

"Time is to our advantage," Jabal agreed. He noticed several extra AK-47s among the slain EPLF rebels. "Apparently they left their rifles here when they climbed down to the satellite. That means they don't have long-range weapons, or at least not many Kalashnikovs."

"One of them managed to hit your man with at least one bullet from a fair distance," the Ethiopian officer reminded him.

"I know," Jabal assured Dawa. "It sounded like the report of a pistol, but we can't assume the enemy scored a lucky shot. Their demolitions man impressed me as being very professional when he blasted off a portion of the satellite to prove he had it wired with explosives. Count on them all being as good at their job as that one is."

"Hopefully they won't be better than we are," Dawa commented as he gazed across the ravine. "We should put some of our people on the other ridge. That way we can cover them better."

"Stay where you are and throw down your weapons!" a voice shouted in Amharic from one of the hills.

Startled, the Ethiopian and Libyan troops swung their weapons toward the voice. A salvo of full-auto bullets suddenly ripped up chunks of earth near the soldiers. Muzzle-flashes of assault rifles blazed from a cluster of bushes three hundred yards to the left.

Dawa, Jabal and their soldiers had used the same tactic to ambush the EPLF guerrillas at the ravine. However, the unit that now threatened them gave them the opportunity of surrendering instead of simply being killed. They could either give up or make a stand.

Hamel's actions left them with only one option. The Libyan commando swung his AG-17 at the muzzle-flash in the bushes and opened fire. Two 30 mm grenades streaked into the foliage and exploded with monstrous fury. Bloodied corpses hurtled from the cover as the bushes caught fire and dust rose from the blast. Hamel shifted the aim of his AG-17 and fired again. Another explosion blasted stone and dirt from the hillside, but no screams or bodies accompanied the eruption.

Automatic fire burst from a rock formation, and a trio of ragged bullet holes blossomed on Hamel's chest. Blood dripped from the exit wounds at his upper back as the Libyan staggered backward and triggered his grenade launcher once more. Another huge shell sailed into the sky and descended into the peak of the hill with a mighty roar. Hamel held on to his AG-17 as he stumbled over the lip of the cliff and plunged into the gorge.

Jabal's other Storm Lions and Dawa's soldiers returned fire at the new opponents. There was no available
cover, and they were forced to duck low to try to present
smaller targets. Two Ethiopians cried out and tumbled
across the ground, propelled by the impact of high-
velocity rifle slugs. Dropping his AK-47, a Libyan commando clasped his bullet-shattered face. He fell onto his
side, twitched feebly and lay still as blood and brains
leaked between his fingers.

Unexpectedly put on the defense, the Ethiopian and
Libyan forces were caught in the open with nowhere to
retreat except into the ravine. Although this was far from
a safe haven, the soldiers crawled to the cliff and climbed
over the edge. Dawa shouted orders to some of his men to
take positions at the rim and use the rocky lip of the cliff
for shelter and return fire at the unknown opponents
above.

"HOLY SHIT!" James exclaimed as he saw the figures at
the top of the rock wall. "They're coming down!"

Descending the incline, Jabal and the remaining Storm
Lions fired down at the ruins of the Argus and surrounding boulders to keep the Phoenix defenders at bay. One
commando hurled a grenade in front of the satellite. The
explosive sphere blasted a hole in the ground and raised
more swirling dust within the gorge.

The grenade thrower didn't get an opportunity to lob
another. He had forgotten about the EPLF rebel who had
fled to the rock ridge along the incline. The guerrilla,
opening fire with his Kalashnikov, hit the Libyan trooper
in the side. Bullets punched through the man's rib cage
and sent him hurtling from the rock wall.

Jabal fired his Stechkin machine pistol at the rebels.
The slugs rearranged the skull and brains of an EPLF

follower into a grisly collage. The captain and the remaining Storm Lions continued to climb into the ravine, followed by Major Dawa and a few Ethiopian soldiers.

"What the hell's going on up there?" Manning wondered aloud as he gazed at the troops above, still engaged in combat with unseen opponents. "Who are they fighting? Another guerrilla faction?"

"Save the questions, Gary," Encizo rasped. The Cuban aimed his Uzi machine pistol at the opponents on the wall. "We've got enough to take care of right now."

He drilled a Storm Lion with a trio of parabellums in the chest. The Libyan slumped against the wall and slid lifelessly to a rock shelf. Jabal scrambled for cover behind some boulders before Encizo could train his Uzi on him. Two Ethiopians, returning fire, raked the metal skin of the Argus with Kalashnikov rounds. A ricochet whined inches from Encizo's ear.

On a rock formation across the ravine, McCarter poked his Uzi around a cone-shaped stone and fired at the soldiers who were targeting Encizo. The British commando sprayed the pair with a long burst and cut them down with half a dozen rounds. The Ethiopians convulsed from the fatal hailstorm and fell from the rock wall.

McCarter's bullets raked stone near Dawa, who was forced to jump from a ledge to a cluster of boulders eight feet below. His boots slipped on the curved surface, and he fell against the stones, grunted as the breath was knocked from his lungs and dropped his AK-47. Dawa rolled from the boulder and dropped to the bottom of the ravine. The six-foot fall added to the Ethiopian officer's bruises, but he was still conscious and didn't suffer any broken bones. Dawa crawled behind a boulder to recover as the sounds of battle continued all around.

Jabal and three of his Storm Lions managed to rush to the bottom of ravine without enduring the battering experienced by Dawa. Sergeant Kiflom scrambled to the boulders where his commanding officer was located to see if Dawa needed help. Other Ethiopian and Libyan warriors fired at the Phoenix commandos' positions to try to keep them pinned down as the soldiers descended into the ravine.

Gary Manning yanked the pin from an M-26 fragmentation grenade and lobbed the explosive over the hull of the Argus at a group of enemies. Most scrambled for cover, but one bold Ethiopian attempted to retrieve the grenade and throw it back at Manning. Katz braced his arm along a rock and aimed the Walther P-88 at the guy who was about to pick up the grenade.

He squeezed the trigger and shot the soldier in the center of the chest. The parabellum knocked him off his feet before he could grab the grenade. The M-26 exploded and shredded the trooper's body. The blast sent two other Ethiopians hurtling backward into the rock wall. Bones cracked and skulls split open on impact. Their bloodied, limp forms slumped to the ground as dust formed a gritty fog across the ravine.

Urging Victoria to stay down, James crept to the edge of a boulder and pointed his Uzi machine pistol at Jabal and his Storm Lion comrades. The Libyan officer ducked behind a stony shelter before James opened fire.

Parabellums ripped into the chest and face of the nearest Storm Lion trooper. The soldier fell backward into the path of the other Libyan commandos. One man literally tripped over the corpse and fell headlong to the ground. This accident saved his life as James triggered another salvo of Uzi rounds. The bullets slashed air above the fallen troopers and smashed into the third soldier, who was too slow to bring his AK-47 into action.

Jabal's Stechkin spit flame three times at James's position. The American warrior ducked as projectiles sang sourly against the boulder. Jabal triggered another volley, and more bullets hammered stone. A chunk of rock broke free from the boulder and struck James in the side of the head.

The stony projectile hit with stunning force, and the pain filled James's head with a brilliant white light. He fell sideways, dazed by the unexpected blow. The Phoenix pro still held the Uzi machine pistol in his fist as he gazed up at a blurred shape that rose before him.

The soldier who had tripped from the path of death rose to his feet and pointed his Kalashnikov at the Chicago badass. The Phoenix warrior raised his Uzi and triggered the last four rounds from the magazine. The Libyan was propelled five feet backward by the force of the blows. Again he stumbled over the corpse of his fallen comrade, but this time he was dead when he hit the ground.

Jabal stepped from cover and fixed his machine pistol on James. The Phoenix warrior's vision had cleared, and he saw the man's stern face and the black muzzle of the Stechkin blaster in his fist. The Libyan officer's features were grim, his mouth pressed into a firm, hard line. Jabal had seen James kill three of his men, and he was about to make the American pay with his life.

Death stared down at Calvin James. He tossed the empty Uzi aside and made a final, desperate grab for the Walther holstered under his left arm. James knew he couldn't hope to reach the pistol before Jabal pulled the trigger, but there was a slight chance he might be able to take the Libyan with him before he died.

The shots barked before James could draw the P-88 from leather. He flinched and clenched his teeth, but no bullets plowed into his prone form. James saw Jabal's head snap violently as two 9 mm slugs punched through his forehead and blew out the back of his skull. A crimson halo spewed from the officer's shattered cranium. Jabal fell, the Russian pistol still tightly gripped in his fist.

Victoria Yatta stared at the slain Libyan. She held the CZ-75 pistol in both hands. Smoke curled from the muzzle as she trembled and slowly turned her gaze toward James. The Phoenix fighter started to rise. The pain in his skull felt like a hot needle. James touched the bleeding bruise above his left temple and immediately wished he hadn't.

"Thank God!" Victoria gasped with relief. "You're alive."

"Oh, yeah," James replied as he got to his feet. "This thing hurts too much for me to be dead. But I'm not complaining."

MAJOR DAWA PULLED his Makarov pistol from leather and leaned around a boulder. Sergeant Kiflom crouched beside the officer, AK-47 held ready. Dawa cursed under his breath as he saw the scattered corpses of Ethiopian soldiers and Libyan commandos in the ravine. It was painfully obvious which side was winning the battle.

Two Ethiopian troops and a Storm Lion survivor charged the wreck of the Argus. They fired their weapons as they ran toward some boulders near the satellite. The trio didn't realize they were headed directly for the cover used by Muhammad and another EPLF rebel until the guerrillas opened fire.

The Libyan commando was struck by three bullets from

Muhammad's pistol and four rounds from another rebel's PPSh-41 chopper. His bloody body was hurled to the
ground. An Ethiopian dropped to one knee and fired two
7.62 mm slugs into the guerrilla rebel's upper chest and
throat. He dropped his PPSh-41 and clawed at the terrible pain in his neck as his mouth opened to vomit globs of
crimson.

Muhammad ducked as the second Ethiopian trooper
fired. Bullets chipped rock from the boulder above his
bowed head. One of the soldiers reached for a grenade
while the other maintained a steady barrage of autofire.

Manning and Encizo saw Muhammad's plight and
trained their weapons on the Ethiopian gunmen. Uzi machine pistols fired in unison. The streams of 9 mm slugs
crashed into the troopers. Bullets severed the spinal cord
of the man who was about to grab a grenade. He fell in a
twitching heap and died with his fingers still poised by the
F-1 blaster on his belt. The other Ethiopian military man
dropped his AK-47 when parabellums burned through his
shoulder muscles and neck.

"Damn them!" Dawa snarled. He scanned the boulders and saw a horseshoe pattern of rock formations that
extended to the satellite.

The major pointed his pistol at the rocks. Kiflom nodded to confirm that he understood. Dawa moved to the
boulders and used them for cover, followed by Kiflom.
The pair circled around to the area by the Argus. Dawa
hoped to get into position to attack the Phoenix pair at the
satellite. If they could hit Encizo and Manning from an
unexpected direction, the chances were good the Ethiopian could take out their opponents and gain control of
the Argus as a bargaining chip with the enemy.

Seeing movement behind a nearby rock formation,
Dawa whirled and swung his Makarov toward the shape

that appeared by the stones. Dawa glimpsed Katz's face above the boulder, but didn't see the Walther P-88 in the Israeli's fist until flame burst from the barrel.

The burning agony of a metal projectile penetrating Dawa's right shoulder spun him around. The Makarov pistol slipped from his trembling fingers as he staggered back. His bone had burst at the shoulder joint, and the major dropped to his knees in terrible pain.

Kiflom pointed his AK-47 at Katz's position and triggered, but the Phoenix commander had ducked. Bullets clipped stone above Katz's head as he leaned around the side of the boulder and thrust his left arm forward, Walther aimed at the Ethiopian NCO.

Katz fired twice, hitting Kiflom in the chest. Still, the sergeant shifted aim and blasted another salvo from his Kalashnikov at his opponent. The bullets pelted the boulder and ricocheted without effect. Katz saw the scarlet stain on Kiflom's uniform shirt. The guy had been shot through a lung and the sternum, yet he was still on his feet. Almost reluctantly the Phoenix pro fired once more.

The third parabellum struck left of the previous bullet holes in Kiflom's torso. The sergeant jerked violently as the missile burrowed into his heart. He fell backward and triggered a final burst from his AK-47. The barrel tilted upward and the bullets streaked harmlessly into the sky. Kiflom landed on the ground and uttered a sigh as the last trace of life bled from his ravaged flesh.

Dawa, grief-stricken and angered, saw his sergeant fall. Kiflom had been a good soldier, a trusted friend and Dawa's most reliable NCO. They had served together for many years. Furious, Dawa jumped to his feet and charged Katz's position.

The Israeli was caught off guard by the attack because Dawa was wounded and had appeared to be out of the fight. The major kicked the Walther autoloader from Katz's single hand. Dawa drew a bayonet from his belt as he rushed around the boulder to confront Katz. The Ethiopian raised his fist with the bayonet held in an overhand grip.

The attack was clumsy. Katz thrust his prosthesis forward and snapped the trident hooks around Dawa's wrist. With his left hand Katz grabbed Dawa's upper right arm, just below the bullet-shattered shoulder. The grip sent a fresh wave of pain through Dawa's damaged limb.

Katz rammed a knee between his opponent's legs. Dawa gasped and trembled as he started to double up. The Phoenix commander held on to the wrist above the bayonet with the viselike grip of his prosthesis and applied more pressure. The steel hooks squeezed muscle and bone until Dawa's hand popped open to drop the big knife.

The Phoenix fighter released Dawa's right arm and jabbed the heel of his palm into the officer's wounded shoulder. Dawa groaned in agony and tried to kick Katz, who nimbly stepped aside. The Israeli, still holding the man's wrist in the talons of his prosthesis, seized Dawa's left arm and yanked it into a hammerlock. Katz stepped behind his opponent and stomped his boot into the back of the major's knee. Dawa's leg buckled and he fell. Katz held the Ethiopian's wrist in the steel grip of the hooks and pushed it between Dawa's shoulder blades while his hand snaked over the officer's shoulder to grab the man's jaw.

Dawa struggled, but Katz planted a boot on his calf to pin the leg and keep him in a kneeling position. Dawa's right arm was useless, his left still pinned. He could do nothing to defend himself as Katz gripped Dawa's jaw and pulled with all his might. The Israeli had been an amputee for more than twenty-five years. His left arm had developed extraordinary strength to compensate for the loss of his right limb. Katz's violent yank twisted Dawa's head forcibly. Bone crunched in the major's neck. The officer's body slumped, his neck broken.

As the Phoenix commander released Major Dawa's corpse, an explosion drew his attention to the top of the ravine. Grenades had blasted away portions of the cliff edge and sent two Ethiopian troopers hurtling to their deaths. Other soldiers stationed at the summit were stunned by the explosions. Two figures appeared at the rim and fired down at the remaining Ethiopians, taking out the last members of Dawa's unit.

The echoes of explosions and gunshots faded to be replaced by stunning quiet. The contrast seemed almost obscene. The sounds of battle and killing were proceeded by the stillness of death.

Although the followers of Dawa and Jabal were dead, Phoenix Force was aware the threat was still alive. The gunmen at the top of the gorge were dressed in military uniforms and didn't appear to be EPLF rebels. The voice that shouted in broken English confirmed this.

"Americans!" it cried. "We have come for the satellite!"

"Oh, shit," James muttered. "Here we go again."

19

"Bo-ker tov!" Katz called out as he again ducked behind the rocks. *"Mah nish ma?"*

The other members of Phoenix Force, Victoria and Muhammad were puzzled by Katz's response. They didn't know what he had said and only McCarter recognized the language as Hebrew. The Briton understood a smattering of Arabic and knew Katz wasn't speaking that language, although it was a Semitic tongue.

"Good morning to you as well, sir," the voice from the top of the ravine replied in Hebrew. "I'm not sure 'how things are.' That will depend on you and your companions."

"It depends on all of us," Katz insisted. "Your side as well as mine."

A pause followed before the voice called out, "How did you guess I was Israeli?"

"I recognized the accent," Katz answered.

"A clever deduction, my friend," the voice declared. "I expected as much. You're the one-armed colonel who formerly served with the Mossad? Correct?"

Katz was surprised by the question. "Yes," he confirmed. "Do I know you?"

"Surely you recall a covert mission into Jordan in the 1980s," the voice replied. "You were in command. There were four other commando experts in your group, and the attack force also included Israeli and Egyptian troops."

"We crushed a terrorist cult of assassins," Katz shouted back. "I remember it quite well."

"So do I," the voice assured him. "I was a sergeant in the paratroopers at the time. You probably don't remember me. My name's Uri Moshin, and I'm now a captain in a special unit."

"Congratulations on your promotion," Katz answered. "Do we have to kill each other, Captain?"

"I sincerely hope not, Colonel," Moshin stated. "I admire you more than I can say with words, but I can't let you leave with the data from the satellite. I'm sure you understand."

"I'm going up to talk to you," Katz announced. "Alone and unarmed. If you intend to start killing us, this will make it very easy."

"You have my word you won't be harmed if you come in peace," Moshin promised.

Katz rose and walked to the Argus. He didn't attempt to conceal himself from the men at the top of the ravine, but warned the others to stay hidden. James urged Victoria to stay put and crawled to the satellite. He joined Manning and Encizo as Katz explained the situation.

"You figure you can make a deal with these guys?" Manning inquired with a frown.

"I'm going to try," Katz answered. "We're not in very good shape to fight them. Moshin's team probably outnumbers us, and we can safely assume they have more supplies and ammunition than we have."

"We've got more than we had before," Encizo announced as he held up an AK-47 assault rifle. "I got this from a dead soldier, and there are lots of others lying around. They were also carrying ammunition, food and canteens of water."

"Yeah," James agreed. He had also confiscated a Kalashnikov from a dead trooper. "But the other guys have the high ground, and it'll be easier for them to blow the hell out of us than the other way around."

"Let's hope it won't be necessary to find out," Katz said. He turned to Manning. "You have the wafer with the microchip data?"

"Of course," the Canadian assured him, patting his shirt pocket. "You're not going to give it to them, are you?"

"I almost wish we could," Katz admitted. "I want you to hold on to that wafer and rig it with some sort of explosive. If anything goes wrong, it's better if nobody gets it than if it falls into the hands of the Israelis."

"Pretty hard on your fellow countrymen," James remarked. "I realize you're a naturalized U.S. citizen, Yakov, but I know you still have a strong sense of loyalty toward Israel, too."

"Yes," Katz admitted, "but I'm not working for their government anymore. My greatest loyalty now is to Phoenix Force. I'm going to try to get us out of Ethiopia and accomplish our mission, at least to a degree."

"What's that mean?" Encizo asked.

"I'll have a better idea myself after I talk with Moshin," the Phoenix commander replied.

"Watch yourself," Manning urged. "They may decide to take you as a hostage."

"If they do," Katz declared, "I don't want any of you to let that get in the way of your job. I know the risk I'm taking and I know I'm expendable if it comes to that."

"Hell, Yakov..." James began.

"You know the rules, Calvin," Katz insisted. "They apply to all of us. You guys stay down, keep out of sight and wait. We'll all find out how things turn out soon enough."

Katz left the others and walked to the rock wall. He climbed up the incline, occasionally stepping over a dead soldier or EPLF rebel. Halfway to the top, Katz encountered a familiar figure draped across a stone ridge. Ebrahim lay on his back, chest torn open by bullet holes. The rebel leader's eyes were open, glassy and lifeless. Katz gently pushed the lids shut and continued his ascent.

Captain Moshin, Kanwonkpa and Sergeant Gehmer watched Katz clamber over the top. The two Israelis and the Liberian mercenary looked grim and scruffy. Their clothes were smeared with dirt and rock dust. Galadi sat on the ground, his left arm wrapped in bandages. Sergeant Rabin was sprawled on his back, his torso stained with blood from a dozen shrapnel wounds in his chest and abdomen. Rabin's feet were elevated on a rock and a blanket covered his mangled body, but he was in a state of physical shock and more dead than alive.

"Is this all that's left of your command, Captain?" Katz inquired.

"I lost some men when that Arab bastard opened fire with a Russian grenade launcher," Moshin admitted. "But there are still enough of us left to put up a fight."

"There are still seven of my people left," Katz told him. "I doubt the three of you can take them. However, if we join forces we'll have a better chance of getting across the border."

"Join forces?" Moshin raised an eyebrow. "Who gets the information from the spy satellite, Colonel? Your side or mine?"

"Maybe both," the Phoenix commander suggested.

"Excuse me," Kanwonkpa began in English. "I don't understand enough Hebrew to know what you're talking about. I'd like to know what the hell's going on here."

"I'm trying to make a deal so we can all have a chance to survive and this mission won't be a total waste for all involved," Katz explained, easily switching to English. "I assume the Mossad has a listening post in Sudan near the border. That would explain how you knew about us."

"Perhaps," Moshin allowed as he cradled his AK-47 in the crook of an elbow. "What if we do? How will that help?"

"Contact your control officer and arrange to have him meet us at the border," Katz suggested. "We'll do likewise and have our NSA contact at the same spot. The data from the microchips can be magnified and recorded. The NSA and the Mossad can do it together."

"Do you think either side will agree to that?" Moshin asked with a frown. "My country won't want your government to have detailed information about our military defenses. Your government won't want Israel to have classified information about the Arab defenses and other countries covered by the satellite."

"So we compromise," Katz said. "Israel gets the data on the Arab nations, whether Uncle Sam likes it or not. That's your only real national security concern. The Mossad would like to have the data on Central and South America or China for the sake of exchanging it for other information or favors from the U.S. But they don't get that extra bargaining chip this time."

"That's what we lose?" Moshin inquired. "What about your people?"

"The NSA doesn't get the information on Israeli defenses," the Phoenix commando replied. "The magnified data will be copied. Information divided between the intelligence operatives and the original data wafer will be destroyed to keep anyone from getting the whole information packet.''

"An interesting proposal,'' Kanwonkpa mused. "Israel and the United States are allies. It seems to me you ought to be able to agree to those terms.''

"The colonel and I certainly could,'' Moshin stated. "But I'm not so sure the NSA and the Mossad will be as willing.''

"There's only one way we'll know,'' Katz replied. "Let's give them a chance to act like rational men instead of greedy children. Maybe they'll surprise us with an uncharacteristic act of maturity.''

"What if they don't?'' Moshin inquired.

"If they're not willing to share the ball,'' Katz answered, "no one will get to play with it.''

Kanwonkpa smiled. "I think I like this man,'' he declared. "I like the way he thinks.''

"I just hope our Mossad and NSA friends will feel the same way,'' Moshin said with a sigh. "Very well, Colonel. Let's try it.''

PHOENIX FORCE, Victoria Yatta and what remained of the Israeli commando team headed west with Muhammad as their guide. Sergeant Rabin was carried on a litter but died before sundown. He was buried in a shallow grave near the capital of Gondar Province. Galadi's left arm was too badly damaged by bullets and shrapnel to be repaired. Fortunately Gehmer had an ample supply of morphine to render the EPLF rebel senseless while James and the Israeli medic amputated the limb.

Muhammad rarely spoke as they trekked across the Gondar region. The only survivor of the Ebrahim guerrilla cell, he quietly mourned the loss of his comrades. When they approached the Sudan border the following morning, Muhammad announced that he wouldn't go any farther.

"My people still have a war to fight," he explained. "They still need me, and I won't leave until we win our independence or die trying."

"Just make sure you or one of your comrades stay close to the border and monitor the radio frequencies from Sudan," Katz urged. "You'll be receiving at least a million dollars' worth of aid within a week."

"Ebrahim would have appreciated that," Muhammad said with a thin smile. "You know he was a Marxist and didn't believe in God. I think Ebrahim will be very surprised when Allah rewards him for his courage and sacrifice in the next world."

"I thought the Koran stated a man couldn't go to paradise if he wasn't a true believer," Moshin remarked.

"I think God believes in some of us even if we don't believe in Him," Muhammad replied. "I wish you all the best and Allah's blessings. Surely none of us will go to hell. We've just been there."

"And you're going back," James said grimly.

"If you were fighting for your freedom," Muhammad began, "I'm sure you'd go back into hell, as well. In fact, you'll probably find other battlefields with the stench of brimstone and willingly engage the enemy again and again. My fight is here, and one day it will finally be over. Your war is everywhere, and it will never end."

"Yeah," McCarter confirmed with a shrug. "I reckon you're right about that, mate. Take care."

Crossing the border into Sudan was easier than expected. Ethiopia had done its best to force refugees into

Sudan, and the major effort to control the border was on the opposite side. Sudan had more than its share of starving people and had also suffered from years of famine. Troops blocked the border, but the NSA and the Mossad had made arrangements to permit Phoenix Force and Moshin's unit into the country.

Chaim Levi and Jerome Halpern were surprised to discover each other at the border. They were both shocked to find Phoenix Force with the Israeli team. The Mossad and NSA agents were taken off guard by this discovery. Katz suggested they go somewhere quiet to discuss the situation.

"This is Qallabat," Halpern replied. "The whole damn town is quiet. Now what the hell are you talking about?"

"A good question," Levi agreed as he glared at Moshin. "Almost as curious a question as why you're with these Americans, Captain."

"We have an idea of dividing up the information from the satellite," Moshin replied.

Stunned, Levi and Halpern listened to Katz's suggestion about sharing data from the Argus and deleting material for the sake of the best interests of both Israel and the United States.

"Where do you think you get the authority to make such a decision?" Halpern demanded. "You and your men are little more than hired guns. You're supposed to follow orders, do your job and leave the thinking to us."

"Making government policies and decisions about intelligence data should be left to those in positions of responsibility who have been given that authority," Levi added. "Captain Moshin, if you have the data, surrender it to me now. If one of the Americans has it, I want you to take it from him this instant. By force if necessary."

Gary Manning removed the wafer from his pocket. A red tube was securely taped to the device. The Canadian gripped one end of the tube with his other hand as the intel officers stared at him, puzzled by his actions.

"This is a magnesium incendiary," Manning announced. "I advise you not to look directly at it."

He snapped the end of the tube to break the fiber fuse. Manning tossed it onto the ground and looked away. A brilliant white light burst from the mini-explosive. Levi cried out and covered his eyes as the glare increased. The sound of plastic and metal sizzling and twisting from the extreme heat announced that the wafer was being consumed by the blast.

"Damn it!" Halpern rasped as he blinked to clear the spots from his vision. "If you really destroyed that information..."

He stared down at the mangled, burned remains of the wafer. Levi muttered something in Hebrew. Halpern stared at Manning, furious to see a smile on the Canadian demolition man's face. The NSA agent turned his attention to Katz. "Do you have any idea what you've done?" he demanded.

"We accomplished the mission to the degree you two would allow," Katz replied. "And you can quote me in your report."

He turned and headed toward the marketplace. The other members of Phoenix Force wearily followed. James wrapped an arm around Victoria's shoulders as the couple trailed behind McCarter and Encizo. Levi continued to moan in Hebrew as if agonized by the loss of the wafer and physically ill from what he'd witnessed.

"You five men have ruined your careers by this stunt!" Halpern snapped at the departing Phoenix Force team. "I'll have your jobs for this!"

"Like hell you will," James replied as he glanced over his shoulder. "And you couldn't do our job, anyway, fella. Not in a million years."

DEATH LASH
by
Dick Stivers

An Able Team novel

PROLOGUE

Despite the chill that was still in the air, spring had finally come to Bucharest, showering the wide boulevards of the city with sunshine. The small squares of rich dirt that bordered the sidewalks were beginning to sprout tiny blades of grass.

Huge crowds still maintained their daily noisy vigil around the government buildings. They shouted their demands past the young uniformed soldiers to the interim leaders who were spending long hours inside trying to plan the future of Romania. Near the university tiny coffee shops still served their bitter blend of chicory and coffee or more expensive cups of instant coffee. As they had since there were universities, students and instructors used them as meeting places.

Now there was a change. Instead of glancing around and wondering who the government informers were before they spoke about anything controversial, the people could shout their political disagreements openly.

In the café Romani, Egon, a young Hungarian from the city of Torda, continued an argument that had been going on since the hated Ceaușescus had been executed.

"We kill the leaders, but we let those who murdered us remain alive," the dark-haired, bearded student complained.

Another student, George, a thin, dark-skinned young man who wore large, thick glasses, looked around nervously to make sure no one was eavesdropping. He noticed the small, neatly dressed elderly man who was folding his morning newspaper and leaving some coins for the waiter. Turning back to the table, George lowered his voice. "Are you talking about the *Securitate?*"

"Of course I'm talking about the secret police. Especially the Draculs."

George began to quiver with fear at the mention of the group.

A young woman with short black hair sneered. "I for one don't believe such a group really exists."

George stared at her. "Do you remember the attempt on the life of the pope in Rome?"

"I remember that somebody tried to kill him."

"Not just somebody. The Draculs," the student said with deep conviction.

"The Italian police said it was the Bulgarian Secret Police," Egon reminded him with a sarcastic smile.

George shook his head. "Do you really believe the Bulgarians are sophisticated enough to attempt such a thing?"

Egon thought about the comment for a moment.

The small, gentle-looking elderly man with the neatly trimmed goatee stopped at the table and nodded.

"Nobody can argue with you, young man," the old man said. "The *Securitate* cancer must be excised. Better they should go someplace else and infect them than stay here and destroy what we're trying to build."

"Well said, comrade," a student agreed.

The small man shook his head. "Not comrade, my friend. Not anymore." He smiled at the group. "Have a pleasant day."

As the old man walked away, the Hungarian student turned to the others at the table. "If everyone in this country was like that gentle old man, it would be a better place," he said with sincerity.

The others nodded in agreement. Hatred and killing still raged on the streets of every city in Romania.

THE SMALL MAN with the goatee walked down the street carefully avoiding the clusters of angry protesters gathered at every corner, still thinking about the conversation he had overheard. He had his raincoat collar raised to keep the chill off his neck.

It was time to leave Romania. Alas, for those who had been captured it was too late.

The small man smiled as he glanced at the rabble-rousers in the streets. If only they knew who he was, he would be their next victim.

No, the only ones who knew were those who worked for him. And they were like his children. He had personally selected them from state orphanages, or from prisons. Now they were loyal only to him.

No, his secret was safe. Nobody knew that the small, mild-mannered man, Michael Demenescu, was also the hated Michael Vlad, leader of the dreaded Draculs. And soon it wouldn't matter. He'd be far away from here.

1

Aaron Kurtzman stopped his power-driven wheelchair at a large window and looked outside at the signs of spring. Beyond the security fences he could see blades of grass and tiny wildflower buds popping up across the wide Shenandoah Valley.

It was a crisp, bright day outside. A good day to be alive. Even Stony Man Mountain, the towering stone peak in the distance, looked pleasant for a change.

Now that spring was here tourists would be returning soon, driving along the narrow roads that crossed the Virginia valley. He wondered what they thought was going on inside the buildings of Stony Man Farm. But he knew they'd never dream for a minute that the complex was the headquarters of Able Team.

Of course, the average American had never heard of Able Team. Operating without publicity or government acknowledgment, the warriors were free to use any means to complete their missions—no holds barred.

Inside the large, windowless conference room Hal Brognola, Stony Man's Washington liaison, waved his cigar impatiently at the double doors as he watched Kurtzman wheel himself into the war room.

"Nice of you to find the time to join us, Bear," the chunky head Fed commented sarcastically.

The other three men around the table looked at one another. Something was bothering Brognola. It was unusual to see him this testy this early into a mission. It had to have something to do with the two-day trip to Washington, D.C., from which he'd only returned two hours ago.

"Sorry, Chief," Kurtzman said, moving himself against the table. He, too, sensed the tension coming from the far end of the long conference table.

"Let's get down to it," Brognola snapped, and opened the folder stamped secret, which sat on the table in front of him. "A question has been raised by some important people in Washington."

The others at the table knew exactly who he meant—the President.

"With the Russians acting as if they want to be friendly, and their satellites kicking out their Communist leaders and governments, is there any need for an operation like Stony Man Farm?"

The brown-haired man sitting closest to Brognola concentrated on fiddling with the small electronic gadget he was holding. "Sometimes I think getting rid of the Commies as a problem—at least for the time being—is like peeling a rotten onion. Under the top layer there's even more poisonous garbage to get rid of," Hermann Schwarz commented wryly.

"You got it, Gadgets," the silver-haired man next to him said. He looked at the beefy Fed at the head of the table. "If we shut down, who's gonna keep an eye on the other federal agencies?" He turned away from Brognola and looked at the others. "Remember those three psychos from the CIA in New Orleans who needed a slap on the wrist from us to remember their places?"

Rosario Blancanales was the glibbest of the men in the conference room. Tall and well built, with wavy silver hair and a military stance, he looked and sounded like a politician, so much so the others nicknamed him Pol, short for Politician.

"This isn't the time for smartass remarks," Brognola snapped angrily. He looked at the blond bull of a man who stared back at him without saying a word. "You got anything you want to say, Lyons?"

Carl "Ironman" Lyons was the most taciturn of the group. "Yeah. Who's ticked off at us?"

"I guess when it comes to popularity we're no Kingston Trio," Gadgets cracked.

The others stared at him coldly.

"That's putting it mildly," Brognola said, glaring at him. "Can you name an agency you haven't butted heads with?"

Pol grinned. "The surgeon general?"

"I don't know," Schwarz commented with a smile, thinking of the vermin they'd eradicated. "We probably forced him to find a new definition for the cause of lead poisoning."

Blancanales and Kurtzman started laughing, and Brognola rapped the table with his fist. "If you clowns are finished, unless the President can demonstrate to the people around him that the country still needs Able Team, he's going to be forced to pull the plug."

The laughter stopped. Bear spoke up. "Like Ironman asked, who's out to get us?"

Gadgets smiled at the computer wizard. "Who isn't?"

Brognola nodded. "That's the problem. The meeting I attended had representatives of all the intelligence organizations there. Each of them went into a long-winded speech about how well they handled their individual jurisdictions without violating the rules. When it was my turn to comment, one of them asked me what rules we followed.''

Kurtzman looked at him. "What'd you say, Chief?"

"What else could I say? The rules of survival." He smiled when he remembered the shocked reactions of the other. "The only one who smiled was the President."

"So they all voted against our staying in business," Ironman commented bitterly. "We probably scare them right out of their three-piece suits."

"No. That would be bad politics. The President took me aside later and told me he was under pressure from his political advisers. We cost too much and there's no way he can tell anybody what the country gets for the money."

None of the others in the room knew what to say. If the source of the recommendation had been the heads of any of the other intelligence agencies, they could have pointed out reasons why they might want Stony Man Farm to vanish.

Ironman spoke up. "You mean the Man is thinking of throwing this country to the wolves on the recommendation of a bunch of politicians and bean counters?"

Brognola nodded. "He's got Congress on his back to cut back on spending."

"Screw 'em," Pol snapped, not bothering to hide his disgust. "I for one won't miss this place. Being here is like being back in Vietnam, only worse."

The others at the table just listened. They knew Blancanales was just venting his frustration, not wanting to face a future that no longer had Able Team.

"Since when did we let the politicians run our show?" Lyons growled. "With or without sanction I say we keep going."

Brognola raised an eyebrow. "That means going underground. No bailouts if you get into trouble."

"We're so underground now that the only deeper we can go is to hell," Ironman muttered.

"The decision isn't final," Brognola commented.

Gadgets jumped in. "How do we get the Man to change his mind?"

Brognola leaned back in his chair and studied his cigar. "We need a big win. I got an unofficial tip last night that might help." The others leaned forward and stared at him. "From somebody who should know what he's talking about." The big Fed rolled his cigar in his fingers.

Pol couldn't stand the silence. "About what?"

"What's one of the biggest problems facing the free world today?" the Stony Man chief asked.

"Drugs?" Pol suggested.

"The threat of nuclear or biological warfare?" Kurtzman added.

Gadgets thought about it for a moment, then asked, "Something to do with the environment?"

Ironman shook his head. "They're too obvious. It's got to be something else." He turned to Brognola. "Feel like letting us in on it?"

The stocky Fed nodded. "I didn't make a mistake when I decided to appoint you team leader." Although the three fighters functioned as a team, Lyons was technically the field boss. "The others are serious problems, but you're right, Lyons," Brognola agreed, "they're the obvious dangers. The one danger nobody talks about is what's going to happen to all the Eastern European secret-police groups now that their Communist dictators have been killed or kicked out."

"They ought to hang all of those butchers," Lyons snarled.

"They would if they could catch them," Brognola said.

"Where are they going to run?" Gadgets asked. "Except Eastern countries run by crazies, who's going to let them in?"

"We are," Brognola said flatly.

Blancanales looked stunned. "Since when do we let garbage like that in?"

"Anytime they can slip past our immigration people with forged passports. A number of them are already inside our borders. If they don't get caught, there's a long waiting list of scum just like them who want to come here."

"Any clues about who they are?" Gadgets asked.

"The first ones coming over are from Romania—the *Securitate*."

"Fancy name for the Commie gestapo," Ironman growled.

Pol looked puzzled. "I thought the Commie government in Romania had been wiped out. What are these secret-police types going to do here?"

"The word I got," Brognola replied, "is go into business for themselves."

Gadgets whistled. "Just what we need, another bunch of trained killers for hire."

Lyons leaned forward and stared at the man at the head of the table. "So what do we do?"

"Find them and stop them."

Ironman nodded. "Did your source have any idea who and where they are?"

"No. Only that they're setting up a base someplace in the United States. Once they're established they plan to market their services to anyone who's willing to pay."

"Too bad there isn't a union for hired assassins," Gadgets complained. "They could picket those scabs."

"Let's get practical," Brognola growled.

Blancanales looked at him. "On the practical side all we have to do is search the whole country to find these creeps."

"First of all," Brognola said, "they're going to need a base of operations. Then they're going to need weapons. Not just handguns, but state-of-the-art automatic weapons and maybe some sophisticated electronic equipment."

"All of that takes money," Bear commented. "Lots of money."

"The source who passed along the tip said they've been hiding money in foreign banks for years just in case a time like this might come."

Schwarz turned to Kurtzman. "You're the walking encyclopedia. How many banks are there around the world?"

"To use the money they'd have to have access to it in this country. And you can't just bring in large sums of money without getting a lot of eyebrows raised. So they'd have to find somebody to bring it in for them in a way that looks legal."

Pol made a face. "You mean like one of those 'anything for a buck' bankers who launder dirty money for drug distributors? I thought the FBI had Treasury put them all away."

The Stony Man chief scowled. "There are still bankers who don't mind dealing with slime for a fat commission. I've had the Treasury boys check out those banks that have been suspected of laundering money for recent unusual transactions."

"Did they find anything?" Bear asked.

"Only that the banking industry just lost another one of that sleazy group."

"Anyone we know?" Gadgets inquired.

"I doubt it. His name is—was—Clarence Matterly. One of those three-piece-suit types who didn't care where the money came from as long as he got his commission. Somebody decided to give him early retirement—with a 9 mm farewell slug."

Lyons smiled. "Good for whoever did it. You think there's a connection between him and these creeps coming into the country?"

"That's still to be determined," Brognola replied. "For what it's worth, the Chicago police report indicates the last visitor this Matterly had was an attractive young woman."

"At least he died happy," Blancanales cracked.

Lyons ignored Pol's remark. "You think she might be one of them?"

"Your guess is as good as mine," Brognola said.

"Like I've always said," Gadgets commented, grinning at Blancanales, "women are the deadlier of the two sexes."

"Speak for yourself. I think they're the best of the two," Pol replied.

"When it comes to women, you don't think," Lyons snapped, glaring at Pol. "At least not with your head."

Gadgets sensed an argument starting as he saw his two partners become tense. He interrupted with a question to Brognola. "What about their base?"

The head Fed glared at Lyons and Blancanales, then turned to Schwarz. "That's a little harder to check out," he admitted. "Thousands of large properties change hands every week. And we don't know exactly what we're looking for."

"How about checking into large-scale weapons deals?" Lyons suggested.

"I can run a check on the various federal and police computer networks to see if there have been any large-scale weapons hijackings or reports of illegal deals," Bear offered. Then he thought of something else. "Talking about computer networks, I have a suggestion. If this group is planning to set up a major operation, they're going to need some way of controlling it."

Lyons stared at the man in the wheelchair. "So?"

"That means they're going to need a computer."

"You can walk into any dealer and buy a computer without being questioned," Gadgets reminded him.

"Not if they wanted a supercomputer," Kurtzman snapped back. "Only a few companies make them, and most of their output is sold to government agencies."

"Interesting thought," Brognola commented. "My source suggested the group might be interested in getting into large-scale theft of government secrets. I thought he meant stealing experimental military equipment."

"Remember the Hanover Hacker, Chief?" Kurtzman asked.

Brognola remembered. So did the others. As the resident computer genius, Bear had presented a seminar on the West German youth who had managed to penetrate many of the country's top-security computer systems and steal classified secrets for Soviet bloc clients.

Gadgets looked concerned. "I hope we're not getting into a wild-goose chase." He turned to Brognola. "How reliable is your source?"

Brognola smiled. "Very reliable. If anybody knows anything about the secret-police groups of Eastern Europe, it's him."

"Yeah?" Ironman looked curious. "Ex-CIA?"

"Ex-KGB," Brognola replied, pausing to watch the reactions.

The others at the table looked stunned.

Gadgets found his voice first. "KGB—like in Russians?"

"The one and only."

"And he gave you the tip? Why?"

Brognola shrugged, still smiling. "Call it *glasnost* if you want."

Gadgets continued his questioning. "Where'd you run into this character?"

"In Washington. We had dinner last night."

Pol couldn't believe what he was hearing. "You and this KGB guy?" He thought about it. "Is he some kind of defector?"

"Hardly," Brognola said, chuckling. "He's still with the Soviet government."

Ironman picked up the questioning. "Still KGB?"

Brognola shook his head. "Supposedly he's now head of their trade mission, trying to talk American companies into opening factories in Russia."

Gadgets laughed. "Isn't that like the Russians? If you can't beat 'em, join 'em."

Pol joined in the laughter. "Makes 'em sound almost like Americans."

Brognola smiled. "We might as well make use of the friendly attitudes while they last." He stood up and started to leave the room.

Bear turned to him. "What about my conference at the NSA? In view of this new assignment should I call it off?"

The National Security Agency was hosting a worldwide conference on computer security in a few days at their Fort Meade, Maryland, headquarters. Top computer experts from around the world would be attending, and Kurtzman was the principal speaker.

Brognola thought about it. "No. Keep the date." He turned to the others. "I want you three to go up there with Bear. I'd hate to have something happen to him—or any of you—right now. And get your asses back here right after."

Gadgets grinned. "Okay if we stop for lunch?"

Brognola stared at him. "If you don't make it a long lunch." He rammed the cigar into the corner of his mouth and strode out of the room. Kurtzman shrugged at the other three and followed him out.

Pol rose from his chair. "Good thing I didn't ask him if I could stay overnight." He sighed. "Oh, well, the young lady will have to wait until another time."

"Maybe I can explain in person to her the reason you couldn't make it," Gadgets suggested, grinning.

Pol turned and stared at him. "You? She was expecting a man, not a boy."

Gadgets ran his hands through his thick brown hair. "Nobody's called me that for a long time." He broadened his grin. "Except for a few young ladies I happen to know." Winking at Ironman, he added, "I think what they actually said when the evening was over was, 'Oh, boy.'"

Pol started to retort, but Lyons stopped him with a glare. "You better make up your mind if you'd rather be without a woman or without a job."

Schwarz stifled a laugh. He looked at Blancanales and asked, "Well, which?"

"You know how I feel about women," Pol snapped haughtily.

"Yeah. You've told me enough times. What's your decision?"

Blancanales struggled with the answer. "I can't decide." He shook his head, as if trying to shake off a massive headache. "Meantime let's go to work."

2

From the outside the rambling complex of buildings looked like any of the other factories around Chippewa Falls. Most of the manufacturing facilities in west-central Wisconsin were built of brick and steel to withstand the cold winters, the last of which was still a fresh memory in the minds of the residents of the area. The snows had been unusually heavy and the temperature had fallen to record lows. But the spring sun had melted the snow and ice, and the flooded rivers and streams had finally settled down to their normal levels at that time of year.

Inside the buildings were room after room of the latest in electronic technology. Huge air conditioners maintained the same temperature and level of humidity twenty-four hours a day. Security safeguards equal to the measures existing at top-secret military installations were present throughout the complex. Guards inspected everything while video cameras maintained a twenty-four hour surveillance. Even those invited to visit the facilities had to pass through a series of inspections before being allowed to enter.

There was good reason for such precautions. Inside the complex the world's most powerful supercomputers were being assembled, most of which were sold to government agencies.

Two guards, wearing company-supplied 9 mm Smith & Wesson automatic pistols in their holsters, maintained a twenty-four-hour vigil on the loading dock, while a shipping team loaded the latest supercomputer into a climate-controlled container for shipment to the National Security Agency.

David Touchberry mopped the sweat from his forehead as he guided the huge crate into the air-conditioned truck container at the loading dock. He turned to the angular young man sitting in the forklift and complained, "How many more crates we got to load, Bill?"

"The last one, Dave-o. Then how about we break for a beer and a brat?"

Touchberry nodded. His idea of heaven was a stein of suds and a bratwurst.

The two armed guards watched them silently, more interested in scanning the parking area than listening to their conversation.

The forklift moved out of the truck interior and stopped inside the loading bay. Bill Kelgower climbed down from his seat and helped Touchberry lock up the rear loading doors of the huge vehicle.

When the locks were firmly in place, Kelgower asked, "Got the seals?"

"Right here." Touchberry held up several foil strips and a crimping device. He slipped a strip through the hasps and crimped it shut, then repeated the procedure several more times.

Waving to the guards, Touchberry turned and walked back into the warehouse, where Kelgower joined him. "Who's installing the unit?"

Touchberry shook his head. "Tomasello. He decided to ride with the trucker. He's invited that summer intern, Heitz, to go with him because he's got NSA clearance."

"Long drive to Washington from here."

"Yeah," Touchberry agreed. "But I hear they made a deal with the brass so they could pocket the airfare. Tomasello's putting money away for his kids' education and the intern's trying to stash away bucks for college."

"When are they taking off?"

"In about an hour. They're just waiting for a guard from the Federal Protective Service to show up and ride shotgun."

Kelgower laughed. "Ain't that like the government? Wasting taxpayers' money. Who the hell would try to steal a computer? You can't hide one of these babies in a closet like you can one of those personal computers."

Touchberry nodded, then turned to one of the guards and cracked, "Keep an eye on that truck, Gorelick, until the FPS guy shows up. We don't want somebody shoplifting it." Laughing at his own joke, the young man led Kelgower back into the factory.

IN ANOTHER PART of the complex, the area where the site engineering group was headquartered, a stocky young man hung up the telephone receiver and stared at the partition in his cubicle. Dressed in jeans and a short-sleeve knit shirt, Steve Heitz took off his glasses and thought about the conversation he'd just completed.

He had just said goodbye to Sylvie, the young Frenchwoman he'd been dating. She had been, as always, sweet and sad that he was going to be away over the weekend. It was the questions she asked about the trip that bothered him. Not one question in particular, just her insistence on specifics.

Something about her had been bothering him from the first time he'd met her. Why, he kept asking himself, would a knockout like Silvie be interested in a computer nerd? He wasn't particularly tall, athletic or good-looking, and he wore glasses and spent his free time reading or in front of a computer.

She'd said she was an exchange student at the University of Wisconsin who spent her weekends visiting her only relative in America, the short, ugly dwarf who usually came with her to the tavern where the people from the computer company hung out after work.

Heitz was also a student. He was working at the company over the summer, putting away enough money to start working on his master's degree in the fall.

The first time he'd seen the pretty sable-haired woman—it had been just about a month ago—the man she called her uncle had sat next to her and glared at the men in the tavern as if they were all potential rapists.

Not that Heitz blamed him. He had wondered what someone so spectacular was doing with the ugly little man.

He could still remember how she looked. She had a thin, haughty face, thick eyelashes and a small upturned nose. Her hair was long and sun-bleached and hung loosely down her back. That night her saucy, unharnessed breasts had poked through a high-cut T-shirt that had hidden nothing and she had worn her skintight jeans low on her hips.

Heitz had been stunned when she walked over to where he was sitting and called him by name. He could still quote her first words.

"Your friend, Tad Silvern, said to look you up when I came here to visit my uncle. You look exactly as he described you."

Tad and he were close friends even if the skinny nerd sometimes acted as if the world owed him special privileges just because his old man was one of the deputy directors of the National Security Agency.

She had told him her name was Sylvie Dessault, a graduate student from France. She never told him how old she was, but she looked twenty-one at most, which was just right for Heitz, since he had just had his twenty-third birthday. She was taking some advanced science courses and Tad, who was staying on campus to start work on his master's degree, had been helping her with her studies.

Every weekend she'd come back to Chippewa Falls and look for him in the tavern. She never said much. She liked to listen to him talk about his work and his dreams. He'd asked her about her relationship with Tad, but she kept assuring Heitz that they were just friends.

He could believe it. Tad had always been backward about girls. Even when Heitz set up a date for him, Tad somehow blew the evening.

On the second weekend, Sylvie's uncle had let her come unescorted. They'd sat and talked until the tavern closed. Then they'd gone back to to Heitz's small, furnished studio.

She wanted to know what a site engineer did. Who had got him interested in computers? Who did he admire in the field?

Naturally he mentioned Aaron Kurtzman, who was his idol. He'd been so since Steve and Tad had spent a summer in Washington, taking a special course in computer security from him.

Kurtzman had "adopted" Tad and himself. He could understand the relationship between Tad and Kurtzman. After all, Tad's dad was one of Kurtzman's closest friends. Heitz had no such connection. His dad, a tool-maker, had died when he was eight, and his mom worked two jobs to help him pay his way through school. Still, Kurtzman seemed to care as much about Heitz's future as he did about Tad's.

To help him save money for the next semester, Kurtzman had contacted someone at corporate headquarters and opened doors for Heitz. Now he was being paid fifteen dollars an hour and had almost enough saved for the next semester.

Yes, everything was going great, except for Sylvie. Before and after they made love she kept asking strange questions about his job. She always managed to get privileged information out of him. For instance, last night, when he announced he was driving with Tomasello to deliver and install the new computer at NSA headquarters, he found himself describing the new model he was going to be installing—and she wouldn't stop asking questions. When were they leaving? What roads would they take? When did they arrive? How much did Steve know about installing something that sophisticated?

When he asked why she was interested, she always had a pat answer. That was what bothered him. She sounded so professional at pumping him for information.

There was no real reason for him to be suspicious. Or was it his fear that she'd find someone else from the company and fall for him? Sylvie was a computer groupie. She said she liked hanging around men who worked with high-tech equipment, even if she didn't know much about it.

From what he'd heard from his rock and roll musician buddies, groupies changed idols like other people changed underwear. He needed to talk to somebody about it. Tad Silvern? Hardly. Heitz felt pretty low about getting involved with the Frenchwoman. He'd find a way to tell Tad about it when they got back together in the fall semester. He owed him that. After all, Tad had found her first.

Jim Tomasello? No, Jim was married with three kids. What would he know about this kind of problem? Besides he might cause unnecessary trouble for Sylvie or himself by talking about her questions to someone from the company.

He knew who he could talk to, if he could reach him. Aaron Kurtzman. He had thought about him all day. The only thing that had stopped him from calling earlier was how Aaron might react when he told him he was sleeping with Tad's girlfriend. But he had to take that chance. Besides, Aaron had said he'd gotten into some pretty strange situations before a gunshot had cost him the use of his legs.

Heitz reached inside his zipper jacket for his wallet. Somewhere in it he had the special number Aaron had given him so that he could call if he ever needed to.

Jim Tomasello knocked on the side of his cubicle. The tall bearded man in baggy jeans and plaid shirt leaned on top of the partition and smiled at him. "Thinking about your girlfriend?"

Heitz turned to look at him. Embarrassed, he grinned. "In a way." He started to say something, but his supervisor held up a hand.

"The answer is no. We can't let her ride to Washington with us. She hasn't got clearance."

The summer intern looked surprised. He had decided to feel Tomasello out about his suspicions concerning the Frenchwoman. Before he could say another word Tomasello straightened up.

"If you want to call her and say goodbye, make it quick. The guard from the Federal Protective Service is here and we want to rock and roll in twenty minutes." The bearded man disappeared.

Heitz turned back to his desk and stared at the phone. With all the long-distance calls people in the company made, he could sneak a long-distance call to Aaron without anyone spotting it.

He wondered if the man in the wheelchair would laugh at his suspicions.

KURTZMAN SMILED as he hung up on the student. If only he had Steve's problems. A beautiful young Frenchwoman found him fascinating, and Heitz was worried if she cared about him or was more interested in his work. Some problem.

He'd made a date to meet Heitz in Washington in two days. He looked forward to seeing Steve. His roommate, Tad, and he were among the brightest of the group Bear had agreed to work with over the past summer.

He would pass on whatever limited advice he had when he met the young man after the international computer-security conference at Fort Meade, not that he understood women any better than Heitz did. To this day they were a mystery, wonderful riddles he suspected no man would ever completely solve.

Kurtzman spun his wheelchair around and glanced at the banks of state-of-the-art computer equipment that lined the walls of the windowless basement room. He focused on the rows of ultrahigh-resolution monitors in front of him. Computer symbols paraded across screens on their march to Kurtzman's computers, where their information would be indexed and stored for future reference.

Each of the monitors represented new data coming in from one of the country's intelligence agencies. One of his tasks was to update their records and maintain easily accessible files so that he could find any information Brognola or the Able Team warriors needed within minutes.

Only a few of the heads of the federal agencies were aware that a computer genius had found ways to invade their top-secret files. But, even if they had, word would have filtered down from the White House to do nothing about it.

Officially Stony Man Farm and Able Team didn't exist. Whenever a congressman or senator asked if such a place or group was more than a rumor, there would be a formal denial from the White House. That was the way it had always been.

Kurtzman continued to watch the smooth flow of symbols on the monitors when the phone rang. He lifted the receiver and heard a familiar harsh voice.

"I called my source to check out your thought," Brognola said. "One group who slipped into this country was the chief secret-police contact with some underground computer-hacker group of crazies in Germany who called themselves Computer Anarchists."

Kurtzman had heard of the Computer Anarchists. Using computers instead of time bombs and automatic weapons, they were very much like the notorious Baader-Meinhof gang in the same country. Both groups lashed out wantonly at establishment individuals and governmental agencies, trying to destroy any semblance of civilization. But this was the first time he'd heard they were involved with a secret-police group.

"Any information about him?"

"Her," Brognola corrected him. "No. All he knew was that she was part of some superspecial inner group in the Romanian *Securitate* whose identities were kept well hidden. Just stay alert while you're at Fort Meade tomorrow. I've already alerted the other three."

"Thanks for the warning, Chief. I'll keep my eyes peeled for any Mata Hari types lurking around the Friedman Auditorium."

"Good. And keep me posted."

3

The truck pulled away slowly from the Chippewa Falls loading dock to minimize shaking the delicate top-secret cargo it was hauling. Only the huge headlights of the semi lighted up the dark road ahead.

Four men sat up front in the cab. The burly driver was behind the steering wheel. Next to him was the beer-bellied guard from the FPS, sucking on an inexpensive cigar. Heitz and his boss, Tomasello, sat on the narrow bench seat behind them.

The bearded man closed his eyes and leaned his head back, while Heitz leaned against his partially opened window to protect his lungs from the strong cigar fumes. He was impatient to get to Washington and talk to Kurtzman.

Inside the climate-controlled aluminum trailer was the six-foot crate that contained nearly twenty million dollars' worth of the latest in computer technology. The huge, sensitive supercomputer was the first of a new generation of extremely fast machines capable of processing billions of bits of data a minute. As usual the National Security Agency was getting the first production model.

Had the guards checked the large, hinged crate carefully they would have noticed a series of tiny holes drilled through the wooden slats, placed so that they weren't easily detected. Inside was a dwarf of a man under four feet in height with a thick black mustache. He sat on the upholstered benchlike insulation that encircled the main part of the supercomputer, gently rocking in time with the motion of the truck.

Despite his lack of height the stunted adult was strong. His arms and legs bulged with thick muscles. His hands were out of proportion with the rest of his body. Large and callused from martial-arts practice, they could easily break a one-inch wooden board or the neck of a full-size enemy. And had.

Janos Dragnan cautiously pushed aside the large attaché case at his feet and reached into the small gym bag next to it. He brought out a flat screwdriver and worked its edge under the upper hinge until it pulled away from the wooden frame of the crate. Then he bent down and did the same with the other hinge. Now he was ready to push the door open when the truck stopped.

He reached over and took out a small bottle of slivovitz from his side pocket. Unscrewing the cap, he took a sip to warm himself up. For another four hours he would have to sit and do nothing, just as he'd done when he was tapping Heitz's home and office telephones. Usually there was more action, more of an opportunity for him to vent his hate, to prove his superiority to the taller idiots who treated him like a child instead of the forty-five-year-old man that he was.

It had been that way with the circuses he'd worked in as a clown until the *Securitate* had discovered and recruited him. Working for the secret police had given him a new sense of dignity and power. He was no longer the subject of jokes and ridicule as he had been when the circus toured Eastern European cities. No, as a special agent— several grades superior to the thickheaded dolts who knocked on doors in the middle of the night and took people away—Dragnan was feared. His presence at a raid or an interrogation meant there would be pain before death.

He remembered the damn Christmas revolution. He had barely escaped from the savage mobs who had sought revenge. Only help from Michael Vlad had saved him from being lynched. Hidden in the trunk of an ancient Mercedes, he'd been smuggled into Hungary and from there flown to Vienna, where he stayed in hiding until Vlad had sneaked him back into Romania.

It was imperative that he prove he was needed. Vlad had a way of eliminating unnecessary baggage. Dragnan thought of the small, neatly dressed man with the goatee. Always smiling. Even when he watched someone die. Yes, Vlad would eliminate anyone. Dragnan supposed that would include his own lover, the young woman who now called herself Sylvie.

She was more than just beautiful. She still looked like a teenage girl, although Dragnan knew she was closer to thirty. She was charged with an animal electricity that would excite a marble statue. He could still feel his shiver when she patted his face with her long, sensual fingers before he'd left for the assignment.

Dragnan tried to erase her image from his mind. It would be difficult, but he needed to be alert when the truck reached the rendezvous point where the others would be waiting. He was prepared for that moment. In his hands he gripped a silenced Uzi machine pistol.

THE YOUNG WOMAN rewound the audiotape and pressed the play button again. There was the young summer intern's voice talking to this Aaron Kurtzman, voicing his suspicions about "Sylvie," the name she'd adopted for this phase of her mission.

It was fortunate Dragnan had been able to place a tap on the site engineer's office phone, or she might have thought he still considered her just a young woman who needed protection and guidance. Where had she over-played her hand?

She had to admit that the dwarf had done a good job. If only he would stop staring at her as if he wanted her to be his next meal. She shivered at the thought of being intimate with him.

She was tempted to place a call to Paris and discuss the situation with Michael Vlad. Then she changed her mind. She could imagine what Vlad would order her to do if he were with her: find someone to kill Heitz.

Find someone? Who? She decided that Heitz and the other engineer would be brought back to their new head-quarters alive. She knew Michael would be furious when she called and told him, but she was certain she could persuade him that her decision had been practical. After all, they could kill them after the installation was completed.

She stopped worrying about what Vlad might say when she glanced in the mirror over the desk. Her hair needed touching up. Streaks of her own mousy-brown hair were beginning to show through the rich sable hair coloring.

She walked into the bathroom and stripped off her clothing. As she applied the bottle of her hair coloring, she thought of all the months she had spent acquiring the equipment needed to run their operations base.

Finding enough weapons to fill their arsenal had taken a long time. Handguns and automatic rifles weren't difficult to buy. Grenades and rocket launchers were. Not every gun dealer was willing to traffic in sophisticated military weaponry. But somehow she had managed to acquire the equipment Vlad had demanded.

It was ironic. She was here, taking the risks, while he remained in Paris and indulged himself in pleasure. And still he made it clear that he didn't trust her when she was out of his sight.

He had sent the dwarf to keep an eye on her. Now that Dragnan was out of the way for the evening, she wondered if she dared go back to the bar and strike up a conversation with the tall, attractive bartender who kept staring at her every time she came in with young Heitz. She thought of an interesting way to spend her last night here.

As she stepped into the shower to rinse the excess coloring from her hair, she thought about Michael again. She was glad she hadn't placed the call to him. He always became livid when she opposed him. He would find out what she'd done from his favorite spy, Janos Dragnan, soon enough.

She stepped out of the shower and began to blow-dry her hair. Then she checked her face in the mirror. It was amazing when she remembered how much she'd accomplished in so few years yet still looked as if she were barely twenty-one.

For thirteen years—since she was sixteen—she'd been carrying out Michael's orders. She could no longer remember what her name had been before Michael had adopted her and renamed her Elena. Elena Demenescu. Not that it mattered to her. She had never known her mother. Michael's mother had been a Demenescu before she'd married his father. It was a special honor that he had given her one of his family's names.

She remembered how surprised she was as a teenager to find out she was being trained to be a member of the *Securitate*. Then Michael had rewarded her with a greater honor. He'd inducted her into the most select unit of the secret police—the Draculs.

There was something about Michael that had excited her in the beginning. The indifference in his eyes when he watched an obstinate prisoner being tortured? The small, gentle voice he used with her when they were alone? The power he had over the lives of millions? She wasn't sure. Perhaps all of them.

Lately she had begun to hate his preoccupation with drugs, his lapses into daydreaming when he should have been trying to line up clients, his seeming lack of concern for her survival when he approved a mission. She had thought he believed she could survive anything; now she realized he didn't care one way or the other.

She went into the bedroom and found a pair of designer jeans that accentuated every soft curve of her body. Struggling into them, she turned her thoughts back to the tape recorder. Steve Heitz had made a date to meet his former teacher, Aaron Kurtzman, after some international computer-security conference he was addressing at the National Security Agency in Fort Meade, Maryland.

She had heard his name mentioned before, from Tad Silvern, the young graduate student at the University of Wisconsin who had been Heitz's college roommate. The way both of them had described the disabled teacher made him sound like the Einstein of computers.

Sylvie made a mental note to meet him someday. He might prove useful.

4

The tired Illinois state trooper sat at the side of the road, watching the headlight glare of cars and trucks racing by his darkened unmarked car on Interstate 94. He kept staring at the radar monitor, checking to see if any of them had exceeded the speed limit by more than ten miles.

It was a warm, cloudy night, and he'd taken off his hat. Glancing at the clock on the dashboard, he was grateful that there was only ten minutes left on his shift. Shirley would be pleased when he showed up on time for a change. He had promised to start stripping the wallpaper in the kitchen of their small house.

A red Porsche tried to reach the speed of sound as it passed him. Ninety-seven miles an hour. He shook his head. That was good for at least three hundred dollars if the driver came up before Judge Clements. The sour-faced judge hated speeders almost as much as he hated having to show up in court three hours a day to collect his salary.

Bill Hershauer picked up the microphone. "A red Porsche coming at you. I clock ninety-seven," he announced, then called out the license plate.

"Read you, Hershauer," the bass voice on the other end replied.

Frank Mariello and Hershauer had graduated from the academy together. The Mariellos were saving up for a down payment on a house down the country road from his.

"I'll pluck this one," Mariello said. "Why don't you head back and check out? As soon as I'm done, I'll meet you there and we can lift a beer, Billy."

"No can do, buddy. Wallpaper tonight."

Frank laughed. "No rest for the married. See you tomorrow."

"Ten-four," Hershauer replied, and shut down his radarscope.

A trailer truck passed by his car. He recognized the name of the company painted on the side. Shirley's brother, Lou, was one of their drivers. He thought he'd recognized him as one of the men in the cab, but the truck had whizzed by so fast that he couldn't be sure.

Even if it was Lou, Hershauer knew that company rules forbade any stops to visit with his in-laws, state trooper or not. Shirley had mentioned that Lou was going to be out on a job for a few days. Oh, well, he'd probably be over for dinner when he got back.

Hershauer started the police car and moved slowly into traffic. It was a ten-mile run from the highway exit to the trooper substation, and he didn't want to be stopped by some hick cop on the way.

THE TRUCK CONTINUED its journey down the interstate. The driver suggested they stop for coffee at the next oasis. He didn't mention the counter girl who worked at the fast-food outlet, a redhead he'd been trying to get close to for months.

The two site engineers vetoed the idea—they wanted to keep moving—but the FPS guard suddenly announced he had to hit the head.

"May as well take a break. We're on company time," the driver cracked as he pointed at the large green sign that announced the car-and-truck oasis coming up.

The large trailer truck rumbled up the ramp and pulled into an empty parking place. The four men got out and stiffly walked past the gasoline pumps toward the one-story brick building in the center of the oasis.

Four somber-looking men in jackets sat in their parked late-model Lincoln and watched them disappear inside. The driver, a large man with a scar that crossed his mouth, asked, "You're sure it's them?"

The man next to him, a stocky bald man in his forties, handed over a photograph of Steve Heitz. "Positive, Sal. The young one looks just like his picture." He tapped the driver on the arm. "Crack open the back door of the trailer and let the short guy out."

The graying thin man in the rear leaned over the top of the front seat. "Gimme the plan again, Frank."

"Jesus, Wiley," the stocky bald man growled. "If you'd stop sniffin' that shit, you'd be able to remember things." He was about to continue his complaint, then changed his mind, forcing himself to sound like a school-teacher. "We wait for them to come back and take them out—*quietly*. We dump their bodies in the trunk. Then you and the shrimp get in the truck and drive it out of here. We'll follow you."

Tony Santangelo, the driver, popped a question of his own. "We never talked about what we do with the bodies."

"Stop somewhere on a side road and dump them. Then we haul ass to the big truck depot on the edge of the city, leave the truck there and take off."

"What about the dwarf?" Wiley asked. "What do we do with him?"

"We leave him there and deliver the money he hands up to Drago."

Wiley's eyes sparkled. "Any chance we can ice the midget and keep the loot?"

"Forget it," the bald man growled. "Drago would have the rest of the boys gunnin' for us if we pulled a double cross."

"Wiley, you're a greedy son of a bitch," Santangelo commented. He turned to the bald man beside him. "Who's Drago's client, Frank?"

The bald man shrugged. "I don't know and I don't care as long as we get paid."

From the rear Wiley complained, "How come we gotta go through Drago for our jobs? He skims off too much."

"At least he keeps us working," the bald man commented. "And compared to pimps who skim sixty percent, he ain't so bad."

"Hey," Wiley snapped angrily. "We ain't whores. We're professionals."

The bald man held up a hand. "Let's fight about it later. We got work to do."

Inside the building the trailer driver huddled at a corner table with the redheaded counter girl. The guard had vanished into the men's room. Surrounding them were tables filled with tired-eyed men wearing peaked caps.

Tomasello and Heitz sat quietly at another table and stared at their cups of coffee. The bearded man looked up at Steve. "So what kind of job are you aiming for when you get your master's?"

"I'm not sure. I'm interested in learning about supercomputers. Maybe I'll go for a PH.D. and teach."

"That pretty French girl you've been dating, she gonna be satisfied settling down on a teacher's salary?"

Heitz grinned. "Hold off, Jim. You got me married to her and we only just met."

"What are you waiting for, boy? Shyness don't get you laid." Tomasello laughed and lightly punched the summer intern on the shoulder. "First time I went out with my old lady we ended up spending a weekend in the sack."

Heitz just nodded. He couldn't get Tad Silvern's face out of his mind.

The guard was tightening his belt under his potbelly as he approached the tables. In one hand he held a sweet roll he'd purchased. "Time we got started," he announced, starting to eat the pastry.

Reluctantly the driver let go of the redhead's hand and stood up. So did Tomasello and Steve.

"See you next trip," the driver told the smiling counter girl. He turned and caught up with the other three.

"Looks like a nice girl," Heitz commented.

"She is," the driver agreed. "Next trip I'm gonna ask her for a date."

Tomasello winked at Heitz. "See what I mean?"

There was no foot traffic when the four men emerged from the building. The half-dozen trucks, including theirs, were parked and dark.

Deep in the shadows Dragnan and the four men from the Lincoln waited as the group came closer.

"They're almost here," the bald man whispered. "Get ready." He saw the gun the dwarf was holding and pushed his hand down. "I'll handle this one," he whispered.

Dragnan looked puzzled until he glanced at the bald man's hands and saw the length of piano wire held taut between them.

"No blood," the bald man whispered harshly.

Tomasello and Heitz had stopped so that the bearded man could point out a star.

"The Big Dipper and the Little Dipper," he told Heitz.

The federal guard paused briefly to listen, then, bored, moved to catch up with the driver. The bald man waited for the driver to walk past where he was hiding and wrapped the wire around his thick neck. As he quickly sawed into the neck, the driver grabbed at his throat and tried to tear the instrument of pain away, but the assassin's hold was too strong. Blood spurted from a dozen ruptured capillaries and dribbled down onto his hands as the bald man raked the razor-sharp wire back and forth.

Desperately the dying man tried to jab his elbows into the killer's stomach. Surprisingly light-footed, the bald man deftly avoided the thrust attempts.

The driver could feel air escaping from a new opening. His windpipe had been severed. He tried screaming, but only soft gurgles came out as the wire continued to cut through the soft tubes and tissue. The terrified man could taste blood as it streamed down his throat and into his lungs. In one last desperate effort he used all the strength he had left to try to tear himself away from the death wire, but he only succeeded in almost severing his head before he slumped forward.

The bald man let the body slide to the ground just as the Federal Protective Service guard walked by. Stunned at the unexpected sight of a nearly separated head, the pot-bellied man started to throw up the sweet roll he'd eaten.

The bald man shoved a thick hand over the guard's mouth, but the FPS guy continued to vomit. Using his free hand to reach under his jacket, the bald man yanked out a hunting knife and rammed it deep into the soft tissue of the guard's thick waistline. The government employee struggled to get free.

Quickly the bald man pulled the blade up toward his victim's intestines. As the overweight guard continued to try to free himself from his attacker's grip, the bald man pulled out the blade and rammed it into the guard's chest. Again and again he chopped at the other man's torso, using the knife as an ice pick.

Wiping his hands on the dead body at this feet, he looked up and saw the two technicians approach.

Tomasello saw some men near their truck. They were half-hidden in the shadows. "Hey, get the hell away from there before I call the cops," he shouted angrily.

Wiley took out a silenced Steyr. He gripped it tightly, ready to fire if the man made a move toward them.

Thinking quickly, the bald man pushed the gun down and called out, "Sorry, mister. We were just standing here talking."

Heitz was right behind Tomasello. He had heard about hijackers loitering at truck stops to steal cargoes.

Shoving his knife back into his waistband, the bald man stepped out of the shadows. He turned back to the rest of his crew. "C'mon, guys, time to get going."

Dragnan was puzzled. He couldn't figure out what the bald man named Frank was up to. But the guy winked at him and gestured for him to follow.

The five men walked past the two site engineers. Tomasello stared at them, then saw the two bodies on the ground. "What the hell?" he yelled.

Wiley grabbed him, and Heitz started to rush to his aid. The bald man turned to face him, silenced gun in hand. Heitz stared at the weapon, then turned and started running back toward the food service building.

The bearded site engineer tried to free himself of the other man's grip. Suddenly Wiley released his hold and giggled as he bounced backward like a boxer. Tomasello raised his clenched fists and threw a punch at the other man's stomach. Expertly Wiley sidestepped the blow and rammed a callused fist at the bearded man's nose. Staggering back from the blow, Tomasello tried to maintain his balance.

Giggling quietly, Wiley chopped at Tomasello's collarbone. The site engineer started to scream from the pain. Quickly Wiley covered the engineer's mouth with his hand, then punched him behind the ear. Tomasello suddenly went limp. The thin man with the cocaine-widened pupils pulled him back into the shadows.

HERSHAUER HAD DECIDED to break the rules just this once. He knew Lou had the hots for the redheaded counter girl at the oasis. He didn't blame him. So did half the truckers who stopped there. He'd stop and needle him for a few minutes before checking in.

As he drove up the ramp to the oasis, he saw the young man race across the parking lot, followed by a bald heavyset man. Damn! What kind of hell was he getting into? He wasn't even supposed to be here. He could hear his sergeant chewing him out for an hour, no matter what kind of trouble he stopped.

He honked his horn as he pulled into a parking spot. The young man turned and ran toward him. The bald man grabbed the young man around the waist and started dragging him back where the trucks were parked.

Hershauer opened his window. "What the hell are you two doing?"

The bald man came back alone. He sounded out of breath as he approached the car. "Sorry, officer. My kid brother gets a little nutty when he's had too much to drink."

The state trooper stared at him skeptically. He started opening his door. "Yeah? Maybe I better check if he's okay."

"Sure, officer," the bald man said. "Only thing is, could you wait a few minutes?" He winked at him. "Right now he's throwing up that garbage he drank."

Hershauer didn't need any more headaches tonight. Shirley would be all over him if she saw puke on his clothes. They'd had enough arguments about his drinking too much when he was off duty. He made a decision. "Just make sure he doesn't get behind a wheel."

"You bet, Officer," the bald man said gratefully. "Sorry to cause trouble. You know how kids are today."

The bald man turned and walked back into the shadows. The state trooper watched him disappear, then remembered why he'd come here. He parked his car and got out. Walking toward the building, he wondered if Lou had done better with the redhead this time than he had before.

He came out of the building a few minutes later, annoyed. The redhead had said Lou had left a few minutes ago. Out of the shadows he saw a trailer truck rumble toward the exit ramp. He read the name on the side. Lou's company. They must have passed each other without knowing it.

Hershauer watched as the truck vanished onto the interstate, followed by a late-model Lincoln. He was tempted to chase after it and turn on his flashers, but decided against it, figuring that one of the head honchos would be on the road, looking for infractions.

Anyway, it was time to check in. He'd talk to Lou when he got back from his trip.

WILEY SAT ALONE in the cab of the truck, expertly steering the huge vehicle down the interstate. He touched his pocket and started to take out the small vial of cocaine he was carrying, then decided to wait until he delivered the truck. It would be his reward for doing a good job to-night.

Inside the trailer the dwarf guarded the computer, the bodies of the two men they'd slain and the two site engineers. He glanced at them briefly, then fondled the attaché case on his lap.

Sitting on the floor, staring at the uncovered corpses, were Tomasello and Heitz, tied up and gagged. Their eyes revealed the fear and horror they were feeling.

Dragnan looked at the two men again and saw the terror on their faces. "You two will be next if you don't cooperate," he said in accented English. The two bound men shivered.

Setting the attaché case on the floor, Dragnan got up and peeked through one of the rear portholes. The sedan with the other three men was still following them. He returned to his makeshift seat and patted the attaché case he would hand to them after they met up with Egon and Lazlo at the deserted gas station.

The driver said it would take a half hour to get to their destination. The dwarf checked his wristwatch. It was eleven o'clock. He opened the attaché case and set the miniature timer for midnight. The men should be in Chicago by the time the plastic explosive, hidden in a secret panel, was detonated.

He shut the case and whispered a dedication. He knew it was an absurd gesture. A bomb wasn't a building or a bridge, but they were works of art, at least the way he made them. And it made him feel good to dedicate each to someone he wanted to remember or please. He placed his hand on the case.

"I dedicate you to Elena," he whispered, and wished the sable-haired woman was next to him tonight so that she could show her gratitude.

WHEN THE PHONE RANG, Elena knew who was calling. Janos Dragnan was checking to see if she was alone.

She was now. The tall, dark-haired bartender had left her bed hours ago. She had been up for hours, making a series of calls.

"Yes?"

She was right. It was the dwarf.

"The equipment is on its way to our base," he reported.

"And the two technicians?"

"Terrified, but alive."

"Good. Where are you?"

"Near Chicago. I have Egon and Lazlo's car. I'll start driving back."

"No. Meet me at O'Hare." She told him what time she'd arrive there so that they could catch a flight to Washington, D.C. "I've made arrangements to attend a computer-security conference tomorrow in Fort Meade."

"What about the place in Chippewa Falls?"

"You can send somebody to clean things up." Every nerve in her body tingled with reawakened excitement. It had been a very good night, and Dragnan had no way of knowing.

"No. When we're finished in Fort Meade, I'll come back and attend to it myself." He paused. "I'll meet you at the airport. I hope you had a good time last night," he said, and hung up.

He knew! Somehow he had found out. Now Michael would know, too.

There was a knock at the door. She wondered who it was. Grabbing a robe, she slipped a small Beretta into her pocket and walked to the front door of the apartment. When she peeked through the security viewer, she saw the bartender from last night. She opened the door and let him in.

"I dropped my wallet when I put on my pants," he apologized. He disappeared into the bedroom and returned holding the thin leather case in his hand. He stopped and smiled at her. "It was really great. Like I told the little guy who hangs out with you the other night, he didn't have to pay me to make a pass. I've wanted to from the first time you walked into the joint."

She was furious. Michael had gotten Dragnan to set her up. As if she needed to have him pay a man to want her!

The bartender sat on the arm of the couch and grinned at her. "I'm not due to show up for work until five, if you get my drift."

She was about to throw him out when an idea began to take form in her mind. So Dragnan was going to come back himself to clean up? She'd leave him one more thing to get rid of, she decided. It wouldn't be smart to leave the bartender behind to describe her intimately.

"Let's go into the bedroom," she whispered, fingering the small pistol in her pocket.

5

Aaron Kurtzman had arrived early to have a private conversation with several of the organizers of the conference. Accompanied by the three Able Team commandos, the wheelchair-bound man looked around the small reception room for a particular face. Blancanales leaned over and whispered that he and the other Able Team members were going outside. Nodding, Bear turned and greeted and NSA assistant director. "General Silvern, isn't he coming?"

"He wouldn't miss it for the world," the beefy NSA official hurriedly assured him. "Unfortunately he couldn't get out of a long-planned Intelligence Coordinating Committee meeting."

Bear was relieved. Tony Silvern and he had been friends for many years. Both were survivors of the political wars that had almost destroyed the intelligence apparatus of the United States over the past fifteen years.

"Tell me about the conference," he said to the NSA officer. "Who's attending? Why was it organized? When Tony called and asked me to be the keynote speaker, he said he'd give me details when I got here."

The chubby man smiled proudly. "There are representatives from virtually every friendly country in the world. Mostly computer specialists who work for the police or intelligence agencies. We hope to establish a computer

network of shared intelligence information similar to the
network Interpol has with its various member police organizations."

The concept made good sense to Kurtzman. "And this
was Tony Silvern's idea?"

"You bet," the other man replied enthusiastically. "It
took him two years to sell it to the top brass. Now they're
a hundred percent behind it." He grinned. "Between you
and me," he added, lowering his voice, "they're already
starting to take credit for coming up with the concept."

"Sounds like bosses around the world," Bear said.
Then he thought of something that might affect how open
he could be with the conference attenders. "Now that
we're almost on a first-name basis with them, are the
Russians sending someone to attend?"

"We thought seriously of inviting them, but at the last
minute the White House decided against the idea."

"Don't worry," Bear commented cynically. "They'll
have somebody here, anyway." He saw the surprised expression on the other man's face. "Disguised as a representative from one of our supposedly good-buddy
countries."

The NSA official nodded, as if to say that after twenty
years as a government employee, nothing would surprise
him anymore.

NOW THAT THEY had delivered Bear to the reception, the
three Able Team hell-raisers had decided to stay outside
and enjoy the fresh air for as long as they could.

"We'd be better off inside," Blancanales said. "At least
it's air-conditioned." The midmorning sun burning
through a thick layer of moisture made being outdoors
uncomfortable.

Lyons grumbled as he wiped the sweat from his face. "Damn weather in Maryland. One day it's cold, next day you need to go around in shorts."

"If we don't get our hands on those foreign creeps, we won't have to worry about the weather around here for much longer," Schwarz reminded him.

"Damn bureaucrats," Lyons muttered.

Pol gazed across the grounds of the NSA's Fort Meade headquarters. "How many bureaucrats do you think it takes to change a light bulb?" He looked at Lyons, who made a face and turned away.

Gadgets grinned and replied, "I give up. How many?"

"Ten," Blancanales replied. "One to change the light bulb, eight to sign the approval forms and one more to take all the credit for it."

Schwarz groaned. He looked around at the numerous buildings. "How many people do you think work here?"

"Too many," Ironman complained. "Get rid of some of them and there wouldn't be any talk of dumping us because of budget problems." He started looking around. There was something about this place that bothered him, but he couldn't figure out what it was.

"Someplace I read that they pay more than sixty-five thousand people," Blancanales commented.

Lyons didn't seem to hear him. He was too busy surveying the NSA complex.

Schwarz shook his head. "I wonder if they all work here?" He pointed to a building. "I think that's the cryptology center. It's amazing. One of the CIA types said they've got close to ten thousand experts just making up and deciphering codes."

"And foreign spies still manage to get into their computers and steal secrets," Pol said sarcastically. "Some experts."

Gadgets nodded. He pointed at the electrified fences that surrounded the complex. "See those fences? The latest in security. They've got a small army of cops who check out everyone going in and coming out. Everybody they hire is checked out by the FBI and given a polygraph test." He looked disgusted. "So how come a large number of people walk out of this place with their pockets stuffed with top-secret documents every year?"

Pol made a face. "What they waste here in one week could keep us in operation for years." He turned to Lyons. "What do you think, homeboy?"

"Something smells wrong," the ex-LAPD cop said. He didn't bother masking his concern.

"The whole place stinks with too much money if you ask me," Gadgets cracked.

Lyons shook his head. "No, not money. It smells more like death."

Blancanales and Schwarz exchanged quick glances, then turned to Lyons. "Maybe we'd better get inside and keep an eye on things," Gadgets said.

THE LARGE STAGE was empty except for the burly man who sat in the wheelchair. The microphone had been lowered so that he could speak into it.

"The real war today isn't being fought on battlefields or in back alleys," Bear told the large gathering inside the Friedman Auditorium. "It's being fought with computers instead of guns and weapons. Someday, long after guns and atomic weapons disappear, computers will attempt to kill each other and the people who support them."

Aaron Kurtzman looked out at the hundreds of men and women staring at him from their seats. He could see agreement in their expressions.

Even in his wheelchair Kurtzman was an impressive figure. From the stage he surveyed the more than five hundred men and women who sat in the hall. Then he continued. "There is no truly secure system. If your computers are linked by telecommunications to the outside—and to be useful they have to be—your system can be invaded." The big man reminded his audience of the ease with which hackers had penetrated military and government-intelligence systems in the past. "Do I need to remind anyone in the audience about the Hanover Hacker?"

Some in the audience winced at the painful reminder of the West German computer terrorist who had managed to penetrate the most secure files of various government agencies before he was apprehended.

"In a time when everything we know and run is stored in the data banks of our computers," Bear continued, "it's essential that we find better ways to prevent the invasion of our systems by those who would use our information to rob us of our money, our liberty and even our lives."

Some of the women in the audience turned occasionally to glance at the silver-haired man standing at the back of the auditorium. He smiled at one of them, a short, mousy woman in her late thirties, and turned to his two companions. "I'm having trouble staying awake," Pol whispered. He glanced at the brown-haired man with the mustache against the back railing, seemingly hypnotized by Kurtzman's words. "You'd think Bear was talking about a woman the way you're staring," he cracked. Gadgets glared at him, then turned back. Blancanales twisted and looked at Lyons. The blond lion was obviously bored. "Gadgets is hooked," he reported.

Lyons lowered his eyes and looked at Schwarz, then turned to Blancanales. "I guess we should be grateful Bear doesn't talk this way back at Stony Man," he commented in a low voice. "I'll be glad when we can take off these flak vests," he added. "I'm starting to sweat up a storm."

Pol glanced at Lyons. "At least Dr. Gadgets seems to be enjoying himself."

Schwarz was an electronics wizard. He loved fooling around with state-of-the-art equipment to find ways to improve it when he wasn't on a mission.

Sounding irritated, Gadgets turned to the others. "Keep it down," he whispered. "This is really important stuff." He glared at Lyons. "If your brains were as developed as your muscles, you'd be listening to what Bear is saying, Ironman."

Blancanales grinned at Lyons. "Our boy, Hermann, has scored another one for the mind."

Ironman nodded and scanned the audience. "We should have made a date to meet Bear for lunch someplace else."

Pol stared at his clothes. Lyons was wearing a pair of jeans. Under a powder-blue sports jacket he wore a bright Hawaiian-style sport shirt. "Aside from the fact that the chief ordered us to stick close to Bear, who would let us in with that shirt?"

Ironman looked offended. "This shirt cost me twenty-five bucks."

Blancanales looked surprised. "You mean they didn't pay you to wear it?"

Gadgets turned away from the stage as Kurtzman finished his presentation. The audience began to applaud enthusiastically. "Are clothes all you two can fight about?" He shook his head in disgust. "Bear was right. You two are becoming obsolete."

"That hurts," Pol said, pretending to look injured.

"If you'd paid attention to Bear," Schwarz said, "you'd have heard him say that computers are replacing guns."

"Yeah?" Ironman made a face, then reached inside his jacket where he wore his modified Colt Python in a shoulder holster.

Two uniformed guards from the Federal Protective Service reached for their holstered side arms. Even though the three casually dressed men wore the tags supplied by Brognola that identified them as federal agents, the officers were edgy. Lyons noticed their movements and pulled his hand away from his jacket.

He smiled at them, then turned to Schwarz. "Until a computer can blow a hole in me I'll stick to guns."

Kurtzman powered himself down the specially constructed ramp in his wheelchair. As he slowly moved up the crowded center aisle, men and women stopped to thank him for his suggestions. An attractive young sable-haired woman, who looked as if she were barely out of her teens, leaned over and kissed Kurtzman's cheek. Bear pushed the switch on the controls to stop the wheelchair.

"C'est magnifique!" she whispered. "An inspiration I shall bring back with me to Paris." She turned to her companion, a tall, stiff man in a tailored pin-striped suit. "Don't you agree, Yves?"

Her companion nodded. "Absolutely. My congratulations, Dr. Kurtzman," he said in a French-accented voice.

Many assumed that Kurtzman held a Ph.D., which wasn't true. Much of his knowledge had come from his years of hands-on experience and a brilliant mind that grasped complex concepts almost instantly. Before the bullet had confined him to a wheelchair, Bear had shared his time between being one of the reserve warriors in Able Team and their computer expert.

"If you're free later, I would love to have a drink with you, Doctor," the woman said softly.

"Sylvie, we have a plane for Paris to catch this afternoon," her companion reminded her harshly.

The woman's laughter sounded like crystal teardrops on a chandelier clinking in a soft breeze. The others were waiting outside, ready to kidnap the man in the wheelchair. It would be so easy if he would agree to join her for a drink.

She turned to the Frenchman and covered her irritation with a smile. "You're so serious, Yves. You go ahead. I can get a flight home in the morning."

The Frenchman glowered at her. He had agreed to bring her to the conference for the thousand-dollar fee he'd been promised. It hadn't been difficult. As a deputy director of the French national police's computer division, it had been easy for him to forge a set of identification papers. He had fulfilled his obligation; it hadn't included personal contacts with the Americans.

Nervously he snapped, "I must insist, Sylvie."

Bear glanced up the aisle to where the Able Team trio waited. They had a lunch date, possibly the last lunch they would have together as members of Able Team if they failed on this new mission. Then he was meeting Steve Heitz.

"I have some appointments I can't break," Bear said, sounding regretful. He could still feel her kiss surging like electricity through him. Her sensuous perfume was making him dizzy.

"Another time," the woman replied sadly, and walked up the aisle with her relieved companion.

Pol was the first to greet Bear at the back of the auditorium. "Who was the beauty?"

"One of his fans," Gadgets commented with a grin.

"A groupie," Pol corrected him trying to keep a straight face. He shook his head at Bear. "And at your age, too. Don't you know groupies are for rock stars?"

Lyons stared at the other two and shook his head in disgust. "If you two clowns are done with your act, I suggest we get our asses out of here."

Kurtzman turned his head and looked back down the aisle. The Frenchwoman had vanished. He could still smell her perfume. There was something about her that he wouldn't forget. What? Kurtzman smiled when he thought of the answer. Everything! Then a familiar voice interrupted his thoughts.

"Kurtzman!"

He looked up at the tall, gray-haired man in a dark gray business suit who was striding toward him. Tony Silvern. Still ramrod-straight despite his age.

Silvern reached their side and shook Bear's hand. "You know these three characters, General," Kurtzman said, nodding at the Able Team trio.

The general had met Ironman, Pol and Gadgets several times in the past when the Able Team warriors had needed background information. The vast NSA computer complex contained billions and billions of bits of data. The agency had the most complete intelligence inventory in the world.

To Ironman and his two partners, Anthony Silvern was a living legend. A brigadier general, he was deputy director of the NSA's Computer Intelligence Division. A much-decorated hero during Vietnam, Silvern preferred leading his troops into combat to sitting behind a desk looking at battle maps. Shifting to intelligence in the early seventies to bring his aggressive attitude to the National Security Agency, he'd put together a task force of computer and intelligence experts to combat the growing incidence of attempts to invade government computers.

The general smiled at them. "Glad to see you're still alive, men."

"We are, too, General," Lyons replied, respect in his voice.

"That's quite a shirt you're wearing," Silvern commented, staring at Lyons. The other two Able Team hell-raisers stifled their laughter.

The tall man turned to Kurtzman. "Never thought I'd be glad to see a computer nerd after raising one. But that was before I became one myself."

"How's Tad doing?" Bear asked.

"He's spending the summer at the university working on a small project for us."

Bear grinned. "No nepotism, is there?"

The general broke into a laugh. "You're damn straight there is." He winked at the computer wizard. "Just like when you agreed to take the two boys on that summer. He's working on his master's degree," Silvern added proudly.

"That's what Steve Heitz said when he called the other night."

"Nice boy, Steve. How's he doing in his summer job?"

"The job's going fine, but he's got girl problems."

The two men laughed.

"If only we had those problems," the general commented, chuckling. "He'll get through them. We always do."

"How about Tad? Does he still prefer computers to girls?"

"Actually he tells me he's found a girl," Silvern bragged.

"If Tad likes her, she must be into computers," Bear commented. "Met her yet?"

"Tad said he'd bring her down here someday soon."

Bear was curious. "What does she look like?"

"Beautiful, according to Tad," the general replied, then winked. "And very European."

"Sounds like the girl who's upsetting Steve," Bear commented. "Must be something about these European girls."

"I'll stick to American women, thank you," Silvern commented.

"I'm sure your wife will be glad to hear that since, as I remember, she was born in Boston."

The general laughed.

Kurtzman thought of the Frenchwoman whose invitation he'd just turned down. A pang of regret raced through him momentarily.

"Excuse me, General," Lyons interrupted, "but we've got to get going. We have a plane to catch."

"A new mission?"

Lyons shrugged. It wasn't anybody's business that Able Team might be going out of business. "No comment."

The general nodded his understanding. Like himself, the Able Team commandos could never speak about their missions.

He exchanged handshakes with all four men. Bear turned to look at the ramrod-straight soldier. "Tell Tad to call me anytime he wants to discuss computers—or girls."

Laughing, Silvern nodded and walked back down the aisle to where a cluster of his staff waited for him.

Pol looked at the wheelchair-bound computer genius. "Maybe you and I can swap stories about girls some night."

Bear grinned at the suave-looking man. "Gentlemen don't swap stories."

Lyons glared at Pol. "It's starting to sound like we've been out of action too long."

Pol shook his head. Brognola's news was still fresh and painful. "It sounds more like we might be going out of action forever."

6

Outside Gatehouse 1 of the NSA complex, near one of the many signs posted on the outer cyclone fence, a dark, late-model Chrysler sedan, its windows open, sat at the side of the road while a parade of vehicles passed in both directions. Its hood was up. A tall, dark-haired man, his suit jacket removed, was tinkering with the carburetor. Inside the car a smartly dressed woman and two men in business suits sat and waited patiently.

A small white car bearing the seal of the Federal Protection Service stopped alongside the Chrysler. One of the uniformed officers leaned out the open window. "Something wrong?"

The shirtsleeved man pulled his head out from under the hood. "It stalled. I'm trying to get it started again," he called out with a slight accent.

"You want us to call a towing service?"

"I've already called one. They can't get here for forty minutes."

The officers nodded and glanced at the three passengers in the large sedan. They looked glum. The two uniformed men understood their discomfort. The inside of their own car, despite the air-conditioning unit that sometimes worked, felt like the interior of a sauna. Without a working air conditioner the poor bastards must be dying in the other car.

The officer leaned out the open window again and smiled at the young woman. "Hang in. With this early hot spell there are a lot of breakdowns on the Washington-Baltimore Parkway," the officer called out again, then nudged his partner to take off.

Inside the sedan the two men relaxed their grips on the automatic weapons they'd been hiding. The shirtsleeved man came around to the side of the car. The attractive woman in the front seat stared out at him. "Close the hood and get back in. He should be coming out in a few minutes," she ordered in a soft foreign accent.

The driver did so.

One of the men in the back seat leaned over and started to speak in Romanian.

"In English," the woman snapped.

"Sorry," the other man apologized. "Do we try to take him here?"

The woman shook her head. "I'll be in another car with Janos. Keep your shortwave radio on. You'll be told when to move against them."

Kurtzman came out of the large building accompanied by Ironman, Pol and Gadgets. The four men moved to where the special van was parked.

The woman and men in the Chrysler watched as one of the other men helped the computer wizard into the van.

"You never told us, comrade," the heavyset man in the back seat complained, "what we're supposed to do with him after we kidnap him."

The woman exploded. "Stupid! Do you wish to get us arrested? Call me anything but comrade, you idiot!"

The men froze with fear.

"Sorry, Comrade," the other man muttered in embarrassment. "I'm still not comfortable speaking English." He turned away to avoid the deathlike stare in the woman's eyes. "I only wanted to know what we should do with the man in the wheelchair."

"You'll bring him to the small airfield in Lowell and turn him over to us."

The driver turned to the woman. "The three men with him, are they his bodyguards?"

"From their appearance I suspect they're more than that. More likely a suicide squad."

The three men looked puzzled.

"As in our country, the Americans must have specially trained squads of men ready to give their lives to protect their more important people."

The driver whistled. "I've heard that Americans go to asylums for criminally insane soldiers to get recruits for such assignments."

"With luck we'll free up three beds in whatever asylum they came from," the woman said, smiling.

"Then you're saying we should kill them?"

"You? No. You concentrate on getting this man Kurtzman. I've made arrangements to take care of the others." She pointed down the road to the silver-gray Oldsmobile that had pulled up behind them. Four dead-eyed men sat inside. The three men in the Chrysler turned their heads and stared back at them.

One of them asked, "Mercenaries?"

"Yes. Until we're more familiar with getting around this country we'll hire them for such jobs."

The driver reached down and patted his automatic weapon. "I haven't used this since we left home."

"I trust you haven't forgotten how," the woman said. "You'll be using it in a few hours when you meet with the mercenaries afterward to pay them." She looked down at the briefcase at his feet. "It's vital that no one can talk about who kidnapped this computer expert."

The driver smiled knowingly. "Not even the mercenaries?"

The woman nodded. "Especially not them."

KURTZMAN WAS WAITING for the other three to get into the van before he asked his question. "Where are we eating?"

Pol grinned at him. "Sorry, Bear, we would have taken you to one of the fancier hotels in town, but they all had their celebrity tables booked."

"Cute," Kurtzman growled. "This is the last time I take you characters out in polite society."

"Promises, promises," Lyons said, smiling.

"Blancanales knows a roadhouse a few miles from here. He called ahead and made a reservation," Gadgets replied.

Lyons and Blancanales walked over to the sedan they'd rented. Gadgets climbed into the front of the van and started the engine.

OUTSIDE THE GATE the woman got out of the car and waited for the van to exit from the NSA complex. Then she gestured for the two vehicles filled with armed men to follow. She looked at the driver of the dark Chrysler. "You understand what you're supposed to do?"

The driver nodded. The woman slapped on the door of the car with her palm. "Then do it. And let the mercenaries deal with these men of the suicide squad. You stay back and watch for an opportunity to grab Kurtzman."

The driver of the Chrysler watched as the woman walked away toward a small car parked at the side of the parkway. He could see the figure waiting in the front seat—Janos Dragnan, the dwarf.

The driver turned back and saw the brown-haired man behind the wheel of the van stop at the guard's station and hand him a pass. The van exited the NSA complex and turned onto the parkway. The driver started to follow, but the other car with Kurtzman's bodyguards zoomed out of the complex and got between him and the van. The driver cursed in Romanian at the intruding car, then waited for the silver-gray Oldsmobile to pull behind him before he moved into traffic.

IRONMAN WAS BEHIND the wheel. He glanced in his rear-view mirror. The car he had cut off was still behind him. He could make out the features of the driver. They were sullen.

Pol turned and looked out the rear window. "Man in that car behind you looks like he'd love to ram into us."

"Probably ticked off that we cut him off at the NSA intersection." Lyons was in no mood to worry about what someone else thought of him. He had arrived at Fort Meade still filled with anger at Brognola's announcement. The terrible humidity hadn't made him feel any better. "What kind of place is this roadhouse?" he asked suddenly.

"I took a lovely young woman there once."

Lyons grunted. "Then how do you know the food is any good?"

"We ate first," Pol said quietly, then grinned.

Lyons studied the vehicles ahead of him. The line of traffic moved slowly along the parkway, then stopped altogether when the traffic light at the next intersection turned red.

Ironman stopped the car. "It's getting hotter," he commented, rolling his window down. "Must be these damn Kevlar sweatshirts Brognola makes us wear."

"Not for much longer," Blancanales reminded him. "You might try turning on the air conditioner. The rental company doesn't charge extra."

"I would have thought you liked the heat," Lyons growled. "You like everything else hot."

Pol grinned. "Only my food and my women." He knew his reputation as a ladies' man, and enjoyed Lyons's and Schwarz's attempts to needle him about it.

Lyons grunted and watched as the green turn signal went on. The dark Chrysler was still behind them. Pol saw him studying the rearview mirror.

"Something bothering you?"

"You think that car's following us?"

Pol turned and studied the car behind them again. "I can't imagine why he'd be interested in a pair of has-beens like us." He turned back. "Probably stuck in traffic like everyone else."

Something bothered Ironman about the car. He couldn't figure out what it was, but he trusted his instincts. They had kept him alive for a lot of years.

Pol stretched. "I'd like to get to the restaurant. I've got a call to make."

Lyons decided to forget the car temporarily. "One of your women?"

Blancanales grinned. "What else?"

The traffic moved a little faster. Pol glanced out the window. "Restaurant's coming up on the right."

Lyons honked the horn and pointed at the roadhouse on the right side of the road. Gadgets stuck his hand out of the window of the van and waved, then pulled off the road and into the parking lot.

Lyons twisted his steering wheel slowly and moved the rental into the space next to the van. He glanced out his rearview mirror again. The Chrysler behind him was turning into the parking lot, too.

ELENA MOVED the rental car into the restaurant lot behind the two cars filled with her men. She circled the lot and found a parking space at the side of the rambling brick-and-wood structure from where she could see the front of the restaurant. Then she turned and looked at Dragnan. He had been staring at her, and from his expression she knew this time he wasn't thinking of ways to entice her into his bed—a thought that made her flesh crawl.

"Is Michael still upset that I decided to bring the two engineers back with the computer?" she asked.

"He didn't say," the dwarf replied coldly.

"But he was annoyed, wasn't he?"

"He seemed to be."

The conversation stopped. Both of them knew that crossing Michael Vlad was tantamount to committing suicide. Even now, when he was preoccupied with living in opium dreams, the head of the Draculs was a deadly foe. Too many people in the *Securitate* were still fanatically loyal to him.

Dragnan turned away from her and watched the four men move toward the restaurant. "What do you suppose they're doing here?"

"Going to lunch, I assume."

"We could go inside and keep an eye on them."

"I don't think so," she commented. "This Kurtzman knows what I look like."

"So does Steve Heitz," he replied bitingly. "Where do we make our move? The airport?"

"No, here."

He showed his surprise. "Here? Out in the open? Isn't that dangerous?"

She smiled at the dwarf indulgently. "You still have much to learn. This is an ideal place. There will be so much confusion when they start shooting that we can grab Kurtzman and vanish before anyone realizes he's gone."

She watched the four men disappear into the restaurant, then opened her door and got out. "I'll be back as soon as I've reviewed the plans with the others."

Dragnan watched her walk to where the steel-gray Oldsmobile was parked. Three of the four men had gotten out to talk to her. The fourth sat behind the wheel and listened through his open window.

The dwarf glanced across the lot to where the dark Chrysler was parked. The three *Securitate* agents looked uncomfortable as they stared at Elena. He supposed they were wondering why Elena had hired mercenaries to handle something as simple as a kidnapping. When she first mentioned it, he'd wondered himself. Elena had explained it on the flight from Chicago.

"If something goes wrong, it wouldn't be wise to have our own people captured. Let it be blamed on some American gang activity."

He had been puzzled. "Then why have our own people even there?"

"Someone has to get rid of the four mercenaries after they've accomplished their task. The fewer who know we're here, the safer we are."

To anybody watching, the four men around the table appeared to be good friends sharing a boisterous lunch.

"Hold it a minute," Kurtzman interrupted.

The others stopped in midlaugh, puzzlement on their faces.

Bear lifted a half-empty beer glass. "I want to propose a toast to the meanest three men I've ever met."

The Able Team hell-raisers looked at one another.

"Us?" Gadgets looked hurt. "Mean?"

"You give new meaning to the word," Bear commented, smiling as he held his glass high. "Olympic-medal mean is what you three are. Thank God you three are on our side."

"Hear, hear," Pol called out as he lifted the glass of wine in front of him.

Silently the four clinked glasses and sipped their drinks.

Kurtzman looked at Pol. "If the ax falls, what are your plans?"

Blancanales didn't bother to hide his dismay at the mere prospect of Able Team's termination. "I don't know. Go home and visit my family."

"That could take months," Lyons cracked.

Pol came from a large family whose members lived near one another on the south side of Los Angeles. One of his rare visits was cause for an endless series of family parties.

Kurtzman continued his questioning. "What about after that?"

Pol shrugged and looked at Schwarz. "I guess you and I could take over our security firm."

"Toni would be waiting for us at the Minneapolis airport with a shotgun," Schwarz said.

Toni Blancanales was Pol's sister. She operated the international corporate-security firm that Pol and Gadgets had started as a side venture several years ago. She had made it obvious that she wanted no interference from the firm's two senior partners about how the company should be run.

"She's been making a tidy profit," Pol admitted to Gadgets. "You got any thoughts?"

"Sandy and I have been talking about getting away sometime when we were both free of assignments. After that?" He shook his head. "I don't know." Sandy Meissner was a DEA agent with whom Schwarz had worked on a Florida assignment. Since then they had become quite friendly.

The three commandos looked at Kurtzman. "You got anything in mind?" Lyons asked.

"Not really. Maybe I'll go into teaching full-time."

The Able Team trio started laughing. "You'd go nuts or drive your students crazy in a few weeks," Pol cracked.

"Probably," Bear admitted sheepishly. "Brognola asked me to join him at the task force if things fall apart." He studied the other three at the table. "You know there's a standing invitation for all of you to join him there."

"Forget it," Ironman snapped. "I've had my fill of bureaucrats."

Pol looked at Lyons. "What about you? You got any plans?"

"If the worst happens, I thought I'd bum around Washington for a while before I put any plans together."

Gadgets grinned. "And do what?"

"Hang out," Lyons said casually.

Pol and Gadgets exchanged knowing glances. Then Blancanales turned to Ironman. "And how is Susan?"

Lyons could feel his face redden. "Susan who?" he snapped.

The other three broke into laughter. Even when he wasn't talking about her, they all knew how much he thought about the FBI undercover agent named Susan Phelan whom he'd worked with recently.

Quickly Lyons looked at his watch. "We better get going. Grimaldi's probably having a heart attack at the airport, wondering where we are." He signaled the waiter, who brought the check.

The four men fought over who was paying, and finally Bear came up with a solution. He looked at Lyons. "We'll use a coin. Heads, Pol and I split it. Tails, you and Gadgets pay." Without waiting for Lyons's comment Kurtzman fished a quarter out of his pocket. He poised the coin between his thumb knuckle and bent index finger. "Ready?"

"Go on," Ironman growled.

Grinning, Bear pushed the coin between two water glasses so that it stood on end. He glanced around the table at the puzzled expressions. "I guess that means we all split the check," he announced, reaching for his wallet.

7

Pol held the restaurant door open so that Bear could wheel himself to the van.

"I still think there was something dishonest in what you did," Lyons told the disabled man as Schwarz started to push him outside.

Kurtzman grinned without replying.

"After you, old man," Blancanales said to Ironman.

Ironman started to snap a retort when he spotted the Oldsmobile with its engine running. He looked at the three men standing next to it, staring at the entrance. There was a fourth man behind the wheel. They were expressionless. He knew who they were the minute he saw them. Mercenaries. Professional hit men.

He saw one of them stare at him, then gesture to the others. Lyons recognized the guy, even after all these years.

Back then the mean-faced man with the permanent smirk had been the chief enforcer for a Los Angeles syndicate chieftain. Thanks to lawyers who were willing to make a joke of justice for enough money he had never been convicted.

Ironman searched his memory for the man's name. Lupo. Wolf. Jackal would have been a better tag. Their last encounter had almost cost Lyons his life. He'd been with the LAPD back then.

Now Lupo was here. Older but no less mean-looking. There could only be one reason. Somebody was going to be killed.

Ironman turned and reached under his jacket. He took out the Colt Python from its shoulder holster and slipped it inside his waistband.

Pol saw the movement. "What's that for?" The square-jawed man nodded in the direction of the Oldsmobile. Pol casually turned and glanced, then turned back to Lyons. "Look like syndicate punks."

"They are," Lyons said with certainty. "I know the real mean-looking one from L.A."

"Who are their target, us?" Pol asked.

"Does it matter?"

The three men shared a hatred for murderers, especially those who killed only for the money.

"I guess not," Blancanales agreed. Pol turned to Kurtzman. "Maybe you should wait inside."

For a moment Schwarz thought Blancanales was about to play a prank on Bear. Then he saw the hard expression on Lyons's face, glanced at the Oldsmobile and moved back to Pol's side. "Think they're waiting for us?"

"Like Ironman said, who cares?" Blancanales replied quietly. He reached under his loosely tailored sport jacket and eased out the Desert Eagle.

Gadgets slipped his hand under his windbreaker and grabbed the Government model .45 he wore in an inside-the-waistband quick-draw holster.

The two men started to stroll toward the suspect car.

"Hold it!" Lyons snapped. "There's something else."

The other two returned.

Gadgets focused on Ironman. "What?"

"There's another car—a Chrysler with the engine running—at the other end of the parking lot. There are three foreign-looking creeps standing next to it," Ironman growled.

Gadgets pretended to scan the clear sky, turning his head slowly so that he could look at the dark sedan. He smiled at the other two warriors. "More hit men," he commented. "They look foreign. What the hell have we walked into? It looks like a scene from a grade B movie." He grinned. "I thought of the perfect title. The Battle of the Creeps." He saw Lyons staring at him coldly. "It was only an idea," he added sheepishly, then turned to Pol to ask him a question. "Think it's going to rain?"

"Maybe bullets," Pol replied.

Gadgets studied his two partners. "Should we get involved?"

"Maybe we can stop the rain before it hits us," Lyons suggested.

"So we're involved." Gadgets's grip tightened on the automatic. "How do you want to play it?"

"Pol and I'll worry about the Oldsmobile," Ironman told Gadgets. "You keep the other punks from interfering."

Bear wheeled close to them. "Don't forget about me."

"You get inside and you'll be okay," Lyons told him.

Kurtzman reached into the side of his wheelchair and grabbed a 9 mm Glock 17. "Hell, no, I'll give you a hand with the punks," he told Lyons.

Ironman looked at the determined expression on Bear's face and remembered how reliable in battle he'd been when Stony Man Farm had been assaulted by a horde of terrorists.

Still, the computer expert was handicapped and confined to a wheelchair. As if he could read Ironman's mind, Bear wrapped his huge hand around the automatic and started wheeling himself toward the Oldsmobile.

"Shit," Lyons muttered, moving quickly to catch up with him.

The three men standing outside the Oldsmobile were stunned at the sight of the disabled man racing toward them with a gun. Their orders were to eliminate his bodyguards, not him.

Lupo had recognized Lyons. Turning to the balding hardman next to him, he snapped, "The guy coming behind the cripple is one of them."

From underneath his open windbreaker the balding man whipped out a MAC-10. He needed to get the cripple out of the way to take care of his bodyguard. Leaning the weapon on the trunk of the car, he started squeezing the trigger, spraying hot lead over Bear's head, trying to scare him away.

"To the left!" Ironman shouted at Kurtzman, who turned his chair quickly and spun out of the hail of lead.

Yanking his Python from his waistband, Lyons had no time for careful sighting. He slid into a two-handed stance and squeezed off two shots in the direction of the balding hardguy who had exposed himself.

The first shot tore into the thug's shoulder, causing him to spin around. The second ricocheted off the metal trim of the rear windshield and slammed into his face, tearing a hole next to the bridge of his nose. Thick red fluid and mucus poured from the wound, and the MAC-10 fell to the ground as the man tumbled out of sight.

Stunned, the other two dropped behind the sedan and tightened their grips on their weapons. Lupo gestured for the men to move to the right while he moved left.

Inside the Oldsmobile the terrified leather-jacketed teenager behind the wheel slid down in his seat. This was his first job. Easy money. No one mentioned anything about easy dying. He reached to grab the automatic weapon he had put on the seat next to him. Shaking with fear, he dropped the MAC-10 onto the floor. Nervously he bent down to fish for it.

Unnoticed, Kurtzman cautiously wheeled his chair so that he had a clear view of the vehicle. His adrenaline pumping, he fired at the man crouching nearest to him.

The first hollowpoint chopped into the man's side. Howling with pain, the would-be killer turned and hosed the area around Bear with a continuous burst of lead death from his 9 mm TEC-9. It no longer mattered that he wasn't supposed to kill the man in the wheelchair. In his eye-for-an-eye world one bullet wound was paid for with another bullet wound.

Even under expert control the compact weapon was inaccurate at distances greater than fifty feet. And in the hands of a wounded wild animal the gun's bullets ricocheted off the cars, the brick walls and the asphalt, slamming indiscriminately into terrified restaurant patrons and passengers in passing cars on the parkway.

One of the wildly fired slugs tore through the fleshy part of Bear's upper right arm. Trying to ignore the pain, Kurtzman fired another 3-shot burst at the hit man's chest. Two of the hollowpoints shattered the killer's collarbone.

The gunman screeched with anger as he felt the pain race through him. Still enraged at the cause of his aching arm, Bear fired another burst. Burning slugs carved grooves in the trunk of the Oldsmobile.

The professional was all animal anger. In rage he let loose an endless stream of 9 mm death at Bear. Two of the slugs chewed through his jacket and shirt, slamming his armored undershirt with a hurricanelike force. The punch of the lead projectiles saved Bear's life, propelling his wheelchair at a diagonal until it spun around and disappeared behind the side of the building.

Kurtzman's weapon fell out of his hand as he tried to cushion the impact with his palms. Momentarily stunned, Bear waited until the waves of nausea ceased before he leaned down and scooped up his gun. Then he wheeled himself back toward the war zone.

There was the man he'd wounded. Despite the blood that covered his face the guy was still standing, still holding his weapon. Suddenly he collapsed like an empty air bag and disappeared from sight.

Surprised, Kurtzman searched the area for the source of the gunshots. Then he saw Ironman crouching behind the front wheel, ejecting spent cartridges, slamming in a plastic speed-loader and shoving six fresh bullets home.

Ignoring the thin curls of smoke floating up from the barrel of the .357, Lyons snapped the cylinder shut, then gently pressed one of the cylinder grooves until it turned slightly, setting the first round in place. Keeping his body close to the ground, Ironman gestured for Kurtzman to move back behind the building. Then, turning away, he carefully worked his way around the bullet-fractured vehicle.

Bear ignored the warning and powered himself toward the open window on the driver's side. Somebody had to take care of him.

Covered with blood from the corpse that had fallen against him, Lupo waited until his fury at losing one of his soldiers consumed him. He jumped to his feet and exposed his AK-47. He concentrated his rage on killing the cripple. Damn the contract!

He swung his automatic weapon toward the rapidly moving wheelchair. One dead cripple coming up, he told himself. It was worth losing the three thousand bucks he was supposed to get. Money was important, but so was getting even.

He sensed a dark shadow behind him and glanced quickly over his shoulder. A man was standing next to him. Swinging his weapon around, he saw the huge death machine in the glowering man's hand. He recognized it immediately—a Colt Python.

Ironman grinned cruelly as he unleashed three lead tumblers at Lupo. "Surprise, shithead!" he yelled fiercely.

All three rounds chewed through the gunman's skin and into his heart cavity. Thick blood oozed from the new cavern. Staring at the gaping hole in his chest, the man died before his body slid to the ground.

Ironman glanced across the top of the car at the blood seeping through Bear's sleeve. He was about to go to his aid when Kurtzman waved him away. "Just a scratch. Let's get this wrapped up first."

Nodding, Lyons turned his attention back to the Oldsmobile. Inside the car, the driver realized he was now the only one of his group still living. He panicked and threw the car into reverse, then stomped on the accelerator. Kurtzman barely got out of the way of the backward-hurling vehicle before it rammed into the handful of hypnotized patrons huddled just outside the restaurant entrance. Two women were shoved back into the brick-framed entrance and crushed between the heavy vehicle and the thick wooden door. Several others threw themselves to the ground, trying to crawl out of the murderous path of the vehicle.

In terror the driver threw the car into forward gear and raced toward the exit. The parkway was thick with traffic. Bracing himself against the anticipated crash, he hunched over the wheel. Then he saw the face. It was cold and unforgiving and had blond hair. It stood between him and escape.

He pointed the front hood ornament at the human barrier and pressed the gas pedal to the floor. At the last possible moment Lyons jumped out of the way. Concentrating on reaching the road outside, the punk behind the wheel didn't feel the three slugs tearing open his body. The Oldsmobile crashed into a parked Mercedes. The driver wasn't upset, though. Nothing would ever bother him again.

The three *Securitate* agents panicked when they heard gunshots from across the parking lot. One of them saw Gadgets rushing forward, Government model Colt in his right hand, and signaled the other two. In unison the three pointed their AK-47's in Schwarz's direction and vented their rage with continuous bursts.

Gadgets fell into a roll and came up near the Chrysler, firing. The nearest of the three gunmen screamed in fury as he felt the burning sensation of the .45 slug cutting a deep groove across his forehead. Angrily turning his weapon on Schwarz, he squeezed the trigger and sprayed the area in front of him with 7.62 mm lead.

Schwarz did a side flip and landed two feet away from where he'd been standing. Pushing his Colt automatic forward, he let two more slugs loose at the livid gunman. The first plowed its way through the man's neck. The second gouged out his left eye and penetrated the thick skull bone.

The gunman clutched his AK-47 tightly as he fell across the trunk of the Chrysler, then slid slowly to the paved ground behind it while the other would-be killers stared at the body. Gadgets took advantage of their momentary shock and ducked behind a nearby Volvo, narrowly missing the hail of hot lead unleashed by the other two vengeance-bent attackers. He peeked around the edge of the Swedish-built car and realized there was no way to reach them without exposing himself. Looking around, he saw Blancanales weaving between the cars to get to him. Pol saw him and waved, then pointed at the corner of the restaurant's brick wall.

Gadgets wasn't sure what Pol was trying to tell him. Finally the smartly dressed Able Team soldier shouted at him, "Watch the bank shot!"

Smiling despite the tight situation, Schwarz watched Blancanales aim his Desert Eagle carefully at the far corner of the brick wall, near where the two gunmen were hiding. Carefully aiming his gun, Pol squeezed off a shot. The slug drilled into the brick. Adjusting his aim, Blancanales fired again. This time the slug clipped the wall at an angle and ricocheted into the rear window of the gunmen's car.

Startled, the two men stood and began to fire wildly in every direction. Schwarz moved to the front of the Volvo. Popping up suddenly, he sprayed the nearest of the assassins with a shower of four rapidly fired shots.

The first two bullets penetrated the chest of one of the hit men, releasing a steady stream of red. The third drilled into his abdomen, rapidly tearing its way into his pancreas. Bits of bloody tissue and splintered bone exploded onto the asphalt.

"Eight ball in the side!" Pol yelled as he rushed forward, preceded by a steady stream of hot lead from his pistol.

Screaming curses in a foreign tongue, the remaining *Securitate* agent tried to rush at Blancanales. He was able to manage a half-dozen steps before he realized he was dead.

"Check 'em out!" Pol yelled to Gadgets. "Ironman may need me!"

Panicking patrons continued to rush out of the front door, creating a traffic jam in the doorway.

"Get back inside," Ironman shouted as he rushed to join his teammates.

Terrified, those patrons who could move trampled the wounded and dead as they rushed back into the safety of the restaurant interior. A young couple in business clothes tried to reach their car and escape the bloodbath, but a squat, pimply man with an AK-47 popped up from behind the Chrysler. His face filled with hate, he began to hose down the front of the restaurant with 7.62 mm death. The young woman in the stylish gray suit was shoved backward into the crowd and cut in half by burning lead.

The sounds of the dying and wounded matched in volume the loud explosions of the gunfire as Ironman and the remaining two mercenaries continued to exchange shots.

Bear had retreated to a corner of the entrance near where the woman and the dwarf had stopped their rental car. He began to feel the white heat of his wounded arm.

Elena watched the slaughter silently, only her eyes revealing the fury she felt at the incompetence of her men.

Dragnan glanced around the area. "The computer expert is over there," he said, pointing at the wheelchair-bound man. "We might be able to grab him while the others are busy."

For a moment it seemed as if she hadn't heard the dwarf, then slowly she turned and stared at him. "And if he resists?"

He showed her the AK-47 he was holding. "This should convince him."

He could see her weighing the idea carefully. "No. The police will be coming soon. We'll find another solution to our problem." She turned the key in the ignition and started the car.

"Better let Brognola know what happened," Lyons told his gray-haired partner as he surveyed the battlefield. Gadgets nodded and worked his way into the restaurant past the dead and living.

Kurtzman began to wheel himself toward the two hell-raisers when he heard the sound of a car pulling out of a parking space behind the building. Two more terrified patrons, he decided. Can't blame them.

The car pulled alongside him and he was stunned to see the face in the driver's seat—the Frenchwoman from the computer conference. For a moment their eyes locked, then she drove away quickly, racing out of the parking lot and into the traffic.

Ironman and Pol rushed to where Kurtzman was sitting. Gently Pol removed Bear's jacket and tore the bloodied shirtsleeve away from the wound. "Good thing you were wearing Kevlar," he commented.

Bear tried to make a joke to mask the pain he was feeling. "I never leave home without it. What if I was in an accident and some good-looking woman had to take my clothes off? It would be like being caught wearing dirty underwear." Glancing at his arm, he looked at the pair of commandos. "We can worry about my arm later. Let's get back to Stony Man." He thought about the French-woman. Was she here by accident? He didn't think so. "I've got a couple of million records I need to check right away."

Pol turned to Ironman. "Isn't that just like Bear? When the going gets tough, the tough get out their computers."

Kurtzman groaned at the attempt of humor as they heard the sounds of police sirens coming closer. He shook his head. "Next time I think I'll lunch alone."

Pol winked at Ironman. "That's the thanks we get for trying to show Bear a good time."

8

Captain Frank Lentraub was furious. The caller had asked him to release the four men he was holding.

"Thirteen bodies in the Howard County Morgue. Another additional fifteen people have been rushed by ambulances to several hospitals for emergency treatment. Eyewitnesses say that the four men were responsible for killing at least seven of the dead people. And you expect me to let them go?"

"Yes," the voice on the other end snapped. "And now."

"I don't know who the hell you think you are, Federal Man, but it'll be a cold day in hell before these characters walk out of this station."

There was a click on the other end. Lentraub stared at the receiver in his hand and set it back in its cradle.

What a mess. In twenty-five years with the Maryland State Police he had never seen such a massacre. One of the witnesses had described the parking lot as a tide of red blood.

He could believe it. By the time he'd gotten there, most of the bodies had been taken away, but the thick, sticky scarlet gore was everywhere. He still remembered how carefully he'd had to move around the area to avoid getting blood on his shoes.

What puzzled him was the man in the wheelchair. At first he had thought the guy was just one of the wounded victims. Then the man admitted he'd killed two of the stiffs. Lentraub found it hard to believe that someone without the use of his legs would be stupid enough to get involved in a shoot-out.

The four men his troopers had taken captive had been fingerprinted and so had the dead men and women. He was waiting for reports from the FBI.

The door to his large, cluttered office opened. Kelly Durkin, the fingerprint specialist, walked in with a stack of reports. He handed them across the desk.

"Sit down," Lentraub ordered. The tall, muscular officer eased his large frame into the worn leather chair. "Anything useful in these?"

"The four we found near the Oldsmobile all had records. Mostly suspicion of murder. Probably syndicate hit men."

"What about the rest?"

"The bodies near the entrance to the restaurant were pretty ordinary citizens. Executives, secretaries, that sort of thing."

Lentraub grunted.

"The three who were killed at the other end of the lot have no records."

"More ordinary citizens?"

Durkin shook his head. "I don't think so. All the labels in their clothes had been cut out. Expensive outfits. Handmade suits, custom-fitted shirts."

"Who the hell are they?" the captain bellowed.

"Want an opinion?"

"Sure. Try me."

"Foreigners."

"Gimme a break, Durkin. That's a pretty wild guess."

The muscular young trooper leaned forward. "The coroner took a look at their dental work. None of it was done in the United States."

"Where was it done?"

"He said he couldn't pin it down yet. But the kind of metal alloys in their mouths are usually found in Communist countries."

Lentraub whistled. What he'd thought was a simple gang war was turning out to be something bigger. "Anything on the four guys we're holding?"

"I saved that for last," the uniformed man replied. "The wounded guy in the wheelchair is pretty famous. Aaron Kurtzman. He's a computer expert—works mostly on government security projects. You know, keeping CIA and NSA computers safe from spies who'd like to get in and steal secrets."

Lentraub threw up his hands. "Okay, but who are the other three? His bodyguards?"

"That's the most puzzling thing. We ran their prints and the names they gave us through the FBI network, and a message came back."

"Well," the captain asked impatiently, "what did it say?"

Durkin handed him a piece of paper. Lentraub stared at the words, unable to accept what he read. "Top security. P clearance only." Lentraub studied the message. "What the hell does P clearance mean?"

"How about President, as in White House?"

Lentraub leaned back in his chair and studied the cracks in the ceiling above him. Someday he'd convince the head of the state police that his office badly needed plastering and painting. He focused his eyes on the young officer sitting in front of his desk. "Who the hell are these guys?"

The phone rang, saving Kelly Durkin from venturing a guess. Lentraub answered it. He recognized the voice—the governor. "Yes, sir," he said, suddenly polite.

"Shut up and just listen," the voice snapped.

Lentraub, as always, did exactly what he was told. As he listened, he tried to interject a protest. "But, Governor, thirteen people are dead—"

The orders were specific. He was to release them.

Finally he was able to ask a question. "Why?"

"Because the President of the United States asked me."

ELENA STARED out of the window of the plane and studied the checkerboard squares far below. Three of her men were dead. They had been told not to get involved in a fight. She couldn't stand people who wouldn't follow orders.

Turning, she glanced at the dwarf. The first thing he would do when they returned to their base was call Michael Vlad in Paris and tell him what had happened.

She knew what Michael's reaction would be the moment he was able to pull himself out of his drug-induced fog. He would be furious with her for the deaths of the three men.

As if it were her fault! But Michael wouldn't listen to her explanation. No, she had to find a way to stop Dragnan from calling Vlad.

"The computer should have arrived by now," she said, trying to engage the dwarf in conversation.

Dragnan grunted, refusing to look at her.

"Michael was anxious that we destroy any files the Americans may have on us. Now we can do it. I'm sure Michael will be pleased."

Dragnan shrugged. He knew from their previous overseas conversations that the man to whom he owed his loyalty still hadn't forgiven the sable-haired woman for going against orders and letting the two computer technicians live. The loss of three of their men would seal her fate. Then only he would be available to represent Vlad in this country.

The one thing he still didn't understand was how she could use a computer to destroy government records. He asked her.

"Once our computer is programmed, I'll plant a time-controlled virus in their computers," she explained.

"Virus? How can that affect machinery?"

"The word is just a way to describe a program capable of destroying computer records."

She could see that the dwarf was having difficulty grasping the concept. "Think of the virus as an eraser, and the records as lists of numbers written in pencil. The way you get rid of the numbers is to use the eraser."

Dragnan smiled. It was beginning to make sense, except for why the virus had to be time-controlled. He asked her about that.

"Imagine that the timing part of the program is a bomb attached to an alarm clock," she explained.

She could see the hard expression on Dragnan's face. He smiled with understanding.

"When the alarm goes off, on the days and at the times we tell it to, the program calls us and asks if it should instruct the virus to start destroying files. That way we can keep destroying any files we want."

It was a simplistic explanation. She had been given a more thorough one by the strange German specialists who called themselves the Computer Anarchists. But she could see that her explanation had satisfied the dwarf.

"And the man we couldn't kidnap? Wasn't he the one you wanted to operate the machine?"

She thought of the graduate student she'd been leading around on a romantic leash. "I have someone else in mind."

The tiny man started smiling. He reached out and squeezed her hand, then released it and stared out at the lush green below the plane. "Michael is expecting me to call him," he reminded her.

"I plan to call him, too," she warned.

He smiled at her. "Of course you will. I'm sure your report will be as complete as mine." He didn't disguise his expression of triumph as he looked out the window again.

"Janos." Her voice was soft and gentle.

He continued staring out the window.

"Would you care to have dinner with me when we get back?"

He looked at her. There was a beguiling suggestion in her eyes.

"Alone," she added.

He nodded. He had waited for this evening for many years. He could call Vlad afterwards.

IN THE SMALL dark red brick house on the Rue Madeleine, the goateed man managed to abstain from smoking the off-white pellets long enough to place a series of overseas calls. After the fifth one, he placed a call to the United States.

The female voice on the other end announced that he had reached Camp Freedom. He asked for Elena, then remembered she was using the name Sylvie and asked for her by that name.

"She is out at the present," the voice reported, sounding cold and suspicious.

"Is Janos there?"

"No, he, too, is not here," the woman said formally. "Who is calling them?"

Vlad identified himself, using the prearranged code words. Suddenly the woman became warm and friendly.

"Comrade Michael—" she started to say.

"Not comrade," he snapped.

The woman sounded embarrassed. "I am still learning not to use that word," she apologized.

Vlad would have lectured her, but there was no time and the call was costing a fortune. "Have them call me when they return," he ordered.

He remembered that the Algerian had promised to bring him some very high-quality opium later that day, and a willing young girl with whom he could share it.

"If I'm not here, please let them know I plan to bring a large number of people to them in three weeks."

Before she could question him Vlad hung up. The calls had fatigued him. He needed a nap so that he would be fresh when the Algerian arrived with his two gifts.

9

"I can't believe it!" Hal Brognola waved his cigar in the air and looked up at the ceiling. "How can four intelligent men go to lunch and end up with thirteen dead people?"

"You won't believe this, Chief," Pol said, shaking his head. "But we were just minding our own business."

Brognola looked at him coldly. "I'll bet." He turned to Kurtzman, whose arm was in a sling. "The doctors say you're healing nicely."

"Does that mean I can get back to my work?"

"They want you to take it easy for a few more days."

Bear was furious. "While that woman gets away," he sputtered bitterly.

"Your description has gone out to every customs agent. She isn't going anyplace for a few days."

Kurtzman didn't bother hiding his frustration. "All I want to do is get started on searching through the computers."

"I hear you," Brognola snapped. He glared at the man in the wheelchair. "What were you doing playing cops and robbers?"

"Protecting myself."

"That's not your job," Brognola growled. "Which reminds me, where'd you get the gun?"

"I talked Cowboy into it," Bear answered sheepishly. "It was all my idea, not his."

Gadgets decided to take the heat off Bear and Cowboy. "Thanks for making those calls. That Maryland state trooper didn't sound anxious to let us go anytime soon."

"Don't thank me," Brognola snapped. "If I didn't need you, the four of you would still be there."

Pol and Ironman exchanged glances, then leaned forward. Lyons looked at Brognola. "Something come up on these foreign agents?"

"Maybe," the Stony Man chief replied. "What do you know about supercomputers?"

Pol shrugged. "They're fast."

Gadgets jumped in. "They're really fast."

Brognola looked disappointed. "You're missing the main point."

Ironman stared at him. "Which is?"

"Every branch of the federal government uses supercomputers to process and store the information it needs to operate."

Kurtzman couldn't contain himself any longer. "The NSA alone has more than six acres of computers to process intelligence files."

"That's a lot of information, Bear," Lyons said.

"They should be able to do spectacular things. One supercomputer with all the peripherals it needs to function can cost twenty million dollars."

Pol whistled. Even Lyons couldn't disguise his surprise. Gadgets just nodded his head, as if he'd known the cost all along.

Brognola took over again. "If you want Able Team to stay in business, you better pay attention carefully. First, some background. For a long time we've had a policy preventing supercomputers from being exported from the

United States. Can you imagine what somebody who had it in for this country could do if they got their hands on one?''

"A lot of damage," Kurtzman observed.

Lyons looked bewildered. "How? They're not weapons."

Bear smiled patiently. "Ironman, if you had listened to what I said at the conference, you would have learned that computers are more powerful weapons than even the—"

"What's all of this got to do with the punks we're trying to find?" Lyons muttered.

"Somebody stole a supercomputer two days ago. They found the abandoned truck and the bodies of a driver and a Federal Protective Service guard," Brognola explained.

Kurtzman looked worried. Brognola glanced at him, then turned back to listen to Schwarz. "If we're going to be looking for these foreign hostiles, maybe the FBI could look for the hijackers," Gadgets suggested.

"No," Brognola snapped. "I have a hunch there's a connection." He turned to Kurtzman. "So does the man in the White House. He wants the foreign agents stopped and the computer found. Not by the FBI. By Able Team."

Brognola handed Bear an envelope. "My contact in Washington had these sent down. Check them out."

Kurtzman took the envelope and opened it. Inside were six computer diskettes.

Ironman looked skeptical. "Anything specific make you think there's a connection between the hijackers and the foreign agents?"

In answer Brognola handed out copies of a report from the Maryland State Police. "Note that four of the dead men had criminal records."

Blancanales shook his head. "All of them were soldiers with the Drago family from Chicago." He looked across the conference table at Brognola. "I'll bet Salvatore Drago isn't a happy man right now."

Brognola smiled. "I wouldn't think so. Especially since he lost another four of his men a few days ago when their car exploded on a highway just outside Chicago."

Ironman posed a question. "Any connection between the two?"

"There could be. The place where their car blew up was only fifteen miles from where the bodies of the FPS guard and the truck driver were found."

Gadgets joined in. "What about the other hit men at the restaurant? Any line on them?"

"All of them were wearing expensive clothing without labels. There wasn't a cleaning tag among the bunch. None of them had ID—not even a phony one." Brognola glanced down at the report again. "There was one thing. The coroner who examined them said their dental work wasn't American."

"Shit," Lyons muttered. "It's like a jigsaw puzzle. Foreign assassins cooperating with local hit men. Who were they after?"

Brognola turned and stared at Kurtzman. "My hunch is you."

Bear looked stunned. "Me? Why?"

"A top-secret computer gets stolen. Whoever took it needs somebody who can run it. Who in the country is more qualified to run it than you?"

The man in the wheelchair smiled and shook his head. "How would they have heard about me? I'm not exactly a celebrity."

Brognola frowned. "Two of the people who were riding in the hijacked truck are missing. One of them is Steve Heitz. That's the kid you took under your wing, isn't it?"

"Yeah. I wonder where he is now."

THE SABLE-HAIRED WOMAN walked out of what had once been the administration building of an Arizona military post and crossed the paved street to the windowless building on the other side. She had slept soundly, exhausted from the trip and the disgusting night with the dwarf. She had let the hot water from the shower scrub the unpleasantness of the evening from her body.

Elena stopped and gazed at what had been accomplished in a few months. What had once been the crumbling shell of a small military base set on the edge of the desert was now a handsome inner core of air-conditioned one-story buildings ready to house more than a hundred people. Offices and storage buildings, including the armory, surrounded the residential units.

A medical and dental clinic had been built. Several of the *Securitate* people expected soon were former doctors and dentists who had used their skills more to torture information from captives than to heal patients.

In the distance she could hear the ricocheting of slugs on the target range. It was good to hear the familiar sounds again. Within the buildings men and women were deep in study, learning the new language, memorizing information about the country where they would now live, being introduced to the latest in electronic communications and surveillance equipment, practicing the thousand and one skills they would need to succeed without the backing of a government.

It would take a lot of work to mold the Draculs into a powerful underground force that would command fear, respect and huge sums of money. Elena had changed Vlad's original plans. He had envisioned the Draculs performing the same things they had done for the Romanian government: blackmail, assassination, intimidation, seduction. Only now they would do it for money.

If Michael would have listened to her, she would have told him that he was out-of-date. There were cheaper sources for murder and intimidation. To survive, the Draculs would need more than just the talents they had employed in the past. They would have to become a strong international force that could provide anything their clients required—from death of a dissident to the secret plans for a new weapon. But Michael had spent too many years as the head of the group. He wouldn't listen to anyone's ideas except his own.

She thought back to her overseas telephone conversation with Vlad. He had been furious at her report, as if she had personally caused the deaths of their agents. But he had softened slightly when she told him about her progress with the computer.

"The files on us will be erased within forty-eight hours," she'd promised, more to shut him up than because she believed it. Now she would have to make good her promise or face Vlad's punishment.

The older computer technician, Jim Tomasello, had been no help in satisfying her demands. When the installation was completed, she had learned quickly that he knew nothing about penetrating government computers. She was certain Heitz would be the same, but she needed to give him one more chance. Tomasello's chances were all used up. Elena had personally witnessed his execution.

The attempt to grab Kurtzman may have been a fiasco, but there was still Tad Silvern. Without Kurtzman she would have to depend on the college student. She had called him earlier, explaining that her "uncle" was ill but that she'd be back at the university in a few days. She had been pleased to hear the hunger in his voice as he'd responded. If Heitz didn't work out, she was pretty certain she could count on Silvern. He'd do anything for her. Anything.

STEVE HEITZ SHIVERED as he sat at the keyboard of the computer under the watchful eye of the armed dwarf who had kidnapped them. He tried to talk to the man. "When are they going to let us go?"

The small man didn't seem to understand English, so Heitz fell silent. For days Tomasello and he had struggled to get the various components installed and tested. Each day the squat, ugly man had stared at them as if he were measuring them for coffins.

Sylvie had assigned another man to work with them, someone who had been trained in mainframe computers. It was obvious to Heitz and Tomasello that he was only there to learn how to keep this computer running.

Now the computer was installed and operating. Sylvie had promised that he and Tomasello would be released soon, and Heitz wanted to believe her. After all, they had been blindfolded all the way to wherever they were. He would never be able to tell the FBI where his kidnappers had taken them.

All he knew was that the air-conditioning was constantly running. In this room that was only sensible. Computers reacted to extreme temperatures. But in the windowless cells where he and Tomasello were kept it made less sense. Unless it was extremely hot outside.

Maybe they just wanted to make them comfortable. He stared at the ugly little man who kept his automatic pointed at him. No, he didn't believe that, no more than he really believed that Sylvie and the dwarf would let them go.

Heitz stood and wandered around the sterile room. He could feel the eyes of the dwarf follow him. Then it suddenly dawned on him that he hadn't seen Tomasello all day. But the door opened before he could speculate on what had happened to the man.

Sylvie walked in and smiled at him. The peasant blouse she wore barely hid her ample breasts.

The only thing he was sure of anymore was that her name wasn't Sylvie. Like everything else she'd told him, he was certain it was a lie. She spoke to the men and women who seemed to live in the complex in a strange language that he couldn't identify.

Now, looking at her, he suddenly asked, "What's your real name?"

She turned away from him and looked around the room. "That's unimportant. The computer—is it really working?"

He was tempted to lie, but he was aware that she knew something about computers, so what was the point? "Yes, it works," he said wearily.

"At least you and your co-worker agree on this."

Heitz became angry. "Where is he?"

"He's gone. You can follow him if you continue to co-operate."

He really didn't believe that they'd let Tomasello go. But perhaps they had. "I've done everything you asked me to do," he said, trying to mask the fear in his voice.

She continued her interrogation. "I've asked you this before. You're certain you don't know how to access government computers?"

He got mad. "I told you before. No! Even if I was willing to, I have no idea how to crack the encrypted passwords they use to protect them."

"I thought you studied under this computer genius, Aaron Kurtzman. Certainly he's an expert on such matters."

Aaron Kurtzman! Heitz looked around the large room filled with sophisticated computer equipment. For no reason he could understand he started to wonder if Kurtzman's computer room had equipment as state-of-the-art as this. "I wasn't interested in learning. My field is superconductors."

"So your friend Tad told me. I was hoping for your sake that he was wrong."

She knew so much. He felt helpless in front of her. "The difference is he was raised to be interested. His father is a big deal with the NSA."

She nodded. "General Silvern. I know." She exhaled a sigh of regret. "So you truly don't know how to do what I've requested."

Given time he could probably figure out how to crack the password, but he wasn't about to tell her that.

She looked at her watch. "I wish I had more time to convince you to help us, but I have to do something about my hair before I get on the plane." She looked at the dwarf. "His work is completed, Janos," she said quietly.

Heitz turned and saw the dwarf leering at him. The woman nodded. In reply the dwarf widened his smile and emptied the clip into the young man's chest.

Heitz could feel the burning agony as the slugs chiseled through his breastbone. Blood splattered in his eyes, and he tried to wipe it away. Then he realized his hand wouldn't obey him.

"Have someone clean up the room and bury the body out in the desert," the young woman ordered as she walked out of the room. "I have a plane to catch."

10

Sitting at the living room desk in his small off-campus apartment, Tad Silvern could feel the excitement build inside him as he stared at the monitor. It was starting to happen now.

He had passed through the first barriers. Now the CIA's computer was asking him to enter the encrypted password for today.

Behind him he could hear the French exchange student laughing with pleasure. She had doubted he could actually do it. Now she had to change her mind. About them, too, he hoped.

"Do you remember my uncle?" Sylvie asked him.

"The dwa—I mean, yes, I remember him."

"Remember I told you he used to work for French intelligence? Well, when he was still an agent, he was arrested in Romania by the *Securitate*, the secret police. The head of the *Securitate* himself interrogated my uncle for days. His identity was evidently once one of the best-kept secrets in Romania. But my uncle found out his name. Is there any computer record of such people in America?"

Silvern smiled at her. "I would think so. Probably in the National Security Agency records. Why?"

"Well, my uncle wouldn't tell me the man's name, but if I could tell him who the man was and where he is now, that would impress him. And please him. I think he still wants to get even with the man.''

Silvern coughed. "Uh, I don't know, Sylvie.''

"Tad, you do like me, don't you?''

"Of course, I do. I love—I mean—''

"My uncle means everything to me, Tad. He's my only living relative. What can it hurt?''

Silvern looked at her, love fever racing through his veins. "I guess it's pretty harmless.'' He punched a few keys, and a NSA menu popped up on the screen with an invitation to enter a password.

"*C'est magnifique!*'' the Frenchwoman squealed. "I'm impressed.''

"More to come,'' Silvern said, tossing the words over his shoulder casually.

She looked at him with what he imagined was awe.

Silvern picked up a framed photograph of Aaron Kurtzman and showed it to her. "Bear taught me how to play a computer like a piano.''

"You admire him greatly.''

"Since I was a little kid, he's been like a second father.''

"You keep calling him 'Bear.' Why?''

"Everyone does. I don't know why. Maybe because he's built like one. He used to move around like a bear until he was . . . in an accident that made it impossible for him to walk.''

"Does he teach full-time?''

"No. Mostly he's a consultant to the government.''

"Oh, doing what?''

Silvern hesitated. "Different sorts of things,'' he replied lamely. "I want you to meet him someday.''

"I'm sure I will. But you were about to prove something to me,'' she reminded him.

Silvern remembered his boast. "The National Security Agency's files. We'll see if there's a file on this group you called—"

"*Securitate,*" she reminded him. "You're wonderful to do all of this just for me."

"For us," he replied. "Be patient. It'll take a little time."

"And I'm sure it's classified information," she said, "so I should go out of the room and let you work in private." She stood and walked to where Silvern had put her case. "Meantime I'll go into the bathroom and take a shower."

"By the time you get back I should have the encrypted passwords deciphered and we can look for the file."

She leaned over and brushed her lips against his cheek. "I'm sure you will," she whispered, then left the room.

After she turned on the shower, Elena opened her small suitcase and checked an electronic recording device inside to make sure that it was still functioning. She had activated it when Silvern had agreed to search the government files.

The technology was known to every serious computer hobbyist. Data sent and received by computers could be recorded by electronic devices planted near the computers. Later the signals could be decoded so that even the most secure computer system could be compromised. She had convinced Silvern's friend, Steve Heitz, to build her such a unit several weekends earlier.

She stripped off her clothes. It had been a long, hot day, and she felt the need of extremely hot water hammering at her skin. As she stood under the shower and moaned at the torture of the scalding water, she kept thinking of Michael Vlad.

He was losing his hard edge as a professional. It worried her. The rest of their comrades would be arriving within the next two weeks. They deserved a leader who hadn't lost contact with reality.

She wondered who was powerful enough to replace Michael? In her mind she ran down the names of all of their group. There was no one she could trust. Then she remembered herself and smiled. Of course, she was the logical person to replace Michael when the time came.

Her shower finished, she put on a robe and poked her head out the bathroom door. "Is it safe to come back?"

Silvern turned and grinned at her. "You're being silly. Come back in here. I missed you. And I'm ready to go searching for the file for your uncle."

"Then I'll get us each a glass of wine to celebrate," she said, and slid by him on her way to the kitchen.

Silvern was too busy concentrating on checking the list of files that flashed before him on the monitor to pick up the drink she handed him on her return. He glanced at her. Her robe didn't leave much to the imagination. Still, she looked so young and vulnerable with her long hair hanging down, wet from the shower.

He smiled at her. "Sit here and help me find the right file."

She studied the menu on the monitor, then pointed to a file. "That one."

"*Securitate,* Romania," Silvern read. "You've got it." He tapped several keys until the file appeared on the screen. "Here it is. Should I make a hard copy?"

"Would you mind?"

He shook his head and turned on the small printer sitting on the desk. As the dot-matrix printer head moved rapidly across the paper, Silvern turned to look at the Frenchwoman.

She was engrossed by the list of names and descriptions on the screen. Had he bothered reading them he would have seen the name Elena Demenescu and a description of a twenty-nine-year-old woman with light brown hair. Had he read the rest of her description he would have learned that the woman spoke five languages, was a member of the Romanian secret police and an expert at seduction and assassination.

The printer completed its task, and he ripped out the pages and handed them to her. Then he suggested, "Let's go into the bedroom."

"Not yet," she said.

He looked surprised. Sylvie had always responded enthusiastically to his suggestions.

"Let's sip our wine first."

He lifted his glass and offered a toast. "To us."

"To us," she whispered back. Pulling up a chair, she sat down and snuggled against him. "I wonder why the NSA has such international records. I would have thought your CIA would keep such things."

"They might, but my father says that most of the government agencies depend on the NSA to maintain a complete intelligence library they can all use. It cuts down on the overhead."

"So if the NSA lost the list, nobody would be able to see them again," she commented.

"Right. But that's not likely to happen. Getting into the NSA system is an almost impossible task." He grinned. "And they keep backup tapes just in case someone happens to get into the system and erases the files."

The Frenchwoman smiled back. "Of course they would have to first find out that a file had been erased."

"Yes," Silvern agreed. He was getting bored talking about computer files when there was something else he wanted to do right now.

The young woman lifted her glass again. "We finish the wine and then..." she smiled.

Silvern gulped his wine down in one swallow.

Sylvie laughed. "You're too anxious."

Silvern began to weave back and forth in his chair. Struggling to stay awake, he grabbed for the edge of the desk and missed. His head smashed against the front of the computer console. Then he dropped the wineglass and slid slowly from his chair to the floor.

The Frenchwoman looked pleased. The drug had worked. It would be at least an hour before Silvern woke up, more than enough time to plant the virus and time-control programs she'd gotten from the German anarchists.

Elena pulled over another chair to the console and inserted the first of two diskettes. Stroking the keys of the computer quickly, she transferred the virus into a little-used section of the NSA computer where it could be distributed to other computers in the intelligence network.

Satisfied, she took out the first diskette and replaced it with the second. In many ways the program it contained was more important than the first.

Again typing, she accessed another sector of the NSA computer. The Germans had told her to find a relatively unused area of the computer's memory where she could plant the time-control program. Searching through the files, she finally found an ideal place—a set of housekeeping programs used occasionally to tidy up computer records. Quickly stroking the keyboard, she transferred the program to the NSA computer.

The time-control command would automatically start calling her regularly at the same time. Unless she signaled it not to proceed, it would activate the virus program and spread its "poison" through the entire network. Only a genius with the right equipment at hand would ever be able to find the two small programs.

Silvern began to stir. There was one last thing she had to do. She put the diskette containing the virus back into the computer and transferred it to the NSA system. It would start destroying the *Securitate* files within an hour. Then, quickly, she manipulated the computer so that it displayed the *Securitate* files again.

Silvern opened his eyes and looked up at her, embarrassed. "Sorry. Wine sometimes does that to me," he told her sheepishly.

She helped him to his feet. "Perhaps I should go home and let you get some sleep."

"No, please stay tonight."

"Of course."

Still embarrassed, Silvern sat down in front of the computer. "First I better get out of the NSA system before they trace the call." He punched several keys and watched as the screen went blank, then pushed his chair out and looked up at her.

She leaned over and kissed him hard on the lips. "Now where were we?" she breathed huskily.

11

Buried deep beneath the heavily guarded Stony Man complex was a series of rooms floating on suspended floors that housed the latest in computer hardware. The control room of the subterranean complex was Aaron Kurtzman's private kingdom. Checking the various keyboards, monitors and consoles, the bearlike man sat in his battery-powered wheelchair, glad to get back to studying the intelligence data he was sucking into his own data banks through telecommunication taps on the NSA computer network.

Usually Bear spent most of his days and nights checking through the systems of various intelligence agencies for new information that might somehow be useful to Able Team. Officially, of course, there were no links between Kurtzman's computer and the data banks in the various intelligence agencies. Only an expert would be able to detect that Bear had successfully cracked the access codes for each of the computer networks and could extract information from them at will.

Unofficially the computer-center managers of the various agencies were aware of the invasion. It had become almost a game between them. They were all on the same side. It was only at the higher echelons of their bureaucracies that the jockeying for position existed.

Bear smiled as he thought of the fun he'd had devising ways of invading secure government computers when he first took over the computer center at Stony Man Farm. He could appreciate how a hacker felt when a code to a password-protected computer system was cracked. Not that he condoned illegal invasion of computer data banks. Too many times what seemed like an innocent prank was really a clever cover for criminal or espionage activities. And Bear agreed that anyone caught should be prosecuted.

Still, he enjoyed seeing data supposedly available to no unauthorized personnel scrolling down his monitors. Someplace in the billions of bits of data he'd stored in his complex computers might be clues to the identity and location of future terrorists and other criminals who were even now plotting to destroy the fragile democracy known as the United States of America.

This time Bear was hunting for specific information. Ignoring the throbbing he still felt in his arm, he searched for the identity of the Frenchwoman who had attempted to seduce him at the computer seminar and later showed up at the restaurant, obviously part of the group involved in the bloody massacre.

They were both professionals; he was sure of that. There was a subliminal aroma that professionals exuded that was absent in ordinary people. The man or woman on the street would never sense it, but its presence could be felt by another professional. Kurtzman was sure he'd felt it at the NSA auditorium when she was working her charms on him.

He had felt something else about her, he admitted to himself—the closeness of a truly beautiful woman.

Her presence at the restaurant parking lot had changed his memory of her. Now she and the man with her were the enemy, daring him to find her.

Kurtzman turned his attention back to his busy monitors. The data continued to flow across the screens in rapid sequence, moving almost too fast to read. Then, suddenly, the screens went blank, as if someone had severed his telephone connection to the NSA network.

"Some new genius at the NSA who spotted my tap," he decided. Turning to the phone on the console, he dialed the unlisted number of the NSA computer center.

He recognized the voice that answered—General Silvern's right-hand man, Bill Jackson.

"Kurtzman here, Bill."

Jackson sounded panicky. "Can it wait, Aaron? We've got a mess here."

"What kind of mess?" He wondered if it had something to do with his blank monitor.

"You tied into our network?"

"That's what I was calling about."

"Somebody's slipped a virus into the system. It's chewing away a section of our data files right now." The NSA computer head's voice trembled with anger.

Bear reacted instantly and hit the off switch on his console. His screen went dark. "Hit the Off switch," he told Jackson.

"Yeah. Good idea." The phone went dead. A moment later the man returned, sounding relieved. "Done."

"I better let you go so you can start looking for the virus," Kurtzman commented.

"It may take days to find it. Maybe weeks, if we ever do. We can't afford to shut the system down for that long."

Kurtzman was sympathetic. So much of the intelligence community depended on information provided by the NSA computers. "How many files were destroyed?"

"Hold on a minute and I'll tell you," Jackson said. Bear could hear him call for a report, then he came back on the line. "So far as they can determine, all we lost is our records of the secret-police personnel in Eastern Europe." He laughed weakly. "Not much of a loss considering how they're being kicked out of power over there." He muttered something under his breath.

"I didn't get that last bit," Kurtzman said.

"I was just cursing all the little snotnoses who get their kicks by penetrating our system and trying to erase our files."

Bear remembered the case of the college hacker who had stood trial for just such an action.

"I'd like to catch all of them and ram their personal computers down their throats, or into any other orifice in their bodies," the NSA computer man snarled.

Kurtzman laughed. Nobody had been able to penetrate the Able Team system—yet. But if they did and wreaked havoc with the files, he was sure he wouldn't have to push the hell-raisers around Stony Man to go out and teach them a painful lesson.

"I'd better let you get back to your mess. I hope your virus didn't find its way into my system," Bear said, and hung up.

He leaned across the console and pressed a series of keys, switching the system to one of the off-line computers that maintained a full set of backup files. Until he checked the records he'd just copied for possible viruses, he'd have to depend on his secondary computers.

Why, he started wondering, would a hacker decide to use a virus to erase something as remote as a file of Eastern European secret police? Then he remembered that they didn't need a logical reason.

No, that was too pat, he reminded himself. Perhaps it hadn't been a hacker. Perhaps it was somebody who wanted those specific files destroyed. But why?

He glanced at the clock on the wall. He was due in the war room in ten minutes. He lifted the phone. "Something's come up. I'll be late," he told Brognola.

The big Fed grunted his consent reluctantly.

Bear replaced the receiver and began to formulate some guesses in his head. He ran his fingers across the keyboard, searching the backup system for copies of the erased files, which immediately popped up on the screen. Leaning back, he studied them. There wasn't much information in them about the secret groups inside the Eastern European police organizations.

He wasn't sure what he was supposed to find. "What or who am I looking for?" he asked out loud. He thought of the Frenchwoman. Was she really French?

He started typing her description into the computer, then pressed the keys that would start the system on a global search of all the files. Even with the speed of his supercomputer the search of the files would take a few minutes to complete. He wasn't sure what, if anything, he would find in them.

BROGNOLA PASSED copies of a two-page report to each Able Team warrior. "This is what we know about the computer hijacking."

Blancanales scanned his copy. "Not much," he commented. "It'll be like looking for a needle in a haystack."

"A loaded needle, pointed right at our country if the computer gets into the wrong hands," Brognola reminded him.

Gadgets looked around the room. "Where's Bear? Shouldn't he be here?"

"He said he'd be up in a few minutes." Brognola shook his head. "Give that man a computer and he forgets about everything else. I don't know how the Frenchwoman even got him casually interested unless she looked like a computer."

"If computers look like that, I might start getting interested in them myself," Pol commented.

Ironman stared at him coldly. "This whole conversation is starting to sound stupid," he snapped.

The head Fed turned to Lyons. "Something bugging you?"

"Yeah," the muscular ex-cop muttered. "Why are we sitting around and talking when we should be out there kicking ass."

Schwarz shrugged. "Whose ass?"

The two teammates glared at each other. Brognola studied their expressions and picked up his copy of the report. "Let's go over what we know, gentlemen," he said in a businesslike voice.

Reluctantly the Able Team commandos went back to reading their copies.

"A trailer truck containing one supercomputer was hijacked at an interstate oasis. No one saw the hijacking. Riding in the truck were the driver, a guard from the Federal Protective Service and two installation engineers. The older one, James Tomasello, has been with the manufacturer for seven years. No personal or financial problems unearthed by the FBI agents who checked him out. No personal or financial problems for any of the four men who were in the truck. Not even Steve Heitz, the summer intern at the company."

"How did Heitz pay for college?" Ironman asked.

"Part-time jobs. According to the people at the company, he was saving up his summer earnings to go back to the University of Wisconsin and start working on his master's degree."

"Sounds like a nice kid," Schwarz commented. "No close friends?"

"Not at the company, although everyone there liked him. His closest friend was his college roommate, Tad Silvern." Brognola glanced over the top of the page at the three men. "You know his father, General Silvern."

The three men nodded without comment.

"How about girls?" Ironman shook his head as Pol asked the question. "I mean," Blancanales added, "did he like girls?"

"No lead there, Pol," Brognola replied casually. "According to the agents who checked him out, he had started dating a girl from the University of Wisconsin." His eyes ran down the page and opened wider as he came across a comment. "Here's something. The girl he'd been dating had a foreign accent. One of the people who'd seen them together said he thought she was French."

Pol whistled. "Like the cutiepie in Washington. If it's her, she gets around."

Lyons leaned across the table and looked at Brognola. "The more we know, the more questions there are. What about the shoot-out at the restaurant? Coincidence? Or is it somehow tied in to this computer hijacking? And this French cutie at the restaurant. She might be the same one who was the missing kid's girlfriend. Were they partners in the hijacking? And who was the bearded creep with her at the restaurant?"

Pol remembered something. "Didn't Bear say he was supposed to meet the missing kid after the conference? Something to do with girl troubles?"

"Given what we were doing after lunch, I don't think Bear had time to worry about giving advice," Lyons replied.

Gadgets threw up his hands. "It's starting to sound like what we need to do is forget the facts and find the girl."

NOTHING. There were long lists of members of the various secret-police groups, but no descriptions. At least none he could use. Bear was frustrated.

He was sure she was on one of those lists. But on which one? Out of the corner of his eye he saw the envelope Brognola had given him—the six diskettes from the Russian contact. As Kurtzman popped the first of them into the disk drive, he wondered if they were filled with false information. The Russians were famous for doing that. He smiled. So was the CIA, he reminded himself. Birds of a feather, he decided.

He typed, and words appeared on the screen. Bear studied them. The six diskettes contained records and descriptions of the various secret-police groups in Eastern Europe, broken down by countries. Poland. Hungary. Bulgaria. Germany. Romania. Yugoslavia. Kurtzman wondered if they were duplicates of the records he already had.

He typed in a description of the Frenchwoman, then waited for the computer to process the information. The computer searched through the diskette without finding anyone who looked like her.

Kurtzman tried a second diskette with the same results. And a third and fourth. Either it was a coincidence that she was at both the conference and the restaurant, or she had managed to avoid having her name on a list of secret agents.

He popped the fifth diskette into the disk drive and typed in a command. Leaning back in his wheelchair, he turned his head away while the computer did its searching. Then, suddenly, he heard the printer clicking away. He turned and studied the monitor. There she was—the Frenchwoman.

THEY'D BEEN EXPLORING ways to handle the mission, and now it was Lyons's turn. "How about sending out bulletins to the various police agencies with descriptions of the girl and the kid who's missing? Maybe they'll have something on one of them."

"I'd like to keep it in the family until we run out of options," Brognola suggested. He was about to continue when the door to the war room was shoved open and Bear raced in. He was holding several sheets of computer paper.

Brognola glanced at him. "You could get a speeding ticket moving that fast. What have you got that can't wait?"

"The girl." He waved the papers in the air. "If you guys think she's something else physically, wait till you read her file!"

12

The three hell-raisers studied the digitized pictures of the woman they'd seen at the conference.

"It looks like the same girl," Pol commented. "Except this one's hair is mousy-brown."

"Women dye their hair," Gadgets said, grinning. He looked at Pol's silver hair. "You should think about it."

Pol smiled enigmatically. "Why? It's my best feature."

Ironman looked up at Kurtzman. "Who does she work for?"

"Really bad dudes."

Gadgets studied the computer genius's smug expression and groaned. He turned to Brognola. "I've got to talk to you about not letting Bear spend another summer with college kids."

Kurtzman repeated the phrase. "Really bad dudes, like in sick creeps. Is that clearer?"

Schwarz grinned. "Now you're speaking my language. What have they done—I mean, aside from what happened at the restaurant?"

Kurtzman glanced down at one of the computer printouts. "The question is, what haven't they done? Ever hear of the *Securitate*?"

"Sounds like some foreign secret-police group," Pol commented.

"The man wins the brass ring," Bear replied. "Romanian secret police. Her real name is Elena Demenescu, and she works directly for a man named Michael Vlad. Sometimes he calls himself Michael Demenescu. He's the head of a super-secret psycho squad."

Pol looked up from the pictures. "Same last name. She his daughter?"

"Adopted daughter. And, according to this report, Demenescu's lover."

"Sounds sick," Gadgets commented.

"Sicker than you think. Most of the Draculs are orphans like the woman. Demenescu raided a bunch of state orphanages for the brightest and most violent kids they had, adopted them and trained them to be loyal to him. The woman was the best of his students."

"Is she supposed to know something about computers?"

"Not enough to run something as complex as the supercomputer. No, she'd need a pro to do that."

Lyons got interested. "Like you."

Kurtzman nodded.

Ironman pushed on. "Or like this kid Steve Heitz and his boss?"

A sad expression crossed Kurtzman's face. "Yes," he replied.

Lyons seemed bothered. "Why the hell would someone like her need a computer?"

"I can think of a lot of reasons," Kurtzman replied. "Sell it to some foreign government that isn't on our friendly list. Fix up tax returns for people. Steal government secrets. Rob banks."

Pol jumped in. "I can see the others. But how do you rob banks with a computer?"

"Not that hard if you know what you're doing. Banks do their business by computer. Transferring money, moving funds from one account to another. Transactions like that."

"It would be too easy to trace," Blancanales commented.

"Sometimes. Some banks would rather swallow the loss than admit they have a less-than-perfect security system in their computers."

"I'm starting to get an uneasy feeling in my stomach," Lyons announced to the others. He focused on Bear. "What else can she do?"

"With the computer that's been hijacked she could penetrate government computers and steal secrets," Kurtzman commented.

"You mean like the ones the military has?"

"And the intelligence agencies," Bear said calmly. "It's been done before. For every spy we catch doing it I suspect there are three who haven't been detected." He looked at Ironman. "Would you like some more examples?"

"I get the picture." He turned to Brognola. "This dame is more dangerous than a hundred armed terrorists."

"Which is what I was talking about at the conference if you'd been listening," Kurtzman commented.

Ironman turned and glared at him.

"There is a bright side," Bear added.

"Yeah?" Lyons showed his skepticism. "What?"

"I don't think that either Steve Heitz or the other man with him have any experience in breaking through the security codes of most of the government agencies. And I don't think Steve would willingly help anyone betray our country. She'd have to find someone who knows how to do it and make him so dependent on her that he'll do anything she wants."

Gadgets displayed a slight smile. "You make her sound like a vampire."

Kurtzman tapped the printouts. "According to these, she is, in a way."

The others in the room looked surprised.

"You better explain that," Brognola growled.

"The group she worked for in Romania is called the Draculs. They were named after a fifteenth-century Romanian, Vlad Tepes or Dracula, who's sort of a legend back there."

"Didn't you say the head of this psycho group was named Michael Vlad?" Pol asked. "Any relation?"

"Supposedly Vlad Dracula's descendant."

Gadgets joined in. "Vlad Dracula any relation to Count Dracula?"

"You got it. The character, Count Dracula, was based on some of the gory actions of the original."

Pol looked skeptical. "He wasn't really a vampire, was he?"

"Probably not. But he was nicknamed the Impaler. He liked sticking his enemies on spikes and draining their blood. Must have seemed to the peasants in Translyvania where he lived that he was planning on drinking it." Bear leaned back in his chair and became a college instructor. "Dracul actually comes from the word for dragon in Latin, but the Romanian peasants applied it to—"

"We don't have time for a lecture on Romanian history," Brognola snapped.

Bear nodded.

"I wonder why this Vlad wasn't at the restaurant," Gadgets said. "You'd think someone like him would want to keep an eye on things."

"Maybe he hasn't gotten his visa to come here yet," Pol cracked.

"This is no time for jokes," Brognola snapped. He became quiet suddenly. "But you've given me an idea. I'll ask Interpol to check the foreign police organizations and see if this character is still abroad."

"Maybe he's still in Romania, hiding out," Lyons suggested.

"I sincerely doubt it," Pol replied. "I bet the new Romanian government would like to get their hands on all the creeps who used to work for the secret police."

"According to CIA reports, more than half of them have been rehired by the Romanians," Bear announced.

The three commandos looked stunned.

"You're kidding," Blancanales finally said in disgust.

"Hold your horses, Pol," Brognola interjected. "There are no secret police anymore according to our snoops. But when all the key jobs like data processing and high-tech communications have been run by branches of the secret police for more than thirty years, and no one else in the country is trained to do them, it's either hire them back or do without for a long time."

"If it was up to me, I'd make them use adding machines and semaphore flags," Lyons commented. He looked as if he was fed up. "What's the point of getting rid of the slave masters if you've got to go and hire back their stooges?"

"It's not up to you, or up to our government. It was their choice," Brognola growled. "Just remember, they didn't rehire any of the Draculs." He turned to Kurtzman. "Any clues on those diskettes I gave you why they're in this country?"

Bear studied the printouts. "For one thing they're on the most-wanted list in their own country for everything from stealing government funds to wholesale massacres.''

Ironman, Pol and Gadgets looked at one another. The wholesale butchery at the restaurant near Fort Meade was still fresh in their minds.

Pol still looked puzzled. "But why our country? Don't we have enough creeps here without them?''

Gadgets smiled bitterly. "Haven't you heard? We're still the land of opportunity, even for creeps.''

Lyons looked at his two partners. "It doesn't matter why they're here. What we need is to find out where they are, then make sure they aren't there or anyplace else ever again.''

Gadgets shook his head. "Where do we start?''

"Let's go talk to the people at the computer company,'' Pol said. "They may have some suggestions.''

"Agreed,'' Brognola seconded.

Kurtzman jumped in. "Then we can talk to Tad Silvern.'' The others turned and looked at him. "Find Steve Heitz and you might find out where she is. Steve and Tad were roommates since they started college.''

"Good thinking,'' Ironman agreed. He gestured to Gadgets and Pol. "Let's get our gear together and get going.''

"It should only take me fifteen minutes to pack,'' Bear said enthusiastically.

The three commandos turned and stared at him.

Pol spoke for all three. "Hey, Bear, you're the brains. We're the muscle.''

Kurtzman started wheeling toward them. "It's about time you muscle types had some brains along to help you.''

Gadgets groaned and looked at Brognola. "You talk to him, Chief.''

Bear turned and locked eyes with the big Fed.

"Your arm okay enough for you to travel?"

Kurtzman nodded.

Brognola turned to the others. "Since he knows computers, having Kurtzman along might be helpful."

"We're not baby-sitters," Lyons complained. "He can't get around without help."

"He's got that fancy cart Gadgets and Cowboy put together. Take it along," the man from Justice suggested.

"Baby-sitters?" Bear looked offended. "Who was it who saved your ass from those creeps near Fort Meade?"

Lyons glared at him. "Saved *my* ass? If I hadn't dropped the third punk, you'd be—"

"Hold it!" Lyons and Kurtzman stopped and turned to Brognola, who waved his cigar at them. "Let's save the anger for the bad guys. Bear goes with you, at least to Wisconsin." He turned to the telephone in front of him. "I'll notify Grimaldi to get the plane ready."

Kurtzman raced ahead of the three warriors before the big Fed could lift the telephone. He stopped and turned back to the others. "See you at the plane. We can talk about how we should handle the situation while we're flying." Then he remembered something. "I better stop and see Cowboy and get him to pick out some guns for me."

He disappeared into the corridor before the others could comment. Gadgets turned to Brognola. "Chief, are you serious about our taking..."

Brognola stared back at him. Schwarz could see nothing but hardness in his eyes. "Not another word about Kurtzman. Deal with it."

"I'M GOING to work for my uncle," Elena said. "I'm sure he would offer you a job, too."

Silvern was surprised at the news. "Doing what?"

"He needs someone to manage a computer center. When he sees what you can do, I know he'll be impressed." They were in bed and she moved closer to Silvern.

"I thought he was retired."

"He was." She leaned over and kissed him lightly on the lips. "Now he's starting his own business."

Silvern sensed something that didn't feel right. "Doing what?"

"I'll let him tell you. You'll love it."

The student looked uncertain. "I want to get my master's degree more than anything in the world."

"We would be together," she reminded him. "Working side by side."

"I'd have to know a lot more about what kind of business he's starting before I'd even consider an offer."

"The latest mainframe computer. State-of-the-art equipment. And you'd have freedom to do what you want most of the time. And power. You'd be one of the most important members of the organization."

She studied his expression. It was obvious she couldn't charm him into leaving with her. She jumped from the bed and started pulling clothes on over her naked body. She had prepared for that possibility. The four men who had flown here with her were downstairs, waiting in the car. Unlike the three who had panicked at Fort Meade, they were used to operating in the States.

Elena had made them wear casual clothes, the kind of clothes that wouldn't look out of place on a campus like this. Each of them was armed and ready to fight if the student resisted and called the police for assistance. Their compact automatic weapons were hidden inside the attaché cases each carried. She was certain they wouldn't be needed, but it was wiser to be cautious.

Now that seduction had failed she fell back on her last verbal weapon before summoning the men from the car. Smiling, she told him about planting the virus and time-control program while he had been unconscious.

Silvern looked shocked. "You did what?"

She repeated what she'd said.

He still couldn't fathom the words. He stared at her, then managed to ask, "Why?"

She felt no need to tell him of her private agenda; not even Michael Vlad knew that. She would have been dead long ago if he knew what she had in mind.

"The why is unimportant. What is important is that you understand that it was done from your computer right here in your apartment."

His mouth fell open. "They'll think I had something to do with it."

She shook her head. "No, they'll think you did it."

"You could tell them the truth."

She thought about it and smiled. "I suppose I could. But why should I? And would they believe me? After all, you're the computer expert, not me."

"You know they'll find the virus and the time-control command," he warned.

"Perhaps. But you can always plant another."

He looked around his tiny living room. She could almost read his mind. To the young student the world he knew had just collapsed. Yesterday he had been a graduate student with a promising career. Now he was a criminal facing a prison term.

She reminded him that his father had been a hero. "How will he feel knowing his son might be a traitor?"

Silvern turned to the Frenchwoman. "This supercomputer you say you have, did Steve Heitz help you steal it?"

"Yes," she lied.

"So he's in it with you."

She nodded pleasantly. "And soon you two will be together again."

The phone rang and interrupted her. He stared at it.

"Answer it," she ordered.

He heard the familiar voice—Aaron Kurtzman's.

"Tad, Aaron," the voice said. "I'm up at the computer plant in Chippewa Falls. I'll be on my way to Madison with a couple of friends in a few hours. I want to talk to you while I'm there, so don't make any plans for this afternoon or evening."

Nervously Silvern mumbled, "I'll be here." He hung up the phone. "Aaron Kurtzman is on his way to talk to me. He's bringing some people with him."

She could sense his confusion. She needed to play on his fears.

"They're coming to arrest you," she said icily. "Prison's a terrible place for a young man to spend his life."

She made a decision. She'd let her four henchmen eliminate the possibility of Kurtzman and his associates following them.

Michael would be pleased with her resourcefulness when she told him. It was important that he realize how well she was carrying out his plans, especially since he was planning to arrive so soon.

Studying the young man's sad expression, she was satisfied that he realized he had no choice but to go with her.

"Okay," he said angrily. "I'll leave with you." His voice got louder. "But I'm warning you. I'm not selling out my country. Not even if it means I'll get killed."

"I understand," the woman assured him. "I suggest we leave before your friend arrives." She watched the student pack a small bag. "Take everything you need," she warned. "You're not going to be able to come back here."

She followed him into the bathroom. He grabbed his razor, and toothbrush, then opened the medicine cabinet and started to take out a vial. He changed his mind and closed the door.

So the young man was no better than other American students, she thought. He took drugs when she wasn't with him. She could provide anything he needed as long as he did what she wanted.

They walked back into the living room. While Silvern looked around, she thought about the message Michael had left. She wished he hadn't made the decision to come over so soon. She only needed a little longer. Then it wouldn't matter when he came. She'd be ready for him.

13

Kurtzman was the first in the Able Team contingent to understand the implications of what Dr. Harold Glover, the white-coated senior scientist for the computer manufacturer, was saying about the equipment that had been stolen. Sitting in the surrealistic surroundings of a windowless "clean" room where air and humidity were electronically controlled, Gadgets, Pol and Ironman felt as if they had temporarily entered the twenty-first century.

Bear responded immediately with a question. "How state-of-the-art was it?"

"The first of a new generation of supercomputers," Glover said. "There's nothing like it anyplace. In fact, we didn't think we'd achieve that many technical breakthroughs for another ten years."

Gadgets asked the next question. "How much better is it than what's in Washington now?"

"It's at least thirty percent faster and more powerful."

"Is there a possibility the thieves have sold the computer abroad?" Gadgets asked.

"There always is," the balding man in the white coat admitted. "But with the Cold War winding down, the obvious customers aren't as interested as they might have been several years ago."

The Able Team group understood that the computer engineer was referring to the dissolution of the Soviet

Union and its Eastern Bloc satellites. Then Pol raised a question. "How about China?"

"Perhaps, although they seem to be having enough problems internally to keep them busy," the scientist replied. "Also I'm not sure they have the kind of reliable energy it takes to keep one of these units functioning properly."

Lyons had been leaning back in his chair, bored by the technical discussions. Suddenly he sat up. "What other special things does your computer need to function?"

"Just a reliable source of electricity." Glover paused for a moment. "Of course, most of our customers link our computers by telephone so they can move information from one unit to another as needed."

Lyons pursued the point. "So, if the thieves decided to use the computer themselves, they'd need a steady flow of electricity."

"Yes," Glover agreed.

"And," Lyons added, "telephone lines."

Kurtzman looked at him. "What's the point?"

"We check with the utility companies and find out if anybody's ordered extra electricity and telephone lines since the hijacking."

Pol laughed. "I wonder how many orders there have been."

"Thousands probably," Kurtzman commented. He turned to Ironman. "The point you made is valid, if they're hiding out in the boonies. But what if they've taken over a factory and set it up there?"

"Then we're back to zero," Ironman growled.

"No, Tad Silvern may know something," Bear reminded him. "So let's go see him and find out before we bang our heads against a wall."

AFTER THE YOUNG MAN and woman had gotten into a taxi and left for the airport, two of the four men she'd left behind had moved into the student's apartment to await the expected visitors. The other two waited in the car parked at the curb.

They checked the apartment carefully, searching for hidden microphones. Failing to find any, they took off their jackets and went into the kitchen to prepare a pot of coffee. The Americans weren't going to arrive for many hours, and they needed to be wide awake when they did come.

"One thing these Americans have is good coffee," the first, a short, stout man in his mid-twenties, commented as the pot began to percolate. "I wonder if there's anything to eat." He went to the refrigerator and opened it.

The other Romanian hardguy, a tall man with pimples, complained, "Pauli, you haven't stopped eating since we came to America."

The short man found a package of ham, took it out and shoved several slices into his mouth.

"Disgusting," the tall man commented.

Swallowing, Pauli belched and grinned. "We haven't had food this good in Romania for years, Peter. Living in that slum apartment in Beirut almost killed me. I thought Michael had forgotten I existed until I got his cable to call."

Peter nodded. "Baghdad was no better. What greedy animals. The money I was given almost ran out. I was thinking of contacting their foreign ministry and trying to hire myself out as an independent when the cable came." He picked up a slice of ham the other had set on the counter. Then they heard three beeps from a horn outside. Shoving the ham into his mouth, he rushed into the living room, followed by the short, stout man.

It was the signal they had arranged. One of the men outside was supposed to let them know when the government people arrived.

They looked out the window. A van had pulled up to the curb. Three men wearing light jackets assisted a fourth man in a wheelchair out of the vehicle. They gathered in a circle on the sidewalk near their van and talked to one another.

"Let's get ready," the acne-faced man said. The two men grabbed their attaché cases and opened them. Reaching inside, they took out the mini-Uzis.

"YOU AND POL wait here," Lyons told the computer wizard, "while Gadgets and I bring the kid downstairs." He looked at the small apartment building. "I don't think there's an elevator, so we'll pick up the kid and go someplace and talk."

Pol was about to protest, but a hard look from Ironman stopped him. Gadgets looked around. "There's got to be a Students' Union somewhere on the campus, or some similar place where students meet and talk."

Kurtzman looked around to get his bearings. "Unless some hothead group burned it down since I was here last, it should be over that way." He pointed to his left. "On University Avenue, right across from the historical library."

"Sounds like you've been here before," Gadgets commented.

"I've given a talk or two here in the past," Bear replied, looking around.

"Let's get to it," Lyons said grimly.

Pol looked at Ironman and Gadgets. "Stay hard," he said quietly.

Lyons nodded. "You, too, homeboy."

As the plane headed west, Elena glanced at the tall, skinny student who divided his time between wiping his eyeglasses and staring out the window at the ground below. The terror showed in the frozen expression on his face.

She had seen the same look on many men. Men weren't equipped to acknowledge fear as comfortably as women, not even Michael, who pretended to be in control of his emotions.

She got up, walked to the front and slid into the seat next to the pilot. "How soon will we arrive?"

He turned and smiled at her. "Between ninety minutes and two hours, depending on head winds."

"Good."

The pilot turned away. She knew he was forcing himself not to stare at her. She was used to men having difficulty not staring at her. She could see the lust in their eyes. It amused her that none of them could allow themselves to admit they wanted her.

She thought of Michael. He had been different. From the time she was sixteen he'd made it clear that she belonged to him. She remembered how he would lend her to important government officials for a night or two. To gain their support for the activities of the Draculs, he would tell her.

In the beginning she was frightened of him and obeyed him out of fear. Then, as her self-confidence grew with the completion of each successful mission, she had become aware of how obsolete he was becoming. A dinosaur in his own way. Soon it wouldn't matter.

Early in her training she had been exposed to the philosophy of Friedrich Nietzsche and his claim that "what doesn't kill me makes me stronger." She had faced dying many times, and survived. And Nietzsche was right. She had become stronger each time. Now the moment was coming when she would have to give Nietzsche's philosophy the final test—with Michael.

But for now she needed him. Even hiding in Paris, wallowing in the opium that had replaced her as his mistress, Michael still had the loyalties of the others. She knew she could lead them only as long as they believed she was carrying out his orders.

Like Michael, Tad Silvern was useful for now. Until she became more familiar with the programming language these new computers used, Silvern would be her translator, telling the machine what she wanted done. She had one idea that she wanted tested immediately. If it worked, the time for Michael's replacement to be named might be sooner than she'd dared to imagine.

Elena pulled out of her private thoughts when the pilot asked a question. "Will you need me the rest of the week?"

She turned to him. "I'm not sure. Why?"

He shrugged. "Someone called before we left and asked if I was available for a trip over the weekend."

She wanted him available whenever she needed to travel. "Turn it down."

He nodded. Her people were paying him enough to reject other clients.

She got up and returned to her seat. Silvern was still staring out the window. "We'll be there soon," she said.

Still focusing on the ground below him, the young student muttered, "It doesn't matter."

She patted his hand. "But it does matter. There is something we need to work on right after we land."

She turned her back on him without explaining and curled up in her seat.

Silvern turned and looked at the young woman next to him. She seemed to be asleep. There was a smile on her face. She hadn't told him what she wanted him to do, but he was sure it was criminal.

How could someone so beautiful be so evil? he wondered.

14

As Lyons and Schwarz climbed the stairs, they kept their hands near their holstered weapons. When they reached Silvern's door, Ironman wrapped his hand around his Python, quickly checking that it was fully loaded, while Schwarz did the same with his Colt Government Model .45. Then Lyons moved to the left of the door and waited until Schwarz did the same on the opposite side of the wooden frame.

"Ready?" Ironman whispered.

Gadgets nodded. He had slipped into a two-handed stance.

Lyons rapped on the door. "Tad!" he shouted. "Tad Silvern?"

The waited for a reply but there was none.

Ironman was positive somebody was inside. Maybe it was the college kid. If it was him, why hadn't he answered? There were several possible reasons. The most obvious was that he wasn't there. Or someone was inside, holding him captive. Or he was inside and dead. There was only one way to find out.

He studied the door. It was made of wood, as was the framing. Typical flimsy construction by developers more interested in profits than quality. Lyons was grateful to whoever had thought saving money was more important than the safety of tenants. He signaled to Gadgets. "On the count of three," he said quietly. "One, two, three!"

Ironman threw his right foot at the door, just below the knob. The two warriors followed up by hitting the wooden door with their shoulders. The shabbily installed panel splintered and tore free from the frame. As the wood fell back into the apartment, Ironman and Gadgets rolled into the room and were greeted by twin waves of searing lead.

Lyons twisted and rolled to the left. Bouncing to his feet, he fired at the dark shadow crouched behind the modern Swedish armchair. His first two shots destroyed the laminated light-blond frame of the three-cushion unit.

The short, stout man hiding behind it popped up and pointed his mini-Uzi at the rapidly moving figure. Before he could squeeze the trigger he saw two more burning flashes from the huge .357 muzzle. He tried to jump out of the way, but the slugs tore into his body, chopping their way into his kidney and liver with great ferocity.

Ironman jumped aside as the gunman fell. Gripping his Python with both hands, the Able Team trooper waited. Too many law-reinforcement friends had died unnecessarily, assuming their enemy was dead when he or she was only wounded and playing possum. Lyons saw the fallen assassin's attempt to push up, so he moved to one side and shouted, "Hold it!"

Concentrating whatever strength was left, the bleeding assassin jerked himself to his knees. The sudden burst of energy surprised Ironman. The Uzi cackled a short message of death. One of the slugs cut into Ironman's leg muscle and came out the other side.

As he fell, Lyons unleashed another shot from the Python. The lead cut through the fallen man's windpipe and esophagus and came out the back of his neck. Gasping sounds replaced words he was trying to shout. Lyons fired again, the last two rounds in his revolver. They destroyed what was left of the man's face. The shots were wasted. The would-be killer was dead.

Lyons dumped the empty shells in his weapon and popped in a speed-loader. His wounded leg refused to support him as he tried to get to his feet and lend Gadgets a hand.

Schwarz had rolled until he was flattened against the wall near the kitchen entrance. The familiar sound of Ironman's .357 and the screams of the wounded man told him he could concentrate on flushing out whoever was in the tiny kitchen.

He turned his head. There was a body lying in a pool of red gore on the floor near the window. Ironman was sitting on the couch. Gadgets looked at the blood leaking from his leg.

"Be right there," Lyons said, wincing from the pain of the wound.

"Call you if I need help," Gadgets replied. Ironman looked as if he needed immediate attention. Schwarz needed to find a sucker play as a lure as fast as possible.

He thought of rushing the kitchen, but common sense told him that would be suicide. He looked around. There was a small desk topped by an expensive computer. On the wall he could see a small frame print, which he could throw, but he didn't dare risk standing. Then he spotted a box of floppy computer diskettes on the desk.

He had an idea. Grabbing the box, he opened it and took out the flexible diskettes. He read the labels. They contained research that General Silvern's son was doing for his master's.

Schwarz hoped the kid was smart enough to make backup copies. Leaning closer to the kitchen doorway, he flipped the diskettes inside like Frisbees. A steady stream of fire chopped into the wall where they landed. Gadgets jumped to his feet and threw himself into the kitchen.

The tall hit man who had been hiding inside was blasting the far wall with a steady stream of searing metal. Gadgets spread his legs and fired a 3-shot burst into the gunman's chest.

A slow, steady trickle of red stained the front of the gunman's shirt. Stunned, the goon turned and faced Schwarz. His face was frozen in shock at the unexpected assault. He tried to turn his weapon on Gadgets, but the Able Team commando ended the movement with a second burst of fire that ripped apart the guy's stomach. The bushwacker hit the floor, lifeless.

Gadgets kicked the mini-Uzi out of the room, then rushed back to the living room. Ironman was sitting on the couch, holding his left leg up. Blood was flowing from a hole in the back of the sinewy muscle and dripping down the leg of his tan slacks.

"You posing for a Bleeding Musclehead of the Month centerfold?" Gadgets cracked.

Lyons tried to smile. "I guess I'll have to postpone giving dancing lessons for a while."

The only times Schwarz had heard Ironman make jokes was when he was hurting and pretending he wasn't. "We better get you to the hospital."

Lyons shook his head. "Later. There may be more of them outside. Got something I can use as a tourniquet?"

Gadgets searched the apartment and came back from the bedroom with a necktie. He formed a slipknot and pulled the makeshift tourniquet tightly above the wound.

Ironman looked down at the now-bloody necktie. "If you were going to force me to wear a tie, couldn't you have picked something I like?"

Gadgets grinned. "Sorry. I searched all over for something that would be more to your liking, but the kid who lived here obviously doesn't believe in wearing ugly clothes."

STARTLED BY THE SERIES of explosions from inside, Pol yanked out his Desert Eagle and rushed toward the building's entrance. Bear followed him in his wheelchair, the modified Glock in hand.

A city workman fixing a drain dropped his pliers, dove for his tool kit and pulled out an Uzi machine pistol. Blancanales spotted the movement out of the corner of his eye and spun to face the unexpected threat. Firing as he brought his weapon around, Pol perforated the gunman's chest with a triple salvo. The workman tumbled forward, firing his Uzi into a clump of bushes.

From inside a parked car a second gunman shoved a Skorpion through the window and squeezed the trigger. Pol, sensing the danger behind him, threw himself into a thicket of shrubs while bullets punched into the wooden front door.

Kurtzman spun his wheelchair around, steadied his weapon with both hands and let loose a 3-shot burst at the car. The gunman dropped out of sight as hot metal slammed into the vehicle. Pol rolled out of the bushes, his face bleeding from a dozen scratches, and sat up, Desert Eagle in hand. He waited patiently.

The muzzle of the Skorpion poked over the edge of the open window. Pol kept perfectly still. A pair of eyes peered cautiously over the edge of the door. Blancanales had waited for this moment. Sighting carefully, he squeezed off a pair of shots at the barely visible gunman's forehead.

His shots were echoed by another pair of shots. He glanced quickly to his right. Bear held his weapon in both hands and was unleasing another 3-shot round at the hidden gunman.

The top of the head vanished again. Pol waited. So did Bear.

"Throw the gun out!" Blancanales shouted. There was no response. "Maybe you'd rather eat lead," he shouted again. Still no reply.

Cautiously Pol moved toward the car, his gun ready to anticipate any movement from inside the parked car. He paused, then moved closer.

Kurtzman began to roll his chair slowly toward the car with one hand, his other hand gripping the Glock. The baptism under fire back East had given Bear new courage.

He looked at Pol for instructions. The Hispanic commando gestured for him to move closer, which he did.

Without waiting for Kurtzman to join him, Blancanales suddenly rushed to the car and jammed his Desert Eagle inside. The gunman was slumped on the floor, a pair of large holes in his forehead.

Blancanales reached inside and gently removed the Skorpion from the hands of the dead hit man. Turning, he saw that Kurtzman was near the fallen assassin who had been disguised as a workman. The computer expert held the dead gunman's Uzi aloft.

Then the front door opened and Gadgets came out, supporting Ironman. Pol stared at the wounded Able Team warrior. "How bad?"

"I'll live," Lyons said, then howled as his wound accidentally scraped against a protruding bush. Schwarz helped him into the van.

"We better make a pit stop at the nearest hospital," Gadgets told Pol.

"After we call Stony Man," Lyons insisted.

They heard the sounds of police sirens coming closer.

"Here we go again," Blancanales announced as two black-and-whites came into view.

"Brognola's going to love getting this call," Gadgets commented. The other two glumly nodded in agreement. It meant another lecture when they got back to headquarters.

Kurtzman kept staring up at the second-floor apartment windows. "What about Tad? Was he..."

Lyons turned and looked at him. "He wasn't there. Only two characters who decided they didn't like our looks even before they saw us."

"Where could he be?" Bear asked.

"I don't know," Schwarz replied. "But I have a feeling that we'll find the missing computer in the same place."

The two police cars pulled up to the curb. Four uniformed offices jumped out, weapons drawn.

A tough, beefy sergeant shoved a Smith & Wesson .38 at the four men. "Get your hands over your heads!" he yelled as the other officers surrounded the Able Team group.

As their hands were being cuffed behind their backs, Pol shook his head. "How come I think I've seen this play before?"

15

Hal Brognola studied the report that Jordan Wilkens, a Treasury Department official, had handed him. There were only two men in the Oval Office with him—the tall, gray-haired man to whom he reported directly, and the worried-looking Treasury official.

Absentmindedly the Able Team chief reached into his jacket and took out a cigar. He rammed it into his mouth, then heard a discreet cough. The Treasury man stared at the brown cylinder Brognola was chewing.

"It's all right, Wilkens. Brognola can't think without one of those things stuck in his face," the man behind the large desk said, smiling.

The big Fed shook his head as he scanned the pages. He looked up at the Treasury man. "When did this happen?"

"Two hours ago. The FBI contacted us as soon as they got the call."

The report was brief. A message had been sent to the International Industrial Bank of Chicago's main computer earlier that afternoon, threatening to destroy all of their records if a ransom of one million dollars wasn't paid within forty-eight hours.

"They thought it was some hacker having a field day, cashing in on the publicity about the murder of their head of international banking," the Treasury representative said, referring to the killing of Clarence Matterly. "At least they did until a major client's entire file began to vanish. That's when they called the FBI."

The Stony Man chief addressed his question to Wilkens. "Why didn't they just cut off the phone lines? No outsider can get into a computer system if there's no phone access."

"It's not that simple. Banks need to communicate with one another and the Federal Reserve Bank on a continuous basis. The only way they can stay on top of the constant flow of numbers and information is through their computers. Without them they would sink under the deluge of information they need to process."

"Sounds like a law-enforcement problem. How did Treasury get involved?"

"As a federally chartered bank, their deposits are insured by one of our agencies." Wilkens smiled in relief. "Only up to one hundred thousand dollars for each depositor. But if whoever planted the threat means it, the bank has forty thousand depositors. The government's bill could run as high as a hundred million dollars." The Treasury man turned to the President. "The bank has asked if we think they should pay the ransom."

Shrugging, the President turned to Brognola. "What do you think, Hal?"

The big Fed looked disgusted. "You know how I feel about blackmailers, but that decision's up to you."

The man behind the desk turned his chair around and stared at the wall behind him. He glanced around the room at the portraits of some of the country's greatest leaders. It was as if he were asking them to help him with his decision.

Brognola looked at the President. "How can we help?"

"Computer experts at the FBI and Treasury think that whoever's behind this was using a supercomputer." He turned to the third man in the room. "Is that right, Wilkens?" The Treasury man nodded. The President turned to Brognola. "It might be the same one your people are currently looking for. Any word from them?"

The Justice man looked uncomfortable. Staring at him, the President suddenly understood why. He turned back to the Treasury representative. "Tell the secretary I've got the best people working on it."

Wilkens nodded, then got up and walked out of the large office.

When they were alone, the President looked up at Brognola. "Have your people gotten any leads yet?"

"They were going to meet with someone who might be able to point them in the right direction, sir." He wondered why they hadn't called in after they'd gotten to Madison. He'd check with Stony Man as soon as he left the Oval Office. "I think the computer theft is tied in with that earlier situation we discussed."

The President looked at him, surprised. "You mean the tip from the Russians about foreign secret police slipping into the country?"

"Yes. Which brings up a serious question. Why would foreign secret-police agents sneaking into the United States need a supercomputer, except to sell it?"

"And nobody has reported anyone trying to smuggle a computer of that size out of the country. It's not like you can slip it inside a briefcase," the gray-haired man reminded Brognola.

"Something's going on that we better stop before it gets out of hand," the Stony Man chief commented.

"Maybe we should call in the rest of the intelligence community for a conference." He saw the disgusted look on Brognola's face.

"It's your decision, sir."

"You don't like it, do you, Hal?"

Brognola shook his head. Using his cigar like a baton, he waved it around as he replied. "I remember somebody describing a platypus as an animal that was designed by a conference of experts."

Despite his worried expression the President smiled. Before he could comment the door opened and his secretary entered. She looked at the Stony Man chief. "There's an urgent call for you from your office, Mr. Brognola."

The Able Team boss started to leave the room to take the call outside, but the President lifted the receiver of the phone on his desk and handed it to Brognola. "Take it in here."

Brognola chewed on his cigar. He was annoyed. What was so important that they had to interrupt a meeting here? "Brognola," he snapped.

The voice on the other end belonged to John "Cowboy" Kissinger, the Stony Man's armorer. He'd volunteered to be Kurtzman's replacement while Bear was out with the Able Team hell-raisers.

"Chief, our wayward kids got themselves busted again," Cowboy announced.

Brognola was about to mouth a string of curses, then he remembered where he was. "Where?"

"Madison, Wisconsin. Ironman has a small hole in his leg. Nothing that'll keep him from playing."

"Any other damage?"

"The other side got wiped out on a pair of sneak-play attempts. Anything you want me to do?"

"I'll take care of it," the Stony Man chief grumbled, and hung up.

The President looked at him. "Anything wrong, Hal?"

"We can talk about it later," Brognola apologized. "I don't think we need to shake up the other agencies until we get a better fix on what we're dealing with."

The President looked uncertain.

"Sometimes the more people who know about a crisis, the more chance everybody outside will also find out. Then you've got a panic on your hands," Brognola added.

There was a long pause, then came the question. "Hal, if they can get into a bank with that damn computer of theirs, what else can they get into?"

"From the little I know, with the right information, anything."

The President looked worried. "We don't need another computer scandal. After those young West Germans cut through our security as if it were cheese, people were wondering if we had any secrets left." He shook his head. "That includes me."

The President came out from behind his desk and put his hand on Brognola's shoulder. "I know you were upset when I said we had to cut back on expenditures, but I had to stop the rest of them from gunning you down behind your back." He smiled. "It would be akin to selling the country down the river to put your group out of business."

Brognola could feel the relief washing over him. He wondered if he should share the news with the others or wait until the mission was completed. He'd think about it later.

"I'll alert the men about what happened," Brognola promised.

"This bank situation can't reach the media. They'll have a field day with it. And the only thing that would hurt would be the public's confidence in their government. You've got to find the people who are behind this thing and put an end to their threats."

Brognola thought about the call from Stony Man. "I could use a small favor," he said quietly.

The President didn't seem to hear him. "Use anybody you need. If they give you a hard time, tell them to call me."

Brognola coughed. "About that small favor..."

"Oh, yes." The President suddenly remembered that his security expert had started to ask for something. "Exactly what was it you wanted?"

"Are you on speaking terms with the governor of Wisconsin?"

"We've had our differences, but, yes. Why?" He saw the sheepish grin on Brognola's face and groaned. "Not again!" Brognola nodded and the President shook his head in wonder. "Can you imagine if the FBI operated by Able Team's rules?" He thought about it. "The country might be in a lot better shape if they did. At least some of the time." He shook his head. "Consider it done," he told the big Fed. "Anything else you need from me right now?"

Brognola worded his question carefully. Deniability was a fact of political life. The President couldn't know exactly what Able Team would do, but Brognola wanted his input. "How far do you want us to go concerning the people involved?"

"You're the expert, Hal," the President commented warily.

Brognola nodded and stood up. He'd gotten his answer.

16

Dragnan was still sleeping. Elena slipped out of her king-size bed quietly. She didn't want him to wake up. As she put on her clothes, she thought back to the previous night.

The call about the death of the four men had come after they'd fallen asleep. As angry as she was at their incompetence, she was enough of a pragmatist to know she couldn't waste time brooding about it.

She had something more immediate to infuriate her. The night with the dwarf had been a disgusting blend of threats and passions. Making love to Michael had been bad enough; Dragnan was even worse. So many times she had been tempted to reach into her purse for the small Beretta and kill him. But the time wasn't right. Not yet.

She had almost shot him when the phone rang. It had been Michael calling for her report. Quickly she'd told him that everything was almost ready for the troops he was planning to send over.

Michael had sounded annoyed. "Almost ready?"

"There were many things that needed to be attended to," she said cautiously.

"And you've been spending all of your time taking care of them?"

She knew what he was asking. Had she found any new lovers? She glanced at the bed and stared at the sleeping dwarf. If Michael only knew.

"Yes." She changed the subject. "The residents of the nearby community love the name you've given our headquarters."

Michael chuckled. "It was a clever choice, wasn't it?"

She hesitated to bring up the issue of funds, but their bank account was getting low. "We'll need some additional funds to keep us going until we can start to receive fees," she said nervously.

Michael controlled the money hidden in Switzerland. It was all the power he had left, but it was enough. Without money the Draculs couldn't survive.

Michael exploded at the mention of money. "We can't keep draining the Swiss accounts," he warned. "Have you found a buyer for the computer yet?"

"Not yet, but we've made some contacts," she lied. She was tempted to warn him that the line he was using could easily be tapped, but Michael would only become more enraged if he felt she was accusing him of being negligent. "In the meantime we do need more funds. In America the only thing that matters is money."

She didn't have the money she needed to take over. If her small test actually worked, she would have enough soon. If it didn't, she would have to come up with another plan.

Still furious, Michael reluctantly agreed to have some additional funds transferred. "Now I wish to speak to Janos."

She glanced at the sleeping dwarf again. "He's in Phoenix checking on our people there," she said glibly.

"When he returns, have him call me," Michael ordered just before hanging up.

She had tried to go back to sleep, but all she could think about was how urgent it was that she get her own plans into operation before Michael arrived.

Now, four sleepless hours later, she checked herself in the full-length bedroom mirror. The T-shirt she'd selected was two sizes too small. She liked showing off her body.

Elena tucked into a pair of tight-fitting jeans, then reached down and pulled on a pair of elk cowboy boots. She looked in the mirror again and approved of what she saw.

She glanced at the bed. Dragnan was unconscious. She was grateful. She shuddered at the thought that the ugly beetle of a man might awaken and want to make love again. Opening the door, she quickly slipped into the corridor.

THE DISHEVELED BEAN POLE of a young man sat up suddenly on the small, sheetless cot that served as his bed. He had heard a noise that sounded like gunshots.

Was someone trying to kill him? He looked around. No, he was alone.

Tad Silvern stared at the narrow slit of thick glass near the ceiling of his concrete room. The sun was beginning to rise. It was morning.

Outside he could hear the sound of a truck. It stopped near his room. He placed the small wooden chair on his cot and carefully climbed up the makeshift ladder. Leaning one hand on the wall to balance himself, he tried to peer outside.

There was a truck outside. He couldn't see all of it. All he could make out was the lower half of one side and door. There were words painted on the door. He squinted through his glasses to make them out. Joshua Trash Collection Service.

Joshua? It was either the name of the trash collection company or the name of a town. He wasn't sure which.

He could see a pair of worn cowboy boots moving past the window. They looked too old to belong to the men who were living here. He tried banging his fist on the window. The boots turned and moved past him in the opposite direction.

Silvern stopped hitting the window. The glass was too thick for his hammering to be heard outside. Then he heard noises in the corridor. Quickly he jumped down from the chair and straightened up the small room.

He looked down at himself. His clothes were sweat-stained. He could hardly stand the stench that permeated them. No one had offered to let him take a shower or even wash. There was a small, nonfunctioning sink in the room, but no soap or towel. The small toilet worked sporadically.

This was his home now, at least until they killed him, if his illness didn't kill him first. He hadn't taken his medicine for five days. Last night he was sure the illness was coming back.

Silvern wondered if he'd had an attack in his sleep. He moved his tongue around his mouth. There were no cuts or bite marks inside. Whatever medicine he'd taken before the woman had brought him here was still protecting him.

He had meant to tell the woman about needing the medicine before they'd left Madison, then had decided not to. He knew why. He would rather die than betray his country.

He became cynical. Who was he kidding? He wasn't a hero. He was afraid to die. If the illness came back, he'd tell her so that she could get him the medication. He didn't want to die.

The rattling of a key in the lock of the thick metal door interrupted his thoughts. The door swung open.

It was the guard who had been watching him through a slit in the steel door. The broad, scar-faced man was expressionless as he spoke in a heavy accent. Silvern glanced down at the powerful-looking automatic rifle the man was carrying. "Come. You are wanted by Elena."

Unable to pull his eyes away from the weapon, Silvern dragged himself to his feet. "Why?"

"She will tell you when I bring you to her."

Silvern knew the woman would. He wondered what her next demands were going to be.

TONY SILVERN LOOKED UP from the papers on his desk as the door to his office opened. He knew the two burly men in the business suits who entered—Kurt Morgan and Stanley Demerest. They were with Internal Affairs.

He wasn't surprised they hadn't knocked. They never did. He smiled at them. "Social or business?"

Neither man returned his smile. Morgan closed the door and turned back to face the general. "Business, Tony," he said. "Potentially nasty business."

Silvern gestured to the chairs in front of his desk. "Sit down."

The two men did.

"What's going on?"

Demerest looked at the heavyset man with whom he'd arrived. "Maybe we should have this conversation someplace else."

Silvern looked puzzled. "Worried about eavesdropping?" He grinned. "Hardly the place a spy could get into and plant a bug."

Morgan took a spiral notebook out of his pocket and opened it. He fished out a pen, then stared at the general. "When was the last time you heard from your son, Tony?"

"Sometime last week. Why?"

The burly man ignored the question. "How often do you usually talk to him?"

"Once or twice a week." He wondered why they were asking about Tad. "Is something wrong?"

"Didn't you wonder when he didn't call you this week?" Morgan asked.

"No," Silvern admitted. "I figured his new girlfriend was keeping him too busy to call his old man." He grinned. "You know how horny these kids get."

"He's disappeared from the campus," Demerest said. "So has his girlfriend."

"Kids probably decided to go somewhere together so they could be alone."

The two visitors glanced at each other. Morgan leaned forward. "I don't think so, Tony."

Silvern was getting tired of fencing. He was used to facing problems head-on. "What's wrong with Tad?"

"We don't know," Demerest answered.

Silvern banged his fist on the desk in anger. "Then why the interrogation?"

"Calm down, Tony," Morgan said quietly. "Did you look at last week's 'super-users' access report?"

"I glanced at it."

"There was a ten-minute access that was unauthorized."

"So? Somebody forgot to get approval to use the computer files. It happens once in a while."

Demerest joined in. "The system operator put a trace on the call."

"That's standard procedure," the general reminded them.

Since the embarrassment of discovering that a West German hacker had been invading their computer system with little difficulty, Silvern had installed an automatic incoming-call recording device that could be activated instantly by whoever was the duty officer in charge of the computers at the time.

"The call was placed from Tad's telephone," Demerest said.

Silvern was stunned. "Why would Tad do something like that? He's not a spy."

"That's what we want to find out," Morgan replied. The two men stood. "If Tad calls you, find out where he is so we can reach him," Morgan added.

After the two men left, Tony Silvern sat back in his huge chair and stared at the large window in his office. Tad a spy? He refused to believe it. There had to be a mistake. But how could he prove it without Tad?

Silvern thought of somebody his son might have called. He picked up his private phone and dialed a number.

A male voice answered. "Who are you calling?"

"This is Anthony Silvern, NSA. Would you leave a message for Aaron Kurtzman to call me at my office or home?"

ELENA WAS WAITING for him in the computer center. The guard led him inside, then disappeared into the corridor.

She looked at the fatigue obvious in his face. "You must get more sleep."

"Check me into a decent hotel and you'll see how much sleep I get," he snapped.

She smiled. "Droll. You know that isn't possible yet."

He hated the way she always dangled a promise in everything she said. He was certain she was lying. He decided to ask another question. "Why can't I take a shower?"

"Oh, that. The plumbing isn't working properly."

He studied her. She looked immaculate. "You don't seem to be suffering."

"The plumbing that serves my room is finally fixed. Yours will be, too, very soon," she replied smoothly.

"Sure," Silvern said cynically. "And I'll get a week-end off soon."

She laughed. "You still have your wonderful American sense of humor." She beckoned him to the computer console. "But enough jokes. It's time to work."

Resigned, Silvern sat down in the swivel chair in front of the monitor. "Who do you want me to hack this time, Fort Knox?"

She looked puzzled. "What is Fort Knox?"

"It's where they keep our gold reserves."

She looked impressed. "Perhaps another time. For now I want you to see if the bank has left a message for us."

He hesitated. He could have explained to the authorities that he had been tricked into betraying his country. But now he was a bank robber, as well.

"We don't have a day to waste," she insisted angrily.

Silvern shrugged. He had no choice. The student tapped away at the keys that would connect him to the computers at the International Industrial Bank of Chicago.

He checked his notes for the proper password. Typing in the symbols, he waited for the computer on the other end of the telephone line to approve his access. Ten seconds later he had his approval. He could sense the woman standing close to his back, staring at the monitor over his shoulder.

"We're in," she whispered. Her voice quavered with excitement.

He could smell her perfume. Instead of lust, all it did was arouse fear in him. Now he smelled the scent of a savage lioness on the hunt.

"Yes, we're in," he agreed. "What next?"

"We told them to leave their reply to our demands in a file named 'ransom.' Find it."

He searched the list of files. They were alphabetical. Finally he spotted it. *Ransom.* "They won't pay the blackmail," he warned her.

"Let's see what they say," she ordered.

He entered the file. The message was brief. "We agree to your demands. Please tell us where and when to send the money."

She laughed loudly. "It worked. They didn't even ask if we would remove the virus."

He turned his chair around to face her. "So? Where do you want them to send the money?"

Still exhilarated by the surrender, Elena hugged the disheveled student. She sniffed him. "You do need a bath and some fresh clothes. You shall have both this afternoon."

"Thanks," he said coldly. "What about the money?"

"The money? I don't want their money."

Silvern was stunned. "You don't?"

"Why take a million when you can get fifty or a hundred times more for the same thing?"

"From the bank?"

"Of course not." Her lips formed into a tight smile. "From your government."

17

"Are you saying that Tad has sold out his country?" Tony Silvern was livid. He turned to Kurtzman. "You know Tad. Do you think he's capable of being a spy?"

Bear shook his head and looked around the general's suburban Virginia living room at the three Able Team hell-raisers. Pol and Gadgets were standing near the large bay window. Ironman was sitting, moving his wounded leg to keep it from stiffening. The trio kept staring coldly at the NSA official.

"It doesn't make a lot of sense," Kurtzman admitted.

"The traced telephone call came from his apartment," Lyons reminded the general.

"It could have been a mistake."

Gadgets joined in the questioning. "You helped develop the tracking device. Could it make that kind of mistake?"

"No," Silvern answered in a whisper. He thought of something. "When you searched his apartment, did you happen to find vials of medicine?"

The Able Team trio glanced at one another. Ironman reached into his pocket and took out a vial. "You mean this?"

Silvern took the vial and studied it. He shook his head, then smiled sadly. "Tad would never have left without this."

Lyons took the vial back and studied the label. "What is it?"

"Tad has a trauma syndrome," the general replied.

Pol looked puzzled. "What's that?"

"He's been an epileptic since he got hurt in a football game when he was ten. He's got to take this medicine, or he's subject to seizures."

Bear reached over and patted Silvern's arm. "We'll find him, Tony." He looked at the others and they nodded.

Silvern walked to his desk and picked up a silver-framed picture of his son. He handed it to the three warriors, then turned to Kurtzman. "He's not a traitor, Aaron," the general insisted.

"I know how you feel," Kurtzman said. His voice was filled with a mixture of sadness and understanding. "I think we'd like to borrow this picture."

The general nodded. "You know he's not a traitor," he repeated.

"The thing we don't know yet is where to look for him," Pol said quietly.

Lyons's voice was cold and hard. "But we'll find out, General. We promise you that."

THE GUARD FOUND him on the floor of his cell. He had come to deliver the sandwich and glass of milk that was the young man's lunch when he heard the strange noises from within and unlocked the door.

Tad Silvern was writhing on the floor, fighting with some invisible demon. For a moment the guard thought he was pretending to be sick.

He edged over to him and kicked him hard on the side. The young man on the floor was too busy with his violent struggles to respond. Then, suddenly, he stopped moving wildly and became still.

Keeping one hand on the automatic he wore in his waistband, the suspicious guard knelt down and listened to see if the fallen man was breathing. Silvern's breathing was irregular and shallow.

What to do? He knew Elena would blame him for being negligent. He'd try to explain, but it would be worse if the student on the floor died.

JINX MAYNARD SAT on the porch of the Lucky Dollar Café, his dusty boots stretched across the wooden railing, and stared at the wide street in front of him. Cars and trucks had begun to crowd the main street of Joshua. And it was only seven. Saturday morning was when all the ranchers came in to do their shopping.

It had been that way ever since Maynard could remember. And he had more than sixty years of remembering behind him. Of course it had been different when he was a little boy. Instead of motor vehicles crowding the streets, horses had pulled open wagons into town on Saturdays.

The lanky, grizzled man hated crowds. He had since he was a child. He'd take the high desert with an occasional sidewinder and a passing jackrabbit or two to keep him company any day.

It used to be acceptable to like to be alone. Nowadays folks thought you were peculiar if you didn't want to socialize. That was why he told people that when he wasn't driving the township's garbage truck he was searching for lost gold mines dug by Indian tribes who used to live in what was now called Pawnee County.

In fact, he did wander around the old Indian burial mounds up in the foothills, looking to see if there was a hidden entrance to some forgotten Indian mine. He hadn't found any yet, not that he really thought he would. What he was really looking for were Indian artifacts. Arrowheads. Bits of pottery. The tourists who came to Joshua paid well for the junk.

The Indian burial mounds were filled with such items. They were considered off-limits to white men. Even those Indians who still lived in the area thought of them as taboo. The state tried to protect them by occasionally sending around state troopers to arrest poachers. But after all these years he'd found lots of ways to get into the Indian grave site without being spotted.

He encouraged people to think of him as another hopeless prospector whose brain had been damaged by too much exposure to the hot Arizona sun. Truth was, if the Indians had really found gold, they would have used it to buy themselves guns and keep the settlers out.

Now when he got into the much-dented jeep he'd bought at a government surplus fifteen years ago, everyone who saw him drive in the direction of the high desert was positive he was off on one of this wild-goose chases, searching for lost gold mines.

Even if there weren't any Indian artifacts to be stolen, Maynard knew he'd still wander out to the high desert. He just plain didn't like most of the people who lived in and around Joshua. He could count the ones he cared about on one hand. Sheriff Matt Devlin was one. Maynard suspected he knew about the artifacts but didn't let on. That pretty dark-haired woman who helped run the new camp for refugees from Eastern Europe was another. She was like him, someone who didn't pry into other people's affairs and didn't like people prying into hers.

She had a funny name—Dessault. He wasn't sure where in Europe she'd come from, but it sounded French. If they all looked like her back there, he hoped a lot more of them would be coming over soon.

Maynard reluctantly lifted his aching bones from the chair. It was time to climb into Ol' Betsy, the name he'd given his jeep, and disappear into the high desert until the crowds went home.

He saw the two uniformed young men walking toward him. He knew them both. The tall one was Bill Proudfoot, a full-blooded Apache. The other was Frank Valdez, who was surprisingly Irish-looking for someone supposedly descended from Mexican stock on both sides. Both of them were Sheriff's deputies, two of the eighteen men who served under Matt Devlin. And, unlike Devlin or most of the other deputies, both were from around the area.

He remembered Proudfoot as a teenager. As arrogant an Apache as you would ever want to meet. Filled with hate for white men, he'd gotten into jam after jam. Right alongside was young Valdez, whose family worked as near slave labor on one of the nearby dude ranches, getting into bloody fistfights every time one of the other teenagers asked him if his mother knew the name of the Irishman who'd been his father.

Something had changed them over the years. They'd served in Vietnam at the very end of that conflict. Two angry eighteen-year-olds taking out their hostility on the North Vietnamese and Vietcong. Now both of them were married with kids. And both of them were respected lawmen.

Life never ceased to amaze Maynard. You never knew how things or people would turn out.

The two deputies waved to him and continued walking down the crowded streets. Maynard waved back and stood. Heading for the alley where he'd parked his jeep, he nodded to the men and women who recognized him. He knew he was considered a character in town, a throwback to the days of an Arizona that had never really existed. The mayor had given him a fancy certificate at a Kiwanis dinner a year ago, designating him "a local treasure." Maynard hadn't liked being singled out, but he had appreciated the free meal and the check for a hundred dollars that came with the fancy hand-drawn piece of paper.

In a way he was a local treasure. Most of the people who lived in Joshua had come from other places. Only a handful of real natives were left. In addition to the two deputies there was "Pawnee" Bill, the old Indian who ran the Indian relics shop. And Tom Wickersham, who published the weekly newspaper. Finally there was him. All of them had been born, raised and educated in and around town.

Even the sheriff was imported from another state. Devlin was born someplace back east and had been with a big-city police department before he'd gone off to Korea to fight.

Maynard hurried past the small brick building that housed the Pawnee County Sheriff's Department, the county jail and the Joshua Volunteer Fire Department. Even though he'd never been forced to spend a night in one of the small cells inside, Maynard felt uncomfortable being so close to them.

It wasn't as if he really did anything dishonest. The worst he'd done was to steal relics from the Indian burial grounds and sell them to Pawnee Bill. Sure, he told himself as he turned into the alley, technically it was against the law. But he didn't think any Indian ghosts would come around and file a complaint with the sheriff.

He checked the back seat of the jeep before he climbed in. The shovel, knapsack and pick were still there. That was what was so nice about living in Joshua. Nobody stole things.

He started the jeep. It coughed and complained but finally sputtered to life. Carefully he backed out into the traffic of Main Street.

He stared at the traffic jam up ahead. Then, out of the corner of his eye, he saw her—the pretty foreign girl. She was walking down the dusty sidewalk. The dwarf was with her. They were talking.

Maynard decided to say hello. "Miss Dessault."

Startled, she turned and saw him. A large smile covered her face. "Mr. Maynard," she murmured.

Maynard could swear that her smile was hotter than the midday Arizona sun. "How's it going back at your place?"

"Fine. We're expecting more people in a few days," she said.

If it wasn't for her accent, Maynard thought, she'd fit right into Joshua. Especially the way she was dressed—cowboy boots, jeans and a tight T-shirt. It was enough to make a man's blood bubble with excitement.

"Missed seeing you when I was out to pick up the garbage last week," he said.

"I had to be out of town for a few days," she replied.

"Yeah, I'll bet it takes a lot of work helping them poor folks get adjusted to our country."

She smiled at him. "Yes, a lot of work. We want to make sure they'll be happy and safe here."

The dwarf next to her tugged at her arm. Annoyed, she turned to him. "Yes, Janos?"

He pointed to the supermarket down the street. She nodded and turned to Maynard. "Janos is right. One of the people at Camp Freedom is ill. We need to get him some medicine." She looked worried. "The problem is that the doctor we helped escape hasn't had time to get an American license yet.''

"You just stop in and see Al Hill at the drugstore. If the old coot gives you a hard time, you tell him Jinx may forget to pick up his garbage for a week.''

She smiled gratefully, then turned and walked down the street. The dwarf glared at Maynard then turned away and moved quickly to catch up with the dark-haired woman.

Maynard moved his jeep into traffic. It was time to get out of town. He thought of heading for the burial mounds, but it was too damn hot. So he decided to head for the tall stands of fragrant pine twenty miles west of Joshua.

As he moved his jeep down Main Street, he saw the foreign woman and the dwarf disappear into Al Hill's store.

18

The police lieutenant recognized them when they walked into his office. "You two again?" He stared at Lyons and Blancanales.

"Good to see you again, Lieutenant," Pol replied, smiling.

"Last time you and your friends came for a visit you left us four bodies to deal with. What are you leaving us this time? Cancer?" He broke into laughter at his own joke.

Pol and Ironman remained expressionless. "We need information," Lyons said.

Lieutenant Michael Harrington suspected the two men and the other two who had been with them were CIA, but knew better than to ask. He'd never get a straight answer if they were. "I can show you our report."

"We've already seen it," Lyons said.

"That's all we got. We don't know who the dead men were or where they came from."

"What about the student?"

"Of course we checked him out," the Madison police official snapped. "Nothing there. You two know who is father is?"

"Yes," Pol answered. "General Silvern."

The lieutenant sounded annoyed. "He had his people come and do their own checking. They went over everything. His apartment. His friends. School records. Now you two show up asking the same questions."

Pol and Ironman exchanged glances. "Tell us about Tad Silvern's friends," Lyons said in a businesslike voice.

The police officer responded coldly. "According to some of the other students, his best friend at school is working over in Chippewa Falls for the summer."

Pol jumped in. "You checked him out?"

"No, not yet," Harrington growled. "We're short-staffed."

Lyons and Blancanales exchanged looks. They knew how anxious Bear was to have Steve Heitz located. Ironman picked up the questioning. "Who else?"

"Some of the students and instructors in the computer department knew him. Not well. Then there's his girl-friend."

"Tell us about her," Lyons insisted.

"Not much to tell. She's an exchange student from France, here for the summer to take some advanced elec-tronics and computer courses. She's supposed to be very pretty."

"Supposed to be?" Blancanales stared at the officer. "Do you think she's pretty?"

"I don't know." The Madison official lowered his voice. "She's disappeared."

Ironman shook his head in disgust. "When?"

"One of my men talked to one of the mechanics at the airport. According to my officer, the mechanic saw someone who looked like this Silvern and a girl get on a twin-engine plane and take off."

"When was this?" Lyons asked.

The lieutenant looked embarrassed. "Supposedly the day of the shooting."

"Did anyone get the plane's registration number?"

"Of course," Harrington replied harshly. "That's standard procedure."

"You check it out?"

The lieutenant nodded. "We ran into a little problem. The number was a phony."

Pol and Ironman looked discouraged. Wearily Lyons stared at the Madison cop. "Did anyone give you a description of the girl Silvern was with?"

"Yes." He fumbled through a folder. "I had our staff artist work up a sketch." He handed it to the hard-faced blond man.

Blancanales and Lyons studied it. It was the same woman Bear had recognized at Fort Meade—the Eastern European assassin. Lyons handed the sketch back to the officer.

"Keep it. I've got copies."

"No, thanks," Lyons said. "So have we." He turned and limped out of the lieutenant's office, followed by Blancanales.

TAD SILVERN OPENED his eyes. Everything was blurry. Elena was standing near his cot.

He had been dreaming about what he would do if she wanted him to help her get into the government computers. He wasn't sure it would work, or that she'd let him live even if it did.

Before he'd collapsed she'd asked him to change the time controls he'd planted. Maybe that was when he could make the other changes.

Now she was here. He must have been talking while he was unconscious. He had heard screams from nearby rooms. This time the screams would be his.

He was only half-conscious. His words came out slowly and muffled. "What happened?"

"You know what happened. You had a seizure. Why didn't you tell me you had epilepsy?"

Silvern struggled to stay awake. Although it hadn't happened for years, he could still remember how exhausted he felt for days after he had an attack. His mouth was dry. "I need something to drink."

She handed him a paper cup filled with water. Greedily he swallowed the contents in one gulp.

"That's better," he said, then turned and looked at her. Her hair was tied back. For the first time since he'd known her she wasn't wearing makeup. "You shouldn't wear anything on your face. You look nicer when you don't."

She ignored his comment. "Aren't you supposed to be on some kind of medication?"

"I forgot it back at my apartment."

She handed him a pill. "I don't know what you were taking, but this is supposed to stop seizures."

He studied the pressed tablet. It looked like the medication he'd been prescribed. He handed the paper cup to her. "More water, please."

She filled the cup with water from a sink tap and gave it back to him. He put the pill on his tongue and let the water wash it back to his throat, then down into his stomach.

"It's time to go to work," she announced.

"I'm still weak," he protested.

"It doesn't take much energy to type on a computer keyboard."

He knew he wasn't going to win this discussion, so he forced himself into a sitting position. For a moment he felt dizzy, but then the dizziness passed. "What's on the agenda?"

"A repeat of the other day."

"You mean what you had me do with the bank's computer?"

"Yes. Only you're going to change the telephone number on the program. And this time it won't be a bank."

He studied her expression. She looked determined. "What are we breaking into now, the White House?"

This was what he feared—that robbing banks wouldn't satisfy her. He waited to hear her response.

"The White House? Why would I want to do that? No, this time we'll start by getting into the computers of the Internal Revenue Service."

BEAR HAD SPENT the day locked up in his computer center. Things had been quiet around the compound since Brognola had shipped Ironman and Pol back to Madison to try to find out where Tad Silvern had gone. He wanted to tag along, but the chief had made it clear that his warrior days were over.

Gadgets was on his way back from Chippewa Falls. He had been spending his time checking out Heitz's missing girlfriend and her dwarf uncle.

Kurtzman was feeling confined in the windowless room. Playing with his computers had suddenly become less appealing than being out where the action was.

Accessing the computer, he had brought up Tad Silvern's telephone records. He focused on the past thirty days. Aside from the calls placed to his father, there were several calls to Steve Heitz's home and office. What had the two of them discussed?

There were only two other long-distance charges. One was to a number in Phoenix, Arizona, and one to the National Security Agency's computer system in Fort Meade.

Something about the date of the call to Maryland bothered Bear. He checked his log for a clue. Of course!

On that date he had witnessed the destruction of NSA data. Flipping through the pages, he found the entry.

There was a moment of sadness as he compared the two times. It was approximately six hours after Silvern had placed his call there that the data had begun to vanish.

Bear picked up the telephone and dialed Brognola's number. "There's something you may want to see," he announced.

Minutes later Brognola stood at his side and stared at a pair of monitors.

"On that date Tad Silvern placed a ten-minute call to the NSA computer," Bear said, pointing out the first monitor, which displayed the record of calls. He shifted his eyes and pointed to the adjacent screen. "The same night a group of files was erased."

Brognola chewed on the end of his cigar. "I saw your report. You remember what files they were?"

"Records of all the Eastern European secret-police personnel."

"Think Tad Silvern was responsible? According to your records, the files were erased hours after the call was logged."

"He could have planted a time-control program with the virus so it would start working later," Bear replied. He could see the puzzled expression on Brognola's face.

"What's it got to do with the scrambling of the NSA files?" the big Fed barked.

"As you know," Bear began, "this virus erases data. If you want to delay erasing the data, you install a time control. That way you can start the virus eating up files at some later time or date. It's like in detective stories when the killer needs to create an alibi. You can be far from the computer when the time control sets off the virus and the data in it starts vanishing."

"You're the computer wizard. Get rid of it."

"The nasty thing about a time control is that it takes a long time to find it. To do it right you've got to cancel all access to the computer."

Brognola remembered the lecture the Treasury man had given him about why the bank couldn't stop its computer.

"Can you imagine," Bear added, "the hell it would cause if those programs were planted in government agency computers?"

Brognola nodded, then shook his head in disgust. "Sometimes I think we're losing the war to high-tech."

Kurtzman smiled. "That's why you hired me. To keep one step ahead of the technology bad guys." He turned back to the monitor. "The thing that bothers me is why Tad planted them," he added quietly.

The Stony Man chief took out a sheet of paper from his jacket pocket. "This might explain it." He handed the paper to Kurtzman. "Lyons and Blancanales faxed this down from Madison. Remember her?"

Bear stared at the sketch he was holding. It was the Frenchwoman.

"According to other students, this is Tad Silvern's girlfriend. Unfortunately we don't know where he or she are."

Bear remembered something. He punched some keys and brought up the long-distance telephone records. "I might be able to help you." He pointed and said, "A call was placed recently to that number."

Brognola studied the screen. "Phoenix? Who's number is it?"

"Coming up," Bear said as he typed a sequence of keys. He glanced at another monitor. "Something called the Indian Research Bureau."

"Get Schwarz out there the minute he gets in." The order wasn't unusual. Bear often acted as Brognola's aide when the big Fed had to be away.

The phone on the computer console rang. Brognola started to leave while Kurtzman answered it. "He's right here." He signaled to Brognola. "It's for you. The red phone calling."

Brognola knew who Kurtzman meant. The Man in the White House. He took the phone from Bear. "Yes, sir," he said into the instrument. As he listened, he grunted quietly several times. "I can be there in less than an hour."

Kurtzman saw the worried expression on his face. "Something happen?"

Brognola nodded. "This is getting out of hand. Now the same group who invaded that bank in Chicago are breaking into the computers at government agencies."

"Who'd they hit?"

"The Internal Revenue Service."

Bear stifled his smile. "It could have been worse."

Brognola turned to him, his eyes filled with fury. "I hate paying taxes just as much as the next guy, but if they can get into the IRS computers, what's to stop them from doing the same at the Department of Energy and stealing our top nuclear secrets?"

The computer wizard could see the rage building in the Justice man.

"We've got to make an example of them fast before anyone else tries to pull the same stunt."

Kurtzman knew what Brognola meant. Find and destroy. With emphasis on *destroy*.

"Anything I can do to help?"

"A lot of praying," Brognola whispered.

19

Michael Vlad's call changed Elena's agenda. Instead of the three weeks he'd previously set as his arrival date he announced that he would be taking over personally in two days. Now she only had forty-eight hours to get ready.

Forcing herself to remain calm and sweet-sounding, Elena asked, "Do you want me to have a private plane meet you?"

"That would be very nice. The less time I spend in the open, the safer I'll feel." He paused, then asked, "You did eliminate the files on us?"

"Of course, Michael. Just as I told you."

"Good," he said, and gave her the arrival information. "I would prefer if Janos and you met me personally."

"We'll be there," she promised. Or someone else will, she added silently.

"One more thing," the quiet voice calling from Paris added. "Naturally I'll be carrying nothing that might arouse the suspicion of the authorities, so can you make sure you bring some of the 'dragon' with you? It will be a very long flight without my pipe."

After she hung up, Elena picked up a heavy paperweight and flung it at the window in her office, fracturing the bulletproof pane. Then she summoned Dragnan and told him the news. He looked pleased until she pointed out a problem. "How long will it take before someone tells him about us?"

The dwarf looked stunned. "What can we do?"

She told him. At first Dragnan objected. Then, as she explained that the choice was between Michael and them, he reluctantly agreed to back her.

"Announce that there will be a meeting at five," she said. "I have something that needs to be taken care of immediately."

Tad Silvern was napping in his tiny cell when she opened his barred door. When she entered, he glanced up at her. Right now she looked like an angel. An angel of death. The smile on her face was cold. Her eyes were filled with anger and hate.

Silvern was worried. "Did I do something wrong?"

"Not yet." She pulled him to his feet. "You have some more work to do."

BROGNOLA STILL COULDN'T believe what the President had told him.

"I've been thinking about it all the way up. It still doesn't make sense. Why would anyone want to get into the IRS computers?"

"According to the message they left, money."

Brognola looked bewildered. "What have they got to trade?"

"If we pay them ten million dollars, they won't destroy the tax records in the main computer up in Martinsburg."

Without meaning to, the Stony Man chief whistled. "That takes nerve."

"The point is, Hal, we need to know if they can really do it."

Brognola let his face become expressionless. "Based on the information I've gotten from one of the real authorities on the subject, yes, sir, they can."

"I suppose we'll have to pay them." He saw Brognola's surprised expression. "Without tax revenue this government stops functioning, Hal." He stood up. "Unless you have a better idea."

"You know it won't stop with the IRS. Give in to their demands and they'll push on to do the same with the Department of Energy computers. And after that maybe the Pentagon."

"What do you suggest?"

"How much time did they give the IRS?"

"Seventy-two hours."

"I think the same bunch who stole the supercomputer blackmailed that Chicago bank. Let my men have a crack at finding them."

The President looked worried. "I was about to call in the FBI until I thought of how the press would handle this if word leaks out." He paced across the large room, then turned and looked at the beefy Fed. "I don't have anyone else I can turn to, Hal."

"We'll stop them," Brognola replied. There was no hint of doubt in his voice. Able Team would be out there, fighting side by side, putting their lives on the line for a country that didn't know they existed, until—

For some reason the last line of the wedding vows came to mind. Until death parted them.

SILVERN REFUSED. Planting a virus in the IRS computers was almost funny. Now she wanted him to do the same thing with the computers at the Pentagon.

"Get someone else," he said stubbornly, staring at the assault weapon the dwarf was pointing at him.

She studied his expression. "There is a doctor among us who gained minor fame for his ability to create excruciating pain without allowing the patient the freedom of passing out. He's been complaining for days that he is getting out of practice."

The college student knew she wasn't lying. He had no doubt she would allow the doctor to refresh his skills on him. "No," he repeated.

She glanced at the dwarf, shrugged and picked up the wall phone. "Tell Dr. Brasacovu to get ready for a patient." She hung up and gestured to Dragnan. "Take him to the infirmary."

Silvern studied her expression. She wasn't trying to scare him. She really meant it. "Okay," he said in resignation. "I'll do it."

"Good. Then you'll do the same with the computers at the FBI, the CIA and the NSA."

Tears filled Silvern's eyes. "Please, not the NSA."

She watched his shoulders slump as he began to weep. Waiting for him to compose himself, she smiled. "I'm moved by your love for your father," she said cynically. "So, instead of the NSA, I want you to plant this message in the computers of the Immigration authorities."

She handed the bespectacled student several typewritten pages. He kept shaking his head in shock as he read the text. Finally he looked up at her. "What a bastard. How did you ever get to meet this—" he looked at the first page again "—this Michael Vlad?"

PETE HOLLIS had celebrated his second year as an agent last night. Sherry had cooked his favorite meal for him for the occasion.

As they drove to the slum section of Phoenix, the young fair-haired ex-Marine had talked about it incessantly to the mustached visitor from Washington.

Hollis was still talking when they parked the car on Madison near Twelfth Street. "Not only a special dinner," he repeated for the third time, "but Sherry gave me a brand-new holster." He started to open his jacket and show Gadgets the hand-tooled spring holster he'd gotten for an anniversary present.

"Enough. I get it. You've got a great wife and kid and they love you."

Hollis looked at the visitor. "You married?"

"No." The response was blunt and cold.

Hollis couldn't figure out the visitor. Ever since Marty Thayer, who ran the Phoenix office, had introduced them, the man who called himself Hermann Schwarz had said almost nothing.

The young FBI agent couldn't understand why a company located in this run-down section of the city would be important enough to interest Washington. What confused him more was the man they'd sent, not your typical agent from Washington. Aside from the fact that he wore casual clothes instead of the business suit uniform everyone else in the Bureau wore, the brown-haired passenger looked more like a professional hit man than a government investigator.

The visitor waited for the young agent's blush to recede, then asked, "Can we talk about what we're supposed to be doing here?"

Embarrassed, Hollis apologized. "Sorry. From what you said back at the office it's just a routine call."

"There's no such thing as a routine check. Things can happen, and we've got to be ready in case they do," Gadgets warned.

Brognola's orders to fly to Phoenix had come without warning. He hadn't specified what Gadgets should try to find out, just that it had something to do with the missing computer. And maybe with an attempt to blackmail the Chicago bank.

Schwarz had tried in vain to convince the big Fed that he worked better alone.

"Let's make the FBI feel useful," Brognola had said, making it clear there was no appeal to his decision.

Hollis grinned as he pushed his jacket aside to reveal the Glock in his new holster. "And I'm ready."

Schwarz decided to ignore the gesture. "Okay. When we get there, let me ask the questions. You just be ready if something goes wrong."

Hollis had scored at the top of his group in boot camp. "No sweat. First wrong move and out this comes," he said, patting the butt of the automatic. He thought of a problem. "What if nobody's in?"

"Then we play it by ear."

They looked at the run-down two-story sandstone building. The entire lower floor was taken up by a large tavern. Several unshaven drunks loitered on the sidewalk outside. One of them started to walk over to the car to try to solicit the price of a drink. He changed his mind when he saw the expression on Gadget's face.

Schwarz and the FBI agent entered the building. The smell of urine permeated the downstairs hallway. There was a directory of tenants mounted on the wall and the FBI agent checked it.

"Second floor," he announced. "Room 12." He looked around for an elevator. There was none. They found the stairs in the back of the filthy lobby.

ON the second floor Gadgets glanced down the dark, narrow corridor. "It must be down there," he said in a low voice as he walked toward a dark wooden door.

The FBI agent followed close behind. "Sure stinks up here," he whispered.

"Like a backed-up sewer," Schwarz agreed. He had spent a lot of time in sewers since joining Able Team. The vermin they fought called it home, he reminded himself.

They came to Room 12. Gadgets tried the handle. The door was locked.

He knocked on the door but no one answered. Hollis took out the warrant they'd picked up at the courthouse on the way over. He was ready to flash it. He looked at the visitor. "What do we do now?"

"Be a shame to have to leave and come back to this stench another time," Schwarz said.

Hollis sniffed the air and made a face. "Sure would."

Gadgets studied the lock. "Old-fashioned spring lock, the kind that opens if you slide a credit card in."

The ex-Marine looked nervous. "Is it okay to do something like that? We have a warrant."

Gadgets stared at him. "And no one to give it to." The Able Team warrior reached into his pocket and took out his wallet. From it he fished out a credit card. Carefully he worked it between the tongue of the lock and the doorframe. "Got it," he whispered.

He withdrew the card and pushed the door open. They looked inside. Except for a few pieces of furniture the room was empty.

NICOLAE RODESCU had been studying a catalog of surplus military equipment when the alarm next door went off. The brutish-looking man opened his desk drawer and took out a MAC-10.

The redheaded woman who sat across the desk from him jumped to her feet. Ana Pastriscanu grabbed a 9 mm SIG-Sauer P-226, similar to the gun her adored Michael Vlad carried, from the small leather satchel she used as a handbag. "Let's go check who's in there," she said.

"First we call Elena and tell her."

"All right. Call her," she said reluctantly.

He dialed the base number and was connected. Quickly he made his report, then listened as she gave him instructions. "I'll call you later." He hung up the phone.

The redhead looked impatient. "What did she say?"

He looked at the gun in her hand. "Put that away. She wants us to check who's in there first."

"And if they're the enemy?"

"Kill them." He looked at her. "But not with guns. They make too much noise."

He opened his desk and took out a large knife in a leather sheath. He had spent at least an hour each day sharpening it. As he stood, he slid his belt through the loop in the sheath. "Do you think you can still break a man's neck?"

She picked up a small thick glass vase from her desk and wrapped her large hand around it. Squeezing slowly, she could see her veins try to push their way out of her skin. Drops of perspiration started trickling down from her forehead, running into her eyes and making her wince from the sting.

She could feel the tendons in her fingers screaming for relief as she applied more pressure to the thick glass vessel. Her muscles stretched and strained as she focused her strength on the small object.

Fascinated, the large man stared at the silent contest. The woman's large hand began to quiver from the intense strain. He was certain this time she would be the loser.

Suddenly the stillness of the room was interrupted by the sharp sound of glass beginning to crack. He looked at the small vase and saw a finger of separation spread the full length of the cylinder.

The determined woman exerted her energy on the captive object until she heard the loud snap and saw the vase split in two. "It's been a while," she said, smiling. "But the answer is, yes, I can."

20

Gadgets led the FBI agent into the small room. "Some Indian Research Bureau," he muttered as he shoved the credit card back into his wallet.

He looked around. There were no filing cabinets. No papers. Nothing except a desk, a chair and lots of dust.

Gadgets was puzzled. Brognola had said Tad Silvern had placed a call here, but there was no phone in sight. Then he recognized a small metal box attached to the wall—one of the call-forwarding devices available in any electronics shop.

Schwarz reached into his pocket and took out the compact portable communicator Brognola insisted they carry on missions. He pressed the code button that hooked the unit into the nationwide telephone network. Another button signaled Stony Man Farm that he was calling.

He placed the unit to his ear. Bear was on the other end, and Gadgets gave him his report. "You might want to cut into the local phone company's computers and find out where calls from here end up," he suggested.

He turned and smiled. The young FBI agent's mouth was hanging open as he watched Gadgets talk into what looked like an oversize pocket calculator. Schwarz turned his back on the Bureau man and glanced at the call-forwarding device. As a confirmed electronics gadgeteer, Schwarz had to force himself to resist taking off the cover and examining the innards. "Ask the chief what I'm supposed to do next. I'll hang on."

While he waited he knelt near the mounted electronics box and studied it. Hollis knelt beside him to watch. He couldn't figure out what Schwarz was doing, but he decided he should keep an eye on him.

Gadgets was still examining the box when he felt a pair of hands squeeze his windpipe. Out of the corner of his eye he could see a man sneaking up behind the young FBI agent. He tried to call out a warning, but the tightening fingers stopped any sound.

Hollis saw the redheaded woman start to strangle the visitor from Washington. He turned to help him. Reaching for the Glock in his waistband, the young agent yanked at the weapon.

It refused to come loose. Somehow it had gotten hung up in the new spring holster. He tugged at the weapon again. The thickset man behind him moved swiftly. With a swift downward thrust he rammed the point of the blade into the young man's back, aiming carefully so that it would slip between the ribs and tear into the lungs.

Hollis stiffened and screamed as the knife skewered him. He had never felt pain like this, not even when a crazed teenager had shot him in the thigh. He fell and hit his forehead against the wall.

Rodescu pulled out his knife and shoved it back into the young agent. Hollis could feel the warm liquid drenching the back of his jacket. He kept wondering if the dry cleaner would be able to get out the stain. Then, with a last burst of anger, he turned, reached up and grabbed the other man's hand. The heavyset attacker clenched his fist and slammed it into the FBI agent's face. The young man suddenly stopped struggling.

Hollis could feel his forehead swelling. As red liquid ran out of his body, he knew Sherry would put an ice pack on it when he got home. That was the last thought he ever had.

Gadgets tried to pull free and help the young man, but the death grip kept him from moving. He could feel his lungs pleading for air.

While the Neanderthal was gloating over the FBI agent, Gadgets forced his head to turn enough so that he could see his enemy. It was a woman. A large, ugly woman with red hair.

She stopped squeezing momentarily while she turned to see how her partner was doing. "Good," she called out. "Is he dead?"

"Almost," the man chortled.

She turned back and glared at Gadgets. "Now it's your turn."

Schwarz let his body go limp. He could feel the thick, sticky blood under his shoes. So could the woman. Gadgets worked his right foot between her legs and pushed.

The woman lost her balance momentarily, then fought to regain it. Gadgets forced a hand between their bodies. Slowly he moved it up her chest. He could feel her flesh. What he had in mind wasn't nice, but it was necessary if he wanted to stay alive.

She tightened her hold, trying to snap the delicate bones that connected his head and torso. Gadgets's fingers rubbed against her large, flabby breast. Turning his hand toward her, he crushed her nipple between his thumb and middle finger.

The woman screamed with pain and tore his fingers away from her breast. Free of her death hold, the Able

Team commando smashed the hardened edge of a hand across the bridge of her nose.

He could hear the bone explode beneath the thick layer of skin. The enraged attacker reached to tear his face as blood and mucus rushed from her nostrils. Gadgets swiftly moved his head aside. As her hands ripped at empty air, he clenched his fist and slammed it at her heart cavity.

Shocked, she stared at him. Despite his dizziness he jumped to his feet. The woman tried to get up, but Schwarz kicked the side of her neck. He could hear the loud noise of her neck snapping as she fell to the floor.

The heavyset man had glanced at the battle before he'd turned to retrieve his blade from the back of the still body on the floor. His partner was obviously winning.

Wiping the knife clean on the jacket of the dead FBI agent, he wrapped his hands around the rough surface of the handle. Now he was ready if Ana needed his assistance.

Schwarz forced air into his lungs and reached for the .45 in his waistband. The thickset man was stunned at the sight of his partner on the floor. He spun around, desperate to find the mustached man.

Ignoring the torture of the torn muscles and ruptured blood vessels in his neck, Gadgets forced an icy smile. "Looking for me?"

The brutish-looking man tried to rush at Schwarz with his still-bloody knife. Gadgets slipped into a combat stance. With no hesitation he let loose three flesh-hunters that plowed through the startled man's chest.

Schwarz glanced at the woman. Her eyes were still staring up at him in surprise. But all she would see from now on was hell.

He knelt beside the body of the FBI agent. As he shut the man's eyes, he cursed the rodents who destroyed decent young guys like Pete Hollis. Then a slight clicking noise caught his attention. It came from the communicator he'd dropped. He picked it up and put it to his ear.

"Yes, I'm okay." He told Kurtzman what had happened, then listened. "I'll meet them at the airport."

He closed the compact unit and slipped it into a pocket of his windbreaker. Shoving the .45 automatic back into its holster, he glanced again at the dead FBI agent. "You didn't die for nothing, Pete Hollis," he said bitterly. "I'll make sure of that."

THE DOCTORS at Saint Luke's had insisted he stay overnight. They wanted to do some more tests on his neck.

"There could be some serious damage where your neck meets your spinal column," the specialist had warned.

Gadgets was still furious at the two "old ladies" who had forced him to come here, just because he'd passed out at the airport. He'd never thought of Ironman and Pol as do-gooders before.

The foam collar the nurse had wrapped around his neck itched. He reached up to unfasten it.

"Touch it and I'll break a rib." He recognized the voice. Lyons was standing at the end of his bed, unsmiling.

Blancanales was next to him. He was carrying some magazines. "I brought you some science magazines."

"Just bring me my clothes and let's get out of here."

"No can do," Ironman answered. "Orders."

Schwarz was angry. "Whose orders? Some jerk doctor's?"

"No, mine." He saw Brognola enter the room. Kurtzman wheeled himself in right behind the cigar-chewing head Fed.

Schwarz wasn't surprised to see the Stony Man boss. Brognola had a way of showing up in the most unlikely places. "We've got work to do, Chief," he complained.

"Tomorrow. If—let me emphasize the *if*—the doctors say you're okay." He checked his watch. "Meantime I've got an appointment with the governor." He studied the three battlers in the hospital room. "I figured I better apologize in advance for what you three are going to do to his state."

"Four," Kurtzman corrected.

Gadgets turned and stared at him. So did the other three. Ironman threw a silent plea at the chief.

Brognola pushed a finger into Bear's chest. "The reason you're here is to stop the computer from doing whatever damage it's been programmed to do." He paused. "*After* these three finish their work."

Kurtzman started to argue, then stopped. One look at Brognola's expression and he knew it was hopeless.

The big Fed turned to Ironman and Pol. "Meantime I've made sleeping arrangements for you two."

Blancanales winked at Lyons. "I think I have a distant cousin who lives in this city. Maybe she can find a friend for you."

"You're staying right here tonight," Brognola continued.

Pol stared back at him in disbelief. "We're not sick."

"That's a matter of opinion. I don't want any of you getting into trouble tonight. Save it for tomorrow."

Lyons started to argue.

"That's an order," Brognola growled, then turned and walked out of the room.

AS HE PULLED his garbage truck out of the front gate of Camp Freedom, Jinx Maynard decided against heading right back to town. The sun had started to go down and the high desert was beginning to cool off.

There was a square dance in Joshua tonight, sponsored by the local chamber of commerce. What it meant was that everybody within thirty miles would be crowding into town, fighting for every available parking space, jamming into the bars and restaurants.

The lanky old man thought he'd head up to the Indian burial mounds and see what he could find before it got too dark. This was a good time to go relic hunting. The state troopers who hung around the mounds to prevent poachers from entering would have their hands full helping Sheriff Devlin handle the crowds in town.

There was time enough later to dump the load he picked up, when the crowds in town thinned out. Nobody cared when he came or went as long as he got his work done and didn't get drunk.

Maynard hadn't gotten drunk in ten years. Not since Doc Morton, who was now buried in the cemetery behind the Methodist church, had told him his liver was almost gone.

The drive along the country road was eventless. Several pickup trucks heading toward Joshua honked greetings at him. Forcing a smile on his face, he honked back.

He parked the truck at the side of the two-lane asphalt road and dug out his small pick and shovel. It wasn't easy getting under the sunbaked top layer of the graves without them.

Wandering among the small mounds that contained the bones of Indian ancients, Maynard inhaled the sweet, clean air of the desert. It reminded him of his younger years when the smell of gasoline was a rarity.

Looking for a likely site to dig, he stepped across several mounds. As he did, his left boot began to sink into the ground. Maynard stopped and looked at the mound he had just crossed. It was freshly dug. Some tourist, he decided, trying to cover his efforts to open a grave. Seasoned poachers didn't give a damn about filling in the open holes they'd dug. Besides, leaving them unfilled made it easier to find fresh graves the next time.

He glanced down at the freshly covered grave. Something was poking up through the dirt. Maynard knelt to see what it was.

He saw the fingers of a hand. Stunned, he kept staring at it. Was it really a hand, or some Indian ghost coming back to get even?

Maynard jumped up, backed away and stared at the hand. It didn't look like an Indian hand. Even with dirt covering it he could see that it belonged to a white man.

For a moment he wondered if someone had looked for a cheap way to bury somebody. That didn't make sense. The town provided a potter's field for anybody who died without means to pay for a funeral.

Moving cautiously, the old man brushed the dirt away from the hand. He could see that it was attached to an arm. And the arm to a body.

The sky had started getting dark. He ran back to his truck and found a flashlight in the glove compartment. Returning to the grave site, he flashed the light on the body.

It was a young man. He could see that. The hot, dry sun did a good job of preserving the dead, and this one was no exception.

Maynard wondered if the guy had died of natural causes. He would have thought so except for one thing. There was a large hole right in the middle of the dead man's chest.

This was one for Matt Devlin. Maynard turned and went back to his truck. He'd let the sheriff handle it. He dealt in old dead bodies. Recent dead bodies were out of his league.

21

Matt Devlin had forgotten about the call he'd received from the state capital, alerting him to the visit by four men from Washington, D.C. He had his hands full trying to make sense out of the body Jinx Maynard had found the previous night.

The weather-worn, gray-haired man had sent a description and the dead man's prints out over the police network hoping the FBI or one of the other police organizations could give him a clue to the man's identity.

Nothing had come back yet, but it had only been nine hours. Among government agencies—even the police—that was about as much time as it took to decide whether or not to have a second cup of coffee.

He had gotten used to the snail's pace of the government. But he still didn't like it. When there was a problem involving the law, he wanted it solved now, not at some time in the future.

He had thought of resigning and finding something else to do. But at fifty-seven there weren't many choices for somebody who had spent his life in law enforcement.

He glanced out his window. Main Street was virtually empty at the moment. He watched as a large van pulled up in front of his office. The driver stopped between two signs that reserved the parking space between them for official cars.

He was about to send one of his deputies out to warn the driver when he saw three powerful-looking men get out. Despite the casual lightweight clothes they were wearing, there was something about how they looked and carried themselves that made him hesitate. Even the one with the mustache who wore a foam orthopedic collar around his neck looked meaner than a nest of mother rattlers.

He'd seen that look before, back in Korea when he was an MP sergeant. They didn't have to say a word to make their feelings known loud and clear.

Two of the men slid open the door and lifted a wheelchair down. Sitting in it was a husky man. The third man limped slightly as he led the way toward the building.

Who were they? he wondered. He didn't have long to find out.

"Carl Lyons," the blond man with the limp said. He pointed at the others and added, "The one with the silver hair is Rosario Blancanales. The guy with the mustache is Hermann Schwarz."

The two men nodded at the lawman.

Lyons turned to face the grizzled-looking sheriff when he heard a soft cough. Twisting around, he saw Bear staring at him icily. He grinned and looked at the Joshua lawman. "Aaron Kurtzman is our technical consultant."

"You the guys from Washington?"

Devlin didn't think they were FBI. He'd met Bureau agents before. All of them were polite to the point of making him want to puke. These four didn't look as if they let good manners ever get in their way.

"You should have been alerted to our visit," Lyons said.

"I was. Right from the governor's office." He was glad he was on their side. Even with one limping and another in a neck brace, they looked like men he'd hate to have to face in a fight. "They didn't say what was up. But it must be pretty important to bring you out here."

"It is," Lyons replied. "What do you know about an abandoned weapons-testing site that was recently sold?"

Devlin smiled. "You must be talking about Camp Freedom out on 60 near the Centennial Wash. Nice bunch of people bought it from the government as a place for refugees to come and get themselves acclimatized to America."

"Have you been out there?"

"Couple of times. They did a nice job remodeling the place." He laughed. "They still get nightmares that some secret-police types are going to break in and try to kidnap them."

Pol joined in. "What makes you think that?"

"They reinforced the cyclone fences around the property and pumped them full of electricity."

Gadgets had been listening. He forced himself to ask a question, although his throat threatened to revolt if he did. "How many people are living out at this place?"

"They started off with about two dozen. But they've been having a steady trickle of people coming in for the past week or so." He scratched his head. "Don't rightly know the exact number." He reached for the phone. "Hell, I can just call Miss Dessault and ask her."

Ironman put his hand on Devlin's to stop him. "Is this the Dessault woman?" Lyons showed him the digitized composite.

"That's her. She's the lady who runs the place. Real pretty. You wouldn't think somebody as pretty as her would give up her life just to help other people." He sighed. "She in some kind of trouble?"

The three Able Team commandos shared a quick glance with the computer wizard in the wheelchair. The same question went through their heads. Was this Miss Dessault Tad Silvern's girlfriend? Steve Heitz's girlfriend? The woman Bear had seen at the conference in Fort Meade?

They came up with the same answer. There was only one way to find out—go into Camp Freedom and look at her.

The sheriff interrupted their meditation. "Washington think something funny's going on in that place?"

"That's what we're here to find out," Lyons said flatly. "I wish somebody had a better idea of how the place is laid out."

Devlin thought about the visitor's request. "There is somebody who does. Jinx Maynard, the local garbage collector. He's out there once a week."

"Where can we find him?"

The sheriff checked his watch. "Wait about thirty minutes and you'll find him with his boots propped up outside of the Lucky Dollar Café. Can't miss him. He looks like a Hollywood version of an old prospector."

Kurtzman started asking a question when they heard the clacking of a Teletypewriter. A uniformed deputy entered the room and handed the sheriff a sheet of paper. "Just came in over the net, Sheriff. Positive identification of that body Jinx found."

Lyons looked interested. "What body, Sheriff?"

"Jinx Maynard found a body buried under some dirt out past the wash last night. Somebody had shot him to death."

Devlin scanned the paper. "Sure ain't from around these parts."

Lyons held out his hand. "Mind if I read it?"

Devlin shrugged and handed him the paper. The only thing in the report that mattered was the name of the dead man—Steve Heitz.

He passed the paper to Aaron Kurtzman. Blood drained from Bear's face. "Those bastards," he muttered, letting the page flutter to his lap.

Schwarz picked it up and read it, then handed it to Blancanales. Pol glanced at it and handed the paper back to the sheriff.

Devlin looked at the death masks on his four visitors. "I've got the annual Apache Powwow coming up in a week. What it means is I'll have a town full of tourists and local drunks getting into brawls all over the place. I don't need any more trouble."

"Like it or not," Ironman said coldly, "you've got it."

"Do I want to know what kind of trouble?"

"You don't want to know, Sheriff," Lyons told him.

"I was afraid of that."

Kurtzman jumped in with a question. "No way we can find this Maynard in less than half an hour?"

Devlin offered his full cooperation. "I'll send one of my deputies to find him and bring him back here." He got up and called in a deputy, then dispatched him to bring back Joshua's garbage collector. After the deputy took off, the sheriff turned back to his visitors. "Officially I can't offer you assistance without some piece of paper requesting it. You got something like that?"

Pol smiled thinly. "That's not how we operate."

Devlin weighed the Hispanic-looking man's reply. "Unofficially I got a couple of local boys who might want to help. Could you use a hand?"

Lyons looked at the others in his group, then made a decision. "Yes."

THE SABLE-HAIRED WOMAN was impatient. She kept pacing back and forth behind Tad Silvern, waving the Beretta she was holding like a witch's wand. Suddenly she stopped and turned to him. Her face was flushed with rage. "You're sure they received the message about erasing their files?"

Silvern was too tired to argue. "Yes, I'm sure. You saw their reply that they have to get approval to do anything."

"Ten million dollars. Your government wastes more than that in ten seconds. Why are they taking so long to ask where they should deposit the money?"

She had made arrangements with a small offshore bank to receive the funds. Through a cleverly constructed network of banks around the world the funds would vanish, only to reappear suitably laundered as legitimate business income.

She needed the funds to operate the base. Only the stubbornness of the American government was in her way.

Elena decided to teach them a lesson. She would erase a portion of the income tax returns in their computer. Turning to the student, she said, "I want you to send them a message that unless we hear from them by morning we'll start erasing their records."

Silvern stared at the gun in her hand. It took all the courage he could find to protest. "You said you'd give them three days."

All the beauty in her face vanished as she spewed her retort. "I changed my mind."

Silvern was grateful he'd taken precautions to prevent the crazed woman from carrying out her threats. Playing around with the IRS computer had tickled him once he'd gotten over his shock. But destroying vital government secrets was something else.

She started to calm down. "Send the viruses in the various computers a message not to activate for now. Then I'll take you back to your room."

"My cell," Silvern reminded her.

"I have a surprise for you," she said, suddenly smiling.

He became interested. This was the first time he'd seen her look even remotely friendly since he'd been brought here.

"I had one of my people purchase a handful of computer magazines for you to read," she said. Then she became coy. "We haven't been together alone for a long time," she added softly.

"Thanks for the magazines," Silvern replied coldly.

IRONMAN SAT on the front hood of their van and studied the fenced-in land in front of them through a pair of high-powered binoculars. The sun had just begun to slip behind the low range of mountains.

Bear rested on the rear bench of the van while Pol and Gadgets leaned against the front door of the vehicle. Blancanales looked over at Lyons. "See anything interesting?"

Ironman shook his head. "Not yet."

"I say we storm the place," Gadgets suggested.

Pol raised an eyebrow. "With three of us?"

"Four of us," Kurtzman called out from inside.

Lyons turned to look at him through the windshield. "Forget it, Bear. I asked you to stay back in town where you'd be safe. You're along strictly as a technical consultant."

Kurtzman stopped talking. When Ironman was in this mood there was no point in arguing with him. "As least help me out of this damn truck."

"No," Ironman snapped. "You're safer inside."

Frustrated, Bear looked at the wheelchair with the oversize tires Gadgets and Cowboy had customized for his use in getting around Stony Man Farm. A lot of good it would do him when he was stuck inside the van.

Gadgets started pacing impatiently. "What are we waiting for?"

"Maynard said he thought there were twenty-five people in there. So far I've counted thirty," Lyons announced, ignoring Schwarz's question.

"What about the sheriff and his men?"

"Devlin said he and three of his best deputies would be standing by, waiting for a radio signal from us to move in. All we have to tell them is when and where. I guess I better work out the where."

He slid down from the hood and fished out a large sheet of paper from inside the van. Using a felt-tipped pen he started drawing a map of the area within the electrified fencing. Pol and Gadgets waited until he was finished. Lyons studied his work, then turned to them.

"Here's how I figure it." He used the pen as a pointer. "This must be the main building. The buildings on either side are living quarters. This building near the front gate must be the garage where they keep their vehicles." He moved the pen away from the buildings to an empty area he'd circled. "This must be their firing range. Which means that the small building near it contains their arsenal."

"I sure wish we knew what kind of weapons they had," Pol commented.

"You can be sure they're state-of-the-art," Lyons said. "We're not dealing with street punks. These are trained professionals."

"That means AK-47s, MAC-10s, grenade launchers," Schwarz started.

"And probably a couple of Browning machine guns," Blancanales added.

"Plus who knows what else," Lyons said.

From inside the van Kurtzman asked, "Can I make a comment?"

The three Able Team warriors looked at him.

Bear was searching through his briefcase. He found the pages he'd been seeking. "Here they are." He handed them to Pol.

Blancanales looked puzzled. "What are they?"

"Before we left Washington I took a pass at Treasury's Alcohol, Firearms and Tobacco unit's computers to see what records they had of illegal weapons movement. Between their files and what I could pluck over the police net I put together this list."

Pols studied it and whistled. "This is enough stuff to arm an entire division."

Kurtzman nodded. "Just about."

Ironman took the list from Pol's hands and glanced at it. "I don't think they got all of these, but even if they have ten percent of what's been peddled in the past month or so, we've got a miniwar on our hands."

Gadgets stared at the cloudless sky as he weighed Lyons's statement. He turned to the blond man. "So what's your plan?"

"We pull an Entebbe," he announced.

Gadgets shook his head. "That's a new one on me."

"No," Lyons corrected him. "An old one."

Kurtzman joined the conversation from inside the van. "You talking about the Israeli raid back in the seventies to save the hostages?"

Lyons's jaw was set and determined. "Exactly."

"I remember that," Pol said. "It took a lot of guts."

Gadgets looked worried. "So do I. And this will, too. There's one difference," he added. "There was a whole lot of them and there's only three of us."

"Plus the two deputies we talked to in town. They promised to be here after they finished their shift," Pol added.

"They can keep an eye on the back end of the property and make sure nobody slips away," Lyons decided.

Gadgets was impatient. "When does all this start happening?"

"We wait until morning, then slip into the compound," Ironman said. "There are three objectives. The first is to find and destroy their computer. The second is to capture or kill the leaders, and the third is to find and rescue Tad Silvern, if possible."

Bear thought about the two students. Steve was dead, but Tad might still be alive. He leaned out of the window. "I wish you could move that last one up, Ironman."

"So do I," Lyons replied.

Kurtzman knew he meant it. He also knew that every war had its innocent victims. He hoped Tad Silvern wasn't going to be one of them.

"One more question," Pol said. "How do we sneak in?"

As if to answer his question, a large garbage truck drove up the dusty road and stopped near the van. The Able Team squad could read the name printed on the side—Joshua Trash Collection Service.

The driver's door opened and the elderly man hopped out. He walked over to Ironman. "Matt Devlin says you could use a favor."

Lyons stared at the man. "What else did he say?"

Maynard swallowed. "He kind of said that robbing Indian graves could cost me a whole bunch of years in jail."

"He tell you what the favor was?"

"Yup."

"It could be dangerous. You willing to do it?"

"No worse than going to jail," Maynard answered. "Yup, I'm willing to do it."

Lyons looked satisfied. He turned to his two sidekicks. "We'll take turns patrolling the area until morning. The rest of us will get some sleep. It might turn out to be a long day."

Not to mention our last day alive, he could have added, but didn't. It wasn't necessary. The three of them already knew that.

22

Something was bothering the dwarf. He stopped by Elena's office to voice his concern.

"It's almost midnight," the sable-haired woman said. "I thought you'd be in bed by now."

"There's something out there beyond the fences," he said.

"You've been listening to the people in town talking about the ghosts of dead Indians," the sable-haired woman replied sarcastically.

"These aren't ghosts. I drove around the fences and saw lights in the hills," Dragnan insisted.

Elena wondered what was frightening the little man. "Didn't that old garbageman say something about an Indian festival about to begin? Perhaps some of the Indians have arrived early and are camping out."

Dragnan wasn't satisfied. "Perhaps. I think I'll post some extra guards tonight."

"Please do what you think's best," she replied sweetly. "I'm not thinking clearly right now."

Behind her pleasant mask Elena knew Dragnan would have to go soon. Like Michael, he was fast becoming obsolete. Her need for him was almost gone. She handed him a newspaper. "Have you seen this?"

The dwarf was surprised at her comment. The sable-haired woman sounded less than her usually confident self. He saw the squat MAC-10 sitting on her desk. A 30-round clip protruded from it.

Dragnan read the headline on the front page: Romanian Secret-Police Chief Caught At Chicago Airport. Commits Suicide. He shrugged. "Did you expect he would let himself be taken alive?"

"No. I just don't want the others to hear about it yet. There was so much dissent when I announced I was taking over that if this news gets out now it could lead to internal revolt."

"I'll make sure the newspaper isn't circulated." She beamed at him and Dragnan smiled back and said, "Why don't you go to bed? I'll be in as soon as I make the rounds again."

"After I'm finished with the student," she said.

He nodded. "How long are you going to keep him alive?"

"Not much longer. I think I now understand how to get into the government computers. His usefulness is almost over."

"Good," the dwarf replied. "Then we can get down to the business we came here for."

THE MOON WAS HIGH over the sloping hill. Gadgets looked up and saw the large glowing circle suspended overhead. He was grateful. It would be hard for someone to sneak up on them without his noticing.

Just then Gadgets felt someone behind him. Swinging around his M-16, he turned slowly and tried to peer into the shadows.

Two dark figures emerged. He recognized both of them—the two deputies Devlin had assigned to assist them, Proudfoot and Valdez. Gadgets lowered his weapon. "Make some kind of noise next time you show up," he complained. "I almost shot both of you."

The two law officers smiled at each other. "We've been here for almost an hour, trying to figure out what this is all about," Proudfoot said.

"Did you?"

"Nope," Valdez answered. "We decided to stick around, anyway."

Gadgets turned away from them and peered through the darkness at the lights that outlined the cyclone fencing. "Happen to see anything going on while you were coming out?"

"They've increased the guards around the camp," Proudfoot reported. "They must be expecting something to happen sometime soon."

Schwarz smiled thinly. "They're right." He looked around. "We thought you'd be here in the morning."

"We came early to stir up some excitement," Valdez said.

"Like how?"

"There are a couple of things we used to do as kids," Proudfoot replied obliquely, "that might get the folks inside just a little bit nervous." His partner smiled at the words.

"Maybe I ought to wake up Lyons and have you tell him," Schwarz said.

"He's awake," a new voice behind them called out.

Gadgets turned. Ironman and Pol were standing nearby, dressed in camouflage fatigues and draped in combat-ready automatic weapons.

The two deputies looked at the assault armament the two were carrying. "Haven't seen anyone carrying that much since Nam," Valdez commented.

In addition to side arms Lyons was cuddling an M-16 while Blancanales gripped a Konzak shotgun. Slung across their backs were Heckler & Koch G-11 caseless automatic rifles. Web belting held an array of grenades and pouches that contained ammo clips for their assault weapons.

"Looks like you're ready to bag some big game," Proudfoot said. "There may be too many for the shotgun."

"You might be right about the Konzak," Pol agreed. "Guess I'll stick with the M-16."

Lyons changed the subject. "You were saying something about stirring up some excitement. How?"

"Show him," Proudfoot told his partner.

Valdez held up a thick canvas sack. Something inside was making a strange noise.

Pol started to reach for the bag. "What've you got inside?"

The Indian deputy sheriff stopped him. "I don't think you want to put your hand in there."

Valdez held the bag open while Proudfoot shone a light inside. Glaring up at them were a pair of diamondback rattlesnakes, hissing angrily at their captors and shaking their tails as a warning to let them free.

Instinctively Blancanales pulled back. "*¡Dios!*" he gasped, then stared at the pair. "You collected them as kids?"

Valdez nodded. "We got tired of being pushed around because we came from the wrong side of the tracks, so we started picking up bagfuls of these things and dropped them into the back seats of the loudmouths' cars at school."

"Sure got them to stop calling us names in a hurry," Proudfoot added.

Lyons stared at them. "What do you plan on doing with them?"

"We'll collect another six or seven and then slip inside the camp," the Hispanic deputy explained. "Never met anybody yet who felt real good about waking up with one of these things crawling around their room."

Gadgets started to laugh. "Talk about guerrilla action." He looked at Ironman. "Any comment?"

Lyons smiled coldly as he studied the canvas sack. "Just one. Don't get caught doing it."

"We haven't been yet," Proudfoot said, signaling the other man that it was time to get busy again. The two deputies seemed to vanish into the darkness.

"I don't know if I approve of what they're doing," Blancanales commented. "But I'm sure glad they're on our side."

"Me, too," Lyons admitted.

OVERHEAD, the moon glowed like a Hollywood searchlight. A shadow moved along the wooden walls of the long building.

Proudfoot stopped and waited for Valdez to catch up with him. They had quietly toured the two housing units, slipping past the dozing guards and leaving little gifts behind.

Valdez looked at the bag Proudfoot was carrying. He whispered his question. "I used up mine. How many you got left?"

"One," the Apache whispered back. "Got any ideas?"

The Irish-looking deputy thought about it and smiled. "How about that big blond woman. You know, the one who keeps looking over the girls in town like she was out shopping."

"Know where she sleeps?"

Valdez nodded and gestured for Proudfoot to follow him. "I peeked in the windows."

EVERY MORNING at five before there was any sunlight Ilona Lupescu would wake up and have to go to the bathroom. It had been going on since she was a little girl, almost thirty-five years. The only difference was that she wore a nightgown as a child. And, now as a woman, she slept naked.

This morning was no different. The tall blond woman threw the covers back and sat up. She started to reach for the lamp on the nightstand, then changed her mind. She could find her way to the bathroom without it.

She still wasn't sure she liked living in the United States. The people and customs were peculiar. But she knew she liked living at the camp. Whatever else was wrong with Elena Demenescu, she'd done a first-class job remodeling the living quarters.

Take this room. For one thing it had its own bathroom. No traipsing down a cold corridor to get to a communal facility.

Then the size of the room. Not a monk-size cell, but a real room. She thought of some of the people she'd known back in Bucharest. A family could make an entire home out of a room this big.

Finally there was food. As much food as she wanted. No having to bully or steal to get a decent meal.

There were only two things missing—a bed companion and action. Elena frowned on her preference for her own sex, so Ilona had abstained so far.

She had filled her days and nights improving her martial-arts skills and practicing on the firing range.

Elena had promised them action. Soon, she had said. As much as she distrusted the woman, Ilona decided to wait and see what kind of action the younger woman had in mind. If it was less than what Michael had provided them, she would join in the already-started clandestine movement to appoint a new leader.

The stirring inside reminded her that she hadn't awakened to think about Elena but to go to the bathroom. Stretching, she let her feet touch the carpeted floor.

The usually springy rug seemed to move more now than it had before. For a moment she wondered if it hadn't been stretched properly. She started to stand when she heard a dry rattling noise near her right foot.

She jumped back onto the bed and pulled the covers up to her neck. Something was on the floor. Something that twisted and moved.

A ghost? No, Ilona didn't believe in ghosts. She left that to the superstitious Transylvanian peasants.

She reached for the light and turned it on. Coiled and staring angrily at her was the largest, meanest snake she'd ever seen. It hissed at her, forcing its forked tongue out of its scaly mouth.

For a moment she was paralyzed. Was this one of those cobras that could spit venom fifty feet? No, it didn't have a hooded head. Numbly she remembered seeing pictures of this creature before. A rattlesnake.

Somebody wanted her to die. She had many enemies, even among the Draculs. But who would wish so hideous a death on anyone?

She had used snake venom before, but only on enemies of the state. Not on people.

Slowly the numbness ebbed away and she realized suddenly that she was only a few feet away from painful death. Ilona Lupescu began to scream.

"How'd it go?" Lyons asked.

The two deputies smiled at each other. "There'll be a lot of nervous folks down there in a little while," Valdez commented.

Pol and Gadgets exchanged glances. Both of them were grateful they weren't on the two deputies' hit list.

Lyons started handing the two men a package of Semtex plastic explosive and a triggering device, then hesitated. "You don't have to do this," he said.

"Hand it over," the Apache deputy replied. "I never told anybody, but that damn camp is sitting on top of my ancestors' bones. They'd probably appreciate getting some sunshine on their graves instead of a bunch of buildings."

Pol joined in. "Let me show you how to set this up."

Proudfoot glanced at his partner. They exchanged smiles. "Ol' Frank here was a demolition expert back in Nam."

The three Able Team commandos looked impressed. They'd gotten a lot more than they bargained for.

"If you two ever want to change jobs—" Gadgets started to say.

"I don't know who you guys work for, but no thanks," Proudfoot replied, rejecting the offer. "If you think we're mean, hell, we've got a couple of old ladies who give mean a whole new twist. They wouldn't like us changing our working hours."

"We need to take out the arsenal and the motor yard," Lyons said.

"Must be that small building that stands alone near the firing range," the Irish-looking law officer replied. "We know where that is."

The other deputy nodded. "What do you want us to do after that?"

"Make sure no one slips out the other side of the complex," Lyons answered.

"We can make sure the electricity's on," Proudfoot said.

"Frightened rabbits have a way of getting around electric fences."

Valdez looked concerned. "All we got with us is a pair of Mossberg 12-gauge and our side arms."

Both were wearing .45 Colt Government models in their holsters.

Ironman slipped his caseless from his shoulder and handed it to the Apache. "We've got plenty of ammo for this baby."

Proudfoot rejected the offer. "I'm an M-16 man myself."

"Me, too," his partner said.

"Our kind of guys," Pol commented with a twinkle in his eye. "I think we can outfit both of you with the latest fashions."

ELENA HEARD the soft movement in her bedroom. At first she thought it was Dragnan walking around in the dark. But, no, the ugly little man was asleep.

She listened carefully. Something was moving across the carpeted floor. She smelled a stale odor in the air, like the stench of a wild creature. She felt for the MAC-10 she'd taken to bed with her. It was still where she'd put it.

Cautiously reaching for the lamp on the nightstand, she snapped on the light. She peered across the floor. Crawling toward the open bathroom door was a huge rattlesnake.

Elena grabbed the MAC-10. She emptied a continuous stream of bullets into the rattler and the carpeting around it until the 30-round clip was empty.

The dwarf sat up suddenly, a Baretta 92-F in his hand. He stared at her and saw the grim expression on her face. Then he turned and looked at the floor. There were bits of rug and snakeskin splattered in every direction. "What was it?"

"Somebody's idea of a joke," she said bitterly. "Their last joke when I find out who." She jumped from the bed and started pulling on her clothes. "Call the guards. I want to find out who was walking around in the past hour."

23

Billy Proudfoot could see the first streaks of morning sunlight sneak in through the small windows of the building. They needed to get done and out of here before anyone came. He crammed a wad of Semtex under the stack of ammo cases, then looked around the weapons warehouse until he spotted his partner. "Haul that wire over here," he called out.

Valdez walked the spool he was holding toward the Apache deputy, letting the wire unravel as he moved. Then he looked around while Proudfoot attached the wires to one of the devices the visitors from Washington had given him. "I think we've got the motor pool and this place covered," he said. "What next?"

"How about we find us a high place so we can get in some varmint shooting?"

Valdez nodded and started to follow the other man out of the arsenal. "You know what?"

Proudfoot turned. "What?"

"I like big-league rat hunting." He grinned. "You think we should reconsider that guy's offer?"

"Sure," Proudfoot replied, "if you're willing to tell my wife about it."

THE THREE WARRIORS waited near the van until they heard the series of explosions from the compound. Lyons peered through his binoculars, then handed them to Gadgets. "It's time to get the show on the road."

Gadgets whistled as he studied the far end of the campsite. "Sure a lot of pollution shooting up into the sky down there," he commented.

Then Pol took the glasses and put them against his eyes. "Beautiful. Even better than when we wired that arsenal in Nam," he muttered.

Ironman signaled Maynard to start the truck, then climbed in and slid down into the narrow space behind the seat.

Bear sat in his chair and watched Blancanales and Schwarz disappear into the truck. He had prevailed upon the three to let him wait for them outside the van.

"Stay hard!" he yelled, fondling the MAC-10 Ironman had left him.

Pol lifted his head and waved. "Stay out of trouble. We'll come and get you when it's over."

The truck moved down the dusty road toward the fenced compound.

DRAGNAN SUPERVISED the men and women trying to put out the fires. It seemed hopeless. Columns of fire and black, suffocating smoke were all around them.

Most of the arsenal had been destroyed, as well as half the trucks and cars in the motor pool.

As he gripped his mini-Uzi, he beckoned an exhausted-looking guard to walk with him. "Who was on duty last night?"

The guard hesitated. "Radu and I were."

The troll's face had no expression. "Were you smoking?"

"No," the fatigued man protested. "I wouldn't smoke around ammunition."

The second guard looked nervous. The dwarf gestured for him to join them. He repeated the question.

"Of course not." The second guard looked offended. "Do you think I'm stupid?"

"No," Dragnan answered. He squeezed the trigger of his Israeli weapon and showered the two men with 9 mm rivets. "Dead."

JINX MAYNARD DROVE his garbage truck up to the main gate and looked around for the guards who were usually waiting for him. Nobody seemed to be around.

He honked his horn several times. A man armed with an AK-47 appeared from inside the small building near the gate. He looked worn and irritated. "Not today," he shouted through the fencing.

Maynard looked over his shoulder for instructions. "What do I do now?"

Ironman, Pol and Gadgets were crouched behind him, fully armed for combat. "Con him into letting you in," Lyons said quietly. "I'm sure you know how."

The occasional prospector nodded and turned back to the guard. "If I don't pick up your stuff now, it'll be two weeks before I can come back. I'm on vacation next week."

The guard seemed unsure what he should do. He started to go back into the building, then changed his mind and opened the gate. "All right, but hurry. We've had some trouble."

Maynard tried to look sympathetic. "Nothing serious, I hope."

"An accident." He hesitated. "A fire. But we have it under control," the guard replied. "Just pick up the trash and leave."

Maynard smiled at the nervous man and drove down the dusty main street of the compound. Usually the main thoroughfare was filled with men and women. Now it was deserted.

He tilted his head back. "Where do you want me to stop?"

"Wherever you start picking up garbage," Ironman answered.

The grizzled old man downshifted the truck and moved slowly around the side of the long building on his left. "I usually start here where they have the kitchen."

"What else is in the building?"

"The dining room and gymnasium. The woman has her office in there. And, from what I could figure out, there are some rooms in the basement. Probably used for storage."

Lyons lifted his head and peered at the building. He could see the narrow slit windows set in the building at ground level. Storage rooms didn't get windows. He wondered what or who was kept down there. "The building across the road. What's in there?"

"Don't know exactly. More offices, I think." He remembered something. "Must be offices. I keep picking up boxes of that large computer paper outside it."

The three Stony Man commandos exchanged glances. They'd located the computer center.

Lyons addressed the driver again. "Where does the woman who runs this place hang out?"

"All over," Maynard replied, keeping his eyes forward as he pulled his truck to a stop. "Mostly she's either in her office or in the building across the street." He opened his door, stepped out and looked around. Nobody was in sight. "The coast is clear," he announced in a low voice.

Lyons, Blancanales and Schwarz worked their way out of the truck. Gadgets felt his neck. The redheaded woman's fingermarks were still embedded in his skin.

The three Able Team commandos reached into the truck for their weapons. All three men wore thick Kevlar armor under their cotton work shirts and had chosen camouflage bush pants that resisted thorns and cactus spines.

Maynard watched as the three donned their battle gear, then looked around nervously. "Need anything else from me?"

"Yeah. Call my girlfriend and tell her I'll be over for dinner," Gadgets cracked.

Maynard looked startled.

"Don't mind him," Blancanales said. "He always gets a little crazy when he's out in the hot sun too long."

Maynard was totally confused. The sun had only just begun to come up.

Lyons shook his head at the other two warriors, then turned to the town garbageman. "You can tell Devlin thanks for the help."

"Should I tell him you'll stop by after this is all over?"

"Yes, if we can," Lyons replied.

THE EXPLOSIVES had awakened Tad Silvern. He had jumped out of bed, convinced he was listening to the end of the world. When the reverberating blasts eased off fifteen minutes later, he sat on the edge of the cot and felt himself to make sure he was still alive.

He wasn't sure what had happened. There was no time to wonder about it. The cell door opened and an armed guard outside signaled for him to step out.

Silvern had never seen this one before. The guy was huge and ugly. As he moved through the door, the student asked, "What does she want?"

He never heard the reply. The guard smashed his rifle against Silvern's head and the student crumpled to the ground.

"She wants to see you," the sour-faced man said sullenly as he threw the human bag of potatoes over his shoulder.

LYONS SURVEYED the compound through his binoculars. He could see a large number of men and women rushing back and forth with buckets of sand to the still-blazing building that had once contained the arsenal. Another group was trying to put out the flames that threatened to consume the motor pool. A dwarf was rushing between the two conflagrations, trying to spur the others into faster action.

Gadgets looked around. "How do we play it? Together or individually?"

"Too much territory to cover as a team," Lyons said. "We'll split up." He pointed at the building that contained the living quarters. "You check that out," he told Pol. Then he pointed at the building with the offices. "You find out what's going on in that one," he told Gadgets. "I'll poke around the building with the computer center."

He reached into a pouch on his web belt. There was another package of Semtex in in. "It's time we wasted another twenty million dollars of the government's money."

He started to move across the street, but Gadgets called out and stopped him. "I just thought of something. What if they've set off those time-controlled viruses? From what

Bear explained they can only be deactivated by someone who knows where they are."

Ironman contemplated the dilemma for a moment. "Maybe I can find somebody inside and convince them to turn the damn things off." He checked around to make sure nobody was watching, then ran across the road.

"Stay hard, homeboy," Pol called out.

"Same to both of you," Lyons replied. "Hopefully I'll see you later."

BLANCANALES SLIPPED into the building through a side door. His M-16 became an extension of his hands as he moved quietly through the single-level structure.

Nobody seemed to be around. Pol thought he could check the place out in a few minutes, then cross the street and lend Lyons a hand.

His plan suddenly changed when an angry couple with TEC-9s opened the front door and stomped into the center hall. They made him the moment they entered, and turned their stubby assault weapons on him.

Diving across the floor to avoid their shower of parabellum poison, the Able Team fighter kicked at a door and rolled into the room. The man and woman charged after him before he could get back onto his feet. A quick body roll and he was facing the attackers.

There was no time to aim. Blancanales emptied his clip at the suddenly surprised couple. As they continued to rush him, Pol's flesh-seekers tore a perforated pattern across their midsections.

Blancanales rose carefully and kicked their weapons out of reach, then he knelt and checked their neck arteries for pulse.

Nothing. Satisfied, he stood up again.

"Drop it!" a sinister male voice ordered from behind.

There was no time to turn and see if the newcomer was armed. Pol assumed he was. He dropped his M-16, listening to its clatter as it made contact with the polished wooden floor.

"Now the gun on your shoulder," the voice said.

Pol let the H&K caseless fall to the floor.

"And the handgun."

Pol started to lift the weapon from its holster.

"Carefully," the voice warned.

As he eased the shotgun out of its leather case, he let his hand grip one of the incendiary grenades on his belt. Jerking it free of its pin, he tossed both the shotgun and the grenade back in an underhand sweep, then dived under the bed and rolled into a tight ball.

There was a sudden flash of light and a wave of extreme heat as the grenade exploded. He could hear the pitiful screams from across the room. He hadn't missed the target.

Flames started to creep across the paneled walls. Pol dragged himself out from under the bed. He could smell his scorched flesh. There was no time to worry about that now. The fire threatened to engulf the room before it spread to the rest of he building. Blancanales scooped up the caseless and high-jumped over the flames.

HOLDING HIS UZI in front of him, Schwarz moved cautiously through the building. It bothered him that he had encountered no one, then he remembered the twin fires. Everybody was out trying to extinguish the flames. Kind of a secret-police volunteer fire department, he decided with a wry smile.

He moved carefully into the gymnasium. It was big and new. Newer than the one at Stony Man Farm.

He left the gym and wandered down the hall until he came to an ornate door. He pushed it open and stared at a lavishly furnished office. Large inlaid desk. Leather chairs. Thick carpeting. Red brocade drapes. A throne room fit for a queen.

He could smell her perfume. A queen's fragrance. This was where she ruled her dark empire. The queen. If he had any choice, she'd be queen for a day, then dead.

He checked her desk. The front-page headline about the suicide of the *Securitate* man caught his attention. Somehow he was sure the woman had something to do with it.

Something else caught his eye—a stack of pages with lists of names, airports and arrival dates. The Immigration and Naturalization Service people would like to see these. He folded them and shoved them into one of the deep pockets in his camouflage pants.

Schwarz left the room and finished checking out the rest of the main floor. The large kitchen was amply stocked. At least the goons were well fed. He wondered if the kitchen help had joined the others at the fires.

He checked the large dining room. Empty. Then he found the stairs that led to the basement and decided to see if anybody was down there before he hooked up with Ironman and Pol.

It took a moment for his eyes to adjust to the dim light. There was a series of metal doors along one wall. He began to open them one by one. They were uninhabited.

The last cell had been occupied. There were scraps of food on the small plastic tray and an empty glass coated with the remains of milk. Schwarz wondered who had been kept here.

He noticed the magazines on the cot. Computer magazines. Now he knew. Tad Silvern.

A thought came into his mind. If the college student had been cooperating, they wouldn't have had to lock him up in a cell. He thought the general would be pleased to know that. Even more pleased if they could find his son alive.

As he climbed back up the stairs, he ran right into a large brute of a man holding a MAC-10. The creature and he were both surprised by the sudden encounter.

Gadgets reacted first. A short burst from his M-16 split the other man's sternum and tore up his lungs. Schwarz stepped over the body and found himself facing a quartet of *Securitate* agents. Several short bursts sent the group scattering for cover.

Gadgets took advantage of their momentary panic and did a forward flip out of the path of a spray of lead from their MAC-10s. Twisting around, he switched his weapon to autofire and felled the four outraged *Securitate* agents with a barrage of flesh-seekers.

One of the men, who was built like a wrestler, started cursing as he struggled to get up. Gadgets dropped the now-empty M-16 and jerked the Colt Elite from his holster. There was no time to aim. He pumped three slugs into the giant, then glanced around at the gore around him. Five up. Five down. And he was still going. That was all that mattered.

He ducked out of the building to see how Pol and Ironman were doing.

24

Elena knew exactly what was happening the minute she heard the gunfire across the road. Someone had betrayed her.

The dwarf? Possibly.

But who were the attackers? Probably mercenaries Dragnan had hired.

How many could she kill with the MAC-10 she wore on her shoulder? She checked the 30-round clip. It was fully loaded.

Then she suddenly remembered that the student was in the room. Turning, she saw him sitting at the computer console, staring at her, his face filled with terror.

"I want the programs that will get me into the government computers," she ordered. "Copy them onto diskettes."

Silvern was frozen with fear.

"Now," she insisted loudly.

"You won't know how to use them," he replied weakly.

"Then I'll take you with me," she decided. "Get them."

Silvern didn't move.

"Get them or die!" she yelled.

Silvern shivered, then shook his head. "No," he said quietly.

She stared at him. His face was strangely calm.

LYONS CHECKED the rooms in the building. They were empty except for the one at the end of the corridor. He could hear voices behind it. Correction—one voice, a woman's.

"Get them or die!"

A second voice—it sounded like the voice of a young man—answered, "No."

Lyons checked his M-16. It was ready, and so was he.

He rammed his shoulder against the door, shoving it open. The woman on the other side swung a MAC-10 toward him.

He recognized her. The lady in the digitized picture. She looked prettier in person. And better dressed. But right now none of that mattered.

"Drop it, lady," he snapped.

He waited for her to ease off on her grip. She smiled at him. A cold smile of hate. He watched her finger as it began to tighten.

The negotiations were over.

He punched a trio of high-powered killers. Two of them tore into her side before she could fire back. The third destroyed her left kneecap.

Blood colored her expensive outfit crimson. Despite the pain on her face she tried to shoot back.

"Don't!" Lyons yelled.

Stubbornly she kept trying. There wasn't time for pity. Ironman let loose another short burst, this time at her face.

Her head exploded like an overripe melon. Bits of blood and brain tissue covered everything, including him.

He heard a noise to his right. Spinning around, he saw a tall, skinny boy puking all over a computer console. "Tad Silvern?"

The young man finally stopped. "Yes, I'm Tad." He stared at Lyons's weapon. "Are you going to kill me?"

"No. Can you eliminate the viruses before they do any more damage?"

The graduate student forced a smile on his face. "I already did a few days ago."

"Come again?" Ironman thought the reverberations had damaged his hearing.

"When I installed them, I changed the programs so they'd self-destruct when they were activated."

Ironman recognized the irony. "Then it's time we got out of here, son."

He remembered something. The Semtex. He took out the plastic explosive and started to press it under the frame of the huge machine.

The young man looked at it. "Explosive?"

"Yes."

"You won't need to use it. I fixed the computer so that it can't be used without extensive repairs from a factory technician."

Lyons smiled. "I guess we better get you home."

GADGETS WAS SMEARING burn ointment on Pol's hands and face when Lyons and the young man emerged from the building.

Schwarz checked with Ironman. "Tad Silvern?"

"Yes. It's about time we left. The locals can handle the rest of them," Ironman announced.

Pol turned and saw a horde of armed men and women rushing toward them from the direction of the still-burning arsenal. "Not yet," he warned.

Lyons shoved the student back toward the door. "Wait inside," he ordered as he snapped a fresh clip into his M-16.

Gadgets and Blancanales also reloaded.

Lyons studied the enemy pack. "I count twenty," he said. "Whites-of-their-eyes time," he snapped, ordering the other two to hold fire until the enemy was closer.

The dwarf was leading the attackers. The ugly little man was carrying a MAC-10. So did most of the others, except for a few who were brandishing AK-47s.

The Able Team squad separated and took cover. Despite the burns Blancanales fired first—a 3-shot burst. A stocky *Securitate* agent in front absorbed two of his shots and dropped.

Schwarz was next. He emptied his clip and stopped four attackers in the prime of their lives.

Kneeling, Ironman was more selective. Carefully he aimed and fired short bursts, making each trio count. Five bodies absorbed his lead and fell.

The dwarf looked at the number who had died and ran to the safety of a nearby building. Lyons spotted him and tried to chop him down with a pair of slugs. The little man disappeared behind the building as the bullets tore into the wooden frame.

"Talk about stubborn," Ironman yelled as the rest of the *Securitate* force pressed forward, emptying their weapons as they moved toward them.

BILLY PROUDFOOT wrapped his arm around an exhaust vent and helped pull Frank Valdez to the peak of the single-story structure. They had just arrived from the other end of the camp. Five fuming goons had made their last stand there. When the rest took off for the other side of the compound, the two deputies had decided the three Washington visitors might need a hand.

Proudfoot checked his M-16. His clip was nearly empty. He slammed home a fresh one and spread-eagled on the roof. Valdez pulled himself up beside him. His assault weapon hung from his neck.

Below them they could see bodies on the ground, and more than a dozen raging men and women firing at the camouflage-clad trio.

"Party time," Proudfoot announced.

Valdez pushed the butt of his M-16 to his shoulder and lined up the sights. "Now I'm dressed for it."

From above, the Able Team squad heard rounds of fire. Turning and shoving their weapons skyward, they were ready to blast the new source of gunfire when they saw the two familiar figures wave to them from the roof.

Proudfoot had his cheek against the stock of his M-16. So did Valdez. They poured a lead shower down on the rapidly approaching *Securitate* force. Three more foot soldiers died.

A ricocheting slug caught Ironman in the right shoulder. The pain made him furious. Enough, he decided, of fighting clean. He reached into his belt and yanked out a frag grenade. Without hesitating he lobbed the metal oval downfield.

Pol and Gadgets dropped to the ground while the two deputies hugged the roof. Chunks of exploding metal tore life from three more opposing agents.

"My turn!" Blancanales yelled, and tossed a frag overhand. Another two fell.

The remaining attackers looked around at the dead and started running in the opposite direction. The two young deputies slid to the edge of the roof and let themselves drop to the ground. The Apache cop checked with Lyons. "You want us to bring them back alive?"

"Your option," Lyons replied.

The two uniformed men took off after the retreating agents, yelling as they pursued them, while Able Team group watched.

"They sound like they're on the warpath," Schwarz commented.

Lyons smiled despite the throbbing in his shoulder. "Aren't they?" He looked around. "Anybody see the dwarf?"

Pol and Gadgets disappeared for ten minutes, then returned. "Vanished," Pol reported.

"He won't get far," Lyons said. He saw the college student peek out from the front door of the nearby building. "Let's blow this pop stand," he decided.

EPILOGUE

Kurtzman was sitting in his motorized wheelchair near the van, waiting for them. His eyes lighted up when he saw the student.

"Hello, Uncle Aaron," Silvern said sheepishly.

"Are you okay?"

The Able Team trio showed up behind Silvern. Gadgets ducked into the van. "He's great," Lyons commented. Then he proceeded to tell Bear what the young man had done.

Kurtzman beckoned the student over and hugged him. Schwarz returned with a first-aid kit and, shoving away Ironman's protesting hands, dressed his shoulder wound.

Kurtzman broke into a loud laugh. "I taught you well," he told the student.

The two deputies showed up. The one with the Irish face asked, "Need anything else?"

"Not now," Lyons replied, wincing as Gadgets taped his shoulder. "But can we take a rain check for the future?"

"Next time give us a few days' warning," the Apache said, laughing. The uniformed pair took off for their parked vehicle.

Pol looked at Bear. "Get to see any of the fight from up here?"

"Some of it," the man in the wheelchair answered. "I missed the very end. I was kind of busy myself."

Schwarz was curious. "Doing what?"

"Getting rid of something that didn't agree with me." The three warriors glanced at one another puzzled. Kurtzman waited until they turned back to him before he continued. "You guys missing a dwarf?"

Pol's eyes sparked. "He go by this way?"

"Almost. We had a disagreement about where he was going." Bear looked satisfied. "I won."

Gadgets checked behind the van and found the dwarf's body, punctured with slugs.

Ironman shook his head. "Sometimes you're too much, Bear."

"Is that supposed to be a compliment?"

"You can take it as one," Lyons conceded.

"Good. So when's our next mission?"

The three warriors groaned and exchanged glances of sympathy. Maybe Brognola could do something with the new Aaron Kurtzman. They couldn't.

DIRTY MISSION

by
Gar Wilson

A Phoenix Force novel

PROLOGUE

As he followed Gary Manning into the large freight shed on the Rotterdam docks, with shots ringing in his ears, Calvin James sensed that the final chapter of the mission was about to unfold. For James this particular strike against the enemy had an added irony. As always the driving force behind any Phoenix mission was a desire for justice. This time, however, the black Phoenix warrior had deeper motives that were driving him passionately. Those motives had almost got him grounded, and only the backing of another Phoenix Force member had prevented his removal from the mission.

David McCarter, the short-tempered, often reckless British member of the Force, had spoken up in James's defense. Not noted for his eloquence or tact, the former SAS man had put into words what James had been feeling and justified the black warrior's intense desire to see the mission through. James had much to thank the cockney rebel for and when the opportunity arose he would make certain the Briton knew it.

James and the rest of Phoenix Force had a hard battle ahead of them. The enemy was ruthless in all aspects. The mission so far had revealed just how deadly and violent that enemy could be. In the past few days Phoenix Force had experienced one of their toughest assignments and found themselves pitted against the human animals who were involved in one of the vilest businesses ever conceived by a twisted criminal mind.

These were the purveyors of nightmares, dealers in drugs, the scourge of the century. One of the fastest growing industries in the supply and demand market, it was a business that dealt misery to the consumer and money to the supplier. Because of the consumer's overwhelming need, drug traffickers grew rich beyond comprehension. Their wealth, built on the wretched pain of drug users, was a constant source of violence, treachery, bribery, coercion and mayhem.

For Calvin James the whole scene had been summed up by an image from a photograph. The black-and-white print had been one of many in a file the Force had been studying at the start of the mission. Hal Brognola had spelled out the mission in the war room at Stony Man. But the Force wasn't presented with the file until they had reached England, and their meeting in London with the team of British police working undercover.

For Calvin James the whole thing had suddenly, shockingly, taken on a chilling, personal involvement. The photograph had shown the face of a girl—a dead girl—someone he had known for a number of years. Angie Martin, the daughter of an Air Force man James had known in Vietnam.

To get the money for the cocaine she'd needed so desperately, Angie Martin had worked the streets as a prostitute. One night a client had turned on her, attacking and killing her. For Calvin James the mission had become real from the moment he'd seen Angie Martin's photograph.

1

"I'll make this as brief as possible," Hal Brognola said. "I hate handing out missions on the run, but I'm in the middle of an Able Team assignment that needs my attention. So let's get to it."

The Stony Man topkick glanced around the war room conference table. The full Phoenix Force team was settling down, waiting to hear the details of their upcoming mission.

Brognola opened the file he was carrying and glanced at the top sheet to remind him of the subject matter. Then he addressed the Force.

"This time around you're going to take on an organization responsible for pushing drugs across Europe and Great Britain. We're involved because some of those drugs are finding their way into the hands of U.S. military personnel. I'm sure you can visualize the kind of problems that could generate. There have already been a number of drug-related incidents—and two deaths to date."

"Do you have any background material?" Yakov Katzenelenbogen, the Phoenix Force commander, asked.

Katz's almost benign appearance, heightened by his gray hair and blue eyes, had fooled many into believing that the middle-aged Israeli was harmless. The fact that he wore a prosthesis on his right arm only added to the deception. Katz happened to be one of the world's top practitioners in the art of warfare and espionage. He had battled the Nazi hordes during the Second World War and the British and the Arabs during Israel's War of Independence. It was during the later Six Day War that Katz had lost his arm. Tragically he had also lost his only son in the same conflict.

The son of Russian Jews, Katz had learned to fight at an early age. Life was a battle, he had found, with a few moments of calm between the hostilities. During those periods of calm, he had mastered English, French, German and Russian. When he moved into espionage and intelligence, he became a top agent in the Mossad, coming into contact with agents of the CIA, British SIS and French Sûreté.

Despite his personal losses—son, wife and arm—Katz held no bitterness. He remained optimistic about life. He was still luckier than many others.

Katz had been more than willing to accept the offer to join Phoenix Force at its conception. The secret commando force had been created to combat terrorism in all its many and varied forms. Katz had been the natural choice for commander of the group. He had taken the position with his usual modesty, quickly earning the respect and loyalty of the others.

"A little, and it's sketchy," Brognola admitted, answering Katz's question. "You'll be liaising with a British police drug team, which has been working on an assignment for a few months, trying to get the goods on the drug trafficking ring. During their investigation, they found evidence of the pipeline feeding our military people. The British government contacted the U.S. Drug Enforcement Agency, which in turn told the Pentagon. When the news reached the President, he called me in and handed the deal to us."

Calvin James leaned forward, his handsome face grim. The black ex-cop and former Navy SEAL had a deep hatred of drug dealers through personal experience. He had lost his sister through a heroin overdose. He kept his feelings under control during mission time, but his inner conflict often spilled over during discussions on the subject.

"How serious have the drug-related incidents been?" he asked.

"An Air Force helicopter almost took off with faulty hydraulics. Luckily someone spotted the problem before the chopper left the ground. It was determined that the guy in charge of servicing the hydraulics was on a cocaine high at the time. That incident took place on a base in England. It's an extreme example, but it shows what could happen if too many servicemen got themselves hooked.

"On another base in the same area live ammunition was handed out during a training exercise. The guy responsible kept telling everyone he figured it would liven things up. When the medics examined him, they found he was almost burned out from drug abuse. When the guy's quarters were searched, enough cocaine and crack were found to make him fly without a damn plane."

"The implication being that the next time could be a big one," Rafael Encizo said.

The fiery Cuban, exiled from his island home because he had disagreed with Castro's takeover, was one of the Force's steadier members. Though he did have a volatile temperament, he was also capable of great restraint in the face of extreme provocation.

When it came to the crunch, Encizo was never found at the back of the queue. He was a hard fighter, something he'd learned during the Castro takeover, and especially during his return to Cuba as a member of the Bay of Pigs invasion force. Captured, he had spent time in the dreaded El Principe political prison. He had resisted all attempts to indoctrinate him.

Eventually he had escaped and returned to the U.S., where he'd become an American citizen. He had worked in a variety of jobs. Despite his unease with their intelligence sources, he'd undertaken assignments for American law-enforcement agencies from time to time. He had been happier when the offer to join Phoenix Force had come along. Encizo liked the freedom the Force gave him, and also the opportunity to work with men he fully trusted.

"Exactly," Brognola agreed in answer to Encizo's question. "All we need is some guy in charge of a sensitive area touching the wrong button because he thinks he sees blips on a radar screen that aren't there."

"Point taken," Gary Manning, the Canadian Phoenix warrior, said.

Ruggedly built, Manning could have been mistaken for a lumberjack from his native Canada. His physical appearance concealed a sharp brain that had allowed him to become a civil engineer of exceptional talent; his forte was heavy construction and explosives. Manning had found he had the magic touch when it came to demolition work. He developed his skill until it became almost an art form. There was little he couldn't do with explosives, and once he joined Phoenix Force he found his skills in constant demand.

A lieutenant in the Canadian Army Corps of Engineers, Manning had served his time in Vietnam as a "special observer." As well as his demolition skill, he was a superb sharpshooter, and became a respected sniper. He was one of the few Canadian nationals to receive the Silver Star from the United States armed forces.

After Vietnam, Manning joined the Royal Canadian Mounted Police's covert intelligence department, traveling to Europe to work with West Germany's newly formed GSG-9 antiterrorist squad. Here he received firsthand experience at urban warfare. Manning stayed with the RCMP until a scandal in 1981 put them out of the intelligence business.

CSIS, Canada's new intelligence service, tried to recruit him after that, but Manning turned his back on the offer, preferring to move into the world of big business. He had a short-lived marriage, then became security consultant and junior executive for North American International.

He had been with NAI when he received the invitation from Stony Man to join Mack Bolan's new combat team—though at first Manning hadn't known Bolan was the guiding light of the Special Operations Group. Initial doubts about committing himself to the project had been swept aside once the Canadian became aware of the real need for a force to combat terrorism and its associated evils.

"How did the deaths occur?" James asked Brognola.

"One was an air force sergeant based in Germany. He was driving along the autobahn at full throttle when his car hit a semitrailer. It took the rescue services three hours to cut him from the wreckage. What got to the medics was the fact that the guy was grinning at them the whole time. Even though he'd lost a leg, he was still grinning in the hospital. He died the next day. An autopsy showed he'd been shot full of coke, and there were a couple of bags of cocaine in his car. Looks like he might have been dealing.

Analysis showed the cocaine to be identical to the stuff found in his belongings in England.''

''And the second death?''

''I don't have any details yet,'' Brognola said. ''My information is basic, just to the effect that a drug-related death has taken place. The victim was the daughter of a U.S. airman based in Germany. She was living in England. You'll have to get the full story from your British contact.

''The incidents are being kept under wraps at the moment. Washington is worried about news getting out. It wouldn't look too good for our image. The incidents in England were easy to conceal, but the one in Germany took some quick thinking and the cooperation of the German administration. Apart from the need to maintain security on these incidents, there's an urgent need to stop the supplier of these drugs.

''The U.S. has been working with the British to nail some of the big drug rings for some time. The British navy has been helping our Coast Guard nab smugglers trying to ship in coke along the Florida coast. In short, we have a good working relationship with the British.

''There've been some heavy investigations, and the DEA has come up with evidence showing a connection between the Colombians and British gang bosses who want to get in on the distribution end of the deal. The problem is the usual one. Even though the drug squads are trying to move fast, they still have to go through due process of law. That generally means delays. They can't just go busting in without hard evidence and all the correct legal papers.''

''What you're trying to say,'' David McCarter interrupted, ''is that they're having a bloody hard time making anything stick.''

Brognola nodded. "Hell, you guys know the problems as well as I do. The drug barons can afford the best lawyers around. They have them on fat retainers. Any law-enforcement agency has got to have its act completely watertight if it expects to win. Trouble is, that they take so long the suspect has time to close shop and move on."

"So we go in and do some corner cutting?" Manning commented. "That it?"

Brognola nodded. "The President wants this particular pipeline shut down, no questions asked. The British will allow us to put in a special team. They have an interest because there also appears to be a similar problem with their own military.

"Once these traffickers get their foot in the door they have the opportunity of expanding their trade. Let's face it, there are weak links in every chain. Even guys in the service can be tempted. Some will have the strength to resist. But others will take the carrot. Some may be content to use drugs for their own enjoyment. A few will see the chance to make some extra bucks. They'll become dealers. And there's a hell of an exploitable market for them.

"But the main point is this—whether the drugs are being peddled by the traffickers or by recruits in the service, they're still harmful to users, the guys in the Army and the Air Force. I don't have to spell out the kind of problems we could face if drug usage got out of hand. And there's another factor to consider. Any guy in the military who gets hooked on drugs is eventually going back home. That could mean quite a lot of men taking their drug problem back to the States. We don't need that. We have enough homegrown drug abuse. The last thing we want is more.

"From the intelligence reports passed to the DEA by the British cops, it looks like the U.S. military forces in

England and Europe are being targeted by these traffickers. This may be just another avenue for the dealers. It could also be deliberate targeting by the Colombians because the U.S. administration is supporting the Colombian government in its war against the cartels. Either way it has to be stopped.

"The President is more than a little concerned. He knows the problems regarding due process of law, but in this case he's given us the green light to move in. To put it bluntly, he's pissed off with these traffickers." The Fed glanced around the table.

"When do we leave?" Katz asked.

"This evening," Brognola replied. "The Air Force will fly you to the U.S. air base at Upper Heyford in Oxford."

"I remember the last time we were there," Manning said. The Oxford air base had been the arrival point for part of Phoenix Force at the commencement of a mission involving hijacked nuclear missiles and a plot to compromise NATO.

"You'll find a familiar face waiting for you," Brognola added. "Andrew Dexter is your contact man again."

McCarter perked up at this news. "At least that means I'll have someone around who'll be able to talk to me in understandable English."

"That's fine for you," James said. "But will he know what *you're* talking about?"

McCarter rolled his eyes toward the ceiling. "Worst thing we ever did was to give up control of the colonies," the hotheaded cockney muttered.

2

"If your last visit is anything to go by, I'm sure we're in for an interesting time," Andrew Dexter remarked, pouring hot coffee into thick china mugs.

Katz turned away from the window of the safehouse, an unimpressive detached house set in badly tended grounds and in need of a paint job. The residence sat on an anonymous little street in Ealing, an area once famous for being the home of the legendary Ealing Film Studios, where much of British movie history had been made. Those days were long gone, and not even Ealing could live forever on faded memories. They had been in the house for almost half an hour. During that time, the Force had freshened up from the long flights, which had landed at 11:30 a.m. on a bright morning.

"We do try to be consistent," the Israeli remarked. "What have you been up to since we were here last?"

Dexter began handing out the drinks. "Being around you fellows gave me a yearning for the old days when I saw some action myself. So I asked for a transfer to an active unit. Ended up on a special government task force to tackle the drug problem."

"Did you get your action?" Encizo asked.

Dexter smiled. "After a fashion. I don't spend so much time behind a desk now, and I did get to draw my gun a couple of times. Never got to fire it, though."

"Lucky guy," Manning said.

"What do you have lined up for us, Andrew?" Katz asked.

"A meeting with the investigating team that heads the task force. They've been conducting long-term investigations into the drug rings here in England. One of their aims has been to pinpoint key people involved in bringing drugs into the country and distributing them nationwide."

"Any success?" James asked.

"On paper, yes," Dexter admitted reluctantly. "But that's not enough."

The black Phoenix pro sighed. He knew what was coming next. Because of legislation, red tape, bureaucratic delays, the British cops were operating with their hands tied, just as they did in the United States.

"It makes me angry," Dexter said. "Those guys are working themselves to the limit, day after day. And every time they reach the point where they want to make a move something stops them. Some legal whiz kid comes up with a point of law that slams the door on a warrant being issued. Or there's a hint that someone's rights are being violated."

Dexter slammed his own mug of coffee down on the table with a bang. "It makes me bloody angry," he snapped. "What about the rights of the poor sods who end up in hospital looking like someone out of a concentration camp? Young kids all screwed up from too much dope? Girls turning to prostitution so they can earn money for their addiction? Users going out the streets and robbing the first poor bastard they see? What about them? Who gives a damn about their rights?"

"We do, chum," McCarter said. "We bloody well do."

Dexter sat down, his face flushed. "Sorry," he apologized. "I don't usually get carried away. But since I've been with the drug squad, my eyes have been opened. It's made me realize there are a lot of evil bastards on the loose who need hitting where it hurts. And to hell with their bloody rights."

"Don't apologize," Encizo said. "We all know what you're talking about. We've all been hamstrung by legal procedure."

Manning scratched his head. "Now governments are seeing the light—they've realized the enormity of the problem and are starting to take action. The trouble is, they're late into the game. The drug business is too well organized to go under in the first round. This is going to be one hell of a fight."

Katz lit a cigarette. "All you have to do is look at Colombia, the main cocaine supplier to the world. The business is so entrenched in Colombian society it practically runs the country. Previous governments have knuckled under to the might of the cartels. Even the army has lost control. Now that the president of Colombia has declared his intention to destroy the drug barons, they've opted for outright war against him."

"I've studied the Colombian situation closely," Dexter said. "The drug cartels own people in the army, the police, even the judiciary. They've built houses, schools, sports complexes for the people. They have a great deal of support in their own country."

"Most of the working class is so poor," Manning explained, "they see the drug barons as heroes. The government can't provide housing or jobs, but the cartels can. The ordinary Colombian peasant, earning a decent wage paid by the cartels, doesn't give a damn about the misery cocaine causes in the United States or Britain. Why should he? His picture of America is of a rich, materialistic country too wrapped up in enjoying itself to care about the poor.''

"What a bloody mess we've got ourselves into," Dexter said.

"It isn't all bad," McCarter said cheerfully. "They still make Player's and I can drink as much Coca-Cola as I want."

"I knew if we waited long enough you'd contribute something useful," James remarked.

The cockney rebel grinned. "I'm here to please."

"What time are we meeting your drug team?" Katz asked.

Dexter glanced at his watch. "In a couple of hours."

"Enough time for us to check our equipment," Katz suggested.

Along with their ordinary luggage had come the Force's additional baggage. This consisted of aluminum cases that contained weapons, ammunition, explosives and an assortment of lethal equipment. Phoenix Force never went deliberately looking for trouble. Their missions, however, were often subject to sudden, violent changes. They had survived for a long time because they never took anything at face value.

The Force preferred using their own weapons. They felt comfortable with familiar firearms. Sometimes, however, they were barred from taking weapons into a country. When that happened, Phoenix Force had to compromise. On a practical level that never worried them. Every member of the Force was conversant with practically all types of firearms. They made it their business to know the workings of foreign and domestic weapons inside out. Not to know could mean the difference between life and death.

Andrew Dexter watched with interest as the members of the Force opened the aluminum cases and removed their weapons. Recently a decision had been reached to equip each member of the team with 9 mm Uzi machine pistols. When it came to a handgun, the Force had opted for the Walther 9 mm P-88 autoloader.

But there had been one note of dissent over the choice of the P-88. David McCarter had refused even to consider changing from his beloved Browning Hi-Power. His objection had been more than just his usual contrariness. His feelings for the Browning were strong, and he made it clear he wasn't about to give it up. In the end, since it used the same 9 mm ammo as the Walthers, he was allowed to keep it.

Other members of the team kept various weapons for the times when something more than a close-quarter firearm was required. Calvin James had his M-16, with the M-203 grenade launcher attached. Gary Manning had a 7.62 mm FAL assault rifle and his most recent addition, the SA-80 5.56 mm rifle. He also had an Anschutz air rifle. This was a high-precision weapon that fired hypodarts loaded with sleep-inducing Thorazine. In separate, smaller cases Manning had blocks of explosives and detonators.

Rafael Encizo had retained his H&K MP-5 SMG, while Katz had brought along his full-size Uzi. David McCarter still used his KG-99, the replacement for the MAC-10 he had reluctantly given up some time back due to its unreliability during firefights. The cockney also maintained a Barnett Commando crossbow, useful for taking out opponents silently. The crossbow provided accuracy over a long distance and was, in McCarter's skilled hands, deadly.

Andrew Dexter watched Phoenix Force go through their ritual of checking each weapon and the loaded magazines that accompanied each firearm. Having seen this secretive group of men at work during their previous mission in Britain, he understood that they were special. They operated in a world of violence and sudden death, confronting desperate individuals in desperate situations. Seeing the Stony Man commandos preparing themselves, Dexter felt there might yet be a little light at the end of the tunnel.

3

The base of the undercover drug unit was situated in a disused factory near the East India Dock Road. There were many vacant factory and office buildings in the area. Although redevelopment was progressing at a surprising rate, there were still many signs of the area's decline.

The drug unit moved unnoticed through the use of panel trucks marked with the logo of a construction company. Their cover was that they were carrying out work inside the factory. Andrew Dexter used a similarly marked panel truck to deliver Phoenix Force to the site. He entered through the sagging metal gates and drove slowly across the debris-littered yard. All around were the drab, deserted buildings of a once-busy factory.

Dexter backed the panel truck up to a loading bay so that the Force could climb out. He led them inside the dusty, gloomy factory and across to stairs leading up. They climbed two flights, then moved along a passage littered with debris, their footsteps making a hollow sound on the concrete floor.

"Can't beat a decent stakeout," James muttered, glancing around their grimy surroundings.

"The glamour of the job," Manning said.

Entering an area divided into offices, they got their first view of the drug unit's setup. Some of the offices were being used as sleeping quarters, a communications room, an information center, a kitchen.

The largest office was the operation center. The walls were covered with maps and photographs. Desks were piled with folders and more photographs. Telephones were everywhere. There were also a number of active computer units. Printers chattered occasionally, disgorging sheets of information.

There were eight people in the room—six men and two women. They were obviously waiting for the arrival of Phoenix Force.

"This is Detective Inspector Tobin," Dexter said, indicating a tough-looking man in shirtsleeves. "He's in charge."

Tobin looked like a nightclub bouncer. His dark hair was cut short and starting to recede. His hands were large and his exposed arms were thick and muscular. His piercing blue eyes regarded Phoenix Force with thinly disguised resentment.

Katz sensed Tobin's antagonism and could well understand it. It was obvious from the amount of paperwork that Tobin's unit had been putting in much hard work, probably beyond what had been expected of them. They may even have been close to a breakthrough. Now they would have to relinquish their independence to a group of strangers who were authorized to override their authority. Katz never liked being in that situation.

"Inspector, my name is Lawrence," Katz said, offering his one good hand, his left. "I must apologize for the way we've been pushed onto you. However, let me say that we're going to need your help, and we'll be grateful for anything you can give us."

Tobin took the Israeli's hand, surprised to find a grip as hard as his own. The one-armed, middle-aged man was no pen pusher, Tobin decided. In Katz's eyes he recognized a kindred spirit, someone familiar with the tough back streets of life who knew how to play down-and-dirty if necessary.

"They didn't tell me much," Tobin said. "Just that a team of American specialists was coming in, and we were to be fully cooperative. No questions asked. All information to be readily accessible to you."

Katz smiled. "I'd have liked to have been a fly on the wall when they told you that."

The line around Tobin's mouth hardened, then he scratched his cropped hair, nodding slightly. He didn't smile, but the corners of his eyes seemed to crinkle.

"You've played this game before?" he asked.

Katz nodded. "Let's say it probably isn't the first time for either of us."

"Bloody hell," Tobin said. "We're after the same thing in the end, I suppose? Hitting the drug traffickers where it hurts?"

"Correct," Katz said.

"Let's get the formalities over," the British cop said, turning to the rest of his team.

"From left to right, Detective Sergeant Vic Lane, and Detective Constables Pearson, Evans, Marchant and Lewis. Our ladies are Detective Sergeant Andrea Renfrew and Detective Constable Barbara Toomey. Every officer in this unit has had experience related to drugs during his or her time with the force. We've been given a wide-ranging brief for this assignment and have also been promised official backup as and when needed. We've been on this a long time, Lawrence, and we feel we're getting close."

"But?" Katz prompted.

"There's always a but, isn't there?" Tobin said bitterly.

"I'd say you weren't getting that official backup as fast as you want it," McCarter observed.

Tobin glanced at him. "You're no Yank."

"Must have been your shrewd powers of observation that got you promoted to detective inspector," the blunt-speaking East Ender wisecracked.

Tobin stepped forward, his eyes fixed on McCarter.

"Excuse Mr. Ransom," Katz butted in. "One of his less than endearing qualities is an immature sense of humor. I'll talk to him about it later."

McCarter, slouching against the edge of a desk as he lit a Player's, muttered, "Sounds like I'll be getting detention again."

Katz, who hadn't heard the Briton's final remark, addressed himself to Tobin. "Is that the problem? Official blockage?"

"Damn right," Tobin snapped. "Every time we reach a point where we feel we could make something stick we get the runaround. It's the old story. Not enough hard evidence. We need more before we can issue a warrant."

"Must be pretty frustrating," Manning sympathized.

Detective Sergeant Vic Lane waved a thick file in the air. "When you've spent all the time we have getting the goods on the bastards, then get told you haven't got enough for a conviction, I'd say it's a bloody sight more than frustrating. You want to know how I feel about drug traffickers? Go ahead—just ask."

"I think we're all agreed," Katz put in, "that there are few redeeming features as far as the suppliers are concerned. We all feel they should be dealt with in—shall we say—a more direct way. Due to your official restraints it isn't possible for you to circumnavigate those restrictions. We, on the other hand, have no such restraints. Official sanction—from both the U.S. and British governments—gives us the power to take whatever action is needed to stop a particular organization."

"No strings attached?" Tobin asked.

Katz shook his head. "Apart from giving consideration to the rights of the innocent—no strings."

"I envy you that freedom," Tobin said. "I take it your interests lie with the people we sent information about?"

"That's right," Katz said. "Your information was passed to Washington. These particular traffickers are targeting U.S. military personnel and their dependents. If you consider it, there's a large market. Thousands of potential customers. One of the problems allied to being part of a large military force in peacetime is the boredom factor. Lots of free time. You also have a percentage of unattached men looking for a little fun. No harm in that.

"But the drug pusher uses that need. He provides entertainment, which is nothing more than bait. The victim is plied with drink, women, whatever is his pleasure, to excess. Somewhere along the line drugs are introduced. They may be offered outright or slipped in casually. It's a gamble on the part of the pusher. He won't get everyone. But some will try it and a percentage will come back for more. Those who become hooked are later used to recruit more potential users. After that it's the old story."

Katz looked from face to face and continued. "What concerns the U.S. government is that any of these military users could be in charge of a high-security department, or in control of an aircraft carrying nuclear weapons. What if he or she overdosed on duty? The result might be horrendous, even tragic. Taking the scenario to its ultimate, we might end up in a war situation."

"Put like that," Tobin said, "I see your point."

"That point being," Encizo said, "we can't afford to wait for due process of law. We're faced with a time bomb. It could go off at any minute."

"What's your feeling on this, Dexter?" Tobin asked.

"I have to go with what Lawrence says. These people don't give a damn about any harm they might cause through their drugs. Appealing to their sense of decency is out. The only surefire way of stopping them is to hit without warning. Cut them off at the source."

"We're not geared up for that sort of exercise," Tobin admitted. "It would take time for us to obtain permission to mount a full-scale raid. That would bring us back to square one."

"You'd have to convince someone you were justified?" Katz asked.

Tobin nodded. "Without permission we can't get the necessary equipment. Right now all we have are handguns."

"Bloody red tape," McCarter snapped. The British commando had strong opinions where bureaucracy was concerned. McCarter was a man of action. He had no time for the formalities of government agencies. Especially when he saw how they often thwarted quick, clean justice. "I sometimes wonder which is the worst offender—the criminal or the law when it drags its heels."

"Let's not get on that tack," Katz warned. "I understand your predicament, Tobin. But we're not under any constraint. And we can be ready to move anytime, day or night. And believe me, move we will."

4

McCarter had been on the periphery of the main conversation. As always, his senses were tuned to what was going on around and beyond the Force, ever ready to pick up a sound or some movement that could be classed as unusual or possibly threatening to the Stony Man commandos. Now the Briton saw something that aroused his suspicions.

One of Tobin's team members—the constable named Marchant—had moved away from the main group. He had casually moved a file from one desk to another, while appearing to listen to the discussion. His action had placed him behind a desk beside a large window. Nothing initially sinister, but then Marchant did something that immediately brought him under McCarter's direct scrutiny.

The constable glanced at his watch with a nervous expression, then glanced out the window, his eyes searching the factory grounds.

What the bloody hell was he looking for? McCarter wondered.

Marchant was beginning to look distinctly uncomfortable. He was acting like someone waiting for an unpleasant incident to occur. McCarter skirted the line of desks and eased up behind Marchant without indicating his presence. "Company coming?" he asked quietly.

Startled, Marchant fumbled his reply, not convincing the cockney rebel.

"Don't play dumb with me," McCarter snapped. He ran a swift bluff. "Do you really believe we'd let you get away with this? Bloody idiot, we've been on to you right from the start."

"How did you find...?" Marchant began to ask, then caught the knowing gleam in McCarter's eyes. He realized then that he had been well and truly suckered.

The cop's face hardened, a muttered obscenity slipping from his lips. Then he made a play for the gun holstered under his jacket.

"Not on your life, chum," McCarter said.

The Briton was ready for such a reaction. Marchant had been exposed in the moments before a surprise attack—of that McCarter was now certain—and he was desperate to extricate himself. McCarter nonchalantly grabbed Marchant's wrist, preventing him from drawing his gun.

"Mine's out first." McCarter grinned, pressing the muzzle of his Browning Hi-Power against Marchant's stomach. "Now what are you going to do?"

Marchant's reaction was surprising. Ignoring McCarter's gun, the cop lunged, making an abortive attempt to head-butt the Phoenix pro.

The agile Brit swayed to one side, still holding Marchant's wrist. Then he slapped the barrel of the Hi-Power across the side of Marchant's skull. The blow drove Marchant to his knees. His upper body struck the edge of the desk, dislodging the piles of paperwork.

By this time the flurry of action had caught the attention of everyone in the room.

Katz took in the situation at a glance. Inwardly he trusted McCarter's instincts. Reckless as he often was, the ex-SAS man wasn't totally insane, and the Israeli knew there would be a rational explanation for his behavior.

"What the hell's going on?" Tobin demanded.

"Something's about to go down," McCarter replied, standing as he relieved the dazed Marchant of his weapon, "and my chum here is part of it."

Deferring further explanations until later, the rest of the Phoenix Force reacted with the instinctive speed that had kept them alive through countless other threatening situations. As one, they drew their autopistols, dropping instantly to the floor.

Andrew Dexter, with the same attitude, unholstered his weapon and ducked behind a desk.

"Would somebody tell me what's happening?" Tobin asked again. To his credit the British cop had the good sense to draw his own gun.

The remaining members of his squad were slower in reacting, unsure of their positions. But they found out scant seconds later. The doors at either end of the large office area burst open, slamming back against the inner walls, glass panels shattering.

Dark-clad figures, wearing gloves and ski masks and brandishing AK-47 assault rifles, erupted into the room. There were five in all—three coming from the right, two from the left.

The moment they were inside, they spread apart and opened fire, raking the office with full autofire. Streams of 7.62 mm bullets crisscrossed the room, seeking human flesh and finding it in the shape of Tobin's squad members.

In the first few seconds three members of the drug squad were driven to the floor by the lash of autofire, flesh and bone torn asunder by the high-velocity slugs.

Phoenix Force and Andrew Dexter, having responded to McCarter's warning, avoided the heavy fire. With their weapons they tracked the hooded attackers. Katz and James were the first to fire, triggering 9 mm responses toward the trio of gunmen they were facing.

Katz's fire struck his target high in the chest, on the left side, shattering the collarbone. The impact knocked the man off balance. He stumbled back, his AK-47 arcing around to spray bullets into the far wall.

McCarter, crouched behind a desk, leveled his Browning and put a second shot into the wounded gunman. The Briton's slug punched through the attacker's throat. The dying man went down in a limp sprawl.

The Walther P-88 in Calvin James's fist cracked three times, sending a trio of lethal slugs into a second gunman. Near Katz and James, Gary Manning and Rafael Encizo returned the withering fire of the attackers. Manning's single 9 mm slug hit dead center between the eyes of his target. The hooded gunman pitched backward, blood staining his ski mask, his AK spinning from his limp fingers.

The P-88 in Encizo's hands exploded twice, knocking out the fourth attacker. The hot projectiles burned into the guy's chest cavity, splintering bone and pulverizing flesh. Another bullet, courtesy of Andrew Dexter, found a home in the attacker's skull. The surviving gunman, deciding that self-preservation was the best option, retreated through the door.

Detective Inspector Tobin, who had remained standing through the brief shoot-out, broke from his trance. He ran across the office in pursuit of the fleeing gunman. McCarter followed.

The hooded man ejected his AK's spent magazine and jammed in a fresh one. With the weapon recocked he twisted around and let loose a long burst as Tobin chased him through the outer offices. The slugs whacked into the wall over Tobin's head, showering him with plaster.

Ignoring the personal risk, Tobin followed his man into a long passageway. He lifted his Browning and fired twice. His shots caught the gunman in the upper body, spinning him round. Tobin fired a third shot into the gunman, tossing him to the floor. The AK-47 bounced out of the guy's hand, clattering across the concrete.

Reaching him, Tobin stood over the wounded gunman. The stunned, bloody attacker stared up at the angry-faced cop. Tobin's Browning angled down, the muzzle settling on the guy's head.

Close on Tobin's heels, McCarter eyed the cop's actions closely. He glanced from Tobin's taut features to his trigger finger, which was well clear of the trigger. The Briton sensed that Tobin wouldn't pull the trigger.

Seconds later Tobin pulled his gun back from the wounded man and jammed it into his holster. Bending over, Tobin dragged the hooded man to his feet, ignoring the captive's moans and protests. He manhandled the gunman back to the main office, dumping him roughly in a chair. McCarter, retrieving the abandoned AK-47, followed Tobin back.

"He didn't need my help," McCarter told Katz. He put away the Browning but kept hold of the AK-47. The other Phoenix warriors had gone to check the area.

"That was good work, Ransom," Katz said, calling McCarter by his cover name. "If you hadn't picked up on Marchant, we might have ended up like those poor devils."

He indicated the motionless bodies of Lane, Evans and Renfrew, lying in bloody pools on the floor.

"Didn't do them much good, though," the cockney replied.

James returned, reporting that there were no more enemy gunmen around. He glanced at the bodies, shaking his head sadly. "This is more like the South Side of Chicago than dear old London town."

"Don't be fooled," McCarter said. "London isn't how it used to be anymore. Forget the changing of the guard and all that quaint crap. More likely to be terrorist bombs and bleedin' rape on the streets these days."

To McCarter, London had long succumbed to the sickness that bedeviled many large metropolitan cities. It had become a battleground for warring factions of extremists. Anyone with a grudge, from the IRA to local supporters of animal rights, used the city to perpetrate their violent deeds. It might be a bomb, or a spate of poisoned food on the shelves of supermarkets. It was innocent citizens who suffered. They could find themselves as victims of faceless cowards who can only express themselves by inflicting senseless suffering on unsuspecting citizens.

"Yeah," James agreed, "I guess you're right."

Andrew Dexter, still holding his Browning, crossed the room to join the Phoenix trio.

"I cuffed Marchant to a radiator on the wall," he informed them. "I didn't want him sneaking away before we had a little chat with him."

"Well done, Andrew," Katz said. "Mr. Marchant has a lot of explaining to do one way or another. I'm looking forward to hearing what he has to say."

5

Twenty minutes later the factory site was the scene of frenzied activity. Police and medical teams appeared. The area was sealed off so that scene-of-crime officers could detail the incident.

Katz made it clear to Dexter that Phoenix Force didn't want to become involved. The liaison man had anticipated the Israeli's request, and the way had already been prepared for the Force to make a quiet withdrawal.

The Phoenix Force commander made an additional suggestion. He wanted Marchant to go with the Force. Dexter didn't hold out too much hope, but Tobin, who had overheard the conversation, agreed.

"Take him," the cop said. "I'll cover you. The less I see of that bastard the better. He'll be safer out of my reach. Just have him handy when my bosses want to talk to him. In the meantime, see what you can get out of him. I owe you that much. If it hadn't been for you blokes, we'd all be dead."

"Thanks," Katz said, "and don't worry, if Marchant has anything we need to know, we'll get it out of him."

The Israeli nodded to Manning and James, and the Stony Man warriors marched the handcuffed Marchant out of the office.

"As soon as we identify the gunmen, I'll pass the information to you," Tobin said.

Phoenix Force and Dexter left the building. Upon reaching their parked panel truck, McCarter got behind the wheel and Katz and Dexter slid in beside him. The others bundled Marchant into the rear compartment.

At the gate two armed police officers stopped the truck, passing hard stares over the occupants.

Dexter climbed out and spoke with them. When he returned, the attitudes of the armed officers had mellowed, and they waved the truck through.

"What did you say to sweeten their disposition?" Manning asked.

"Nothing much," Dexter replied. "I simply explained how you had saved their mates."

"I like this guy," James said.

"Oh, my bleeding heart," McCarter muttered. The grinning cockney drove the panel truck through London's busy streets, heading back toward Ealing and the safehouse.

"Dexter," Katz asked, "as a matter of interest, who knows the location of the safehouse?"

"No one on Tobin's team," Dexter assured him.

Encizo glanced at Marchant. The rogue cop scowled. "We have to face the fact that there's a security breach, Andrew," the Cuban pointed out.

"Don't remind me. I feel bad enough when I realize I could have led you fellows into early funerals."

"Don't get too obsessed about that," McCarter said cheerfully. "We're still alive and kicking."

"That's fine," Katz said, "but we shouldn't assume all's well until we've checked things out."

"I agree with Lawrence," Encizo said. "We have to be sure."

There was a general round of agreement.

"Okay," McCarter joined in. "You know, riding with you guys is getting to be bloody dull."

Rear access to the safehouse was through a narrow, tree-lined lane. At Dexter's suggestion McCarter parked the truck out of sight some distance from the house. With the vehicle hidden the Force armed themselves with their Uzi machine pistols, taken from the weapons cases that had been placed in the truck's tool lockers. Dexter stayed behind to keep an eye on Marchant.

The extensive, untended garden behind the house provided the Force with plenty of cover on their approach. They found no sign that anyone had visited the house during their absence. The grounds were deserted. Even so, Phoenix Force made a thorough appraisal before entering.

Once inside they made a floor-by-floor inspection. Again they found nothing unusual. The rooms were undisturbed.

"Looks okay," McCarter stated as they assembled in the main room.

"We could spend days checking," Katz said. "I don't think anyone has had time to do any sophisticated bugging, so we'll just have to suppose I'm right."

"Dexter could probably have the place swept by his people," Manning suggested.

"If we can trust them," James said. "After today's little exhibition, who do we trust?"

"We have to start somewhere," Manning said.

"The drug business generates such staggering amounts of money that bribery becomes a high-value lever," Katz pointed out. "We already have one cop who has sold out his partners. For all we know there may be others."

MANNING WENT to get Dexter. When he returned, Calvin James was ready to interrogate Marchant.

The rogue cop was secured in a straight-backed chair, one of his shirtsleeves rolled up. James checked the man's heart and blood pressure. The drug he was about to administer, scopolamine, was one of the most powerful truth serums known. As a side effect, it frequently increased the rate of the subject's heart. This could be fatal if the subject had a weak heart. However, Marchant had no such problem.

"I've heard about this stuff," Dexter said. "Never seen it used, though."

"Coleman has used this many times, and always gets results," Katz explained, using James's cover name.

"Never lost a patient either," McCarter said with a hard grin. "But there's always a first time."

"Let's go back to the other room," Katz suggested. "It's better for Coleman if there are no distractions."

They returned to the main room, settling into chairs.

"Tobin gave me something for you," Dexter said. "He figured you'd probably be able to make more use of it right now." Dexter passed a thick file and binder to Katz. "The manila file has all the current information the team had to date. The binder is a sort of manual on the drug business. Tobin's team put it together. To be honest, it's bloody awful reading, but I think you'll understand why they're so dedicated."

Katz handed the manila file to Manning, who began to distribute the paperwork to the other Phoenix warriors. The Israeli settled back, opened the thick binder and began to read.

It was all there, just as Dexter had said. Countless hours had evidently gone into compiling it. Tobin and his team had gone beyond the normal requirements of gathering evidence to create this chilling, graphic catalog of the drug business.

Tobin had covered the whole scene. Nothing had been missed. There were interviews with the medical profession, the legal people, the users, the addicts, the sick and the suicidal. There were photographs, too, images frozen for all time of ravaged, despairing faces. The haunted eyes of an eighteen-year-old who had been to hell and back. A corpse covered in scabs and bruises, the twenty-year-old face gaunt and sunken.

The Israeli immersed himself in the material, aware of the case it made against the drug trade. Tobin's probing had uncovered some of the faces behind the business, the shadowy bosses who controlled the thriving drug rings. From their expensive offices and exclusive homes they commanded their armies of importers and distributors while keeping themselves apart from the sordid day-to-day dealings. They delegated authority, then sat back and counted the money as it poured in. Much of the income realized was quickly channeled into legitimate enterprises—restaurants, clubs, chains of video stores. The drug barons became richer with each passing day, filling their bank accounts on the misery of others.

The countless thousands hooked on heroin and cocaine, existing simply to feed the hungry monster that dominated them, were the ones that paid. They sank into the depths of despair as they struggled to support their habits.

So they borrowed, then turned to crime—mugging, burglary, stealing anything they could turn into cash. Others turned to prostitution, selling themselves in order to pay for the drugs they needed. In the process they exposed themselves to disease, perversion and latent violence.

The deeper he delved into Tobin's material the more Katz felt for the families and friends of the users. They were all helpless victims.

Katz scanned page after page, viewed picture after picture, growing increasingly horrified. Tobin's team had uncovered statistics that showed an increasing corruption of young children by the traffickers. Addicts as young as nine and ten years of age were being discovered. Kids who should have been experiencing the joy and wonder of childhood were being drawn into the nightmare world of drug dependency. Some had even descended into the ugly business of child pornography to earn the cash they so desperately needed.

Katz closed the binder. He remained silent for a while, regaining control of his emotions before he spoke. "If I was ever in doubt as to the need to exterminate the drug traffickers, I'm not any longer."

Dexter nodded. "It hit me pretty hard when I read it myself."

"This stuff is pretty grim reading as well," Manning said.

"This isn't exactly sweetness and light," James said as he entered. He was holding the notepad on which he had written Marchant's replies to his carefully phrased questions.

"Just give us the highlights," Katz said.

"Our boy Marchant is bought and paid for. It appears he ran up some gambling debts that brought him to the attention of some local hoods in the drug business. The main man is Charley Yale."

"That name's in this file," Encizo said.

"Yale came on to Marchant strong. Made it clear he wasn't about to forget Marchant's gambling tab. Then made him an offer. If Marchant became Yale's inside man, he would earn his debt a hundred times over. Marchant took the carrot. His job was to keep Yale informed of how close the drug team was to any breakthroughs. Also to let him know if anything special was happening."

"Like us turning up?" McCarter suggested.

James nodded. "Tipping off Yale about a team of specialists flying in from the States earned Marchant a fat bonus."

"Did he know that the hit men were going to take out everybody in the room?" Manning asked.

"They told him they were only interested in the specialists. Marchant's own people weren't to be touched."

"And he believed that?" Encizo asked. "The guy is not only a scumbag, he's loco, as well. Didn't he realize it would be an ideal time to take out the drug squad, as well? Kill off everyone involved in the investigation?"

"The guy is blinded by dollar signs," James said. "He's obsessed by money, totally materialistic. His loyalty count is so low it's underground."

"What do you know about this Yale character?" Manning asked Dexter.

"A real hard nut," Dexter explained. "A typical East London gangster. Local boy. Never strayed far off his own doorstep. Vicious type not to be crossed. But clever."

"Any connection with the Colombians?"

"Yes. But we haven't come up with evidence that could get him into court."

Calvin James took a seat next to McCarter. He picked up the manila file and flipped through it. He came across one report, realizing that it referred to the recent death of an American girl, the daughter of an Air Force man. It was the case Brognola had mentioned. The black warrior read the details. Turning a page, he was confronted with the dead girl's personal details and photograph.

David McCarter, sitting close to James, heard the barely repressed groan of anguish that escaped the black man's lips. He turned to see James staring at the file with an expression of pure shock on his face. McCarter was about to make a flippant remark, but something stopped him. The Briton realized that James's shock had been caused by more than just a photograph. The black warrior was deeply upset. McCarter waited until James put the file down, then retrieved the file and quickly scanned it.

He wasn't quite sure what had upset James. But one thing was certain: he was going to find out.

6

A short while later, during the lull in the conversation, the Briton caught Katz's eye. "Why don't I do a little snooping round my old stomping grounds? No telling what I might pick up from the street talk."

Katz glanced at him with a slight frown. "I would have thought you'd be out of touch having been away so much."

The irrepressible Briton grinned. "It hasn't been that long. And I do come back from time to time. People in my neck of the woods have long memories, and they don't miss much that's going on."

"All right," Katz agreed. "Just try to stay out of trouble and don't upset too many people."

"Anything you say, boss," McCarter said. "Tell you what, I'll take Coleman along. He'll keep me on the straight and narrow."

James looked startled, almost as if he didn't want to become involved in one of McCarter's escapades.

"Fine," Katz said. "Get moving then. By the way, Ransom, no telephone calls here. Just in case anyone's listening in."

McCarter nodded. He turned to Dexter. "Any transport around?"

"Yes. There's a Vauxhall Cavalier in the garage." He located the keys and handed them to the Briton.

As McCarter and James left, Katz settled back in his chair, a thoughtful expression on his face. What was the cockney up to now? he wondered.

MCCARTER AND JAMES got into the car. McCarter negotiated the narrow street with ease, heading for the main road.

"Who is she, Cal?" he asked.

James glanced at his British partner. "What are you talking about?"

McCarter sighed. "Let's not play silly bloody games, chum," he snapped. "We both know someone in one of those photographs meant more to you than just another picture."

"There's nothing to talk about," James replied.

He was trying to pass over the subject, but the tone of his voice betrayed his true feelings.

"I think there's a lot to talk about," McCarter insisted. "Cal, I got a look at that photo. Showed a young girl. Looked like she'd been through hell before she died. You want to know something else? You know who she is. Now tell me I'm wrong."

James was silent as the British commando eased the car across an intersection. "Who is she, Cal?" he asked in a gentler tone.

Calvin James's eyes were fixed on the windshield, but he was seeing the girl's image. Only this image had the girl smiling and alive.

"Her name is—*was*—Angie Martin. She would have been twenty-two or three when she died. I've known her most of her life, on and off, though I hadn't had much contact over the past year. Her father is in the U.S. Air Force. I met him in Nam. Harry was flying helicopters then, and I was with the SEALs. A mutual friend introduced us. We were both from Chicago, so we had a lot in common. Plenty to talk about. It made home seem a little closer knowing someone who was familiar with the old neighborhood.

"After we got back to the States, we kept in touch as much as we could. Harry stayed on in the service, so I didn't see him for a while. Then his wife died. It hit Harry pretty hard, but he weathered it and brought up Angie himself, despite being moved around by the Air Force. We met up a few times, and I got to know Angie pretty well, watched her grow up. Then Harry got posted to Europe. He took her with him, and she finished her schooling and went to art college in Germany. After she graduated, she moved here to London to work in an advertising agency. Last I heard she was doing pretty well for herself."

"Bloody awful way to find out what happened to her," McCarter said, referring to the police file.

James nodded. "I'm going to find out who's responsible."

McCarter heard the determined tone in James's voice. "No. Hold on, Cal," he warned. "Personal vendettas aren't part of our job."

"I can't just walk away from it, David. No way. I don't give a damn what anyone says."

"Cal, we have to think about this. Bloody hell, man, do you want to throw it all away? Everything you've done since you joined the Force?"

"It doesn't wash," James said. "All that duty crap. Sticking to the rules. *They* don't stick to any rules. The bastards who sell the shit that killed Angie. What about them? Do they get off? Free and clear?"

"No. We go after them. But we do it by the book, Cal, the way we've always done it. That's why we're here. To put these slimeballs out of business."

"Not enough," James raged. "I want to pull the trigger myself on the bastard who got Angie hooked. A long-distance kill won't do it this time."

"It's wrong, Cal," McCarter said. "You can't functions properly if you're running on revenge. Look, I know how you feel—"

"Do you?" James turned to the Briton. "Okay. Then tell me you wouldn't do the same if you were in my shoes. Go ahead, David, tell me you'd turn around and walk away."

McCarter's hesitation convinced James he had been right. He had put the Briton on the spot, and McCarter hadn't been able to lie outright despite his argument against James's intention.

"I was hoping you wouldn't ask that," McCarter said. "That was bloody unfair."

"Yeah? It's a hard world, David, my man."

McCarter pulled the car over to the curb and parked. He pulled on the brake and turned to James. "I'll go so far with you on this, Cal. But if you step too far over the line, I'm going to scream bloody murder."

"I want to talk with Angie's roommate," James said. "She shared with a girl named Jenny Barlow."

"You got the address?" McCarter asked.

James nodded. "I've got it."

The house was in London's Camden Town area. It was an old building, like those around it, a relic of Victorian London when the fashion was for large, rambling family houses. Now the cost of maintaining such edifices was too much for most people, and the big houses had been converted into rented flats.

The house where Angie Martin had lived had been recently refurbished. The outside shone with fresh paintwork. Angie had shared the basement flat with her friend.

The entrance was through an iron gate set in the railing fronting the house and down stone steps. The door to the flat was painted a deep, rich maroon. The only thing odd about it was that it was open.

McCarter and James stood at the door. The Briton eased his Browning Hi-Power from its holster. "You don't leave your front door open these days," he said.

James pulled out his P-88 and followed his partner through the open door. They were in a tiled entrance hall. On the wall facing them was a row of hooks for hanging coats. Pairs of shoes lay scattered across the floor.

James was about to speak when McCarter held up a hand. In the silence the black warrior heard the soft sound of someone crying. Someone in pain.

A man's voice reached them. "I believe she's got the message now, Eddie."

"Just let me remind her a bit more," came a second voice.

There was the sound of a hard slap, then a ragged cry of pain.

"That's it," James muttered, and shouldered open the door that led into the flat.

There were two men in the room and one college-aged woman. One of the men had her by the arm, holding her as his open palm swung toward her already bruised face. The second man, tall, blond-haired and expensively dressed, arched his upper body around as James burst into the room.

The black warrior moved toward them in long, angry strides. The guy shoved the girl away, reaching under his jacket. James got to him first, looping the barrel of the Walther in a backhand curve that crunched against the guy's jaw, sending a wash of blood over the guy's lower face and shirt.

The guy staggered away from James, clawed for his holstered gun. James hit him again, slamming the steel barrel of the P-88 against the back of his skull. This time the guy crashed to his knees. James booted him in the ribs, flipping him onto his back, then jammed the P-88's muzzle into the man's neck. With his free hand James relieved the guy of his holstered gun.

"Move an inch, pal, and you're dead," James snapped into the guy's ear.

McCarter had entered the room close on James's heels and had seen the situation as it was. Grabbing a straight-backed chair, he hurled it at the blond man, who crashed to the floor. The fallen man was kicking and struggling with the chair as McCarter reached him. His lean face registering wild anger, McCarter drove his clenched fist into the guy's mouth, knocking him back off his feet. He lay staring up at McCarter, blood bubbling from his lips.

"Nothing like a cozy evening at home," McCarter remarked, bending over the blond guy and searching him for weapons.

"You won't find anything," the girl said huskily. "He hasn't the guts to do his own dirty work. That's why he pays Grogan to do it for him."

"Why don't we all sit down and try to sort out this mess?" McCarter suggested. He hauled the blond man to his feet and shoved him onto a couch. James did the same with the man named Grogan.

"Give me a minute," McCarter said. He went out to close the open front door. "I feel better now."

James was examining the girl's face. She had a number of angry marks on her cheeks that would turn into bruises. "You hurt anywhere else?" he asked.

The girl shook her head. "I'll live, thanks to you two. Who are you? Police?"

"Do I look like a copper?" McCarter asked defensively.

"My name's Coleman," James said. "He's Ransom. We came to talk to you about Angie."

"The way you said her name makes me believe you knew her."

"I did," James said. "And I know her father. We were in Vietnam together. I saw Angie a number of times while she was growing up. I also know about you, Jenny Barlow."

Jenny studied the black Phoenix warrior.

"Now I know you," she said. "Angie showed me a photograph of her father and you standing beside a helicopter in the jungle. But you—"

James held up a hand, suspecting she was about to reveal that his name hadn't been Coleman then, and wanting to keep his real identity from Jenny's assailants. "Later," he said softly.

McCarter pointed a finger at the pair on the couch. "And what do we need to know about these dropouts?"

"The blond one is Archie Cadel," Jenny said.

"He have anything to do with Angie's death?" James asked.

"He's the one who got her started on drugs," Jenny said. "And he supplied her ever since."

"How did it start?" James inquired.

"Cadel arranges parties for American servicemen and provides drugs for those willing to try them. Angie got invited to one of the parties by some people she knew. It was a way of keeping contact with service people. I went along with her. During the evening, Cadel started passing drugs around. The idea scared me, but Angie wanted to give it a try. The trouble was, she liked it and wanted more.

"I didn't find out until a month after the party that she was taking the stuff regularly. By then the party was really over. Cadel was raising the price all the time, and Angie was desperate for more. She started borrowing, then taking. I didn't know what to do. She begged and pleaded with me not to let her father know. I realize now I should have ignored her. But she was in such a state.

"Finally I got her to agree to get treatment. She promised she would. Then she disappeared for a while. I got a couple of phone calls from her. She said she was at a clinic getting treatment and I wasn't to worry. As soon as she was well, she was coming home. What I didn't know was that by this time Cadel had her on the streets selling herself so that she could earn more money for his damn drugs.

"The next time I saw Angie was when I went to identify her body. The police told me one of her clients had attacked her with a knife. It was terrible what he'd done to her."

McCarter realized James was about to move. The Briton lunged toward his Phoenix Force partner, missing James by a fraction.

Cadel, slumped on the couch, saw James coming for him and tried to shrink away. James took hold of him by the front of his expensive jacket and swung him upright. He drove hard, crippling blows to Cadel's face, slamming him to the floor. Cadel rolled away, but the agile black warrior closed in on him. As Cadel made an attempt to rise, James slammed his foot into the man's side. The dealer curled up, groaning.

McCarter reached his partner, slamming a shoulder into James's back. James stumbled across the room, struggling to maintain his balance.

Taking advantage of the distraction, Grogan sprang to his feet and dashed across the room. He threw his hands up in front of his face and took a headlong dive through the nearest window.

As the guy disappeared in a shower of broken glass and splintered window frame, McCarter ran toward the window. He was in time to see Grogan vanish up the steps that led to street level.

"Bloody great," McCarter groaned.

He turned back into the room. James was staring down at Cadel, his face taut with barely restrained fury.

"It's over," McCarter snapped. "Just leave it, mate. Don't make it any worse than it already is."

"Stay out of this," James retorted, his voice trembling with rage. "It's my business. Got nothing to do with anybody else."

"Like hell," McCarter said. "You let one of our captives escape because of your bloody childish outburst. For all we know he could have backup waiting down the street. Any minute now we could be up to our ears in a firefight. And we have an innocent civilian with us. What if she gets hurt because of your stunt? How are you going to feel about that?"

Calvin James glanced at Jenny. She was white-faced, still partly in shock after her own experience at Cadel's hands. The black warrior felt a sudden pang. He had allowed his feelings to get the better of him. And in doing so he had broken two cardinal rules of the Force. He had used violence against an unarmed captive and had also put someone at risk. Feeling remorse, James glanced at McCarter for reassurance, receiving only a hostile scowl.

"Let's get the hell out of here," McCarter growled. He tossed the car keys to James. "You look after Jenny if you think you can manage not the screw up again. Jenny, grab a coat and go with him. We have a car across the street.''

McCarter turned his attention to Cadel. The drug dealer was on his knees, clutching his body. Blood streamed from his face, staining his shirt and coat. The Briton didn't feel any sympathy for him; he deserved everything he got. But the cockney was concerned about their safety during the next few minutes.

''Get up, chum. You're a long way from being dead.'' He caught hold of Cadel's jacket and hauled the man to his feet. ''Hurt does it? Bloody well should. I don't approve of what my mate did, but if it had been me, I'd have hit you a bloody sight harder. Now move it, pal.''

McCarter propelled Cadel to the door, shoving him toward the steps. He kept behind the drug dealer, urging him up the steps. As they reached the street, McCarter saw that James and Jenny were already nearing the parked Vauxhall.

Cadel was stumbling, complaining about his injured face. McCarter was tired of his whining. He began to speak, but was interrupted by the shrill howl of squealing car tires accompanied by the rising growl of a high-revved engine.

A sleek black Jaguar was fishtailing in their direction. Even though the light was starting to fade, McCarter saw the gleaming tubes of gun barrels poking out the windows.

James grabbed Jenny and pulled her behind the Vauxhall. The Jaguar swept in close. Autofire filled the air. The Vauxhall rocked as slugs pounded the metalwork, raising sparks. Glass exploded from the rear window. The Jaguar cleared the front of the car and roared on toward McCarter and Cadel.

"Get down!" McCarter yelled, trying to grab Cadel. The drug dealer wriggled away, stepping into the street as the Jaguar closed on him.

The look of expectation on Cadel's face turned to abject terror as he realized that the Jaguar wasn't going to slow to pick him up. A shrill scream rose in his throat as the first slugs hammered his flesh, kicking him back across the sidewalk and up against the iron railing. The dealer hung there as a second volley of slugs tore into him, blasting his life away in an instant.

McCarter, flat on the sidewalk, angled the Browning Hi-Power at the Jaguar and triggered. A side window shattered and a dark shape inside the car jerked out of sight. The Briton's final shot took out the rear window as the Jaguar accelerated down the street.

7

Sanctuary vanished in the first burst of autofire. The safehouse was no longer safe.

Twilight had fallen, shrouding the overgrown grounds around the building. In the lengthening shadows the intruders almost made it to the house before they were seen.

Katz, with his obsessive need for caution, had decided to maintain a constant watch. To that end he had Gary Manning and Rafael Encizo watching the grounds from concealed vantage points at windows at the front and rear of the house. Manning, at the front, spotted the hit team in the overgrown garden.

"Here they come!" he yelled as he caught the gleam of raised weapons. His shout reached the ears of the invaders.

Once their approach was noticed, the hit team opened fire, raking the windows with a murderous volley of full autofire.

Without questioning the Canadian's command Katz and Andrew Dexter sought the safety of the floor. Over their heads the windows exploded inwardly, showering glass across the room. Bullets howled inches above them, striking the far wall. The heavy stream of fire filled the room with racket.

Manning, ignoring the hail of fire, crawled across the floor toward the weapons cases against the far wall.

Reaching them, he flipped open a case to a standard Uzi SMG and snatched up a couple of magazines. He slid them across the floor to Dexter, then turned to another case, retrieving a metal box holding concussion grenades. He took a couple of the flash grenades and eased them into his pocket.

As Katz cocked the Uzi he had snatched from the table, his eyes caught movement at one of the windows. The glass and most of the frame had been ripped away by the heavy autofire. In the frame a dark figure appeared. Turning, Katz braced the Uzi across his prosthesis and triggered a short burst. The body crashed to the ground outside and there was a temporary lull.

The firing from outside flared up again as the unseen gunners recovered. Once again the room was riddled with heavy fire.

"Take the wall between the two windows," Katz told Dexter.

Dexter crawled across the glass-strewn floor, ignoring the cuts he received. Once between the windows, he stood, his Uzi cocked and ready. Katz placed himself at the side of one of the windows.

"Steed, you join up with Arnez and cover the rear," Katz said, using Manning's and Encizo's cover names.

The Canadian nodded and crouch-walked to the door, vanishing from sight.

There was more gunfire from the unseen gunners. Eventually it tapered off. The sound of running feet reached Katz's ears. Dexter had heard it, as well.

One intruder leaped in by the window and turned right as his feet hit the floor. He found himself staring into the muzzle of Dexter's Uzi. The British cop triggered, riddling the guy's lower torso and spilling his blood onto the carpet. As the guy went down, Dexter turned back toward the window as a second man tried to scramble inside. Slugs from Dexter's Uzi caught the intruder full in the face, driving him back over the sill.

Katz confronted a pair of intruders that reached the window simultaneously. Each seemed reluctant to let the other go first. Their ill-timed moment of hesitation gave Katz the opportunity to make the decision for them. His Uzi spit and the pair were driven back in a bloody haze, crashing outside.

From behind Katz and Dexter, somewhere in the house, came more gunfire. Katz thought of Manning and Encizo, and hoped they were all right.

SECONDS AFTER Manning reached Encizo in the rear parlor, the large patio doors opened up. From the deepening gloom three armed men appeared on the patio. One of them opened up with an automatic weapon, raking the partially opened patio doors. The toughened glass imploded, filling the room with flittering fragments.

Rafael Encizo returned fire with his MP-5. The H&K crackled with flame in the gloom as Encizo triggered at the guy who had destroyed the patio doors. A stream of slugs stitched the guy's middle, twisting him around in midstride before dropping him, lifeless, to the ground.

Manning's SA-80 felled a second man. Slugs in his chest, the guy stumbled blindly, forgetting his own weapon as he clawed at his wounds. Colliding with the wall, he slithered along the brickwork until he fell facedown on the paving slabs. His legs moved in slow, spasmodic jerks even after his breathing had stopped.

The surviving invader jammed back the trigger of his MAC-10 and ran headlong toward Manning and Encizo, yelling incoherently. The slugs from his weapon chewed and chipped at the woodwork and plaster, missing the Phoenix pair who had dropped behind a couch.

Manning put a single shot through the running man's brain. The guy continued to move, but his senses were out of sync and he turned and twisted in a jerky dance. The muzzle of the Ingram sank toward the ground, the last burst of fire crackling against the stone slabs. As the weapon clicked empty, the MAC-10 dropped from the man's fingers and he followed it down, staring out at the darkening world through dull eyes.

Encizo took cover at the edge of the patio doors, scanning the grounds beyond the house. It was difficult to discern anything due to the rapidly approaching darkness. The deep shadows were blending with the tangled shrubbery, blurring outlines.

"You want to go flush 'em out?" Manning asked.

"Do you?" was the Cuban's reply.

The Canadian smiled. "Hell, no," he said. "Let's wait and see if they figure another try is worth the price their buddies paid."

KATZ STUDIED the front garden, watching for further movement. Nothing appeared to be happening. However, it wasn't wise to accept anything on face value. There might easily be others out there, just biding their time.

Across the room, his back to the wall, Andrew Dexter had pulled the telephone down to floor level and was dialing a number. "I've bloody well had it with all this so-called security crap," he said forcibly. "Safehouse my arse! We'd be safer in the middle of bloody Belfast."

Despite his amusement at Dexter's remarks, Katz couldn't help being somewhat disturbed at the obvious breach of security. First Tobin's undercover base. Now the safehouse. Both coming under armed attack within a few hours of each other. Either British security was in need of review, or the opposition had better intelligence than anyone had expected. Knowing the way the British operated, Katz had to suspect the latter. The way things were shaping up, it looked as if the drug traffickers had someone else on their payroll. Unless Marchant had known more than even Dexter had been led to believe. The drug squad wasn't supposed to know the whereabouts of the safehouse, but someone had passed the location to the opposition. The questions was—who?

"That you, Franklin? Good. Just shut up and listen. The safehouse has been hit. We've held them back, and up to now we haven't had a second strike, but we can't be sure there aren't others outside. Get some assistance over and be bloody quick about it. What? Of course armed, you fucking idiot! Now get your finger out, because I'm timing you." Dexter slammed the phone down, staring at it for long seconds, his head shaking from side to side.

"He actually asked me if the backup needed to be armed! Jesus Christ, what have I got myself into?"

Katz didn't reply. His mind was busy with the implications of the attacks. Phoenix Force was used to sudden, unexpected violence erupting around them. It came, as the saying went, with the territory. The physical side didn't worry him as much as the reasons. There was nothing worse than carrying out a mission in an atmosphere of mistrust and suspicion. Nothing was ever black and white; varying shades of gray always intruded. On this mission nothing seemed to be gelling. The whole affair was rapidly becoming a shadow mix, with the players carrying big question marks pinned to their backs.

It was time, Katz decided, for the Force to make an unobtrusive retreat. To find their own base. Locate themselves and make their own decisions, away from all interested parties—good or bad or indifferent. The Israeli kept his decision to himself. He wouldn't even let Dexter in on it.

Not that Katz didn't trust the man. The Phoenix Force commander felt he had the knack of being able to judge a man's worth, and Dexter had proved himself on a previous assignment and was doing the same this time round. When the chips were down, Katz looked out for the safety of Phoenix Force first and foremost. His fellow warriors were an extension of himself, physically and spiritually. They had gone through too much fighting and suffering together. The invisible bond of the warrior held them together.

The security of the group was of prime importance to Katz. The only way he could ensure control of their own destiny was by removing the Force from outside influences. And that meant going it alone until such time as it became safe to come in. Such a situation wasn't new to the Stony Man commandos. They were fully capable of operating outside society. If doing so meant surviving, then it had to be so.

Encizo eased into the room, keeping well away from the windows. He located Katz and crouched beside him. "We took out three back there," he said. "Steed's keeping watch in case there are any more. I think we dealt with them all."

Katz nodded. "Dexter and I held them here. I believe we terminated most of the ones who tried to force an entry. It's hard to tell whether there are more. Too dark to see. So we're just sitting tight until Dexter's cavalry responds to his telephone call."

"Sometimes even the telephone can be helpful," the Cuban replied. He glanced at Katz. "What's our next move?"

Lowering his voice so that Dexter wouldn't be able to hear, Katz said, "We do what the Invisible Man does. We disappear. And we don't leave a forwarding address."

"Who the hell are these guys?" Encizo asked. "They keep popping up as if there's a damn sale on. Looks like somebody is hiring them in boxes by the dozen."

"Maybe we'll get a chance to see when Dexter's people arrive."

Half an hour later the police vehicles finally appeared, lights flashing and sirens wailing into the night. They rolled up the drive and screeched to a halt outside. Armed police sprang from the vehicles, and the grounds of the house were flooded with light from portable lamps. Anyone hiding in the grounds would have been able to slip away during the confusion and racket as the police teams made their presence known.

Dexter was on his feet as armed police entered the room. They were led by a fresh-faced young officer in plainclothes. He was tall and powerfully built, with red hair, and he looked immensely pleased with himself.

"The idea, Franklin," Dexter explained with great restraint, "was to make a silent approach in the hope of apprehending any of the miscreants still in the area. All you've succeeded in doing is to warn them you were coming. Most probably you did the same for every criminal in the metropolitan district."

Franklin thought about Dexter's explanation for a moment, his face earnest. "On the other hand, sir," he countered, "we've avoided further usage of weapons."

Dexter nodded in resignation. "There's no answer to that, Franklin. No bloody answer at all."

Manning returned to the room with more armed police in tow. He indicated the police officers with a jerk of his thumb.

"These fellers came in the back way. Searched the grounds in back as they moved up to the house. If there had been anyone there, they would have flushed them out."

Katz led the way outside. There, under the glaring lights, the bodies of the hit team were being laid out. The Israeli knelt beside one body, examining the man. He moved to a second and third body. "South American," he said softly to Manning and Encizo. "I'll go further and hazard a guess that these guys are Colombian."

"Colombians," Encizo echoed. "No wonder the game's getting so dirty."

"What do you expect with those crazy buggers involved?" Manning exclaimed. "They have one set of rules and they stick with them regardless. And they've been getting nastier since their own government started cracking down on them. The drug barons have been having a hard time. Problem is, it's made those still around tougher than ever."

"They've certainly built a reputation as ruthless businessmen," Katz observed.

"Ruthless I'd agree with," Encizo said. "But these creeps aren't businessmen. They're just trigger-happy gangsters."

"I'm not trying to justify their actions," Katz said. "All I meant was that they market their product well, which is unfortunate for everyone involved—except the Colombians."

Encizo sighed. He found it hard to reconcile himself to the fact that the Colombians were actually good businessmen. They had all aspects of the drug trade worked out, from growing the crop to final delivery. Added to that was their forceful way of handling problems. The Colombians always took direct action if someone opposed them. Swift, brutal and without remorse, the Colombian dealers took out the problem in the most permanent way. The severe methods removed opposition and served to warn others of the folly of resistance.

Up until recently the Colombian drug kings even had control over certain sections of their country's administration. It had gone on until world opinion had forced the Colombian government to do something. The military had been brought in and had waged a tough war on the traffickers. There had been some success, but the battle was far from over. The Colombian drug barons weren't going to allow their fantastically lucrative business to go under without a fight, and they were striking back with indiscriminate violence.

As far as Rafael Encizo was concerned, the drug dealers were still nothing more than crooks, evil parasites who made fortunes from the misery of others. They were without conscience. They wouldn't hesitate to bring their brutal acts of violence to the European continent. A whole new market lay before them, where the sale of drugs would net them limitless amounts of cash. With that sort of wealth at stake the bribery of a relatively minor police official was all in a day's work. The killing of a few more would have been decided upon with little concern.

The Vauxhall Cavalier, driven by David McCarter, edged up the drive, threading between the parked police vehicles. It pulled up short of the Phoenix commandos, and McCarter climbed out. "What's been going on here?" the Briton asked. "Party got out of hand?"

"Nothing so simple," Katz said. He took McCarter to the bodies and showed him.

"That's all we need," McCarter said. "The South American Mafia."

"At least it all starts to make sense," Katz pointed out. "The Colombians have been wanting to open the European market for a while now. These could be the opening moves. Establishing contact with criminal elements to be their local distributors. Sending over some muscle to provide backup. Sort out problems in their peculiarly subtle way."

James appeared, joining Katz and McCarter. The Israeli sensed almost at once the tension between the two. "How did you get on?"

"Fine," McCarter said lamely.

"Cut the crap, David," James snapped, forgetting to use McCarter's cover name. "You might as well tell him. I screwed up, and he has to know sometime."

Katz turned his steely gaze on the cockney. "Well?" he demanded.

Reluctantly McCarter related the events that had taken place from the moment he and James had driven away from the safehouse. The Israeli listened with increasing annoyance. By the time McCarter had completed his report, Katz was visibly angry.

"Did it happen that way?" he asked James.

The black warrior nodded. "Just as he said."

"This isn't the place or time to discuss this," Katz said. "But once we're resettled there are a few matters we need to resolve." There was a hardness in his tone as he concluded, "The main one being whether you remain a part of Phoenix Force."

The Israeli turned away, leaving James staring after him, his expression one of total shock. Whatever he had been expecting, Katz's statement had left him stunned. The black commando glanced across at McCarter.

The brash cockney had no answer for his partner. For once, he too, was speechless.

8

Mejia was waiting in his pajamas, a cup of hot black coffee in his hand and an expression of displeasure on his handsome brown face. He sat back in the comfortable leather armchair that had become his favorite piece of furniture in the house's booklined study, watching in silence as Torrejon was shown into the room.

The broad-shouldered Torrejon, a bull of a man who had no need to fear anyone on a purely physical level, approached his employer with the timidity of a child anticipating a severe beating.

The silence stretched on. Mejia had long since become aware of the power of silence. It had the capability of unnerving the best. He eyed Torrejon over the rim of his cup, drinking the rich Colombian coffee and savoring its flavor. It was hard to resist the temptation to allow the silence to drag on. It would have been interesting to see how long Torrejon could hold out. The Colombian drug trafficker had pressing business, however, which didn't allow much time for games.

"Well?" he demanded abruptly.

"They failed," Torrejon stated, realizing the folly of attempting to offer any excuses. "The attack failed. The men were wiped out."

Mejia put down his coffee cup. The flavor had suddenly vanished.

"This is becoming a habit," he said, keeping his voice steady. "First the hit against the drug squad. Then interference with Cadel's visit to that talkative English girl. Now we're made to look stupid for a third time. And all in one day. I think you've achieved a record, Jorge."

Torrejon kept his mouth shut. He wanted to tell Mejia he wasn't to blame. All he did was assign the men to carry out the various tasks. If they failed, it wasn't his fault. How could it be when he wasn't even present? The only thing he might have achieved by going along would have been to get himself killed along with the others.

He wanted to say these things and more to Mejia, but he knew Mejia's violent temper. The man was capable of erupting without warning, turning into a raving homicidal maniac. Torrejon had seen it happen more than once. He had seen Mejia beat two people to death with his bare hands.

The Colombian drug trafficker had little respect for human life and would end it as casually as one might swat a fly. His ferocious moods were known and feared, and such knowledge kept those around him in constant awareness of their own frailty. So, despite his personal feelings, Torrejon kept his own counsel.

Mejia gestured toward a chair facing his own. "Sit down, Jorge."

Torrejon sat, feeling some of the tension drain out of him.

"This team of special investigators from the States seems to be giving us problems," Mejia said. "Have we had word about them yet?"

Torrejon shook his head. "Our inside man with the British police hasn't been able to find out anything. His information covered the location of the safehouse where they were staying and their arrival time in the country.

From Marchant's information we knew they were to meet with the British drug squad. But we had no idea they would be armed and ready to use those arms."

"We cannot undo what has already happened," Mejia said. "But let's learn from it. These people are different from most law-enforcement teams. They appear to work on their own, making decisions and acting on them, especially when it comes to using direct force. I don't like it. It makes life uncertain, and I don't have time for uncertainties at the moment."

"Do you want me to assign more men to take them out?" Torrejon asked.

"Yes," Mejia said. "But this time make them aware that they're dealing with professionals. Any operation against this team requires planning. If they go in hard, without preparing themselves, they'll end up dead. Try to think ahead. These specialists are clever, so we have to anticipate their moves."

"Now that Cadel is dead," Torrejon pointed out, "they've lost a major lead. He was the main connection to our supplier to the American servicemen based here in Britain."

"I agree. It was wise to kill him once it was realized he might talk. On the other hand, I'm sure our specialists will read all the information gathered by the drug squad. If there was anything in there that might have connections, they'll obviously pick up on it." Mejia gave an exasperated sigh. "It was a great pity the strike at the factory failed. The destruction of the drug squad and all their information would have gained us a great deal of time."

"If we had been able to recruit Marchant sooner and found out just how much information had been gathered, we would have tried to destroy it much earlier," Torrejon replied.

"There isn't much we can do about Marchant at the moment," Mejia said. "He'll be in close custody. Make a note to have him eliminated the moment an opportunity presents itself. He's no longer of any use to us, but he could become a liability."

"I'll arrange it," Torrejon said.

"Where are these specialists now?"

"No one knows," Torrejon admitted. "They left the safehouse together and haven't been seen or heard from since."

Mejia smiled. He was beginning to appreciate the utter professionalism of the American team. The two breaks in the supposed security cordon had obviously alarmed them. The Colombian trafficker felt certain the specialists had taken off for an unknown destination where they could regroup and formulate their next moves in safety. Finding their own safehouse, known only to themselves, would allow them breathing space, give them time to ready themselves for whatever lay ahead. A grudging respect for his adversaries began to grow within Mejia. It wouldn't suppress his desire to see them dead, but there was nothing that denied a man from admiring the skills of his enemy.

He dismissed Torrejon with a flick of his lean brown hand. Alone once more, Mejia crossed to the percolator and poured himself a fresh cup of coffee. He wandered to the main window and eased back the heavy curtain. Dawn was edging its way over the rooftops of London, fingering its way down through the dark buildings to cast light over the streets.

Mejia stroked a hand through his thick black hair. There was much to be done. People to see. Places to go. The tall Colombian reflected on the fast pace of his life. There wasn't enough time in each day to accomplish everything he needed to do. He smiled at his reflection in the window. Given time it would all come together. And when it did, he could return to Medellín and present the cartel with their latest prize. It would bring him respect and even more wealth.

Carlos Mejia had experienced poverty and deprivation during his childhood. As a teenager, he had broken away from his family, striking out on his own. He had always possessed a natural ability to survive, and once on the streets of Medellín he had quickly absorbed its rules. At eighteen he was running his own street gang, pulling in a reasonable income from various rackets. He had also built himself a reputation as a man to be wary of. Mejia was known as a man who always honored his deals but tolerated no kind of nonsense from anyone. He was his own enforcer, having the strength to back his threats and the cold nerve to carry them out. He killed his first man before he was twenty, and over the next few years repeated the act several times.

In his early twenties he was recruited by one of the Medellín drug cartels. The cartel saw great potential in Mejia. Their faith was justified. Over the next four years Mejia progressed through the ranks with ease. He never made a wrong move, and he was loyal to his employers. The cartel was his family and his religion. It came first. All else was secondary. Mejia carried out the tasks assigned to him with ruthless efficiency, whether it was a drug delivery or an assassination. He spent time in Miami and New York and traveled to other parts of the globe on cartel business. Wherever he went, business improved.

When the European market began to expand, Mejia was chosen to oversee the operation. Things began to move when the energetic Colombian based himself on the

Continent and also in Great Britain, commuting between the two as he established his chain of command. One of Mejia's own ideas was the targeting of American service personnel in Europe and Britain as a large, almost captive market.

It hadn't taken long for Mejia to find the right people to front his idea. He was already negotiating with London's criminal fraternity, establishing contacts. One of his best was Charley Yale, a product of London's East End gangster quarter. Yale was a streetwise hood with many diverse acquaintances. Greedy for money, he was more than willing to accommodate Mejia.

Yale also came up with Cadel, the man with the social connections. Cadel's problem was that he had no money, which was something Mejia changed. The playboy Englishman found Mejia's offer impossible to refuse. It was easy work. Just organize parties and invite along the sort of guests Mejia wanted.

If he had no other talent, Cadel's organizational abilities were more than adequate. Before long his weekend parties were all the rage. And as they were slanted toward the unattached Americans serving at bases around London, they drew in plenty of clients. Cadel had laid his plans carefully, promoting his parties in the local towns and villages around the bases, attracting the Americans by his promises of lively entertainment set in luxurious London homes, where everyone could forget their day-to-day routine and have an evening of relaxation.

The first few parties were conducted strictly by the book, giving everyone a memorable evening and making certain that the guests were returned to their bases intact. After the third weekend, the drug pushing started. By this time people were starting to look for that something different. Once the drugs were introduced the future pattern for the parties was established, and Cadel's pushers began to target the most likely individuals. After that it went much easier.

As the London parties were going on, similar weekends were taking place on the Continent. American bases in Germany were the first to be targeted. Caution at the outset allowed a gradual buildup of regular clients. Then, just as in England, the dealers moved in and began to distribute free samples of coke.

The hooks were baited, the lines ready to be reeled in. Mejia's strategy appeared to be working. Then things began to go wrong.

A U.S. Air Force man killed himself in Germany. He had rammed his car into a trailer. Drugs were found in his bloodstream and packs of coke were found in his car. The daughter of an Air Force man was found murdered in England. She was identified as a drug addict, selling herself to obtain money to feed her habit.

As well, there was an ongoing police investigation into nationwide drug dealing. A special squad operating in London had been quietly gathering information and had tapped in on the party racket.

Mejia hadn't panicked. Problems were there to be overcome. He had gained access to informants inside the police force. From them he learned details about the drug squad such as the location of their London base. He was even informed about a team of special investigators coming in from the states, which would be based at a safehouse in Ealing. As far as Mejia was concerned, he had the situation under control. It had seemed that way—until now.

The matters could still be handled, but it would probably take longer than he had anticipated. It would be worth the wait to see the American specialists destroyed.

He knew his patrons back in Medellín would be pleased when that happened. The Americans were behind much of the vigorous action being waged against the cartels in Colombia. The U.S. administration had put itself behind the Colombian government in trying to destroy the Medellín connection. Cocaine trafficking in the United States was beyond control. It had established itself to the degree that it had almost become part of the fabric of everyday life, and now the Americans were desperate to rid themselves of its cancer. However, they weren't finding it easy, nor were the Colombians doing anything to ease the situation. Infiltrating American military life in Europe was both another market and a means to make the U.S. pay for their interference.

Cadel's loss, though serious in one respect, wasn't the end of the matter. The openings had been made, and there were already significant numbers of Americans drawn into the habit. Some were already selling drugs on behalf of dealers, while others had developed strong cravings and would continue to buy for themselves. Cadel would soon be replaced. New talent was always ready to step into vacated shoes.

Mejia glanced at his watch. It was hardly worth going back to bed, he thought, then changed his mind. He had almost forgotten about the beautiful girl with the red hair and green eyes. A smile ghosted across Mejia's handsome face. Now there was a girl who made the prospect of bed all too welcoming. Just the thought of her excited him. He had time to spare before his first meeting. And if he was a little late, who was going to question him? No one, he reminded himself. Because he, Carlos Mejia, was the man.

The top man.

And who was there to better him?

9

Phoenix Force relocated to a motor lodge situated at the South Mimms service area on the M25. The M25 was the London Orbital Motorway, a freeway that ringed the capital city, allowing access and exit to the sprawling metropolis and its environs.

It was close to ten-thirty by the time the Force checked in. They passed themselves off as a group of businessmen on their way to a conference in the city. Once installed in the neat, functional rooms, they went to the brightly lit cafeteria. Here they picked up trays and moved to the self-service counters. Soon they were selecting a table from which they could observe the entrance, and which was also close to an emergency exit.

Although it was late and they had experienced a hectic day, even by their standards, the Stony Man commandos had restricted themselves to a light meal of sandwiches and salad. Katz had chosen tea to drink, McCarter a couple of cans of chilled Coke. The rest had coffee.

The meal was eaten in silence. No one had much to say. They were all waiting for Katz to broach the subject foremost in their thoughts.

Stirring his third cup of tea, the Israeli raised his head to catch Calvin James's eye. The black warrior met Katz's stare and held it.

"I have to say, Cal, that I'm very disappointed in your performance. What you did could have jeopardized David and risked the life of an innocent girl. As it is, a prisoner escaped and another was killed. The murder of Cadel was done by his own people in order to prevent him from being questioned, and it's entirely possible that would have happened, anyway." Katz placed his cup back on the table, allowing himself a moment's thought before he continued. "That apart, you went completely against our operational procedure. You allowed personal motives to take over. Damn it, Cal, you made a violent attack on an unarmed prisoner. You know how we view the rights of captives."

"You want to hear about *right?*" James replied, struggling to control his emotions. "I saw what had been done to a young girl's rights because of Cadel."

"We're not discussing the rights of anyone except Cadel," Katz snapped. "You violated *his* rights, Cal, and the moment you do that we're on the slippery slope to becoming the kind of people we're fighting. Don't get me wrong. I'm as outraged as you about what happened to Angie Martin. But we have to step back from that and stay detached. The fact that you knew the dead girl has no relevance as far as Phoenix Force is concerned."

"Am I hearing you right?" James asked. "I just forget I ever knew her?"

"If you can't separate personal feelings from Stony Man business, how can anyone be confident of your support in a crisis?" Katz asked. "We operate as a unit. Each man contributes his effort toward the collective good. It has to be that way. If it doesn't work, we'll go under. We have to be able to trust each other all the way down the line, without ever having even to think about it."

Calvin James glanced at the other Phoenix Force members around the table. They returned his gaze with unflinching hardness, giving nothing away as to their feelings. James felt certain they agreed with Katz. As they had a right to, he admitted. Katz had expressed the teams' feelings, and the black warrior accepted that criticism. He had been wrong—that he knew. His actions at Jenny's flat had put both McCarter and Jenny at risk. James just wished he could put the clock back. He would give anything to correct his mistake.

"You've put me in a difficult spot, Cal," Katz said. "To the extent that I'm not convinced you should continue with this assignment."

"You can't mean that," James protested. "Okay, I screwed up. I'm guilty as charged. But this mission is important to me. Don't cut me out, man. Not on this one."

"Your personal feelings don't come into this, Cal. Not when they could compromise the survival of the team."

Calvin James had never felt so bad in his life. There was no way he could express his feelings for the members of Phoenix Force. They were his life, his family, and he would never have willingly done anything to endanger them. His rash action in attacking Cadel had tarnished his image. His fellow warriors doubted his credibility now—and that hurt more than anything. The black warrior had great respect for his Phoenix partners.

James glanced from Katz to the others. Across the table David McCarter sat back in his seat, a Player's cigarette in his hand and a faraway look in his eyes. He didn't even acknowledge James.

"I have to look out for the safety of the others, Cal," Katz concluded. "The slightest suspicion that one of us may be functioning irregularly is justification for removing him from action."

"Meaning I'm out?" James asked.

"Until I decide otherwise," the Israeli stated grimly, hating himself for what he had to do.

James stood and left the cafeteria without a word. Silence hung over the table, forming a barrier between the Phoenix warriors as each wrestled with his private thoughts.

David McCarter leaned forward, forearms resting on the tabletop. He stared directly at Katz. "I think you called this one wrong," the Briton said. "You have the best judgment of any man I know, but you shouldn't drop Cal. Not on this one. I'm not condoning Cal's behavior. He needs a bloody good rollicking. Make his ears burn, but don't cut him out of the mission. He doesn't deserve that."

"Why not?" Katz asked evenly, prepared to listen to McCarter's side of the story.

McCarter took a long drag of his cigarette. "We all know Cal's relationship with drug traffickers. Cal has never come to terms with the way his sister, Susie, died. He doesn't make a show of it, but he still carries a lot of grief and guilt around. I'd say he handles it bloody well most of the time."

"I have to agree with that," Katz said. "But what's your point?"

"I saw Cal's expression when he read the report of Angie Martin's death. He told me later how much that girl had meant to him. Maybe subconsciously she was a substitute for his sister. Angie's death must have been like a rerun of Susie's. When we visited Jenny and Cal confronted Cadel, the guy responsible for supplying Angie's drugs, it must have all come together. For once, his emotions overcame his good sense. He let his feelings direct his actions.

"Yes, it was stupid and irresponsible. I told him so and I still think you should kick his arse around the block. Having said that, I believe Cal is still as dependable as he's always been. Say what you bloody like, but I'd still trust him any day as my backup. Cal is one of the best. A bloke couldn't have a better partner. Present company accepted." McCarter looked around to see several of his colleagues nodding in approval.

"All I can add to that is my agreement," Gary Manning said.

"Same goes for me," Encizo added.

Katz studied each man in turn, seeing the same earnest expression on their faces. Their loyalty for Calvin James was a confirmation of something he had felt for a long time. The closeness that had developed between the Phoenix Force warriors in the years they had been together had become more than just words. It was a true bonding, an intangible thing that went beyond physical expression. These men, hard-fighting and ruthless when the need arose, were as caring for each other as men could be. It was, as far as Katz was concerned, an affirmation of the Stony Man concept. Good men coming together as one to combat evil, and finding true comradeship in that coming together.

"I'm glad you all feel that way," Katz said. "The last thing I wanted was to stand Cal down, but for the good of the group something had to be said."

"We understand, Katz," Manning said. "Being the boss can be a lousy job."

"It has its perks," McCarter remarked. "He always gets first choice when it comes to hotel rooms. Have you noticed I always get the smallest room with two single beds instead of a large double?"

Encizo grinned. "That's because nobody wants to sleep with you, amigo."

Katz held up his hand, waving them to silence. "Sounds like everything is getting back to normal."

"So go and tell Cal," McCarter suggested.

Katz got up and left the cafeteria.

He found the tall black man in the car park, wandering up and down the lines of vehicles. Katz fell in beside him, and they walked on for a while in silence.

"Before I say anything," Katz began, his voice hard, "I just want to finish what I started in there. That play of yours was completely unprofessional, and I don't ever want to have to remind you of it again. I could have expected it from a rookie straight out of training college, not from one of my Phoenix Force men. It's a first and last. No excuses next time. If it ever does happen, I'll come down on you so hard we'll both regret it, and you'll end up sweeping dead leaves back at Stony Man. Got it?"

"Got it," James answered.

"I'm truly sorry about Angie. No young life should be snuffed out like hers. Or Susie's. Twice in a man's life is unfair. You reacted out of pure frustration, and in honesty, I might have done the same thing myself. You realize that I'm now talking off the record, just to show you that I'm not the unfeeling bastard you believe I am."

"I know you're not," James replied. "And I feel bad about letting you guys down."

"It's over," Katz said. "There was a decision reached after you left. Totally spontaneous and generated by a few well-chosen words by David that obviously echoed the way everyone feels about you."

"McCarter?" James said.

Katz smiled. "I must admit I was a little surprised myself. He made us realize we're all human, and everyone's allowed the occasional lapse."

"McCarter?" James repeated.

"Don't get me wrong," Katz said. "He said you still needed your butt kicked for such a bonehead play. But that came at the tail end of quite a speech on David's part."

"After I almost got him killed?"

"Something to think about. You have good friends in there, Cal."

The black warrior turned to Katz. "And out here, I hope."

"I did my job, Cal. I think our friendship can weather it. Don't you?"

"Does that mean I'm still on the team?"

"What do you think?"

As they returned to the cafeteria, James asked, "What do I say to them? Hell, how do you say anything after this?"

"You just take it as it comes, and prove they were right." Katz grinned. "I'll tell you one thing, Cal. McCarter is going to be a pain."

10

By nine o'clock the following morning Phoenix Force was on the move. A great deal had happened since their quick breakfast in the cafeteria.

They had decided to abandon the car Dexter had provided—in case its identity was known to the opposition, making the Force easily traceable. The unmarked police vehicle was moved to a busy parking lot in the area. Meanwhile, David McCarter telephoned for a taxi and went to the nearest car rental agency.

While the rest of the Force packed their bags and prepared to leave, Katz located a public telephone and rang a number Andrew Dexter had given him. This was a private number known only to Dexter, one he used in dire emergencies. He had given the number to Katz the previous evening after the Israeli had informed him that the Force was moving on to a new location. "Get yourselves settled somewhere," Dexter had said, understandingly. "I'll be waiting for your call."

Dexter answered after the first ring.

"Lawrence here," Katz said. "I've decided we need to get moving. The fact that Cadel is dead isn't going to shut down the organization. So we're going to go for the top men. As soon as you and I finish speaking, we'll be leaving for Charley Yale's place. Can you have someone ready to move in once we complete?"

"Can do," Dexter answered. "You guys watch out. Yale's a hard case. The man is mean and devious. Been around a long time and knows all the tricks. Time someone brought him down. The legal way never works. He's got too many contacts in high places."

"They won't do him a bit of good today. By the way, how's Jenny?"

"She's fine. We have a policewoman staying with her. She insisted on returning home. She'd a tough kid. From what she told us it looks as if Cadel was starting to panic. He was scared Jenny might tip off the police about his involvement. That's why he visited her. The idea was to scare her into silence."

"Damn fool," Katz said. "He only made it worse for himself. Anything on the hit teams?"

"Colombians and some local talent," Dexter said. "No ID on any of the Colombians. You can be sure they were all in the country without papers."

"Has Marchant said any more?"

"Tobin has him back now. There might be a chance of getting him to cooperate. He realizes he's in too deep to wriggle free, so we may even persuade him to give us a line on the other man we're after."

"Thanks, Andrew. I'll be in touch."

Katz returned to the others near the main exit.

"There's one reason I hate this damn country," Encizo grumbled. Katz followed his gaze. Beyond the glass doors rain was pouring from a slate-gray sky.

"It's one of the reasons why the grass is so green," Katz advised.

"That's fine if you're a grass lover," James murmured. It was the longest speech he had made since the previous night. Obviously, James was still feeling down.

He was trying to keep a low profile until he felt he could hold up his head in front of his partners again.

A large car drew up and McCarter climbed out. He dashed inside, shaking the rain from his hair. "All set for the mystery tour?" he asked, picking up his suitcase.

The car was a Ford Granada, allowing ample room in the rear seat for Manning, Encizo and James. Katz sat up front with McCarter.

The Israeli guided McCarter to the car Dexter had provided. The Briton jumped out, followed by Manning. They unlocked the trunk and took out the Force's aluminum cases, which they had been forced to leave in the vehicle overnight. It would have created suspicion if they'd carted all that into the hotel. A collection of aluminum cases, some quite large, wasn't normal, and Britain had its terrorist problems like most countries. It could have been extremely embarrassing for the Force to have been raided by the British police.

As soon as the cases were placed in the Granada's trunk, McCarter drove onto the M25. After a few miles, he left the motorway and picked up the Southgate Road. Despite the rain, the cockney kept up a steady pace through Tottenham and Hackney, bypassing the famous Hackney Marshes. Here the Briton's knowledge of London served him well, and he used countless side streets, twisting and turning until the other Phoenix Force members were well and truly lost. They reached their destination without mishap as the brash cockney, thoroughly at home, announced, "Here you are, boys, the good old Mile End Road." Reverting to an excellent impression, McCarter mimicked John Wayne as he added, "This is God's country, men, as far as the eye can see."

He eased the Granada to the curb and switched off the engine. Heavy rain drummed against the roof, bouncing off the street around them. Despite the rain, the Mile End Road was busy, with streams of traffic edging along in both directions. The sidewalks were less crowded than usual, the downpour having driven pedestrians to seek shelter.

"This is how I want to remember England," McCarter sighed in mock wistfulness.

"If you like it so much, why did you leave?" Encizo asked.

"I said I wanted to remember it like this," McCarter replied. "I didn't say anything about bloody well liking it, you idiot."

Encizo gestured at the Briton's back.

"Tut-tut," McCarter chided. "I saw that. One day your finger will stay in that position."

"Cut the patter," Katz warned. He leaned across the car to study the area.

"Yale's street is across the road," McCarter informed him. "The one down the side of the pub. See it?"

Katz nodded. "Doesn't look all that elegant for someone in Yale's position."

McCarter grinned. "You have to remember that Yale is still a local boy. It's tradition down here. A bloke can be a villain, but he stays where his roots are. He's a mate to everyone in the area. They know he's a bad 'un, but so what? He's a local boy made good. Gives to all the local charities. Helps people in trouble. Keeps the peace on the manor. Still drinks at the local with the other blokes. And I'll bet you next month's salary he loves his old mum."

"You kidding?" James asked.

The cockney shook his head. "It's the way down here. Family is very important. You can be the meanest bas-tard under the sun, but all will be forgiven if you look after the family. Bit like the Mafia with an East End accent.''

"Didn't the Kray twins come from around this area?" Katz asked. "I recall reading about them somewhere."

"That's right," McCarter said. "They were local boys. Real vicious bastards who ran the local rackets. They were real Jack the Lads. Walked round as if they owned the place. Mind, no one would have challenged them if they said they did. They were pals to all kinds of celebrities. Had their photographs taken in clubs with singers, actors, boxers. Local heroes Ron and Reggie Kray. Even when they were arrested for murder they were still Ma Kray's boys. They doted on her, loved her, and she never believed a thing that was said against them. Even after the murder was proved in court she still maintained they were innocent."

"What happened to them?" Manning asked.

"For once the cops got it right. The Krays were banged up for life. They're both still inside, and folk still talk about them as if they were bleedin' pop stars. The point I'm trying to make is—don't expect too much community spirit if push comes to shove. Charley Yale is the good guy down here. We're the enemy."

"As far as we're concerned," Katz said, "Charley Yale is definitely one of the bad guys. Tobin's file implicates him in the drug ring. The evidence wasn't strong enough to allow them to go after him, but they linked him with the Colombian group working in this country. Yale controls distribution of the Colombian cocaine for this part of England. Yale brought in Cadel. The fact that Cadel is out of the picture isn't going to stop Yale. He'll simply bring in another front man and maintain the connections."

"Meaning that the drug supply will continue," Manning observed.

"Yes," Katz admitted. "Unless we do something to stop it."

McCarter restarted the car and made a reckless dive through a gap in the traffic, cutting down the side street where Charley Yale's house was located. "Tell you what," he said, "let's use plan B."

"What's he talking about?" Manning asked.

"Plan B," McCarter repeated. "It must be a good one because they're always saying it in those spy movies."

"The guy is definitely nuts," Manning decided.

McCarter eased the Granada to a stop well short of Yale's house, checking that there was a way out at the far end of the street. Then shut off the engine.

During the trip from the service area, waterproof coats had been pulled from the Force's luggage. The Stony Man commandos donned them in the car. Each Phoenix warrior carried his handgun and Uzi machine pistol. The Uzis and other items were easily concealed in the large pockets of the waterproofs.

"David, you and Cal go round the back. The rest of us will take the front. I don't want this to end up a shooting match if we can avoid it. If Yale has any backup, let's try and put them out of action with a minimum of fuss."

McCarter nodded. "Remember what I said about these guys and their mums. If Yale's old lady is at home, we'll let Cal deal with her. He has such a winning way."

Katz glanced at James, relieved to see a wry smile on his lips. "David," he said.

"Yeah?"

"Just go."

Phoenix Force moved across the street, staying close to the brick front of the houses.

Yale's was a detached building with three floors, originally built in the mid-nineteenth century. To one side was a short drive. A black three-year-old Daimler automobile sat in the driveway.

"Looks deserted to me," Manning said as he glanced at the house.

"What do you want? Charley Yale hanging out the window waving a Union Jack?" McCarter asked.

"David, we'll give you four minutes before we go in by the front door," Katz said.

McCarter tapped James on the shoulder. "Come on, Mr. Tact and Diplomacy."

The Phoenix pair moved past the parked car, using it for cover as they made for the path to the rear of the house. They had to ease through a wrought-iron gate first. Luckily there were no windows on the end wall of the house, save for one high up.

Rain sluiced down off the roof overhang as McCarter and James reached the rear of the old house. They stuck close to the wall as they surveyed the layout. There was no garden to speak of, just a small, sodden lawn enclosed by high brick walls that separated Yale's house from its neighbors.

"I don't care if Yale has a bloody squad of Colombians in the place," the cockney grumbled. "All I want is to get out of this damn rain."

"I'm beginning to grow gills myself," an equally wet James answered.

The rear door opened onto an enclosed porch. McCarter found the outer door unlocked. Easing it open, he slipped inside, James behind him. The inner door opened just as freely. McCarter edged it open a couple of inches so that he could peer into the room beyond.

It was a kitchen, fully modernized and equipped with every household gadget imaginable. A rush of warm air greeted the Phoenix warriors as the slipped silently into the room. Closing the outer door, McCarter crossed to the kitchen door, which stood ajar. He looked down the long passage to the front door—other doors to other rooms. At the far end of the passage he could see the rise of the banister rails and stairs leading to the upper floor. Somewhere in the depths of the house music was playing. McCarter recognized the strains of an old Stan Getz composition.

"We'd better check the rooms in case Yale has company," the Briton suggested.

James nodded, easing his Uzi machine pistol from his coat.

Armed with his own Uzi, McCarter slipped out of the kitchen. At the first door he paused to listen. He couldn't detect any sound inside the room. He reached for the doorknob, glancing at James who nodded. McCarter turned the knob and thrust the door open. James went in fast, his Uzi up, sweeping from wall to wall. The room was fitted with a large pool table and plush, comfortable chairs, with a small bar at one end.

"No home should be without one," James remarked.

McCarter and James tried another room. It looked like an office. It held a couple of desks, filing cabinets, shelves, files, telephones and even a fax machine. Two men occupied the room.

One man, a fiftyish accountant type, sat behind the desk, bend over a sheaf of papers. The other, young and lean, sporting a shoulder-holstered automatic, was standing over the seated man. He held a china mug in his right hand.

"This is cozy," McCarter said, moving into the center of the room. "Coleman, go and let the others in."

The seated man stared at McCarter, his dark eyes full of anger. Neither he nor the younger man made any move under the threat of McCarter's Uzi.

"This is a mistake," he rasped in a deep, husky voice. "You know who owns this house?"

McCarter grinned. "Some local tearaway called Charley Yale, isn't it?"

"You won't be laughing so much when he gets through with you."

"Who are you?" the younger man asked. "Bleedin' cops, I'll bet."

"The cops know better," the seated man countered.

"You see a warrant?" McCarter asked. He turned to the younger man. "Take out the gun and put the magazine on the carpet."

The young man did as he was told. He ejected the magazine and threw it across the carpet. On McCarter's further instruction he tossed the empty automatic down, as well.

"Now sit down," McCarter said. "I want you both with your hands on your heads."

"Charley isn't going to like this," the main behind the desk said.

McCarter grinned wolfishly. "You want to call him in?"

"Call him yourself," the young man said.

James entered the room, taking in the scene. Behind him McCarter could see the others.

"We checked the living room," the black man said. "Empty."

"Charley boy must be upstairs," McCarter said.

James fished several pairs of plastic cuffs from his pocket as he crossed the room.

"Okay, boys," McCarter said breezily. "On the carpet, face down, hands behind backs."

James quickly cuffed both men at the wrists and ankles. "Be wise if you stay put," he suggested. "We won't be far away. You get my drift, boys?"

The older man stared at James. "Is this a hit on Charley?"

"No. This is just his retirement day. Didn't he tell you he's quitting? I hope you boys have plenty of unemployment insurance, 'cause you're going to be out of a job."

Rafael Encizo leaned over the young man and pressed his autopistol's muzzle against the man's temple. "Is he alone up there? Think carefully before you answer, amigo, because if you lie I'll come back and cancel your ticket."

The man nodded vigorously. "Christ, yes, he's alone. Honest to God, he's alone."

"Fine," Encizo said. "I'm sure you feel better for telling the truth."

The Force gathered in the hall. Katz led the way up the carpeted stairs. On the landing they turned along the passage, moving toward the room from which the music was emanating. Katz stopped at the appropriate door, eased the handle and pushed it open.

The room was tastefully decorated as a luxurious study, with thick pile carpet underfoot. The walls held book-lined shelves. In an alcove stood an expensive stacking stereo unit. The speakers were mounted on the wall. On the wall facing the door were French windows overlooking the rear of the house. There was a narrow balcony outside, with an iron railing edging it. Set a few feet from the French windows was a large executive-type desk.

Behind the desk, in a soft black leather chair, sat Charley Yale. Katz recognized him from a police photograph. Yale was in his mid-forties. He was of average height but very broad across the chest and shoulders. His physique gave him a stocky appearance. His face was round and ruddy, set on a short neck. He wore his dark hair short. He was dressed in light blue slacks, loafers and a monogrammed short-sleeved shirt. Around his right wrist was an expensive gold watch. He was pouring a cup of coffee from a heavy silver coffeepot when he realized he was no longer alone. He put the coffeepot back on the desk.

"Your taste in music is better than your choice of profession, Mr. Yale," Katz said as he led the Force into the room. James, the last man in, closed the door.

Yale burst from his seat, ignoring the weapons directed at him, face flushing with anger. "Who the fuck are you bastards? And what do you want?"

Gary Manning walked across to the stereo and switched it off.

"I asked you a bloody question," Yale ranted. "I don't know who you are, but you made a bad mistake coming in here like this. I'll have your bleedin' heads for it."

"Charley, think of your blood pressure," McCarter said. "Just shut up and listen." McCarter leaned across the desk. He placed a hand against Yale's thick chest and pushed him back into his leather chair.

"All right, all right," Yale said, holding up his beefy hands. "I take your point. You're all tough guys. I still want to know where you're from."

"Uncle Sam sent us," Gary Manning couldn't resist saying.

"Uncle bloody who?"

"Someone you've upset pretty badly," Encizo said.

Charley Yale's taut expression remained in place. "I don't give a bleedin' shit who sent you," he snapped. "All I know is you're causing me a pile of grief."

"Listen, chum," McCarter said, "we haven't even started yet. Wait until we get really warmed up."

Yale turned to the Briton. "You sound like a local boy. What are you doing with this bunch of jokers?"

"A yob like you wouldn't understand," McCarter replied. "Your problem, Charley boy, is that you're a dinosaur who hasn't caught on to the fact he's extinct yet."

Yale laughed contemptuously. "Am I supposed to be scared?"

"You ought to be," Manning said. "But a dumbhead like you hasn't got the brains to realize his time is over."

"Dumbhead!" Yale roared, his ruddy face darkening with rage. "I'll show you who's a fuckin' dumbhead. You reckon all you have to do is come crashin' in here wavin' those bleeding guns around and I'm supposed to wet my pants? And you call me dumb. Let's face facts, boys. I'm the boss around this manor. All I have to do is snap my fingers and I can have a dozen guns after you. Nobody—*nobody*—tells me what do to. Sweet Jesus Christ, even the police have given up trying to collar me. They know I'm way ahead of them. Charley Yale is too smart to get caught. And you clowns think you can make a difference."

"Yes, Mr. Yale, we can make a difference," Katz said, his voice restrained. "You see, we're not restricted by the law of the land. We don't have to play by any rules. Our directive is to locate the source of a problem and deal with it any way we feel to be right and proper. I do hope you understand what I'm getting at."

"Little like your way of doing things, chum," McCarter pointed out. "When was the last time you concerned yourself with the law, Charley?"

Yale began to realize he was in the presence of a group that operated on a level far removed from law-enforcement agencies. He was also quick to assess the need for a different attitude toward them. Charley Yale, if nothing else, was a survivor. "So what do you want? A deal?"

Katz shook his head. "No deal, Yale. But we do want something from you."

"Like the name of the guy who's been leaking top-level information," Encizo said. "Information, for example, on our presence at what was supposed to be a safe-house."

"You want me to snitch?"

Encizo nodded. "It's better than being dead."

Yale wasn't convinced.

"There is another matter we have to attend to," Katz said.

"I can't wait to hear," Yale said.

"Perhaps we forgot to mention it, but we're closing you down," the Israeli explained. "As of now you're out of the drug business."

Yale was unable to suppress his amusement. "Just like that? You walk in here and tell me I'm out of business? Maybe you haven't realized my connections."

"The Colombians?" Manning asked. "That didn't take too long to figure out."

"Okay," Yale sneered, "then you'll know those people don't take kindly to interference. You don't tell them they're out of bleedin' business. You bastards must live in fairyland."

"First you, then your Colombian buddies," Encizo said. "Believe it—because it's going to happen."

"Your mistake," Katz said, "was in going for U.S. military personnel. Right now you have the United States administration on your case. And they don't take kindly to the kind of activity you're involved in."

"I'd say you were up to your arse in trouble," McCarter remarked. "I'm surprised an East End boy hasn't figured it out for himself. Your Colombian chums have placed you smack in the middle. They're using you, Charley. Wait till the shit hits the fan. You'll be all on your own. Can't you see? They're the smart ones. Taking all the gravy and leaving you to catch the grief."

"It ain't like that," Yale protested, jumping up, hands splayed on the surface of the desk.

No one answered. Yale stared hard into McCarter's eyes. With an awkward gesture he drew the back of his hand across lips that were suddenly very dry. His position seemed a little less secure than it had a few minutes ago.

"Your choice, mate," McCarter said softly, persuasively.

The gangster stared at each face in turn, as if expecting sympathy. Realizing his position, Yale used the animal instincts that had ensured his survival over many years. With a speed that caught even the Phoenix warriors unprepared, Yale's fist connected with David McCarter's jaw, sending the dazed Briton stumbling back against Katz and Manning.

Yale turned, grabbed the silver coffeepot and sent it spinning at Rafael Encizo. The Cuban ducked, feeling the heavy vessel strike his shoulder. Luckily the thick padding of his waterproof jacket softened the blow and prevented the hot liquid from soaking through to his flesh.

Yale bent behind the desk. Clipped in place, loaded and ready for use, was a 9 mm Uzi. The weapon had helped pull him out of a couple of sticky situations, and he was banking on it doing the same again.

Calvin James, who had remained in the background, was the only member of the Force not directly in Yale's line of fire. Understanding that the gangster had been pushed into a corner and was desperate to strike out against his tormentors, James acted impulsively, thrusting in front of his teammates, reaching out across the desk to grip the Uzi's stubby barrel and forcing it toward the ceiling.

Maintaining the momentum, James sprang across the desk, crashing against Yale. He clamped a hand around the gangster's throat as the two of them staggered away from the desk.

The forefinger of Yale's right hand tightened against the trigger. The Uzi spit half a magazine into the ceiling. Slugs chewed into the plaster, showering the room with debris. James heard someone yell some kind of warning, but it came too late.

He recalled the French windows directly behind Yale's desk an instant before they hit them. Wood splintered and glass shattered. Yale and James, locked together, slithered across the narrow balcony. Such was their momentum that they toppled over, and vanished from sight.

11

Rafael Encizo reached the French windows first. He crossed the narrow balcony to the iron rail and looked down. Charley Yale lay in a crumpled heap on the concrete. Rain was washing away the blood seeping from beneath his head. There was no sign of Calvin James.

"Come on, man, give me a hand."

Encizo altered his gaze. At his feet he saw one of Calvin James's hands, the fingers curled around an upright of the balcony railing.

The rest of the Force joined the Cuban.

"Hang on to me," Encizo said, leaning over the railing. He reached out to James's outstretched free hand. Encizo felt hands latch onto his clothing as he leaned far over the railing. Then he had James's hand, gripping it tightly.

Using the combined strength of the other Stony Man warriors, Encizo hauled James up inch by inch until the black man was able to grab the upper rail. Everyone breathed a sigh of relief when James stepped back on the balcony.

"Thanks, guys," James said.

"Trust you," McCarter muttered. "Always hanging around somewhere."

His remark drew a concerted groan from the others. McCarter's wit had the ability to plummet the depths on occasions.

"How about getting inside," Katz suggested.

Katz picked up the telephone and punched out Dexter's special number. When Dexter answered, Katz gave him the okay to send the police. He also asked for an ambulance for Yale. Dexter didn't ask why; he simply said he would arrange it and rang off.

"Before we give this place a thorough search," Katz said, "I'd like to say something. It's simply this. Thanks to Cal's quick thinking we weren't hurt. I have no doubt Yale was about to fire. Regardless of his own safety, Cal prevented that. We owe him a vote of thanks."

The others were quick to agree.

"I suppose that means I have to be nice to him again?" McCarter said, unable to resist adding his own tag line.

"What do you mean *again?*" James asked.

"Cal, see what you can do for Yale until the ambulance arrives," Katz said.

James nodded and hurried from the room.

"Someone had better stand watch," Katz decided. "It would be unfortunate if any of Yale's associates arrived before the police."

"Leave that to me," McCarter said. "At least I can understand the lingo."

Katz, Manning and Encizo began a methodical search of the room.

"I don't expect Yale will have any direct references to his drug contacts," Manning said. "There may be telephone numbers."

After ten minutes, the Phoenix men had gathered an assortment of paperwork, files, invoices.

"Dexter can have the bulk of this stuff," Katz said. "His people will probably be able to glean any useful information from them. What we need is something that will point us in the direction of Yale's main supplier."

Encizo, going through Yale's desk, located a small, locked drawer. He went to work on the lock with the blade of a letter opener, patiently levering the drawer open. "Hey, guys, maybe this is what we're looking for."

Katz and Manning joined him. Inside the drawer was a leather-covered address book. Beneath it were a couple of computer disks.

Dexter and Inspector Tobin arrived. David McCarter was close behind them.

"I never thought I'd ever have the excuse to get inside this place," Tobin said. "I won't ask how you did it. Have you found anything we can use against Yale?"

Manning held up the gathered paperwork and files. "Have your people go through this lot," the Canadian said. "They might be able to pick something out of it."

"There may be more," Katz suggested. "Two of Yale's men are tied up in another office downstairs. One was armed, and I'd be surprised if he has a permit. By the way, Yale pulled an Uzi on us. Surely that's an illegal weapon. At least it gives you a reason to be here."

"A foot in the door was all I ever needed," Tobin agreed with a barely suppressed smile.

"How is Yale?" Katz asked.

"He'll live," Dexter said. "Broken leg and arm. Fractured ribs. Cracked his skull pretty hard, but he's a tough son of a bitch. And a lucky bastard."

"A damn sight luckier than some of his clients," Encizo pointed out.

"I'm going to take a look downstairs," Tobin said.

Once they were alone Katz showed Dexter the address book and the disks. "Do you know anyone who could read these for us?" the Israeli asked. "Preferably someone not involved with the authorities, Andrew."

Dexter smiled. "You won't hurt my feelings. I'm careful who I talk to myself at the moment. And I do know a chap who could help. I've used him a couple of times before. He's a bloody great computer hacker. If anyone can get these disks to talk, he will."

"I'm hoping we might pick up some lead to Yale's main source of supply, the people who are bringing the drugs into the country," Katz explained. "There has to be some organization in existence somewhere."

EDDIE CRANWELL had been conducting a love affair with computers ever since he was old enough to reach a keyboard. He learned to work a computer before conquering riding a bike. As far as Eddie was concerned, there were only computers. Nothing else mattered to him. He shunned television and disco dancing through his teenage years, preferring the glowing monitor screen. Out of necessity he mastered mathematics and the English language because they were prerequisites to the computer world.

As the years passed and Eddie's skill grew, he took a job in a computer company. The problem was that Eddie was too good for the place. In six months he had outgrown the company. Bigger and better things beckoned. The main problem was that Eddie liked to explore. He wasn't content simply to follow the rules. He needed to push himself to the limit, to experiment. So he moved into development and research, his talent expanding all the time. His skills earned him good money, so much that he was able to open his own business by the time he was twenty-five.

This was what Eddie had always dreamed of. He gathered a small, dedicated team around him, guiding and nurturing them. His business was a great success, and that success allowed Eddie time to indulge in his favorite pastime—sitting at his keyboard, letting his imagination run free. His business brought him in contact with people from all walks of life. Andrew Dexter was one of those people. He had often used Eddie's computer wizardry on official and not-so-official work.

It was no surprise when Dexter arrived at Eddie's office, along with five strangers and a couple of computer disks.

"We need your help, Eddie," Dexter said. "This is official police business. We need to know what's on these disks, and we need to know bloody quick."

Eddie examined the disks, determining the type of system they belonged to. His office was equipped with an impressive array of machines, all interlinked to a variety of monitors and printers. His computing skills had enabled him to create a configuration of peripherals that allowed him to move information from one system to another with ease.

"Pretty basic setup," he said. "Nothing very sophisticated."

He rolled his wheeled seat along the bank of computers, pausing at one. Then he fed one of the disks into the drive slot and touched the keyboard. The glowing screen threw up a menu. Eddie studied it, then keyed in more instructions. The screen image changed.

"Somebody's trying to be clever," Eddie said, pleased that he was being challenged. "There's a code to enter before the disk will cough up."

"Can you break it?" Katz asked.

The smile on Eddie's face widened. "Can a duck quack? It may take a little while. There's a coffee machine on the desk down there. Help yourselves." With that he turned back to the computer, his fingers flying across the keyboard.

Dexter and Phoenix Force helped themselves to the coffee.

"Can I have a look at the book you found?" Dexter asked.

Katz passed it over, and Dexter went through it page by page.

"A lot of telephone numbers," he remarked. "Either Charley has plenty of friends or he's suffering from a number fetish. I'd be surprised if any of them belonged to his business associates. We're more likely to find the juicy stuff on the computer disks."

"I daresay you're right," Katz replied.

The minutes drifted by. Phoenix Force was restless. They were reluctant to lose their momentum. Once the opposition accepted that they could be in a threatening situation they were likely to react quickly. Evidence could be destroyed, people might vanish, and the Force could find themselves on a losing streak.

"Here we go," Eddie suddenly called. He punched a button, and one of his printers began to disgorge paper.

"This is the first disk," Eddie explained. "Looks like an account disk. We've got all kinds of cash accounts. Money received. Money moved from one source to another. Here we've got bank account numbers. There are some pretty substantial amounts of money being handled." He tore off some completed sheets and passed them out. "I'll print out the other disk now."

Katz and the other Phoenix members examined the printed sheets. Eddie hadn't been exaggerating. The money being pushed from account to account was in large amounts, running into hundreds of thousands.

"I'll have these account numbers checked," Dexter said. "I'll guarantee we'll find some Swiss bank numbers here."

"This is the printout of the other disk," Eddie said, handing over more printed sheets. "Is any of it making sense?"

"I think we're getting some ideas," Katz said.

Eddie returned the disks to Dexter.

"Many thanks, Eddie," he said. "You'll remember to forget we've been here—like before."

"No problem, Andrew."

Katz shook Eddie's hand.

The Force returned to their car. McCarter took the wheel and drove through the rain-streaked streets while the others scanned the printouts Eddie had provided.

"What we seem to have here," Katz said, "are lists of names, addresses and telephone numbers. Do you recognize any of them, Andrew?"

Dexter read out a few names. "All these are known drug dealers and pushers. This guy, Johnson, runs a small freight company. He's been convicted a couple of times for handling stolen goods. Always wanted to get into the big time. Drugs would do that for him."

"What about this one?" Manning asked.

"Now that is interesting," Dexter said, making no attempt to conceal his excitement.

"Come on, Andrew, spill the beans," Katz urged.

"Ralph Massey," Dexter said. "We've been looking for a connection between Massey and the drug business. This has to be it."

"Is this Massey an important dude?" James inquired.

"International businessman. He operates a large haulage company that imports and exports perishable food. Fresh vegetables, meat, fish, cheese. Has his own processing plant outside Felixstowe. There have been murmurs about him for some time, but nothing substantial. Nothing has ever been found on any of his trucks during routine stops at customs. The feeling is that Massey has contacts at a high level who are able to warn him of planned searches. One of the problems is that Massey uses contract drivers as well as his own. These independents run their own vehicles, so it's hard to know who's running for whom. And, of course, there's an elaborate freighting system operating in Europe. Containers can be hauled partway by one company, then handed over to another for the completion of a journey. Makes it hard to keep track of a particular load."

"You only need a few people open to a little bribery to look the other way at customs posts and the job becomes even easier," Katz said.

Dexter nodded. "Massey is a clever man, no doubt about that. A British-European police and customs operation has failed to come up with anything so far. It's one of those situations where everyone knows the man is involved but can't touch him."

"With luck we might be able to change that," Katz said.

Dexter held up the disks. "You already have."

Manning, who had been studying one of the printout sheets, said, "I've found a couple of interesting telephone numbers. First one is in Rotterdam, in the Netherlands. The other is in Spain."

"How do you know that from just a number?" Encizo asked.

"It's surprising what you pick up working for an international company," the Canadian replied, referring to his time with North American International. "I spent some time in London during my stint. Did some dealing with European clients, a lot of it by telephone. It's surprising the sort of things you remember. Like the international dialing codes. The country code for Spain is 34. The Netherlands is 31 and the area code for Rotterdam is 10."

"Don't bother to ask," Dexter said. "I'll have the numbers tracked to their source. We'll find out who Charley Yale knows in Spain and Rotterdam."

"In the meantime we have another visit to make," Katz said. "I think we have enough to justify a look at Mr. Massey's setup. My instinct tells me we could be getting closer to the main distribution for this drug ring."

"There's one thing everyone seems to have missed," McCarter said smugly.

"What's that?" Encizo asked.

"Just the fact that Rotterdam is the main port on the continent for commercial traffic. It's where the ferries take all the freight trucks and containers across to England. To Felixstowe, as a matter of fact, where our chum Massey has his base. Is that a coincidence or just plain lucky?"

12

"What is it this time" Carlos Mejia demanded, extremely annoyed because he had been summoned from an important meeting.

Aware of his superior's anger, Jorge Torrejon apologized profusely. "I felt certain you would want to know what has happened," he said quickly. "Yale has been arrested."

"Damn! How?"

"The team of American specialists made a visit to Yale's home this morning. It appears that during the visit Yale fell, or was pushed, from an upstairs window. He's in hospital now under police guard."

Mejia paced up and down the corridor, his mind working furiously.

"Is he expected to live?"

"His injuries aren't fatal," Torrejon said.

"More's the pity," Mejia mused. "It would solve a security problem for us if he died."

"A dead man can't talk," Torrejon agreed. "Perhaps we could intervene to change his condition."

"Precisely what I was thinking."

"It won't be easy," Torrejon said. "On the other hand, it isn't impossible."

"We have to do it. Yale knows too much. His information would delight the British police. It's far too risky to allow him to live, which is a pity, because he was a good businessman. But there will be others we can employ."

"I'll attend to it myself," Torrejon said.

"Do it as soon as possible," Mejia ordered.

"I'll start immediately."

"As soon as I've completed negotiations with our greedy Australian friends next door, I'll be leaving for Felixstowe. Massey and I are flying to Spain to finalize payment of the next drug shipment."

"I'll contact you as soon as Yale has been dealt with."

"It would be useful if that stupid policeman Marchant could also be taken care of," Mejia suggested. "Two problems eliminated with one stroke, Jorge. See what you can arrange. Talk to our other inside man. He should be able to find out where Marchant is being held."

Torrejon nodded. He waited until Mejia had returned to his guests, the Australians, yet another market the Colombian was exploring.

Torrejon picked up a telephone receiver and dialed their inside man at Scotland Yard. Brushing aside the other's protest that it was too short notice, he set up a meeting. Torrejon made it clear to the man that for the money he was being paid, inconvenience was something to be handled.

Torrejon made a second call. He spoke to the man named Grogan, the heavy who had worked with Cadel. Grogan listened as Torrejon explained what he wanted. By the time he put down the receiver, Torrejon had completed the arrangements that would solve the problems created by Charley Yale's arrest.

An hour later Carlos Mejia sat in the rear seat of the Jaguar limousine, vacantly watching the London scenery drift by. It was still raining. The weather didn't concern him. He was too involved with his thoughts. The next couple of days were going to be extremely busy. Much was riding on the success of his deal with Ralph Massey. Mejia wasn't anticipating any difficulties. Massey was a hard man certainly, but also a good man to deal with. Everything was straightforward with Massey. He kept his business negotiations up-front, never trying to trick his partners, and always came up with the right figures. Mejia settled back in the comfortable leather upholstery. He enjoyed riding in the Jaguar. He had two Jaguars back home. The luxury automobile was supreme in its class. No one, not even the Americans, could beat the British when it came to creating really plush, indulgent vehicles.

The only thing the Americans were good at was creating wealth, Mejia thought, smiling at his own insight. And he enjoyed separating them from that wealth by selling them a product they apparently craved to the point of ruin. It made the Colombian trafficker shiver with excitement when he thought of the unending torrents of Yankee dollars flowing into the pockets of the Colombian drug cartel. So much for so little, he thought. All that wealth, just for little packets of white powder that cost so little to produce.

The white powder made dreams come true, Mejia thought. Although for the poor fools who indulged their reckless habits, those dreams became nightmares. Images of black, formless horrors grew in the minds of addicts, relentlessly demanding more and more of the substance that had become as necessary as air. The stronger the addiction, the richer Mejia and his masters became.

A man of conscience might have worried over how his product ruined lives, how it corrupted and destroyed, how it turned people into rabid animals who would kill and maim. Mejia was blessed by having no such social awareness. As far as he was concerned, he provided a commodity to those who required it. No more than that. His only concern was to keep turning such a handsome profit.

He turned on the built-in compact disc player, closing his eyes as the Boston Symphony Orchestra swept into the haunting music of Tchaikovsky's *Romeo and Juliet*. It was one of Mejia's favorite pieces, and he allowed the rich sound to envelope him, forgetting for the moment that he was driving through the rain-swept chill of England. It was a brief escape, but enough.

13

"First we take a look," Katz said. "No profit in going in without assessing the odds."

McCarter didn't particularly agree, but for once the irreverent Briton resisted the urge to comment.

The other Phoenix Force members agreed with Katz's suggestion. It would have been too easy to barrel straight in on Massey's base. The difficulty lay in staying alive once they were there. For all they knew there might well be a small army defending the place. Gathering some intelligence would cost only a little time, which might later mean the difference between dying and staying alive.

"You agreed, David?" Katz asked, aware that McCarter had yet to add his voice to the others.

"I suppose," the cockney replied impatiently.

"So who goes in?" Manning asked.

"Cal, will you take it, along with Gary?"

The black warrior nodded. He and Manning moved off to prepare themselves for the probe.

McCarter, briefly alone with Katz, said, "He'll appreciate that."

"Cal?" Katz smiled. "I noticed he was still down. He's been keeping unusually quiet. Time he had something to occupy his mind."

McCarter glanced up and down the narrow country lane. The Ford Granada was hidden behind a thick tangle of bushes and trees near the road. "Could be a problem if we get ourselves spotted," he muttered.

"Spotted by whom?" Katz inquired.

"Maybe a mobile patrol keeping an eye on the property from this side of the fence."

The Israeli turned. "What makes you say something like that?"

"Because it's what I'd do in Massey's shoes," the Briton said.

Standing close by, Encizo moved closer, nodding. "You know how these drug traffickers are," he said. "They tend to get a little paranoid at times."

"Point taken," Katz said. "Let's cover Gary and Cal as they go in."

Ralph Massey's estate was situated in lush, green country some twenty miles from Felixstowe. The property, a sprawling complex, included a modern processing plant with facilities for freezing the prepared produce and meat that arrived from various sources in England and Europe. The processing plant also handled prefrozen goods from Europe, which meant that semitrailers, fitted with refrigerated units, moved in and out of the place day and night to fill the contracts Massey had with national food distributors.

Tobin's intelligence reports, drawn from observations by the British Customs and Excise Service, which often worked closely with the police, suggested that Massey used the vast fleets of delivery vehicles to import drugs from Europe. Somewhere on the estate the drugs were cut and packed, then reshipped across the country. Tobin suspected that Massey's trucks transported the drugs in marked cartons among the regular goods. At various drop-off points couriers would pick up the cartons after a delivery had been made, probably without the driver of the vehicle even knowing.

Police and customs officials had been unable to plant an undercover man on the premises who could gather enough solid evidence to obtain a warrant for a raid. The slow pace of justice was making life exceedingly frustrating for the police drug teams. Despite the existence of special police drug squads, legal procedures had to be rigorously followed.

Their special status allowed Phoenix Force to bypass many of the legal restraints. They were able to go directly to the corrupt heart of illegal setups and strike hard and fast before the enemy had time to shut up shop and vanish.

Such was the case with the Massey organization. Having studied Tobin's information and the detailed layout of the Massey estate that Dexter had provided in London, the Force was ready to enter the lair of the dragon and confront him face-to-face.

The light was fading fast as the Force made their approach along the western perimeter of the Massey plant. Fortunately it wasn't raining in the Felixstowe area.

Clad in black combat gear, faces darkened, the Force had equipped themselves for what might easily turn into a hard probe. They carried their 9 mm Uzi machine pistols and handguns in shoulder rigs. Each man wore a combat harness, its pouches filled with extra magazines for each weapon as well as stun and fragmentation grenades. Knives were strapped in place.

As they stood together in the deepening shadows of the trees, Katz went over their plan of action again. "From the police file it appears that there's a cocaine distribution setup somewhere on this estate. The stuff comes in from the Continent, then is shipped across country. Now this is no nickel-and-dime operation, so the setup must be pretty large. We could find some Colombians on the scene, and they might be jumpy, ready to shoot at shadows. Our aim is to destroy any drug setup we find and get out alive. If we can pick up any information on the organization, that will be a bonus. But no heroics or unnecessary risks doing it.

"We wait here while Cal and Gary carry out their probe," Katz concluded. "When they return, we go in."

The perimeter fence was of chain-link construction, some twelve feet high. Rafael Encizo and Gary Manning spent some time checking for alarm sensors.

"It's clear," Encizo finally announced.

McCarter, who had gone to the car for a pair of wire cutters, quickly cut through enough links for the Force to breach the fence. Once James and Manning were inside, concealed by the darkness, McCarter closed the flap in the fence.

"Let's find some cover," Katz said.

They concealed themselves in the tall, untended grass along the road, patiently waiting for their partners to make their probe and return. After several minutes, Encizo hissed a warning.

A dark-painted Land Rover, lights dimmed, approached slowly along the narrow road. It moved at a pace that made it clear it was there for far more than simple sight-seeing. As it closed in on the section of road where Phoenix Force lay concealed, Encizo glimpsed the automatic weapon in the hands of the guy beside the driver. The Land Rover rolled by, taillights gradually fading from sight along the unlit road.

"Close," Encizo said, aware that his knuckles were almost white from gripping his Uzi.

"They could be a problem," McCarter said. "If they're out here and there's shooting later, we're likely to find them waiting when we leave."

"Then we put them out of action *before* we go in," Katz stated.

McCarter volunteered for the job.

James and Manning returned within twenty minutes. The Canadian summarized the findings. "We counted three armed guards patrolling the grounds. They shouldn't be too hard to handle. One could be Colombian. There appear to be others guarding a section of the big house."

The land on which Massey had built his processing plant had originally been the home of a local landowner. The vast grounds held wooded and landscaped areas, even a man-made lake. The ancestral home was a massive stone mansion three floors high, with endless corridors and countless rooms. Massey maintained an apartment within the place, though he was seldom in residence.

Katz unfolded the plan of the estate that Dexter had provided, and Manning pointed to one section. "About here is an area being used as a parking lot. Just down here is the entrance to the basement vaults, or cellars, running beneath the house. There seems to be a fair amount of activity around this point. The entrance is guarded by two guys with SMGs."

"Did you do anything about the guards on patrol?" Katz asked.

Manning shook his head. "I decided to leave that until we all went in. If I'd done it earlier, someone might have missed them."

"Heads up," McCarter warned. "Here comes Car 54."

They waited until the Land Rover rolled beyond them. McCarter and Katz eased from cover, moving quickly to opposite sides of the road.

The startled driver and his armed passenger abruptly found themselves staring at the muzzles of Uzi machine pistols thrust in through the open windows.

"Just put your foot on the brake," Katz advised the driver. "Keep both hands on the wheel."

"As for you, chum, let's see you put that gun down. All the way, joker, and get your finger off the trigger."

McCarter whistled sharply, and the rest of the Force surrounded the Land Rover. The driver and his mate were removed from the vehicle, searched, then bound hand and foot with plastic riot cuffs. Dumped into the rear of their own vehicle, the immobilized pair suffered a bumpy journey as the car was driven into the undergrowth.

Back at the fence, the Force reopened the flap and filed through one by one. McCarter, the last in, eased the flap back into place and followed his comrades onto the estate.

14

Two hundred yards farther, Katz raised his hand, indicating that he wanted the Force to halt. He gestured for them to drop out of sight. Facedown in the grass, they lay, watching an armed guard approach.

Carrying an Ingram MAC-10, the guard looked bored. He wasn't fully alert, as if he was at the wrong end of a long stretch of duty. The monotonous routine of being on watch had mind-numbing long-term effects no matter how well-intentioned a man might be at the outset. After a certain period of alertness, the mind inevitably drifted.

Katz touched Manning's arm, indicating the approaching guard. The Canadian nodded, unlimbering the Anschutz air rifle he carried. The silent performance of the Anschutz, coupled with its sleep-inducing load, made it the ideal instrument for taking out the opposition without arousing others. He snugged the weapon to his shoulder, taking careful aim, then eased back on the trigger. The rifle expelled its Thorazine-loaded hypodart with a soft hiss. The guard paused in midstride as the dart struck, instantly injecting the swift-acting liquid. He managed a single, faltering step before the Thorazine gained control. Then he fell flat on his face.

The Phoenix warriors looped and tightened plastic riot cuffs around the unconscious man's wrists and ankles and dragged him into some nearby bushes.

Ten yards farther, Manning repeated the performance with the Anschutz. The second guard was dispensed with as swiftly as the first.

Fifty yards from the house the Force crouched in the shadows cast by a stand of gnarled old trees. From this vantage point they observed several armed men patrol the west side of the large stone-built house. A number of parked cars and panel trucks were parked out front. A stone ramp led down to wide wooden doors below a carved arch. The doors allowed access to vaults beneath the house that at one time might have been used to store wines and perishable foodstuffs.

"I'd say they have more down there than frozen turkeys," Gary Manning said as he observed the armed guards along the ramp.

"How many soldiers do you make?" Katz asked.

"Seven," Encizo replied.

"Eight," Calvin James corrected. "One just came from the house."

Encizo nodded. "I missed that one. Eight it is."

"And there may be more inside," McCarter said.

"And still others patrolling the grounds," James reminded them.

"This is shaping up nicely," McCarter said with a wry grin.

"Don't get too excited," Manning warned. "I forgot to bring your antihysteria pills."

"When you two have completed your vaudeville act, we need a diversion," Katz interrupted. "Something to draw those people away from that entrance."

"That can be easily arranged," McCarter said. "Give me a hand, Rafael."

The Cuban nodded.

"When we set the diversion, you go," McCarter said.

"Take care," Katz told them.

The Phoenix pair moved around the outside of the house. Encizo, though unsure of their destination, had enough faith in his partner to follow him without question.

McCarter dropped to a crouch. Encizo did likewise, following the Briton's gaze. Ten yards farther on were the parked vehicles, including a pair of sleek Jaguars.

"Have you noticed the noise a blown gas tank makes?" McCarter asked.

Encizo's smile was bright even in the shadows. "Like fireworks," he said.

McCarter and Encizo simultaneously plucked M-26 fragmentation grenades from their webbing and pulled the pins. Lobbing the grenades toward the parked cars, they watched as the projectiles hit the ground. Upon hitting the concrete, the M-26s rolled beneath their respective targets.

They exploded within seconds of each other. McCarter's lifted the rear of a panel truck amid a flash of light that illuminated the other vehicles. Buffeted by the fiery blast, the truck began to disintegrate, a process hastened as the gas tank blossomed in an orange-yellow ball of fire. The brilliant flash lit up the evening sky, casting dense black shadows against the house. As the fireball scorched paintwork and cracked window glass on neighboring vehicles, Encizo's grenade ripped open the Jaguar, tearing through to the fuel tank. The subsequent blast flipped the heavy machine onto its roof, spraying blazing fuel in a wide arc. Shouts of alarm filled the air, followed by the thud of running feet as the armed guards hurried over to investigate.

"Do you think the guys will have heard the bang?" McCarter asked dryly.

"Hell, I reckon Hal will have heard it," Encizo replied.

TWO MEN REMAINED at the vault entrance, weapons up and ready.

Katz had a concussion grenade at the ready. He tossed it at their feet. The two guards were staring toward the burning vehicles, and failed to hear the sound of the grenade as it struck the ground. It exploded, momentarily blinding them with its brilliant flash and throwing them back.

Katz leaped to his feet and charged, Manning and James close on his heels. The incapacitated guards were rubbing their stinging eyes and shaking their heads. Manning clubbed one with his Uzi and, as he fell, quickly looped plastic cuffs around his wrists, pulling them tight. James dealt with the second man in a similar fashion.

"In we go," Katz ordered, covering the Phoenix warriors as they descended the ramp and entered the vault. The Israeli followed them.

The entrance opened onto a wide concrete area. There was a makeshift office, subdivided by cinder blocks, to one side; it was deserted. Through soundproof glass could be seen a computer desk. Beyond the office block the vault area spread out beneath Modern strip lighting that threw an unreal stark light over everything.

Bags and cartons of raw cocaine were stacked on wooden tables and on the floor. White-coated workers were busy preparing and weighing the white powder and filling small plastic bags with it. Farther along the illicit assembly line other workers were packing the bags in a variety of containers for final distribution.

The Phoenix warriors, carrying Uzi SMGs, threaded their way through the tables, roughly pushing aside the white-coated workers in their attempt to reach the exit.

Seeing Phoenix Force, a few armed guards opened fire. Slugs pounded the walls, filling the air with stone chips and dust.

Katz's Uzi replied viciously. His first volley cut down one guard, tearing into his lower chest. He tumbled across one of the trestle tables, scattering open bags of white powder.

Manning took out another gunman, his bullets destroying most of the man's lower jaw and throat. The maimed human creature clutched his ruined flesh desperately, pathetically, as he dropped.

James turned his weapon on the remaining two guards. Ignoring the slugs whistling by, he fired with deliberate calm. The guards were driven off their feet, crashing into tables, hands clawing at the holes appearing in their flesh.

Katz stepped deeper into the underground room. He gestured at the white-coated workers. "You have thirty seconds to clear out of here. If you don't, I won't be responsible for your safety."

There was no argument as the workers rushed for the exit.

The chatter of autofire filled the air. It came from the far side of the vault. Bullets smacked against the trestles, dispatching rough slivers of wood into the air. The Phoenix warriors separated, each going his own way as he tracked in on the concealed gunman.

James kicked over one of the trestles, crouching behind it as he reloaded. The moment his Uzi was ready he crawled to the end and peered around the edge. He was rewarded by the sight of a grim-faced Colombian stepping out from behind a stone pillar, his Ingram searching for Katz's moving form. James stood upright, swiveled his Uzi at the Colombian thug, and triggered, ruining the drug trafficker's light tan suit. Riddled with holes, the ex-thug sprawled across the dusty floor, eyes wide but unseeing.

Katz turned to Manning. "Get those charges set," he barked.

Manning nodded. While James guarded against interruption and Katz investigated the office, Manning moved among the rows of tables. He overturned them, tipping the assorted bags and cartons of cocaine onto the floor. He kicked the thick plastic bags into a rough pile and went in search of more. He found some others stacked to head height.

Opening his backpack, he removed an explosive device comprised of a C-4 block of plastic explosive and a timer-detonator. He wedged the explosive between two of the bags and set the timer for four minutes. Satisfied there were no other cocaine caches in the room, he returned to the pile of cocaine he had dumped from the tables. Here he placed another explosive device. One minute had elapsed. Checking his watch, he set the timer for three minutes. Both charges were set to detonate at the same time.

Manning returned to James and touched his arm. "All set here."

James nodded. "Just waiting for the boss."

Manning glanced through the glass. Katz was at the computer terminal, his fingers busy with the keys. The Canadian moved to the door of the office. "Any luck?" he asked.

Katz rose from the terminal. He touched a button and the computer ejected a disc from its slot. Katz pocketed it, plus a number of others he had located in a plastic box.

"Maybe. We'll pass these to the authorities. Leave one of your little devices in here."

Manning placed one of the explosive charges beside the terminal. He checked his watch again and set the timer to detonate as close to the other devices as he could. Then he followed Katz back to the entrance.

Autofire erupted from the general direction of the parking area.

"Let's get out of here," Manning said, glancing at his watch. "We have fifty seconds left."

They moved to the door. The gunfire had intensified.

Flattened against the wall, James peered out. "They're still engaging David and Rafael," he reported.

"Then let's get the bloody hell away from here before one of them figures out what's going on," Manning said.

The Phoenix trio broke cover, moving quickly along the side of the house. Ahead of them the night was further illuminated as another parked vehicles blew, sending a brilliant incandescent trail of fire into the sky.

The sudden eruption of flame provided enough light for the Stony Man warriors to make out the shapes of scurrying figures darting back and forth with guns. Behind them Manning's charges blew. The explosion in the office ripped out the wall, spewing stony debris. A cloud of thick dust rolled into the night. From the vault area the other charges added their destructive power and noise. The rumble of falling masonry could be heard as the solid thump of the detonations faded.

As the charges went off, Katz, James and Manning charged toward the group of guards. Their autofire scattered them. Calvin James fired a fusillade of shots and retired two traders in human misery from their profession and from the land of the living. The tattered corpses tumbled twisting and squirming.

As Manning ducked and weaved, his weapon blasted a stocky thug off his feet in a mist of red. While the guy fell, Manning twisted and crouched to avoid the probing muzzle of another gunner's full-size Uzi. Triggering up into the gunner's torso, Manning heard his high scream as the doomed criminal struggled to remain on his feet. But his limbs refused and he crashed to the concrete, his blood fanning out across the ground as he jerked his way to oblivion.

Phoenix Force thrived on this close-quarter combat with the drug peddlers. Katz extinguished one man, then quickly pushed his body away as another attempted to butt him with the wooden barrel of a rifle. The Israeli rammed the muzzle of his Uzi into the guy's groin, then drove his steel prosthesis deep into his throat, twisting the steel hooks and drawing blood.

As his victim began to choke, Katz yanked the prosthesis out. The stricken guard slumped to his knees, head sinking to his chest. Sensing someone close by, Katz whirled, coming almost face-to-face with a dark-skinned Colombian. The guy, yelling in incoherent Spanish, pointed the muzzle of his Uzi at him. Katz thrust his Uzi up into the soft flesh under the guy's jaw. He emptied the magazine in one long burst. The slugs cored up through the mouth and into the upper skull, pulping brain tissue and splintering bone. The Colombian keeled over on his back, one shoe rapping against the concrete in response to the nerve-shredding pain.

15

Joining the fray at the moment of the explosions, David McCarter and Rafael Encizo cut into the far flank of the guards as they sought to rejoin their Phoenix companions.

Briefly together the Force exchanged quick words.

"Let's head for the fence," Katz snapped, unwilling to waste time now on idle chatter. "I have a feeling there may be more of these guys around."

The Force headed away from the house, aware that they were visible as silhouettes against the flames coming from the wrecked cars. It wasn't the best situation, but they had little choice.

Lights were going on, shining from windows. Distant, angry voices could be heard.

"Sounds like the reserve team waking up," Manning remarked.

Three gunmen, outlined by flames, opened up with auto weapons. Bullets sizzled through the air, chewing at the grass around the Force.

Encizo and James broke their stride, turning their Uzi machine pistols on the gunners, who were just in range. The Stony Man commandos triggered a wedge of slugs at the attackers, felling them.

To the right twin beams of light cut through the shadows. The sound of a car engine filled the air.

"Now that's bloody unfair," McCarter growled.

The dark bulk of a heavy Mercedes came at them, headlights probing the night.

"Keep going!" James yelled, turning toward the approaching car.

When the Mercedes was dangerously close, James raked the front of the car, taking out the headlights and puncturing the radiator. Steam erupted from beneath the hood. His next burst penetrated the driver's side of the windshield.

The Mercedes suddenly swerved violently, its heavy tires digging into the soft earth. With ponderous slowness the car turned over on its roof, sliding for yards before it flipped onto its side. A rear door, twisted from its frame by the impact, sprang open, and the head and shoulders of an armed man appeared. Despite the streaks of blood marking his face, he maintained enough control to turn his Uzi at James, triggering an angry burst.

James felt the warm slugs tug against his shirtsleeve. He returned fire, which burned into the gunner's throat and head. The guy jerked, coughed blood and became an ugly corpse wedged in the door opening, staring fishlike at the night sky.

Meanwhile, the rest of the Force faced attack from armed men from the house. The attackers were well armed with automatic weapons but seemed to lack the tactical know-how that might have saved them. Their offensive action was noteworthy only for its lack of coordination. The group acted as if it was each man for himself. Their autofire, fired at random and seemingly without aiming, fell well short of the moving targets.

Rafael Encizo threw a fragmentation grenade at the attack group. It landed just ahead of the group. A few at the front, realizing what the object was, yelled an ineffectual warning. Then the explosive device did its deadly work, sending its mass of searing fragments into the attack group. Flesh and clothing were shredded by the whirling debris as the awful power of the grenade wreaked its devastation.

The rest of the Force added their firepower to the grenade, taking out the remaining members of the attack group. As Calvin James rejoined the Force, Katz looked grim. "Enough," he said. "They've had enough."

With weapons reloaded Phoenix Force moved through the darkness, making for the point in the fence where they had breached the estate.

They were about to go through the fence when Katz called a halt. "Is that what I think it is?" he asked.

McCarter followed his finger. "Telephone pole. Well done, Katz. You recognized it."

The Israeli ignored the sarcasm. He followed the cables snaking back into the darkness. "They supply the house. Gary, have you got any explosives left?"

The Canadian needed no further instruction. He crossed to the pole and placed one of his C-4 blocks, setting the timer for fifteen seconds. Back with the others, the Canadian watched as the blast shattered the pole and sent it toppling to the ground, ripping the telephone cables free as it did so.

"We don't want anyone making calls for help," Katz said. "Do we?"

They met no further resistance, reaching their parked car and driving off without firing another shot. McCarter drove back to the main road about a mile away. He followed the road past the front of the estate. Katz eventually told the Briton to stop at a pay phone.

The Israeli called a number Dexter had given him. It was to the commander of a combined police-customs task force, which was waiting for Katz's word to go in. When the commander answered, Katz gave him the response he had been anticipating.

"How did it go?" the commander asked after Katz's opening statement.

"We encountered armed resistance. They had automatic weapons. There may still be some fight left in a few, so go in prepared. I have some computer disks that might give you some handy information. We discovered a large cache of cocaine, which we destroyed, but there's bound to be some around you can use as evidence. We'll meet you at the main entrance to the processing plant. The house itself is about three-quarters of a mile from the plant."

"We're ready to move. It shouldn't take us more than five minutes."

Katz returned to the Granada and settled into the seat beside McCarter.

The cavalcade of police vehicles rolled up after just four minutes. Most of the vehicles sped into the grounds of the processing plant, sirens wailing and lights flashing as they cut toward the house, where the light from burning cars could still be seen against the night sky. Two cars remained at the entrance, angled across the gateway to prevent anyone getting out.

Katz climbed from the Ford to greet a tall, uniformed man who had emerged from one of the police cars. "Commander Shaw?"

The police officer nodded. "Andrew Dexter described you perfectly, Mr. Lawrence."

Katz raised his prosthesis. "It isn't easy to miss."

"By the look of you, I'd say you've had a busy night."

"We weren't exactly welcomed with open arms."

"By the way, Mr. Lawrence, I'd like to express my thanks. It's nice to know we were right about the place, even if we weren't able to do anything about it."

"The main thing is, we've put Massey out of business here," Katz said. "Both our countries have gained from that. What we have to do now is follow this through and nail the lid on his European operation."

"I've already been in touch with our counterparts in Rotterdam. They're more than willing to allow you to lead an operation against Massey's base over there. The telephone number you provided belongs to a freighting company on the Rotterdam docks. The police over there have been doing some checking. Although it isn't in his name, Ralph Massey owns the majority of stock."

"This gets more complicated as it goes on," Katz remarked. "Oh, while I remember. We cut the telephone lines to prevent any of Massey's people sending out warnings. It would help if we could keep news of this event from leaking out."

"We'll do our best. Don't want to drive Massey underground. Just before I left my office I was told that Massey and a foreign-looking man took the ferry to Rotterdam late this afternoon. So he's still on the loose."

"We don't want him hearing about this, if we can avoid it," Katz said.

Shaw glanced at the Granada. "Do you or your men need anything?"

"Only a fast ride to Rotterdam and a chance to catch our breath."

"The ride is already arranged. The RAF is sending a helicopter over from the Woodbridge air force base. It will fly you to a prearranged location near the Rotterdam docks where you'll be met by the Dutch police squad assigned to work with you. The fellow in charge is an Inspector Hooten. I know him quite well from our work together on drug investigations. He's a good man. He may appear gruff, but that's just his way."

"That all sounds fine," Katz said.

"As to your other request, I have a room set up for you at headquarters. There are bunk beds for you and your men, and there will be hot food and drink. I'll have one of my officers escort you there. As soon as I finish here, I'll join you."

"You may want to send someone to the west section of the boundary fence," Katz suggested to Shaw. "We left a couple of Massey's guards tied up in their Land Rover. They're off the road in some undergrowth."

"I'll have them seen to."

Shaw called a young police officer across. "This is Police Constable Francis. Follow his patrol car to HQ. Mr. Lawrence and his people are to be given whatever they want, Francis. They're your responsibility."

"Yes, sir," Francis replied. He turned to Katz. "Just follow me, sir."

"See you later," Katz said to Shaw. The Israeli returned to the Granada.

"David, follow that patrol car. It looks as if we're going to have the opportunity to get some rest before we go after Massey's base in Rotterdam."

"That," Encizo said, "is the best thing I've heard all day."

"Make the most of it," Katz warned. "I have a feeling it's going to be the *only* good thing about today."

16

Andrew Dexter climbed from the car, feeling the cool evening air against his face. He turned and looked slowly around the hospital parking lot, seeing nothing unusual. He couldn't rest until he had seen Charley Yale safe and well in his hospital bed. Dexter couldn't explain the gut feeling that had brought him to the London hospital. The need to check on Yale was pure instinct. Something was telling him things weren't right.

Like any good police officer, Dexter had developed his instinct over the years. During his career, Dexter had come to rely on instinct more and more.

This time his instinct had been triggered by a specific event. The second informer within the police force had been identified. He had been caught out as he attempted to draw away the officers guarding Marchant so that the rogue cop could be eliminated. However, the police officers protecting Marchant had become suspicious, resisting the phony instructions.

There had been a short, furious firefight. At its conclusion two hit men were dead, and the informer—Detective Sergeant Wallace Crosby of the National Drug Information Unit—was under arrest. The moment he realized he wasn't getting away free and clear, Crosby broke down and began to talk. He named names and places, admitting freely that he was on the take and that he had passed along vital information liable to endanger the lives of fellow officers.

The reason was simple. Crosby was a homosexual who had been set up and blackmailed by Charley Yale. The gangster had videotape evidence of Crosby's involvement with a teenage boy. The police officer, terrified of being exposed and losing his job, had fallen for the oldest trick in the book—agreeing to be Yale's eyes and ears on the inside.

Crosby had provided Yale and Mejia with information about Tobin's drug squad and its progress in building a dossier on the expanding drug organization in Britain. The increasing evidence the drug squad was collecting had forced Mejia to move against them.

Whether, in retrospect, it had been the correct move was open to debate. But Mejia was under pressure from his Colombian bosses. They were expecting results. Any police action against Mejia and his drug trafficking business wouldn't go down well with the cartel leaders in Medellín. They had limited patience when it came to delays or setbacks. The previous successes of any employee would have little effect when blame was being handed out. Mercy wasn't a characteristic of the Colombian drug barons.

The strike against the drug squad, intended to destroy evidence, had failed, mainly due to the presence of the American specialist team. And Marchant had been exposed and taken prisoner. Archie Cadel, captured by the American specialists, could have talked, so he was dealt with on the spot. Marchant, in police custody, might talk at any time, so he, too, was marked for elimination.

Crosby provided the police with the name of the Colombian behind the drug ring. The crooked cop had accepted the bitter fact that his life was ruined. He was finished in the force and would probably go to jail for his part in the events of the past few days. He saw no reason why he should be the only one to suffer. So he gave the name the police wanted: Carlos Mejia.

It meant nothing to the police, since Mejia had entered the country illegally, with false identification, as had his team of Colombian enforcers. The British police passed the name to the National Drug Intelligence Unit, a department set up exclusively to hunt drug traffickers, in coordination with other countries. If Mejia was part of the Colombian drug scene, someone, somewhere, would know about him.

Andrew Dexter, as a member of the drug squad, picked up the information as it came in. He noticed the peculiar omission of Charley Yale's name in intelligence reports. The fact stuck in the back of his mind. The more he thought about it the stronger his instinct told him something was out of place.

The Colombian, now known as Mejia, had left no loose ends, obviously, so how could he be indifferent where Yale was concerned? The gangster was in a hospital, under police guard, soon to be charged with a number of weapons and drug-related offenses. The computer printout had linked Yale with a number of known drug dealers, and had also pinpointed distribution sites around London and the adjoining counties. Yale had built up a thriving drug business that was on the verge of expanding even farther across the country.

So why had Mejia left him alive?

It didn't fit the pattern, Dexter decided. He had quietly collected Franklin. The young police officer was one man Dexter could trust. Together they had left Scotland Yard, picked up Dexter's car and had made for the hospital where Charley Yale was recovering.

Franklin was curious about what was going on. He had the sense not to ask. He knew Dexter would tell him at the opportune moment. One thing troubled him slightly. Dexter had made him bring along his gun. Franklin smelled trouble.

Standing beside Dexter in the parking lot, Franklin shuffled his feet impatiently. He shivered slightly. It had become quite cool with the onset of evening. "We going in, sir?" he asked.

Dexter nodded. "Just keep your eyes open, Franklin," he said as they approached the entrance.

The reception area was fairly busy since it was peak visiting time—the most likely time for Charley Yale to have callers, Dexter thought.

He led the way to Charley Yale's private room on the second floor. The landing at the second floor led off to both left and right. To the left were regular wards, the passage leading to them brightly lit. To the right the passage lay in shadows, illuminated only by subdued lights.

Dexter drew his automatic pistol, making sure it was ready for use. After a moment's hesitation, Franklin did likewise.

They reached the swing doors that gave access to the passage along which Yale's room was located. "I could be completely wrong about this," Dexter said. "So let's take it easy until we know one way or the other. Okay?"

"Understood," Franklin replied.

They went along the passage to a brightly lit area that housed the nurses' station. The desk was deserted.

Dexter's gut feeling began to work overtime. He reached the station and peered over the desk. Two uniformed nurses and a uniformed police officer lay on the floor dead, each shot once through the head.

"Christ," Dexter moaned softly.

"What is it, sir?" Franklin asked, glancing over Dexter's shoulder. Then, seeing, he groaned.

"There should be another officer," Dexter said, scanning the passage. "They must have him inside the room. You ever shot at a real target, Franklin?"

Franklin, his face pale, shook his head.

"Well, it looks as if you may get to alter that fact. If you feel like freezing, remember just one thing—the other guy wouldn't and he'll be alive when you're stone cold dead. Just remember what they've already done. Your choice, Franklin."

Dexter broke away from the desk and started down the hall. He was angry, enraged, sick and bloody tired at the casual, brutal way these drug traffickers operated. He pushed opened the door to Yale's room with his shoulder, the muzzle of the Browning Hi-Power tracking ahead of him.

The missing police officer was sprawled on the floor, blood seeping from beneath his head. There were three other occupants of the room besides Charley Yale: the man named Grogan, one of Grogan's soulless hit men and Jorge Torrejon.

Charley Yale was sitting up in bed, his face registering the shock of knowing he was likely moments from death at the hands of these men. But Dexter's entrance postponed that. The guns trained on the gangster turned as Dexter burst into the room.

Grogan was closest to Yale. Dexter shot him high in the chest, kicking him into a bedside cabinet that toppled noisily. Then Dexter swung his gun arm toward the hit man, stroking the trigger twice. His target fell across the bed, his face a bloody mask.

Jorge Torrejon got off a single shot, the bullet thudding into the wall above Dexter's head. Franklin's Browning spit out three closely spaced shots that hammered into Torrejon's chest above his heart. The Colombian killer was dead before he hit the floor.

Movement on the far side of the room caught Dexter's attention. Grogan, on his knees, pumped at least four bullets in Dexter's direction, then Franklin shot him twice through the head. Grogan tumbled backward, striking his skull against the wall, crashing to the floor and shuddering in ugly spasms.

Franklin, his gun hand trembling, turned. Dexter was down on the floor. There was blood on the front of his shirt.

"Jesus, no," Franklin said, kneeling beside Dexter.

Andrew Dexter stared up at the young police officer through a wavering mist that threatened to obscure his vision. Oddly he felt little pain, though he knew it would come.

"I know it's asking a lot, young Franklin, but do you think we might be able to find a doctor in this bloody place?"

Franklin snapped out of his daze, ran to the bed and pressed the emergency button. Then he remembered the dead nurses at the desk. He snatched up the phone and dialed the switchboard.

"Hey, what about me?" Charley Yale suddenly yelled, his earlier fear evaporating.

Franklin raised his Hi-Power and let Yale see it. "Open your mouth again, Yale, and I'll finish what those bastards started." The switchboard answered at that moment. "Room 17, second floor, get someone up here fast. There's been a shooting. Do it now!"

Dropping the phone, Franklin returned to where Dexter lay. He knew the moment he knelt beside him that there was no need for anyone to hurry any longer.

It was too late.

Andrew Dexter was dead.

17

Katz replaced the telephone receiver and turned.

"That was Inspector Tobin," he told the others. "There have been a number of developments since we left London. The second informer has been discovered. He was a member of the National Drug Intelligence Unit by the name of Wallace Crosby. He was arrested during an attempt to assassinate Marchant. Crosby has been doing a lot of talking since he was caught, probably hoping to lessen his sentence. He's identified a Colombian in the employ of one of the Medellín cartels as the head of the drug importing organization. His name is Carlos Mejia. Tobin is waiting for positive ID on him from the Colombian authorities. Mejia is unknown over here. The feeling is that he must have come into the country illegally, the same as his hit teams."

"Is Mejia the guy who left the country with Massey?" Encizo asked.

"Possibly," Katz said.

"What else did Tobin say?" Calvin James asked.

"An attempt was made on Yale's life," Katz said. "A three-man team killed two nurses and two police officers who interfered. The killers might have completed their hit if Andrew Dexter hadn't decided to go to the hospital and check on Yale. It appears Dexter and his partner arrived at the right moment. They took out the three hit men."

"Good for Andrew," Manning said.

Katz's grim expression indicated the opposite. "I'm afraid not. Andrew was hit during the exchange and died almost immediately."

The room fell silent, indicating the depth of the Stony Man warriors' feelings at the loss of Andrew Dexter. The British police officer had been involved with them on a previous mission and had always played his part with true professionalism.

"Another good man wasted," James said.

"Maybe not wasted, Cal," Manning said. "Andrew died for a cause he believed in. The only way we have of combating evil is by physically confronting it."

"It still comes down to a lot of good men dying," James went on.

"That's the hard part, Cal," Katz said. "The sacrifice of personal safety and even life is the price many have to pay to protect the ideals we cherish. It's always been that way. The death of a fellow warrior is never easy to bear. It doesn't get any easier, no matter how many times you face it."

"We have to make sure that Andrew's death isn't a waste," Encizo said. "We do that by carrying on. By never giving in to those who threaten us."

James accepted the words of his Phoenix partners. They were right. It would have been an injustice to Andrew Dexter's memory if they allowed his death to fall by the wayside. The thing to do was to keep on pushing, to use the death of a good man as a spur.

"David, you're very quiet," Katz said.

McCarter, slumped in a chair, with an unlit cigarette in his fingers, glanced across the room. "Takes something like this to make you realize nothing is forever. It has to end for us all one day."

The Briton's uncharacteristically somber mood was reflected in the eyes of the other Phoenix commandos. Each harbored private thoughts on McCarter's observation.

Phoenix Force missions were apt to be hectic, fast-moving affairs, with little time for reflection on the frailties of human existence. For once, caught in a period of calm, they were left to contemplate their own fates.

The mood was destined to be short-lived. It was McCarter himself who broke the silence. "Oh, come on, you blokes," the Briton said. "We'll be asking for handfuls of bleedin' Valium tablets next. If Andrew Dexter could see us now, he'd think we'd gone and retired."

Katz looked at his watch. "The helicopter will be ready for us in thirty minutes. Come on, guys, let's move."

As the group broke up to collect equipment and luggage, Katz felt Calvin James's eyes on him. The black warrior confronted Katz.

"That was why you were so mad at me. Because you hate the thought of anyone losing their life by a thoughtless act. Like me losing control with Cadel." The ex-cop held Katz's steady gaze. "Lesson learned, Katz, the hard way. I'm not liable to forget. Okay? Peace, man, huh?"

Katz's expression softened. He patted James on the shoulder as he moved by him. "*Shalom*, my friend," he said gently.

THE INCLEMENT WEATHER had finally rolled away, leaving the new day bright and calm. A few small white clouds marked the blue sky.

Phoenix Force, dressed in civilian clothes, crossed to the Royal Air Force Sikorsky-Westland helicopter waiting for them behind the police headquarters. Between them the Force carried their assorted aluminum cases and personal luggage slung from shoulder straps.

Commander Shaw walked with them, briefing them about the previous evening's events.

"We managed to locate some cocaine you hadn't blown to the four winds," Shaw said with a little sarcasm in his voice. "That, plus the information we're getting from those computer disks, has given us a hell of a boost as far as evidence goes. My intelligence people are compiling quite a list of dealers and suppliers. We even have details of the setup supplying your military bases. We also found enough weapons to equip a small army."

"The Colombians tend to go in for overkill," Katz said. "Their methods are unlike anyone else's. Once they target a location, it's all systems go. Talking with them is out of the question. Make no mistake, Commander Shaw, if they get a toehold in this country, you can expect the worst."

"I'd hazard a guess and say you've loosened their grip somewhat," Shaw said. "Especially after what happened at Massey's base last night."

"Make sure they don't regain it," McCarter snapped. "For Christ's sake, get your bloody heads out of the sand. Forget the Queensbury rules. This isn't gentlemen playing cricket. It's a dirty bloody war, and you have to get down in the crap with the rest of the rats if you expect to win." The Briton strode toward the helicopter, leaving Shaw behind.

"Ransom has a rather direct way of expressing himself," Katz explained. "He does, however, always get his point across. In simple terms, you'll have to get your people to toughen up their act. The drug cartels are waging a war back in Colombia with their own government. That should indicate how far they're prepared to go."

"Then it's up to us to keep them off our island," Shaw answered. He took Katz's hand as they reached the helicopter. "Good luck, Lawrence."

As Katz settled into his seat, the Sikorsky-Westland began to lift off. Moments later it swept forward and up, angling out toward the coast and the gray waters of the North Sea.

18

Maintaining an outer calm, Carlos Mejia crossed the yard of Massey's freight company in Rotterdam. He caught the eye of one of his men and beckoned the Colombian to his side.

"We may soon be having visitors," Mejia said. "Have the men position themselves. I want our best shots with rifles high up. This time we end it."

"Who's coming?" the Colombian asked.

"It will be those accursed American specialists. I've just spoken with one of Yale's men. He's managed to elude the British police and called to inform me that both Yale and Marchant are still alive. The assassination attempts failed. Jorge is dead. Yale's man tried to contact me at Massey's plant, not realizing I had left England, and discovered the lines are inoperative."

"Do you think it's significant?"

Mejia smiled tightly. "I'm certain Massey's place has been hit. The police are trying to keep the fact concealed so as not to alarm us."

"Wouldn't it be wiser to leave here now?" the Colombian asked. "Get out while we can?"

"And let it be known in Medellín that I ran away? I have no choice, Escobar. Even if the English base has been destroyed, we still have enough cocaine stored here to sink the damn island. There's also another, more im-

portant consideration. The weapons. They must be dispatched safely for Colombia before we leave.''

Escobar acknowledged the wisdom of his leader's
words. Cocaine itself was available in abundance. But the
large cache of weapons, ammunition and explosive stored
in the freight shed wasn't so easily replaceable. The
weapons, supplied by Ralph Massey as part payment for
large consignments of cocaine, were destined for Colombia to help the drug barons in their relentless battle with
the Colombian government.

''Go and place the men, Escobar. Warn them to be on
the alert.''

Mejia joined Ralph Massey, who was conversing with
the foreman of the loading gang. Beyond Massey, berthed
alongside the quay, was the freighter that would carry the
weapons cache to Colombia. The vessel was due to set sail
on the evening tide.

The Colombian trafficker zipped up his expensive
leather jacket and slid his hands deep into the pockets. A
warm breeze blew in from the sea, stirring his thick black
hair. Mejia drew in a deep breath, exhaling slowly. The
possibility of confrontation with the Americans excited
him. He wanted to test himself against these men. He was
intrigued by their doggedness, the way they pushed forward against all odds. Very determined men, capable and
fearless. Mejia admired those qualities. It wouldn't prevent him from destroying them. He vowed that this time
they would lose the game. They had to, because Carlos
Mejia refused to be defeated.

RALPH MASSEY FINISHED with the foreman, who turned
and walked away. Massey drew a thick cigar from a silver
case, which he replaced in his pocket. He lit it. Becoming

aware of someone watching him, he turned. "Carlos, you look rather serious."

"I have reason," Mejia said.

He told Massey all of his suspicions. The British drug dealer listened in frustrated silence, drawing heavily on the cigar clamped between his teeth. His strong-boned face darkened with anger.

"Bloody hell, Carlos, I thought you had everything under control! That's what you've been telling me. Your so-called hit men were going to get rid of this American team and settle with Marchant and Yale."

Mejia shrugged his shoulders, still smiling. "We can't always have what we want, my friend."

"Oh, that's bloody good. Very comforting. It isn't you who may have had his home and business wiped out. All you've lost are a few sacks of cocaine and some inefficient men, both of which you can replace very easily. What the fuck do I do? From the sound of it, I'll be lucky if I can ever go back to England."

"You're always telling me you don't like the place. Be honest, Ralph, you haven't lost all that much. The freight business has been running at a loss for years. You've only been using it as a cover for your profitable enterprises. Are you telling me you're going to shed tears over losing a plant that freezes chickens? Your interests are all based here in Europe, anyway. Illegal arms shipments, drugs, the pornographic video production company in Denmark—have I missed anything?"

"Actually you have," Massey replied, his temper abating slightly. "All that may be true, Carlos. But I liked my British setup. It was a wonderful escape for me. Every man has to have a bolt hole, somewhere he can go and shut the door against the world."

"What about your villa in Spain, overlooking the Mediterranean? With that beautiful French girl, Cecille?" Mejia asked.

"I hadn't forgotten. But surely you understand, Carlos. England is *home* for me. The same as Colombia is for you. The native soil always draws you back."

Mejia understood. No matter where he went, no matter what he experienced, Colombia was always deep in his subconscious, always summoning him home.

"We both have things we miss," Mejia agreed. "However, they're of little importance right now. Our priority is to protect our investments here."

"What are you planning to do? Start a war here on the docks? The foreman and his gang are going to commence loading in two hours."

"I'll do whatever is needed," Mejia replied. "I think we can forget about the regular loading gang. The first thing is to move the arms to a safer place. A ship could easily be stopped. We must load it into freight containers and have it moved."

"Where to?" Massey asked.

"Away from here," Mejia answered. "We must move the cocaine, as well."

The Colombian, his mind made up, hurried toward the freight shed.

Ralph Massey watched him go. He had to admit that Mejia's decision was the best under the circumstances. Too much was at stake to take risks. The cocaine shipment in the freight shed was the largest single consignment Massey had ever accepted. Once cut and distributed it would keep him solvent for the next couple of years. The money he would make from it would compensate for any loss he might suffer back in England. So as Mejia had said—they had to look after their investments.

Turning away from the moored freighter, Massey crossed the yard and made for the freight shed.

Ralph Massey had realized long ago that worrying over something that had already happened did little good. Born in near poverty close to Liverpool's waterfront, he had suffered a brutal childhood at the hands of a father who drank away every penny he earned. Massey's mother gave him little more. She blotted out her awful life by going with every man she could get her hands on. Young Ralph Massey had had to fend for himself because there had been no one else to help him. It forced him to become self-reliant.

After school, Massey joined the Royal Navy and spent the next eight years at sea. He met a man in Copenhagen during shore leave once who made pornographic movies and became his partner. Later he set up house in Copenhagen, arranging distribution deals for the movies worldwide, using the contacts he had established during his naval days.

As the porn business expanded, so did Massey's business empire. He was soon supplying a growing list of illegal commodities. Some Arabs convinced him to handle an illegal arms deal, and within a year he was a dealer in armaments. Massey quickly grasped the concept that supply and demand was the key, the actual merchandise—movies, guns, ivory, diamonds—made little difference. True, there were often borders to cross, custom posts to go through, police and military officials to bribe. To Massey it was all part of the great challenge.

Massey had purchased the processing plant near Felixstowe as a legitimate business. But soon the freight trucks were used to carry illicit goods of a varied nature back and forth across the North Sea. Massey's business reached across Europe, North Africa and the Near East.

He was already into drugs when Carlos Mejia came to see him one day at his Spanish villa. During the Colombian's visit, they struck a deal to open the way for a full-scale invasion of Europe and Great Britain by the Colombian drug traffickers. Within a year the ring was fully operational, and for a while everything went according to plan.

Then a team of American specialists arrived in London. From that moment the rot began to set in. The American team was totally unlike any other group of law enforcers Massey or Mejia had come across. They appeared to operate without restrictions, and they went straight for the heart of the matter. It was this blitzlike approach that took everyone by surprise. Though he wouldn't admit it, even Mejia was caught off guard.

If they showed up in Rotterdam before the arms and drugs were moved, they would net the biggest haul of all time.

Massey wasn't usually prone to looking on the black side. On this occasion he felt sure the Americans would turn up. They were either blessed with good luck, or they had impeccable timing.

Entering the freight shed, Massey beckoned to one of his men, a large Dutchman named Bruno van Eycke. It was Van Eycke who ran the Rotterdam business for Massey during his absence. Though an uneducated, brutal man who had spent many years in prison, he was loyal to the Briton and would do anything for him.

"I want at least three of the largest freight containers brought around here as soon as possible," Massey said. "Make sure they're fully fueled. One will be loaded with the Colombian cocaine. The other two should take the arms shipment."

Van Eyck's broad features moved as he digested the orders. "Aren't the weapons going on the boat?"

"They were," Massey said. "But there's been a change of plan. They may not be safe here. We have to get them away from the docks to a place where we can store them for a while. See to it, Bruno. I also want as many as possible of our people armed and standing by."

Van Eyck nodded and hurried away.

Within ten minutes diesel-powered tractor units were pushing the freight containers into the large freight shed. The moment they were in place the combined Colombian-Dutch loading team went to work.

As Mejia and Massey watched, Mejia gestured toward the activity. "Ralph, my friend, I'm feeling better already. Within the hour those trucks will be traveling the roads along with many others. Who will know what they're carrying? Who will care? We'll be safe again."

Massey simply nodded. He just wished his twisting guts were in sympathy with the smile on his face.

19

"They're up to something!" Gary Manning exclaimed. Lowering the binoculars from his eyes, he rolled away from the edge of the roof on which he was lying. The Canadian handed the glasses to one of the Dutch police officers, who took Manning's place near the edge of the roof.

"Let's assess what we have," Katz suggested. "We've spotted men on the roof of the freight shed."

"Don't forget, they were *armed* men," Encizo said.

Katz nodded. "Right, Arnez. *Armed* men on the roof. A great deal of high activity all of a sudden. Now three freight containers have been reversed into the place. Someone's in a hell of a hurry to move something. I wonder just what it is."

"Maybe they have a few tons of thawing gourmet dinners to deliver?" McCarter suggested brightly.

A grunt of disapproval emanated from Inspector Hooten, the Dutch police officer assigned to work with Phoenix Force. Hooten was a large, heavy man with a solid, square face. He was polite but distant, and spoke only when necessary. Katz had detected a trace of animosity in the Dutch police officer. Presumably he resented their presence but was under instructions to cooperate with them.

Phoenix Force had touched down in Rotterdam just under an hour earlier. Unmarked police cars had whisked them through the outskirts of the city, the second largest in the Netherlands and the country's chief port. During their flight in from the North Sea, the men of Phoenix Force had looked down on the great port of Europoort and the city beyond it. Observing the port from the air allowed them to appreciate its size.

Now the Force was inside the port area, on the roof of an empty storage warehouse. They were able to observe the Massey freight shed and its surroundings from a safe distance. Dressed again in combat gear and carrying all the equipment they might need, the Force was prepared for any eventuality.

"They could be moving drugs out of that place," Encizo said. "The way they're acting, maybe they got a tip-off from England."

"It's possible," Katz agreed. "The police were hoping to prevent any news leaking out, but that can be difficult."

"If that's so," Hooten said, "we should stop them from leaving the port area. I don't want any violence on the city streets."

"Do you think we do, chum?" McCarter asked.

"We would prefer to contain any action right here," Katz said.

"If we stand here jabbering much longer," McCarter snapped, "those bloody trucks will be in Berlin."

Manning unlimbered his Anschutz. "Give me a chance to get closer to those guys on the roof, then you can move in. They could pick us off one at a time if we don't put them on ice."

Katz accepted the Canadian's offer. "Coleman, you go with him and provide cover."

The Force synchronized their watches.

"How long do you want?" Katz asked.

"Ten minutes," Manning said. "You go in at twenty minutes past."

With James on his heels the Canadian set off across the roof. Katz, McCarter and Encizo crossed to the iron ladder that led to the ground.

"How do you wish us to help?" Hooten asked.

Katz indicated the route the loaded freight trucks would probably use to leave the area. "Can you set up roadblocks in case they manage to give us the slip? If you can stop them before they reach the main road, all the better."

Hooten nodded. "Leave that to me." He sounded relieved not to be getting involved in any direct action.

Katz, McCarter and Encizo quickly descended the ladder. They moved nearer the Massey freight shed to a spot where they were able to see across the yard.

Directly across from them was the freight yard. To one side was a stack of steel fuel drums. On the opposite side a portable office building had been erected. A few yards from the portable were a number of large freight containers. The Massey freight base was contained within a high perimeter fence. The yard extended to the edge of the dock where a medium-size cargo ship was berthed. The ship looked deserted.

The doors of the freight shed were open, and the Force could see the dark, bulky shapes of the three freight trucks inside. Movement could be seen around the containers and the sound of voices could be heard.

Encizo glanced at his watch. "Four minutes to go."

"FOUR MINUTES," James said in answer to Manning's question.

It had taken the Phoenix pair longer than expected to reach the freight shed and find the ladder to the roof. Because of the open layout of the buildings, they had been forced to take a longer route to avoid being seen.

James climbed the ladder first. Reaching the top, he peered over the edge of the roof. There were three men on the flat roof. Two were at the front of the building, while the third had taken a roving watch and was presently on the far side with his back to James. The black commando waved Manning up the ladder.

"Take him first," James said, indicating the mobile guard. "Once he starts across the far end he's going to spot us easy."

Manning shouldered the Anschutz, snugging the butt to his shoulder. He aimed carefully, allowing for distance, then touched the trigger.

The hypodart struck the guard in the neck. The stricken guard tried to reach the object that had created the sudden stab of pain. He was slower with the Thorazine injected into his body. With what seemed infinite slowness he slid to the surface of the roof, rolling onto his side.

Manning reloaded, checked the distance to the other guards and shook his head. "I need to get closer."

"Here we go," James murmured, leading the way across the roof, his Uzi machine pistol in a two-handed grip.

The moment they were within range Manning raised the air rifle, aimed and fired. The dart struck the target between his shoulder blades. The guard, a brown-skinned Colombian with shoulder-length hair, straightened up, jerking his head as he attempted to see what had hit him. Before he could call out the Thorazine dropped him to the roof.

Manning and James had already started forward, the Canadian reloading the Anschutz on the run. As the second man fell, he dropped his SMG and it made a distinct clatter.

James threw a desperate glance toward the remaining guard and realized, as he saw the man begin to turn, that Manning was almost out of time. There was no way he could reload and fire before the guard became aware of what was happening.

The black warrior dug in his heels, thrusting forward. He gauged the distance he had to cover, a sinking feeling in his stomach telling him he wasn't going to make it. The distance was too great. But James had to try. There was no going back. No surrender even to something that seemed inevitable.

Manning completed his reload. He pulled the barrel of the Anschutz toward the guard.

The Colombian spotted his fallen partner. His head snapped around, eyes blazing as he saw Manning. His MAC-10 swung into position, a finger already on the trigger.

Channeling all his energy into a final burst, Calvin James closed in on the Colombian. The drug trafficker sensed James's presence and froze in a trap of indecision, caught between the Phoenix pair. Whichever Stony Man commando he chose to attack would leave him open to retaliation from the other.

The Colombian's hesitation proved to be his downfall. Had he responded quicker he might have had a fighting chance. By the time the Colombian settled his weapon on Gary Manning, James rushed headlong, smashing into the guard and knocking the guy off his feet. The Colombian rolled across the roof, moving perilously close to the edge.

James, too, was being carried by momentum toward the edge of the roof.

Seeing his partner's predicament, Manning dropped the Anschutz, grabbed James's combat harness and hauled him away from the edge. A moment later the Colombian slid over the roof. His yells didn't cease until he smashed into the concrete.

"You almost took the expressway to the ground yourself," Manning said, retrieving his Anschutz.

James, his face beaded with sweat, said, "Thanks for the hand, Gary."

They heard voices at ground level.

"You figure anyone noticed the guy's dive?" Manning asked.

James grimaced.

"I knew he wouldn't reach the water from up here," the Canadian said. "Let's get off this damn roof. I have a feeling the guys are going to need us."

"OUCH!" David McCarter muttered as he saw the Colombian guard fall from the roof. "I think we've lost some of our element of surprise."

Armed men appeared from the shadowy interior of the freight shed. The dead guard was examined. Excited voices were raised. Orders were snapped out and the armed men spread across the yard.

"Think we can sneak by 'em?" McCarter asked, checking his equipment with the maternal interest of a mother fussing with her child.

"No," Katz said. "But we have to make a move. If they figure they might be under attack, they're going to want to move those trucks out pretty fast. I don't want them out of this yard."

"In that case," Encizo suggested, "I think we should go and get it done."

"You know," McCarter observed, "I believe there's hope for this bloke yet."

Encizo plucked a smoke canister from his harness, pulled the pin and hurled the canister across the yard. It bounced a couple of times, then rolled. There was a soft sound and then thick white smoke began to issue from the smoke grenade. A faint breeze coming in off the water caught the smoke and spread it across the yard. McCarter also launched a canister, which landed yards from Encizo's. It's smoke also began to drift, adding to the confusion.

"We'll split as we approach them. Come together at the shed door," Katz ordered.

"I'll take the middle ground," McCarter said, relishing the idea of getting into action.

"Rafael, you break right. I'll cover the left side of the yard," Katz said. "Just remember that our priority is stopping those trucks from leaving."

The Phoenix warriors reached halfway across the yard before anyone spotted them. There was a chorus of yells, then gunfire.

The swirling smoke made target selection difficult.

Katz attempted to cross the yard without engaging the enemy. He made it three-quarters of the way before the drifting smoke thinned out and left him completely exposed. He was confronted by two armed men, one a Dutchman, the other a dark-skinned Colombian. Both drug traffickers opened fire.

Katz went down on one knee, bullets whizzing overhead. Bracing the machine pistol across his prosthesis, he returned a long volley of shots. Aimed with deadly accuracy, they caught the Dutchman in the stomach and chest.

He fell to the ground in a writhing heap. Katz switched his aim to the Colombian and triggered another burst. He caught the guy in the side, splintering ribs, mutilating internal organs.

Ejecting the near-empty magazine, Katz snapped a fresh one into place, cocking the Uzi.

RAFAEL ENCIZO dropped into a crouch as he reached the center of the smoke cloud. Dark shapes were moving around. He waited for the burst of gunfire to indicate he had been seen. He had already heard the exchange farther off to his left. The shadowy figures moved by him. Encizo started forward again. Sensing someone very close, the muscular Cuban twisted toward a dark looming shape.

The muzzle of an Ingram MAC-10 seemed to fill Encizo's field of vision. Resisting the urge to panic, the Cuban fighter triggered his Uzi at the dark shape behind the Ingram. Flame belched at him from the MAC-10. He felt something tug at his jacket, then saw the bloodied form of the man he had shot fall.

Alerted by the gunfire, two local Dutch hoodlums who worked for Ralph Massey peered through the swirl of smoke, probing ahead with their automatic weapons.

Encizo saw them as they emerged from the smoke. His Uzi crackling fiercely, he caught them full-blast. Tumbling, the drug pushers dropped their weapons, writhing, slipping from life.

Turning toward the freight shed, Encizo emerged from the smoke, confronted by a tall man dressed in dark workclothes who was rudely pointing a Franchi SPAS-12 combat shotgun at him. Encizo dropped to the concrete, tucking in his shoulder and rolling. He heard the savage boom of the shotgun. The charge hit the concrete so close to him that he felt the sting of concrete chips against his cheek. The sensation was followed by the warm wash of blood down his face.

Flat on his stomach, Encizo tipped the Uzi upward, stroked the trigger and was rewarded by the sight of cloth fragments flying away from his target's left shoulder. The wound was slight; Encizo's bullets only clipped the top of the man's shoulder. Encizo dropped the Uzi, dug under his coat and drew his P-88. Steadying the gun in a two-handed grip, he pumped three slugs into the shotgunner's chest.

The guy seemed astonished. He stepped back, his SPAS-12 trailing the ground, its weight forcing the trigger against the guy's finger. The weapon exploded, the major part of the blast tearing into the shotgunner's right leg below his knee. At close range the effect was deadly. It shredded the flesh from the limb and shattered the bone. The shotgunner crashed to the concrete in agony.

Regaining his feet, Encizo snatched up his Uzi and fed in a fresh magazine as he ran for the open door of the freight shed, his ears picking up the sound of revving diesel engines within.

20

Departing from his Phoenix partners, David McCarter plunged into the swirling smoke. The Briton's blood raced with the thrill of combat. McCarter's addiction was strenuous activity and personal risk.

Peering into the smoke, McCarter moved toward the freight shed. His head moved from side to side, searching for any slight movement. The scrape of leather on concrete announced a hulking figure with a heavy .357 Desert Eagle in one big hand.

Bruno van Eycke eyed the tall Briton and growled with anger. He swung the powerful handgun at McCarter's chest, pulling back on the trigger.

The cockney had already taken evasive action. His lean body turned sideways, reducing the target the Dutchman had to hit, allowing the Briton to bring his Uzi into play.

The Desert Eagle cracked, and the bullet burned the air a half inch of McCarter's chest. The single blast from the Desert Eagle was answered by McCarter's Uzi. The mini-weapon spit bullets into van Eycke's left side, twisting him off his feet. He struck the concrete, blood spraying from his body, the pistol flying from his fingers.

McCarter moved on, his ears ringing with gunfire, the smoke thinning around him. Spotting him, two Colombian drug warriors swung their MAC-10s. They were no match for McCarter's superb reflexes. His Uzi lined up and stitched a row of slugs in one guy's chest and the upper chest and throat of the other, canceling their contracts with life in an instant.

As his burst struck the second Colombian, McCarter felt something hit him in the right side, above his hip. It was like being struck by a heavy length of wood. Heading for the freight shed, he ignored the dull ache across his lower torso. He dropped the used clip from his Uzi, replacing it as he ran, cocking the weapon.

The high, wide entrance to the freight shed yawned before him. Within the vast shed he could make out figures dashing back and forth. Gleaming diesel tractors stood in a neat row. McCarter heard the chugging drone of an engine turning over, then the burst of power as it caught.

The sound spurred him on, despite the weariness spreading through him. He caught sight of Encizo and Katz closing in on the shed entrance. There seemed to be something wrong with his legs. Though he was pumping hard, he didn't seem to be making much headway. The ache in his side intensified. Touching the spot, he felt warm, sticky liquid soaking through his combat jacket. He knew what it was without seeing it. Damn! He'd taken a bullet. The realization annoyed him more than anything else. He could feel the sticky wetness spreading down his thigh.

McCarter heard his name being called, saw Katz waving. The Israeli's voice was fading even as McCarter caught his eye. Over everything else McCarter heard the pulsing roar of a diesel engine. He stared into the freight shed through blurred eyes. One of the tractor units was picking up speed as it approached the doorway. Behind it the thirty-foot container rocked on its double set of heavy tires. The Briton fumbled with his Uzi and pulled the trigger, pumping bullets at the front tires. He stood his ground, swaying drunkenly, striving to keep the Uzi leveled at the wheels. The left front tire burst with a solid thump, fragments of rubber spinning across the shed. McCarter fired into the opposite tire, seeing the rubber burst apart. The front of the tractor dipped, the huge steel wheels striking sparks as they came into contact with the concrete floor. The driver hauled on the steering wheel as the bulk of his machine slewed to one side.

Too late, McCarter realized the tractor was heading directly for him. He tried to get out of its way, but his rapidly weakening condition had robbed him of his agility. Blinding pain washed over the Briton as the tractor sideswiped him. McCarter was lifted off his feet and hurled across the concrete. He slammed into the wall of the shed, twisting and turning before crashing to the ground in a loose sprawl.

He didn't see the tractor swerve violently, the front crashing against the steel girder that formed the upright for the entrance to the freight shed. Upon impact, the driver slammed against the toughened windshield. He slumped unconscious over the wheel. The diesel engine roared briefly, then juddered and stalled into silence.

JAMES AND MANNING reached ground level as the shots rang out from the freight shed. They sprinted along the building to a side door. It was locked. Manning emptied half a magazine into the wood around the lock, then drove his booted foot against it. The door crashed against the inner wall.

The Phoenix warriors dashed inside, crouching. The shed was filled with stacks of goods of all shapes and sizes. They threaded their way through rows of boxes, barrels, sacks, some stacked twelve feet high.

Ahead of them the high doors of the entrance were wide open. Three diesel tractors, coupled to large aluminum containers, had been reversed up to the shed's loading dock, where several men were loading boxes and cases into their cavernous interiors. Thick white smoke was rolling across the concrete apron fronting the freight shed, and armed men were running around in the smoke. The firing intensified.

One of the diesel engines burst into life. The doors of its container were hastily closed. Moments later the rig rolled forward, the driver giving the machine all the power he could muster.

Figures burst from the smoke cloud—Katz, Encizo, McCarter. They were running toward the entrance. Even from a distance James and Manning saw that McCarter appeared to be in trouble. The tall Briton was weaving as he ran. Then he stopped, confronting the moving tractor. The cockney held his ground, firing at the tires, which exploded, causing the rig to lurch to one side. The truck was closing on McCarter with frightening speed.

James wanted to yell but knew it could jeopardize both Manning and himself. And it wouldn't change a damn thing, he realized.

The careening rig reached McCarter. A second later the Briton was hurled through the air like a limp rag doll, crashing against the wall, then dropping to the ground where he lay without moving.

"No!" James groaned. It couldn't be happening. Not now. Not to McCarter.

The black warrior glanced at Manning. The Canadian, his face grim, nodded. As one, the two Phoenix warriors burst from cover and entered the battle.

21

Carlos Mejia witnessed the rig crash, cursing as he realized the stalled tractor and container were blocking the doorway.

He spotted the surviving American specialists as they skirted the rig. Mejia lifted the Heckler & Koch MP-5 from a packing case beside him. The SMG was his personal weapon, a favorite, one that he had used many times during his violent career. The Colombian worked the cocking mechanism. "This time we stop them!" he yelled.

Close by, Ralph Massey, who had just seen his container of drugs put out of action, faced Mejia. "How do you plan to get out of this?"

"Like men," Mejia snapped. "We fight—or we die!"

Mejia picked up a spare Ingram MAC-10 and thrust it into Massey's hands.

"Make your choice, Ralph. As I said, fight or die. Freedom of choice." He smiled without humor. "Democracy in action."

There was no more time for talk as the combined Colombian and Dutch group moved to clash with the American specialists.

Mejia realized only two of the Americans were visible. Even with one out of action there should have been four. "There are two more," he called.

Behind him came a shout from Massey. "Here!" he called, seeing James and Manning approach from the rear.

Although he was no gunman, Massey raised the Ingram in desperation and pulled the trigger. Unfamiliar with such a weapon, he failed to allow for the Ingram's rate of fire. The muzzle climbed, sending the 9 mm bullets sailing over the heads of the advancing Phoenix warriors.

James and Manning competently returned fire, reducing Massey to a blood-soaked corpse, his world of illicit dealing and drug smuggling wiped out in seconds. He died without really knowing what had hit him, his dreams vaporizing as quickly as the smoke from the barrels of the guns that had killed him.

Several gunmen, confronting James and Manning, opened fire while scrambling up the steps of the loading dock. Their jerky movements fouled their aim. James swung his Uzi at a pair who had mounted the steps, then triggered. The unwary pair were swept from the steps. They crashed to the floor, writhing.

Manning's target managed to elude him at first. The enemy gunman leaped from the steps, firing from the hip as he gained his feet. Bullets sizzled past Manning's face, slamming into a wooden crate. The Canadian dropped to a half crouch, triggering his Uzi, turning the Colombian into a human disaster area.

Katz and Encizo, with David McCarter strongly on their minds, clashed head-on with the remnants of Mejia's group. The Phoenix warriors skirted the stalled rig, weapons up and ready.

With their automatic weapons blazing, Dutch and Colombian drug traffickers burst into sight. Bullets struck the concrete around Katz and Encizo, filling the air with splinters and dust. Both Stony Man commandos came to a dead stop, giving themselves time to aim.

Katz triggered a short burst at a Colombian. The guy dropped his weapon and clutched his hands to his ruined face, blood oozing between his fingers. Katz shot him again, a burst to the heart that stopped the agony. Swiveling on his heel, Katz met the rush of another gunman whose weapon jammed. With an enraged roar the Dutchman swung the Ingram at Katz, missed and stumbled. Katz lashed out with his prosthesis, the steel tips gouging the Dutchman's throat. Soft flesh gave way to cold steel and the Dutch gangster let out a shrill, gurgling screech. Katz pushed his right leg out and tripped the man, sending him to the floor.

Rafael Encizo, his Uzi in a two-handed grip, took out two gunmen with his superb marksmanship. He blasted one, then switched to the other in only a few seconds. Neither gunman had the opportunity to challenge the deadly Cuban.

There was a sudden lull in the gunfire. From the loading dock Calvin James called out, "There's one more! Guy in a leather jacket carrying an MP-5. He's between the containers."

Katz ran forward, clipping a fresh magazine into his Uzi. He cocked the weapon. Reaching the front end of the rig, the Israeli crouched, peering beneath the vehicle. About halfway along the rig he could see a man's legs.

The Israeli slowly rose, flattening against the front of the tractor.

"If you come out with your hands up, we won't harm you," he called.

Silence greeted his challenge.

Up on the loading dock, Calvin James edged slowly around the container, his Uzi held before him.

"Surrender is the only course left open to you," Katz called, again giving the unseen gunman the opportunity to give himself up.

"No!" came the reply. "I can't surrender. If I don't die here, I surely will on my return to Colombia. My employers don't look kindly on failure."

"Don't force us to open fire," Katz warned.

The soft scrape of leather on concrete warned Katz that the concealed man was moving. The Israeli stepped around the front of the tractor, his Uzi leveled. Mejia had decided to make a break for the loading dock. He was still yards from the steps when Calvin James stepped into view.

"Not this way, brother," James snapped.

"Do you know who I am?" Mejia demanded, still not ready to give in to the inevitable.

"Yeah, I know who you are," James said. "A goddamn scumbag. A guy who sells shit to poor suckers and gets rich while they die."

Mejia whirled around, facing Katz. Some twenty feet away, the Israeli had his Uzi aimed directly at Mejia.

"I am Carlos Mejia," the Colombian said. "I don't expect you to allow me to walk away free, but I could make you all rich men. I have the money to do it."

"The king rat himself," Calvin James said through tight lips. He felt the rage welling up again, his finger tightening on the trigger of his Uzi.

Gary Manning placed a hand on James's shoulder. "It wouldn't be worth it, Cal," he said softly. "Murder is murder, no matter how strongly you figure you can justify it.''

James relaxed, knowing full well that Manning was right. It didn't make him feel any better.

"We don't make deals with criminals," Katz replied. "You are responsible for a great deal of suffering and death, Mejia. There isn't enough money in the world to buy yourself out. It's time you and your kind realized the world will only tolerate your evil for so long. Then it starts to fight back. That fight has just started. The time is coming, for you and your cartel bosses. The way you go is up to you."

Mejia took a deep breath. His finger tightened against the trigger of the MP-5, which he held loosely. He prepared himself for what he had to do.

There was only one option open to him. No other solution would do. There was no question of him going to prison. He wouldn't tolerate that. Nor could he return to Colombia. Death would be his only reward.

Katz saw the MP-5 start to rise. It was tracking him with deliberate precision. The Israeli responded instantly. His Uzi crackled harshly, briefly, sending a stream of 9 mm slugs into Carlos Mejia. The Colombian drug trafficker fell back, one arm flying wide to slap against the side of the container. The expensive leather jacket, full of ragged holes, began to streak with blood.

Mejia collapsed facedown on the floor. The unfired MP-5 slipped from his hand. His body moved with jerky spasms, his left hand scrabbling against the floor, nails gouging into the oil and dirt. Finally he became still, his fingers stiffening. Under his nails was caked dirt from the floor. It was the first time Mejia had gotten dirt on his hands since those early years on the streets when he had broken away from his family to make his own way in the world. He had come full circle. His life had started in the dirt. Now it ended in the dirt.

"Before any of you ask, I've just had the latest report on David," Hal Brognola said as he entered the war room of Stony Man Farm in Virginia.

Phoenix Force, minus David McCarter, was seated around the conference table. They had been summoned for a debriefing on the mission.

Katz opened a fresh pack of cigarettes and extracted one. He lit it while Brognola made his way to his chair and sat down.

"I spoke with the doctor looking after David," the Fed said. "He's very pleased with his condition."

Phoenix Force had been back in the United States for three days. McCarter, after initial treatment at a U.S. base in Holland, had been flown back to the Medical Institute at Arlington, Virginia. Stony Man had used the institute before. Katz had spent some time there after being blinded during a mission in Quebec. The medical teams at the Institute were the best available, and as far as Brognola was concerned, only the best would do for his Phoenix warriors.

"The bullet clipped his lower rib on the right side but luckily only cracked it. Apparently the rib deflected it back out of his body without it damaging any organs. He lost a lot of blood—but that was mainly because he insisted on continuing instead of lying down like any normal person."

"Would you expect David to act like a *normal* person? Shot or not?" Gary Manning asked.

"Getting hit by the truck did him no good, of course," Brognola added. "One broken arm and a fractured skull. Countless abrasions. Badly bruised spine."

"He was lucky," Encizo said. "But that guy *is* lucky. He can do the craziest things and come out smiling."

"How long will he be in the hospital?" James asked.

"Knowing David, the shortest time possible," Katz answered.

"Be a few weeks," Brognola said. "I believe some of the nurses are also asking how long it will be before he can leave."

Manning laughed. "Sounds as if he's getting better already."

"Okay," Brognola said, tapping the file on the table before him. "Mission update time, guys."

"This should be good," Manning murmured softly to James.

"Talking of luck," the Fed said, "you guys must have a monopoly on it. Despite starting a couple of small-scale wars in England and Holland, and leaving a hell of a body count, you seem to have gathered quite a fan club."

"We didn't have much choice, Hal," Katz pointed out. "You have to accept that the attacks at the factory site and the safehouse were the work of the drug ring. All we did was defend ourselves."

"Point taken," Brognola conceded. "The little bust-up at Massey's place near Felixstowe? Who twisted your arm on that one?"

"We had an objective," Encizo said. "It was to be expected there would be resistance."

"Same goes for Rotterdam," Manning said. "Come on, Hal, we weren't exactly up against a bunch of nuns."

"I guess you're right," Brognola sighed. "You'll probably be pleased to know that the British prime minister sends congratulations. So does the Dutch government. Regardless of how you did it, a major drug ring has been smashed. The information the authorities have got from the computer disks has enabled them to pick up a lot of the small fish—pushers, collectors. They've also uncovered a considerable number of drop-off points, where they've confiscated consignments of drugs."

"What about the U.S. connection?" Katz asked.

"We've scored there, as well. Names on the disks have enabled military authorities to break up the organization that was pushing drugs within U.S. bases. Unfortunately that meant arresting a number of active servicemen. But better that than having them spread the stuff even more."

"This has been a dirty mission right from the start," Katz said. "It highlights the problems large-scale drug pushing creates, for example, corruption within the British police that cost the lives of honest officers, bribery and assassination attempts. Maybe we did hit hard, Hal, but at least we showed everyone that pussyfooting around with drug traffickers isn't going to achieve a damn thing. The Colombians have no scruples when it comes to maintaining their markets. They'll go to any lengths. At least this time we showed them there comes a point when *we* have had enough and will play their game."

"At least you stopped that arms shipment reaching Colombia," Brognola said. "The weapons found in Massey's freight shed were all stolen U.S. equipment. Serial numbers were checked and traced back to a series of thefts from U.S. stores all over Europe. It's beginning to look like Massey had been along that road before. Some of his people in Holland are being questioned, and they're talking. It's going to take a long time to sort out all the details, but that's for other departments. All in all, guys, a successful mission. The President sends his thanks."

"Pity it can't be the end of it, period," Manning said. "For all we know someone could be starting afresh already."

"We can't afford to look at it that way," Katz said. "We take each victory on its merits and worry about tomorrow when it comes."

"I suppose we're lucky to be able to do that," James remarked. "I was thinking about Andrew Dexter."

"Yes," Katz said, "at least we're still alive." He glanced across the table at James, smiling briefly. "And still a team to be reckoned with."

James knew what the Israeli meant.

"Okay, guys," Brognola said, standing up, "that'll be all for now. By the way, we have a visitor dropping in shortly. He'll be here on a flying visit for a briefing. I believe you may have met on the odd occasion. Name of Bolan. Mack Bolan."

"Be good to see him again," Katz said.

"Yeah," Manning agreed.

"You guys mind if I bow out?" James said. "I have something that needs doing. I've missed a couple of opportunities, so I don't want to let it slide."

"You go ahead, Cal," Brognola said. "Anything we can do?"

James shook his head. "No. This has to be personal. Okay, Katz?"

The Israeli nodded. "You carry on, Cal. Give him our best, as well."

"Sure," James said as he left the war room.

Brognola, intrigued, followed Katz from the room. "What was that all about, Katz?"

"Nothing much," the Phoenix Force commander replied. "Cal just has to says thanks to someone." Brognola's puzzled expression drew a smile from the Israeli. "I'll tell you all about it one day."

These heroes can't be beat!

Continue to celebrate the American hero with this collection of never-before-published installments of America's finest action teams—ABLE TEAM, PHOENIX FORCE and VIETNAM: GROUND ZERO—only in Gold Eagle's

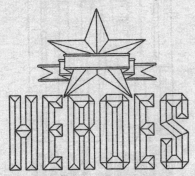

HEROES: Book III   September $4.99   448 pages

ABLE TEAM: Secret Justice by Dick Stivers
PHOENIX FORCE: Terror in Warsaw by Gar Wilson

Celebrate the finest hour of the American hero with your copy of the Gold Eagle HEROES collection.

Available in retail stores in September.

In the Deathlands, the only
thing that gets easier is dying.

JAMES AXLER

DEATH LANDS®
Moon Fate

Out of the ruins of nuclear-torn America emerges a band of warrior-
survivalists, led by a one-eyed man called Ryan Cawdor. In their quest
to find a better life, they embark on a perilous odyssey across the ravaged wasteland known as Deathlands.

An ambush by a roving group of mutant Stickies puts Ryan in the clutches
of a tyrant who plans a human sacrifice as a symbol of his power. With
the rise of the new moon, Ryan Cawdor must meet his fate or chance
an escape through a deadly maze of uncharted canyons.

GOLD
EAGLE ®

DL16

Collect all three titles of the HEROES collection and add a free preview copy of WARKEEP 2030 by Michael Kasner to your library!

The year is 2030 and the world is in a state of extreme political and territorial unrest. Under a joint Russian-American initiative, an elite military force—The Keepers—has been dispatched to contain the damage. With the ultimate in 21st-century weaponry, they complete their mission: strike first, strike hard and give no quarter.

Retail value $4.99, 352 pages